FROM HELL TO MARION COUNTY

BY MARY YARBROUGH DEAN

This book is dedicated
to the brave men and women
who settled Marion County Florida
and to their descendants
in whom the spirit
of the pioneer still
lives.

Published by
BenAura Publishing
P. O. Box 606
Anthony, FL

ISBN 0-9748012-0-8

Chapter 1

By sundown the whole world had seemed tinged with red, it was the color of the powder smoke that hung so heavily along Chickamauga creek. The waters of the creek flowed red with blood as the creek lived up to its name. It was indeed a river of blood.

Captain Matthew Kendall shivered as the frosty air of midnight seeped into his very bones. With his mouth pressed into a grim line, he strove to ignore the body of a dead soldier, lying face down in the stream next to him. He knelt down wearily and submerged his canteen and listened with undue fascination to the sound the air bubbles made as they drifted to the surface.

Feeling more weary than he had ever felt in his life, Matthew stood up. The heel of his worn out boot caught on an obstacle hidden in the darkness. With difficulty, he regained his balance and knelt down stiffly in order to find out what had tripped him. With a hand that was numb from the cold, he reached out to touch the stiff cold body of the soldier who lay at his feet. He felt sickened by it all, so much death and dying. There were so many bodies scattered upon the ground that one had to step over and around them, in order to get from one place to another.

Clinching his teeth to still their chattering, Matthew tried in vain to shake off the grimness of his thoughts. Death was all around him but he knew in his heart that there were worse things than being dead. Worse than death were the screams and moans of the dying. Since full dark had fallen at Chickamauga Creek the rumbling of the ambulance wheels had not ceased. Darkness as black as death itself, hindered the stretcher-bearers in their search for the wounded and Matthew had no doubt that they would be at it all night.

Matthew sat down wearily and rested his back against a tree. As was his custom after each day's fighting, he reviewed the day's happenings one by one. They had gained ground that day but still had not succeeded in cutting off the Yankees from Chattanooga. Even after suffering heavy losses, they still had managed to hold their own. Still there was no end in sight and Matthew refused to even speculate on the final outcome. Their own General Bragg was a man to be reckoned with, but the Union's General Rosecrans was a formidable opponent in any man's army.

After a time, Matthew grew tired of rehashing the day's fighting and stretched out on the hard, cold ground to sleep. His hand encountered a damp patch of soil and his hand tightened convulsively around it. It felt faintly sticky and he knew instinctively that it was soaked with blood. It mattered little whether the blood had come from a fellow Confederate or a Yankee. Matthew loosened his fingers, letting it drop from his hand.

A cannon boomed nearby, shattering the comparative stillness of the night. Matthew's body tensed, then relaxed. Since nightfall, the pickets had kept up a nearly steady firing among themselves and the ringing of axes could be heard throughout the entire area as breastworks were hastily thrown up in preparation for the next day's fighting. Somewhere nearby, a wounded soldier moaned pitifully in pain. Along Lafayette road, wheels rumbled as artillery was moved and an overworked mule brayed in protest. Sounds all familiar yet haunting. With a great deal of effort Matthew managed to close his mind to them. He listened instead to the twittering of a bird that was roosting in the branches over his head. In the background, Chickamauga Creek made a whispering sound as if it were unaware of the dead and dying that littered it's banks.

Matthew shifted his weary body restlessly as a muted rumble sounded from the region of his empty belly. He'd gone to bed hungry before, a man was always hungry on army rations. Food was unimportant to him but his aching body longed for the sleep it had been denied. Lack of sleep made a man fuzzy headed and careless and either condition could prove fatal. A tired man made mistakes and in this war, there was no room for error.

Tomorrow wouldn't be his first battle and God willing, it wouldn't be his last. God only knew, he ought to be used to it by now; so what was keeping him awake? Sleeping on the hard ground was old hat by now and even though the cold was brutal, he had slept cold before. Matthew turned over and stared up into the tangle of tree branches over his head. He closed his eyes, forcing himself to search his mind and emotions for a clue.

Physical discomfort was seldom enough to keep him awake and he accurately laid the blame on his tangled emotions. Relentlessly, he questioned himself. Was it fear that kept him awake? Of course he was afraid but fear was almost an old friend by now. He had lived with it long enough to grow accustomed to it. Besides, a man who wasn't afraid wasn't cautious and a man who wasn't cautious didn't

2

live long.

The reason for his wakeful state came to him reluctantly. It was the doubts that haunted him. What the hell was he doing here anyhow? He was born to be a gentleman, not a warrior. There was a lot of difference between war and marching down the streets of Atlanta, as proud as a peacock, to the stirring beat of a drum. Heaven knew, they had all been caught up in it, chock full of Southern pride and righteous indignation. They had all dressed up in sharp new uniforms of Confederate gray, their heads filled with visions of glory. Cocksure of a swift and easy victory, they had marched off like boys to a Sunday school picnic. No damn Yankee was going to tell them how to run their lives and plantations.

The war had raged on for two years now and still there was no end in sight. By now, both North and South knew the meaning of hell. Lately, he had begun to question everything he had once believed in. He was raised up with slavery and accepted it as a way of life, never questioning the right or wrong of it. Slaves were necessary, but there was nothing right about it. Still, how else could the South survive? Matthew didn't know the answer; he wasn't even sure there was one.

What was he fighting for then? A way of life that he wasn't even sure he believed in anymore? Hatred? Hell yes! He hated Yankees, arrogant bastards, what did they know? How to pillage, kill and destroy; sometimes it seemed that this was what it was all about. Whoever could kill and destroy the most would win the war. Kill or be killed, it got to be a sickness, that unholy thrill of battle. He'd been caught up in it himself; it reduced a man into something he could not later recognize as himself. It left a man hard eyed and even harder hearted. Nothing much mattered anymore, just win the damn war and go home.

Matthew closed his eyes and for a precious moment in time, he was no longer at Chickamauga but at home. As if it were only yesterday, he saw himself seated at the library desk working on the plantation accounts. A soft knock sounded at the door, just before it opened to admit Elizabeth. She crossed the floor gracefully even though her still shapely body had already begun to thicken with their child. Setting his pen aside, he allowed his eyes to drink in the blond beauty of her. Within her grew the all-important heir to Silver Oaks and the adjoining plantation belonging to her parents as well.

3

Elizabeth smiled at him charmingly, "Don't let me disturb your work, Matthew. I only came to find something to read." she said. Her silk petticoats made a swishing sound as she crossed the room and began to scan book titles as she made her selection.

Matthew remembered picking up his pen and finishing adding the column of numbers. He was through with his work long before she found her book and left the room. Still, he lingered, using it as an excuse to delay going to bed. In most ways, Elizabeth was all a man could wish for in a wife. She was beautiful, charming and a good hostess. She would make a good mother for his sons. He was fond of her in a brotherly sort of way but lovers they were not. Theirs was a marriage of convenience, brought about to insure the joining of two plantations. Silver Oaks and the plantation belonging to her parents would one day be joined and would become the largest in the state of Georgia. In the past, he had fought bitterly with his father over the arrangement but had ultimately done his duty.

Matthew's thoughts returned reluctantly to the present as a bugle sounded nearby. The sound was repeated over and over, throughout the surrounding woods and all up and down Lafayette Road. He arose from the ground and finger combed his unruly brown hair. It was months since it had last been cut and by necessity he tied it back in a cue with a piece of leather thong. He rubbed wearily at his bloodshot eyes and briefly scratched at his beard. He encountered a tick and quickly made short work of the creature by crushing it between his thumbnails.

The memory of home had turned his thoughts to Elizabeth and he smiled a bit ironically to himself. The slight stirring of his body at thoughts of her was more of an annoyance than anything else. He stepped behind a tree and quickly relieved both his full bladder and the other discomfort as well.

The early morning fog proved to be as much help as it was a hindrance. Matthew's division was in one of the first assaults of the day. Hidden by the thick veil of fog, they managed to sneak up on Negley's troops. The fighting was hand to hand and as bloody as any cockfight. By some miracle they managed to break up Negley's division before the fog had cleared.

By sunup they found themselves face to face with a division of Yankees hidden behind a log breastwork that they had built during the night. It was like beating one's head against a brick wall.

Later that day, Matthew was amazed to see that a gap had formed in the Yankee lines. Though they didn't understand it, the opportunity was too good to pass up. Before the day was over, they had driven off Rosecrans and half his army. Much of the Union artillery was in their possession as well as an ammunition train and Rosecrans' headquarters.

Late on the third day of battle, the Yankees were out of ammunition and after dark, by the light of a full moon, the fighting raged hand to hand. The South had won the battle but didn't know it yet.

Chapter 2

Matthew had dodged bullets for three days without a scratch but was not so lucky during the final skirmish. A blow to the back of his head laid him low. He awakened to a raging pain in his head and a burning in his left arm. Lying very still, he surveyed the scene within his immediate range of vision. The moon still shone as bright as day and he could see that the ground around him was littered with soldiers, dead and wounded. He could make out the color of the uniforms of those closest at hand, butternut brown and the darker Union blue.

Matthew turned over carefully onto his back, keeping a firm hold on his musket and fighting off dizziness and nausea. The moonlit sky overhead spun crazily for a moment and he had to fight to remain conscious. After a short rest, he was able to reload his musket and try to get up. He was driven back down by dizziness and pain. His arm like fire and he ran his hand gingerly over the wound. There was a four-inch gash, sealed off with clotted blood and to his relief the arm still functioned as it should. He breathed a sigh of relief, for a severe wound of any kind to a limb, usually led to amputation. His luck had held, so far.

A man lying nearby cried out for water. The voice was unfamiliar, yet definitely southern. Matthew realized that he too was thirsty. He took a long drink from his canteen, though it made his stomach turn. He rolled over and fought down the dizziness and nausea. When he was able, he crawled to the side of the man who was

5

still begging for water. With difficulty, he held the canteen to the man's lips. Now that he was closer, he could see that the wounded soldier was only a boy, probably no more than seventeen. The boy swallowed the water gratefully, choked and coughed up red froth. He weakly wiped his mouth on his sleeve and tried to talk, choked again and at last managed to speak. "Letter for Ma in my pocket. See she gets it." he gasped. The young soldier placed his hand over the pocket containing the letter, drew one more gurgling breath and died. Matthew rested his hand over the still heart of the boy for a moment before finding the letter and putting it in his shirt pocket. A wave of sadness washed over him and he dropped his aching head down on his outstretched arm to rest.

Seeing the boy die had made him think of his own son, now only two years old. Only once had he laid eyes on the boy, only an infant then, but strong and healthy. The child had his own dark hair and the blue eyes of his mother.

Matthew seldom thought of death but when he did it was related to a fear he had that he would never live to see his son again. Upon first sight of the boy, he was filled with such pride and love that it both surprised and overwhelmed him. That little boy-child was what he fought for, what this war was all about. He was willing to die to preserve his heritage, so that his son could carry on in his place.

A wave of pure homesickness swept over him and he turned his thoughts purposely away from his family, only to have other equally nostalgic thoughts enter his mind. His thoughts now centered on his personal servant, Lum. Lum had been given to him as a present from his father on his twelfth birthday. They grew up together, swam together and fished and hunted. They were like brothers, one white and the other as black as the ace of spades.

Their relationship was that of friends, rather than master and slave. Matthew's father had not approved of the friendship but was powerless to stop it. As far as Lum was concerned, Matthew had but one regret, and that was that he had not freed his black friend before he left to go to war. Matthew's thoughts bothered him and he turned his head as if to get away from them. It was a mistake for pain exploded in his head and he couldn't remember later whether he had slept or lost consciousness.

Matthew awakened as pain exploded in his side. His eyes flew open but he was unable to focus them well enough to see what had caused his pain. Fortunately, his ears were in somewhat better working order and what he heard made his blood run cold. Yankee voices sounded all around him and one in particular was just above him. "Get up!" the voice commanded, just before the hard toe of a booted foot connected once more with his unprotected ribs. In spite of himself, Matthew grunted in pain, though the shock of the blow served to somewhat clear his head. With what little strength he had, Matthew pushed against the ground with both arms in an attempt to get up. Half way up, he was overcome with dizziness. He would have fallen except the Yankee soldier who gripped his collar was holding on too tight. At first, Matthew's blurred vision registered two of them but as his head cleared, he could see that there was only one.

Swaying but determined to stay on his feet, Matthew looked straight into the eyes of his antagonist. The cruelty that he beheld in the eyes of the other man shocked him to the core; never had he seen such evil in the eyes of another human being. The hand at his collar tightened, shutting off his breath and he swayed dizzily once more. The Yankee sergeant jerked Matthew hard, pulling him to within inches of his snarling face. "Fall! You Rebel bastard! Give me an excuse to kill you. You're not worth the powder it'd take to blow you clean to hell!" he roared. Matthew found a reserve of strength that he didn't know he had and stood glaring back into the evil eyes of the Yankee before him.

Their staring match was ended when a Yankee private interrupted them. "Sarge, this one over here can't get up. What do you want me to do with him?" he asked.

The Yankee let go of Matthew's collar and turned to answer the private. "Watch this one," he commanded." I'll take care of the other one."

Matthew stood helplessly at gunpoint as he watched in horror as the evil eyed Yankee sergeant cold bloodedly finished off the young Rebel soldier who was unable to rise. Sickened, he watched as the scene was repeated over and over until only the walking wounded were left alive.

The Yankee sergeant seemed to take fiendish pleasure in the killing of his helpless victims. When he had finally finished his gruesome detail, there were only six men in butternut brown and gray left alive. They were the fortunate ones, alive, able to walk and prisoners of the Yankees.

The forced march to the holding pens began and Matthew managed to stay on his feet by concentrating on putting one foot in front of the other. Right, left, right, left, his vision blurred, causing him to stumble. The pain of a bayonet piercing the skin of his back, cleared his head and his vision and he stumbled on. A man beside him was less lucky, he fell to the ground and when it became evident that he would not be able to rise, he was unceremoniously pierced through with a bayonet.

The march seemed to go on forever and only the knowledge that to fall was to die kept Matthew going. He was scarcely aware of his surroundings as he plodded along, putting one foot in front of the other. After a time the back of his shirt was soaked with blood as he bled from half a dozen cuts from the point of the Yankee's bayonet. Each time he stumbled, the bayonet point pierced him again until at last he came to expect it. After a time, he no longer even felt it, for the pain in his head overrode it all. Reasonable thought was becoming impossible and it crossed his mind that if he were to fall, they would kill him and in death he would find ease for his head.

Matthew stumbled once more, this time falling to his knees. This time the expected prod of the bayonet came and by now, he hardly felt it at all. For long seconds, he hesitated and at last a mental picture of his son's face came to his rescue. With every ounce of strength left in him, Matthew attempted to rise, failed and tried again. Behind him, the voice of the Yankee sergeant rang in his ears, " Go ahead and fall, you Rebel scum. It would give me great pleasure to ram this pig sticker in you clear up to the hilt."

The sharp point of the bayonet bit into Matthew's back once more and he made yet another valiant effort to rise. It wasn't so much that he was afraid of dying; it had become a matter of pride that he not go at the hands of this particular Yankee. Helpless rage consumed him, so bitter that it tasted like gall upon his tongue. Hatred for the sergeant with the bayonet so filled him that he dug his fingernails into the palms of his hands so deeply that he drew blood. Deep in his heart, Matthew made a vow; he would get that bastard if it was the last thing he ever did.

With a strength born of rage, he managed to rise half way up. He suddenly felt himself being lifted the rest of the way by a strong arm, clothed in butternut brown. A rich southern voice penetrated through to his befuddled mind, though the word was softly spoken, "Walk!" It was a command and used to obeying, his body followed orders.

Even with the strong arm of the other man supporting him, Matthew doubted that he could have gone on much longer. The Yankees halted beneath sheltering trees at high noon and the prisoners were allowed to rest. They were given neither food nor water before they were secured to trees and left guarded by one sleepy guard.

Matthew's arms were tied behind him and the position caused the cut on his arm to open and bleed, fortunately not for long. The light beneath the tree was not so blinding and he looked to find the man who had supported him the last weary mile or so.

Tied to a tree just opposite him sat a Confederate private and Matthew recognized him by a peculiar bloodstain on his sleeve. The stain was roughly in the shape of a horse's head and this was the only thing he had seen clearly about the man up until now. His first thought was to thank him but he appeared to be sleeping. Instead, Matthew studied the dark face, memorizing it for future reference. A cap of confederate gray was pulled low over a nut-brown forehead with straight black hair spilling from beneath it. The features of the young private were those of a white man but the skin was Indian dark. As he looked, eyes as black as a Negro's suddenly opened and gazed back at him seriously for a moment. The jet black eyes suddenly broke into a twinkle and the dark face was lit by a white toothed smile.

"Hell of a fix we're in." he said. "I thought that damn Yankee never would quit usin' you for a pin cushion."

"My back feels like a pin cushion. I'm Captain Matthew Kendall and I owe you a favor for your help back there."

"Private Todd O'Mally at your service. Captain. If you're thinkin' that's a strange name for a Cherokee, you're right. My father was Irish and my mother was an Indian. I reckon that's why their children turned out as wild as bucks." Todd explained with a grin.

In spite of his headache, Matthew managed to return the grin. "Well, this is one fellow that's damn glad to meet you. They raise some pretty wild offspring here in Georgia too. My home's down south of here. Where did you come from? " Matthew asked.

"About as far south as you can get and still be in civilized territory." Todd said, with a laugh.

"My sister and I have a small plantation in Florida. I came up here with McCant's Marion Light Artillery."

Todd shifted his weight, dislodging his cap and as it fell to the ground, Matthew could see that a blood soaked neckerchief was tied around his head. Matthew didn't have to ask why Todd hadn't left the battlefield the night before.

The noon break was short and the forced march to the holding pens continued. The short rest had done Matthew a world of good and he was able to continue the rest of the way unaided. The pain from his various injuries continued but to his intense relief, much of the dizziness had subsided.

They arrived at the holding pens at sundown and were put in with some fifty or so other Confederate prisoners to be shipped to a federal prison somewhere up north.

The prisoners were given a meal of hardtack and shared dippers of water from a common bucket. The scanty meal somewhat revived Matthew and he, along with Todd sought a place to rest along the stockade walls. In the opposite corner of the holding pen, someone began playing a harmonica. The talk among the prisoners died down so that the only other sound was that of the sentries as they made their rounds. The last notes of a ballad were followed by "Dixie", the sweet notes of the song of the South rang out in the still Georgia air. After a while, the player grew silent and softly spoken conversations once more sprang up among the men.

Matthew laid down on the hard, cold ground and closed his eyes. His head was still throbbing as well as his bruised ribs and his back felt as if it had been stung by at least a hundred bees. He was a quiet man by nature, but the urge to talk was upon him. Curiosity about his newly found friend was foremost on his mind and it was an easy curiosity to satisfy. He had but to ask the more talkative man a question and the answer was most likely to be long and informative.

"When you left Florida, did you figure on bein' gone this long?" Matthew asked.

Todd shook his head and an ironic grin split his face. "Hell no, I figgered like everybody else, that we'd whip them damn Yankees in six months time. Me'n my sister had just graduated from the academy. She went on home but me and the rest of the boys, including the teacher joined up with the Confederacy. I reckon we all thought it'd be a lark." Todd sighed and wrapped his arms around himself against the evening chill. A far away look came into his dark eyes as he continued to talk. "I got a letter from her a couple of months ago, she wrote to tell me our Daddy had died. She's got the place to run all by herself now. It's not the biggest I ever seen but I reckon it'll do. What about you Captain? You from one of them big plantations?" Todd asked.

"We're not on duty, call me Matthew." Matthew invited. "I'm from Silver Oaks, just south of Atlanta. It'll go to my son one day. I guess that's what this war's all about."

Todd's voice was still wistful as he replied. "I ain't got a wife yet but there's a little gal I reckon I'll marry if I ever get back home. Now my sister's a different story, that girl's too wild for any man to tame. She's one tough little gal though."

Todd grew silent but Matthew wanted to hear more. "I haven't been home in two years. My son was just a baby when I left. I've passed within a couple of miles of home and still couldn't get leave. I'll be glad when this thing's over. I sure do want to see my boy." Matthew's voice had become as wistful as Todd's.

"And your wife too," Todd prompted. "Is she pretty?" he asked.

"Yeah." Matthew replied but didn't elaborate.

"Hell," Todd continued, "it's bad enough missin' my girl. Reckon it'd be even harder if she was my wife. But then, we got other things to worry about now I reckon."

Matthew looked and sounded half asleep when he replied. "I sure as hell don't intend to spend the rest of the war in a Yankee prison, if that's what you mean. It could take forever before we get exchanged and I sure as hell don't want to be used as trading fodder to pay for getting some Yankee free to kill more of our boys.

There ought'a be some way out of this glorified pig pen they got us in. Come mornin' I reckon we'll have to see if these boys don't have a gap in their lines big enough to walk through. I still haven't got over Rosecrans leaving his door wide open for us like that. He had to have been drunk or crazy one. Thomas sure as hell gave us a run for our money though." Matthew concluded what for him was a very long speech.

Todd arched an eyebrow, his thoughts apparently ran along the same lines. "Well, if you come up with anything, let me know. I got better things to do than spend my time getting' jerked around by these bluebellies."

Matthew didn't answer right away, he'd discovered that he'd been

11

still too long and his shirt was sticking to his back. "Damn, I can hardly move. How about pouring a dipper of water on my back, before I completely grow to this shirt." he told Todd. His voice grew harsh as he continued, "I'm going to get that bastard with the bayonet, if it takes me the rest of my life." he growled.

The bucket was nearly empty but Todd managed to fill the dipper. "Damn bucket's empty, you better drink a swallow of this before I pour it out." he suggested. "We ain't likely to get any more before mornin'."

They shared a drink of water before Todd carefully poured the remainder over Matthew's back. The water burned the cuts on Matthew's back like fire and he sucked air between his teeth. Todd returned the dipper to the bucket and proceeded to peel the shirt from the wounds on Matthew's back. "You're damn lucky, the bastard didn't shoot you." he said. "I reckon he probably would'a but I got the feelin' they ain't got enough ammunition to spare."

"My thoughts exactly." Matthew agreed. "I sure would like to get my hands on one of those Spencer rifles. If Jeff Davis could get his hands on enough of them, we'd win this war for old Dixie for sure."

Todd pulled the last of the stuck places loose. "There you go." he said. "Too bad I ain't got a jar of ol' Granny's salve to smear on. It'd probably draw out the soreness by mornin'."

"You got a point there," agreed Matthew." I'd rather have a black root woman doctor me any day, than one of these army surgeons. Hell, they kill more than they cure. I'm going to try to get some sleep, no tellin' what tomorrow will bring."

After another moonlit night, the prisoners awakened to early morning fog. The Confederate prisoners shivered in the early morning dampness. They breakfasted on gruel and water, refraining from excessive complaints, lest even that be taken away. Through the cracks in the upright log walls of the holding pen, Matthew and Todd, along with the others watched as the majority of the Yankee troops at the encampment marched off to Chattanooga. The number of soldiers left to guard the Rebel prisoners was comparatively small and many of them took heart. A cocky feeling of superiority sprang up among them and a dozen different plans of escape were concocted among the ragged, unarmed men.

Matthew and Todd listened to the variety of schemes and rejected most of them as mere foolishness. After some discussion on the subject, they decided to bide their time and hope for the right opportunity to present itself.

Todd was in relatively good spirits, but Matthew, still suffering from his wounds ran a low-grade fever. He suffered from chills early in the morning but began to improve as the sun began to bake the stiffness from his body. Later, in the afternoon, the rumor spread among the Rebel prisoners that they would be moved out early the next morning.

Throughout the day, constant conversation had strengthened the budding friendship between Matthew and Todd. There was a natural merging of like spirits, as if the two men were cut from the same pattern, if not the same piece of cloth. This was a new experience for Matthew. He wasn't a man to form close friendships easily but he was rapidly finding in Todd the person of the brother he had never had.

By the end of the day, there was little that was worth knowing about either one of them that hadn't been told. Matthew found himself almost envying Todd. They were almost equal in education and neither of them had ever known poverty. It was the growing up years that were different for the two. While Matthew was brought up to take his place in the aristocracy of the south, Todd, other than getting an education, was allowed to grow up, more or less a free spirit. Though Matthew reasoned that the war years had little changed Todd, he himself had come into being his own person. In the army of the Confederacy, no one was concerned with how he talked or dressed, or if his manners were less than perfect. Before the war, the only living person who knew the real Matthew Kendall, was his servant and companion, Lum. Todd, on the other hand was free to be himself. He'd gone to school, learned perfect manners and English, along with the three "R's", kept the knowledge and left the refinement in the classroom. Refinement was something that Todd put on when needed and took off when he didn't, like changing shirts. For Matthew, it had was a thing he had to wear, day after day.

While Matthew loved Silver Oaks, with the love any man has for his home; Todd loved his small plantation with an affection that bordered on passion. Todd's vivid descriptions of the state of Florida, still sparsely settled and for the most part still virtually a wilderness, fired Matthew's imagination. In his mind grew a mental picture that was a cross between Paradise and the Garden of Eden. He fell asleep that night, listening to Todd talk about a place near his plantation,

13

called Silver Spring. In the night, Matthew dreamed of it and awakened briefly to wonder just how accurate the dream had been. No place could be like that, he finally decided and chalked the whole thing up to utter bullshit. No water could be so clear that a pebble could be seen sixty feet below the surface. How could enough water boil up out of the ground to make a river a hundred feet wide? Matthew decided that he would have to take some things Todd talked about with a grain of salt.

Chapter 3

The prisoners were marched out of the holding pens at gunpoint early the next morning. Breakfast was a repeat of the morning before and for once, there was no fog. Matthew's wounds were healing and he felt strong and ready for what lay ahead. He and Todd marched along with the others, keeping quiet for the most part and keeping their eyes and ears open. There was no chance of escape during the day, but perhaps if they had to camp before reaching the train, they might find an opportunity.

As they had hoped, the Yankees stopped for the night. The prisoners were secured to trees on a wooded hillside and there were not enough guards to watch them all closely. It was here that luck was on their side. The Union soldier who tied Matthew's hands behind his back, was fooled into thinking that the wound on his arm was much worse than it really was. Matthew had allowed his arm hang apparently limp and useless all day. The tattered, blood soaked sleeve of his shirt added credence to the appearance of a severe wound. The Yankee soldier, kinder than most, took pity on him and tied him loosely.

Under the cover of darkness, Matthew was able to work both hands free and while one of the guards was occupied elsewhere, he was able to free Todd.

From there on it was a matter of waiting patiently for the right moment to slip away. It came at last, when one of the guards fell asleep and the other was distracted by sounds in the bushes, perhaps made by some small animal.

Their escape would have been a total success if the sleeping guard had not woken up at the last minute and shouted an alarm. They ran through the dark woods, dodging trees and musket fire, making poor targets for the pursuing Yankees. It was apparent that the Yankees' hearts weren't in the chase, for they didn't search long or very hard for the escapees.

Though they could no longer hear any signs of further pursuit, Matthew and Todd continued to run until they had stitches in their sides and were completely winded. Still, they would have kept moving, had not Todd called out breathlessly for Matthew to wait. Something in the other man's voice brought Matthew quickly to his side.

Todd was clutching his left arm, just below the elbow and a stream of blood dripped from his fingertips onto the ground.

"Tie something around this damn thing! I'm leaving a trail a child could follow." Todd gasped.

Matthew examined the arm as best he could in the poor light. "Hell, man. Why didn't you say something sooner? You've lost a lot of blood already." Matthew pulled a handkerchief from his pocket and tied it tightly around the bleeding arm above the wound. Fortunately the mini ball had gone through and only nicked the bone.

Todd made light of the whole thing. "Didn't seem like the right time to be stopping to fuss with a scratch. I doubt if them sons-of-bitches'll bother following us anyhow. No use to tempt them with a clear marked trail though. Damn, I ain't had nothing hurt this much since a snapping turtle bit my big toe when I was just a young'un. I thought the bastard never would let go."

Matthew smiled wryly. "Hell, that's no turtle bite you've got there! You damn near lost your arm! A half inch over and that bone would have looked like kindling wood. You sure as hell have a talent for understating a situation."

Todd plunged his injured arm between the buttons of his shirt to give it some support and shrugged. "It ain't nothing I tell you. You worry worse than an old woman, Matthew." he stated flatly.

"The hell I do," Matthew denied. "Let's put a few more miles between us and those Yankees before daylight. Maybe by then we can find a place to lay up and rest for a while."

They kept moving until daylight and stopped at a stream to drink. At least for the time being the area was deserted. They bathed in the stream, ridding themselves of several days accumulation of dirt. Todd lay belly down in the cold water and soaked his arm.

Matthew was concerned about the wound, even though Todd kept insisting that it wasn't much worse than a mosquito bite. Though the bone was only nicked, there was a chunk of flesh and muscle that were completely torn away. The third and forth fingers on Todd's hand wouldn't move at all and he probably never would have full use of that arm again. Matthew bandaged Todd's arm as best he could and they wallowed themselves out a place in a thicket to sleep.

After a few hours, Matthew was awakened by Todd's moans. Todd still insisted on making light of the wound but was obviously in great pain.

"Go soak it again." Matthew suggested. "Maybe it'll help. Skeeter bite huh! You must have some damn big mosquitoes where you come from."

Todd spent a few minutes soaking his arm. It helped somewhat and they decided to move on.

Along about sundown, they came upon a farm house where a lone woman hoed in a garden. They watched the house for a while before deciding it was safe to approach it.

The old woman greeted them warmly when she saw their uniforms. She was stooped and motherly and more than glad to offer shelter to two southern boys in need.

When they were inside the shabby but comfortable house, the old woman seemed torn between feeding them and tending their wounds. Seeing Todd's distress, she decided on the latter.

"Why law' boy," she said kindly to Todd. "Let ol' Granny take a look at that there arm. You done gone and got yourself shot by one of them there Yankees. I doctored a few shot wounds in my day, got durn good at it too. My ol' man, rest his ornery soul, used to git likkered up and got hisself shot a time'r two."

She lifted a brown jug down from a shelf in the corner, uncorked it and sniffed its contents appreciatively. "This here's good stuff for what ails ya, whether ya take it inside or pour it on straight out'a th' jug." she said.

She filled two tin cups and handed one to each of them. They sipped it carefully, for to do otherwise would take a man's breath away. Todd emptied his cup first and set it down. Matthew, feeling less in need of it's rejuvenating effects, sipped his more slowly. Todd blinked owlishly, straightened his backbone and laid his arm out on the plank table for the old woman to look at. She untied the bandage and let out a low whistle at the sight of the wound. She uncorked the jug once more and was about to upend it over Todd's arm when he restrained her. "Ma'am, you certainly don't intend to pour that liquid fire on my arm do you?" Todd asked, with great dignity.

Matthew put a hand over his mouth to hide his smile of amusement. It was apparent that Todd had acquired an abundance of culture along with the White lightning.

The old woman braced her hands on her bony hips and glared down at Todd like an irate school marm. "Don't you git uppity with me boy!" she snapped. "If you know what's good fer ya, you'll let me git on with my doctorin' else you'll git gangrene an th' dang thing'll rot off."

Todd looked at her a bit taken aback but held out his arm obediently. The old woman poured a good proportion of the White lightning in and around the wound and Todd let out a yell that was loud enough to bring every Yankee down on them, from miles around.

The old woman didn't seem a bit upset by Todd's yell. "Now don't carry on so sonny, stuff does smart a might but not that fearsome. Now, let's see, a thang like that ought'a be wet healt. I got just th' thang here." She scooped up a handful of salve from a jar and packed the wound full of it. When this was done, she tied it up in a clean bandage, dabbed a smear of the salve on the cut on Todd's forehead and stood back to admire her work.

By now, more of the White lightning had soaked into Todd's system and though he was a bit white around the mouth, he gathered his instant culture around him. He kissed the old woman's hand with all the grace and pomp of an English lord. "I'm most grateful Ma 'am," he said with great dignity.

The old woman gave Todd a look that was a curious combination of pleasure and indignation and turned her attention to Matthew.

"Now, son, let ol' Granny see what she can be doin' to fix you up a might." she offered kindly.

Matthew set his cup down without finishing it's contents and took off his shirt. The old lady didn't even try to hide her bewilderment when she looked at his back.

"I ain't never seen th' likes of this in all my born days." she stated.

"What'n th' heck done this to ya?"

Matthew's gray eyes turned as dark and hard as steel but he answered the old woman calmly. "The point of a Yankee's bayonet. It seems I couldn't move fast enough to suit them."

The old woman clucked over Matthew's back and coated it with some of the same ointment she had used on Todd. The cut on his arm was given much the same treatment and she produced a clean but faded man's shirt to replace his tattered one. Matthew thanked her and wished that he had a way of repaying her for her kindness. All he had was Confederate money and it was hardly worth the paper it was written on.

The old woman fed them the best meal either of them had had in months and they spent the night on pallets on her floor.

Chapter 4

The next morning, they announced their intentions to leave but the old woman insisted that Todd stay on so that she could look after him until his arm had healed. After giving the matter some thought and discussing it at length, they decided that she was right.

When Matthew was ready to leave, Todd followed him outside. "Where do you aim to go?" he asked.

The pleasant expression on Matthew's face faded and his gray eyes grew as dark as thunder clouds. "I'm going to find that bayonet happy Yankee snake and kill the son-of-a-bitch." Matthew replied.

"How the heck do you think you're gonna do that?" Todd asked incredulously. "We don't even know where he went."

"I know where he went. That bunch he left out with was going to Virginia. I didn't sleep too good that first night and I heard them talking about it." Matthew replied.

Todd raised a raven black eyebrow. "Look buddy, I know how you feel. I'd like nothin' better than to get my hands on that scum myself but the chances of you catchin' up with him ain't good. You could spend the rest of the war huntin' that piece of trash and all you'd get out of it is shot for desertion."

Matthew had no choice but to admit that Todd was right. "I know and I reckon he's not worth it. Since I'm already missing, I think I'll slip off to Silver Oaks and see how that boy of mine's doing."

"Yeah," Todd replied. "I reckon you could get away with it. A man needs to see his wife once in a while too."

Matthew gave no reply to Todd's last statement. "I'll concoct some kind of story to tell my regiment when I get back to them." he said.

Todd didn't even try to hide the fact that he hated to see Matthew go. "Look," he said "if I don't see you again before this war's over, I want you to promise to look me up, if we both live through this thing. Come see me and I'll show you huntin' and fishin' like you ain't never seen." he promised.

Matthew shook Todd's hand and took him up on the offer. "I'll do just that." he said. He turned to go but the old woman called him back.

"I got me some stuff here you might be needin' boy. Reckon th' feller that had it won't be needin' it no more." She presented Matthew with a full knapsack and a nearly new rifle. He was at a loss for words, not knowing how to thank her. At last, he simply hugged her and walked away, without looking back.

Early the next morning, Matthew found a horse that had perhaps wandered off during the fighting at Chickamauga. Now, well armed and mounted and with a knapsack full of food, he set off at a mile eating pace for Silver Oaks. His journey, for the most part, was unimpeded. He kept to the back roads and since the Yankee army was mostly in Tennessee, he made good time.

As he drew nearer to home, his thoughts raced ahead of him. Things were bound to be different since the war was getting so close to home. The Union navy had all the ports blockaded and it was next to impossible to export the cotton. It would not bring in nearly as much profit on the local market. Matthew's father was a good businessman and had trained him well in the running of the plantation. He resolved to talk with his father about freeing the slaves and working out some kind of sharecropping arrangement with them. The Kendall family had always treated their slaves well. There was a strong bond between them and the slaves, who among themselves referred to the white family as 'their people.'

Due to the war, there were no letters passed between Matthew and his family. Still, he had high hopes of finding them all well. And then there was Lum, his personal slave and closest friend. Matthew had long since decided to give Lum his freedom, no matter what the situation was at Silver Oaks.

Matthew spurred the horse to greater speed as he drew closer to home. Silver Oaks was located just south of the city of Atlanta and Matthew skirted the town lest he be found without furlough papers.

As he topped the hill overlooking the house, he stopped to look and catch his breath. The white mansion looked as stately as ever, with it's tall columns rising majestically. As he drew nearer, it became clear that the grounds were not as well kept as before and only a handful of blacks could be seen working in the fields.

It was apparent that the plantation had suffered during his absence. As he entered the yard, Matthew's heart skipped a beat, then began to pound in alarm. Upon the front door was a black funeral wreath.

Matthew dismounted, ignoring the pain in his wounds caused by the sudden movement. He ran up the steps to the porch, two at a time and when he reached the front door, he found that it was locked. Pounding impatiently upon the carved panels, he waited to be let in.

The door was at last opened by a young black girl who had once been a field hand. She stared at him for a moment before opening the door all the way and he could tell by her expression that at first she didn't recognize him. Surely, he hadn't changed that much in only two years, he thought.

The girl's black eyes suddenly lit with recognition and she began to talk excitedly. "Massa Matthew! Lawd, it be you! Miz 'Lizabeth say you not gwine get no message she sends, but you sho' did. Lawdy, I'se sho' glad you done come home! Miz 'Lizabeth, she sho' be in a sorry state heah lately."

"Liza, what in heaven's name are you talking about?" Matthew asked. "I haven't received any messages from here in months and what is Elizabeth in a state about?"

"Oh Lawd, Massa. Oh Lawd!" Liza moaned and covered her face with her hands.

Matthew drew on patience that he didn't know he had and gently pulled the black girl's hands away from her face. "Liza," he said, in a soft but commanding voice, "what is going on here?"

Liza shook her head sadly. "I takes you to Miz 'Lizabeth, she be de one what ought'a be doin' de tellin'." she said sadly.

Matthew followed her up the winding flight of stairs to the door of the master bedroom. Liza went quickly back down the stairs, leaving him to enter the room alone. He tapped lightly on the door and entered without waiting for his knock to be answered.

The heavy drapes were closed over the windows and it was a moment before Matthew made out the huddled form of Elizabeth on the massive bed. She was propped up by at least half a dozen pillows. Even in the dimly lit room, Matthew could see that her hair was in total disarray and that her face was blotched from weeping.

When Elizabeth saw him she cried out, "Matthew!" and held out her hands to him.

Matthew crossed the floor and clasped his wife's hands as he sat down on the side of the bed. Before he could say anything, she began to speak. "Matthew, I tried, I tried so hard! I got a doctor out of Atlanta! I did everything I could." Elizabeth's voice broke and she began to weep.

"A doctor for who? For God's sake woman! What's going on here?" Matthew demanded.

Elizabeth grew hysterical and Matthew lost what little patience he had left. Though it was not in his nature to strike a woman, he gave her enough of a slap across the face to bring her to her senses.

She looked at him in stunned surprise and answered him quite calmly. "Little Matthew and your Daddy. A fever took them both. Oh God, Matthew. I tried to save them. I tried so hard."

Matthew was too stunned to even cry and he stared at her in utter disbelief. He sat without moving for so long that Elizabeth, thinking he hadn't understood her, repeated herself. "They're dead Matthew. Our son and your father, they're both gone. Matthew, say something, oh please say something!" She put her arms around him and began to cry once more.

Matthew held his wife's shaking body and stared blindly over her shoulder. At last the numbness inside of him began to dissolve and he felt something in him crumble and fall into a million pieces. As if he was in a trance, he pulled away from her and stood up.

Elizabeth held out her arms to him in a gesture of pleading. "Don't leave me, Matthew. Please don't hate me for failing you." she begged.

A wave of pity swept through Matthew and he held Elizabeth's hand gently. "I don't blame you, Elizabeth. I know that you did everything that could be done. You've been a good wife and a good mother. It's just that I am so empty inside." Matthew drew in a deep breath and let it out in a sigh that was almost a sob.

Matthew left the room and went to seek out his mother. He found her in her bedroom, sitting by a window and sewing peacefully. She looked up as he entered the room and eyed him sharply. "Son you're late and look how dirty you've gotten your clothes! You've been out playing with that boy, Lum again. I can tell. Your Daddy is going to be mad. You know he wants you to take more of an interest in the plantation." At this point her voice sounded even more discontented. "Matthew, your Daddy works mighty hard to make this the finest plantation in the state of Georgia and all you want to do is play with that slave Lum."

Considering his mother's obvious state of mind, Matthew had no choice but to humor her. She had retreated into the past and he saw no reason to attempt to bring her back. The present was nothing short of hell and the future was not guaranteed. "I'll try to do better Mother." he promised. This seemed to satisfy her and Matthew left her to her sewing. As he walked out the door, he felt yet another part of himself crumble into nothing.

Matthew went in search of Lum. He needed his black friend's love and understanding more than he had ever needed anything in his life. He found the quarters nearly deserted as he wandered through them. He asked someone where Lum was and was told that he was out supervising the work in the fields.

Only a few acres were under cultivation and as Matthew approached them, Lum saw him and came running to meet him. Of all the things on the plantation that he had seen thus far, Lum was the least changed. He was still as black as the ace of spades and as big and tall as a mountain.

Lum greeted his master with a bear hug and warm affection. "Massa Matthew." he said with feeling. "I'se sho' sorry you gots to come home to so much sorrow. Ol' Massa and de boy too. It sho' be sad times heah but dis be one man what be glad to hab you home."

Some of Matthew's closely guarded emotions broke free under the influence of Lum's sympathy. "Lum, how can I go on?" he asked. "My Daddy was an old man and I can see why God saw fit to take him, but why little Matthew? It just doesn't seem like I've got anything left worth living for."

Lum scratched at his woolly head and patted Matthew's shoulder awkwardly. "Massa, dis world done be spinnin' all out ob control. But one ob dease days it's gwine stop an' settle back wheah it s'pose to be. Things be bettah when dat day come. We all gwine get by someways, I guesses. You an' Miz 'Lizabeth still be young, you can hab a whole wagon load ob chillen 'fore you gets too ol'." Lum said philosophically.

"I know that Lum, but it doesn't make losing this one any easier and as for Silver Oaks, I just don't know what's to become of this place. I can't stay here. I'm not even on leave, I just slipped off. Now that Daddy's dead there's nobody but Elizabeth to run it and she doesn't have the foggiest idea how to go about it. Lum, what's a man to do?" Matthew asked.

"Massa," Lum replied, "We gots 'bout thirty ob us left heah, dat's what be left aftah de rest ob dem done took off for de nawth. Ol' Massa done give what ob us dat stays cash money an' we be doin' jus' fine. What I be tryin' to say be dis. I'se gwine help Miz 'Lizabeth on de place. De people what we got be 'nough to hol' dis place togetha till de wah be ovah."

"Lum, I don't know what I'd do without you." Matthew said with feeling. "I should have given you your freedom papers before I left. I've kicked myself a thousand times for not doing it. I've got to go back to my unit tomorrow, but I'll tell Elizabeth to take care of the legal paperwork. You are free, Lum. You can do whatever you want with your life."

"Lawd, Massa Matthew. What I'se gwine do, I be free? I likes it jus' where I'se at." Lum replied.

"If that's what you want Lum, then I'm grateful. But you're a free man now, you can go where you please."

"It please me to stay heah." Lum replied. In spite of the sad occasion, he gave his former master and friend a white toothed grin.

After talking with Lum for several more minutes about his sharecropping plans, Matthew made his way to the family cemetery. He stood for a long while gazing down at the fresh graves and steeled himself against the pain that washed over him in waves. He dreaded going back to the house to a mother who was lost in the past and a wife that he hardly knew. At last he turned his back on the fresh mounds of earth where Silver Oak's memories of the past and dreams of the future lay buried.

Elizabeth was coming down the stairs when he entered the house.

She had changed her clothes and combed her hair. Though her face was still puffy from weeping, it was fresh and clean. As she saw him come in, she straightened her shoulders and lifted her chin. "Did you see Mother Kendall?" she asked.

"I saw her." Matthew replied. "How long has she been like that?"

Elizabeth shrugged her shoulders. "Since Papa Kendall and little Matthew died. She just couldn't accept it. My folks couldn't either, they left everything and went to New Orleans until after the war is over. They wanted me to go with them but I felt like I belonged here, looking after things in your absence." Her face crumpled momentarily and she controlled herself with obvious effort. "Fine job I'm doing! I need you here Matthew."

"Elizabeth, you know I have to go back, though Lord knows there's not much left to fight for." Matthew said dispiritedly.

"Don't say that, Matthew." she pleaded. "We can have more children. We'll win this war and then we can rebuild." She took his hand in both her own and held it.

"Elizabeth, I wonder, I just wonder." Matthew looked down at her sadly.

She took his hand and began leading him up the stairs. "I had Tilly fix you some food and the boys prepare a bath for you. Come eat and bathe, Matthew, you've been through hell."

Matthew looked at his wife in surprise, she had never used a word like hell in front of him in her life. "So have you." he conceded. "I am pleased with you Elizabeth."

Elizabeth gave him a small but appreciative smile. "Thank you Matthew." she said.

Elizabeth left Matthew alone to eat the food she had brought up for him. It would soon be dark and she had another duty to attend to and only one night in which to get it done. More than anything, she wanted another child and she was eager to do what must be done in order to achieve it. True, she was fond of Matthew and if not for the war, she would be quite happy with him. She was content with him and her marriage before the war broke out, though she could have done without the wifely duty part. But then, how else was one to have children? Her heart would always ache for the son they had lost and she was sorry that Matthew had not had a chance to get to know him. Her bright little boy child, such a sweet, good boy. He could never be replaced but perhaps another would help to fill the empty spot in her heart.

Elizabeth gave Matthew an hour in which to bathe and eat then slowly ascended the stairs. She closed and locked the bedroom door behind her. Matthew was asleep on the bed and she stood looking at him for a moment. There were new lines on his face that hadn't been there before and there was a touch of premature gray in his hair. He was lying on his stomach so that his bare back was exposed to her. She saw the wounds from the bayonet and the still raw gash on his arm. A rush of tenderness swept over her such as she had never felt for Matthew before. For the first time in her marriage to him, she was filled with an urge to love her husband. In a way, she was trying to make up for his suffering and her own shortcomings.

There was a sense of urgency to her feelings, their time together would be so short and she must make the most of it. She undressed quickly and dropped a silk nightgown over her head. Sitting before her dressing table mirror, she brushed out her hair, so that it fell in silky waves down her back. Elizabeth blew out the candles and took a deep breath to give herself courage. She was about to seduce her own husband and it was an experience that was entirely new to her.

Matthew awakened slowly, emerging from a realm of deep sleep, induced by physical and emotional exhaustion. He felt the soft hands that stroked him and for a time, he simply enjoyed the soothing sensation of being touched. His sleep-clouded brain did not question what he felt, it only absorbed the comforting feeling of being soothed and cared for. Part of his mind told him that he was dreaming, for this kind of behavior was not in the nature of his wife. Yet as the soft touching continued, he became more aware that the dream was real. With this realization came a rush of desire that swept over his body like wildfire. With a groan, he turned over and gathered Elizabeth in his arms. To his delight, she responded in kind, pulling him closer to her and tangling her fingers in his hair.

The woman, who had not kissed him hello after an absence of two long years, now kissed him of her own accord. Her lips were warm and willing, though lacking in passion. However when he attempted to deepen the kiss, she stiffened and drew away. He restrained himself, kissing her more carefully and was rewarded when her hands drifted like butterflies down his back. She inadvertently touched a sore spot and Matthew flinched. "Did I hurt you?" she inquired softly.

"Um, I'm a little sore." Matthew admitted.

"Matthew, I missed you." she purred.

"I believe you did." he said, a bit surprised.

Elizabeth didn't comment, she only moved her body against him in a way that she never had before. He had gone too long without a woman to be overly patient and when he began to touch her more intimately, a bit of her old reticence came back. Still, she offered no resistance when he stripped the nightgown from her body and positioned himself above her. Her response was affectionate, though without passion and she submitted to his loving freely, if not helpfully. Matthew's passion was quickly spent and he was overcome with sleep immediately thereafter.

Chapter 5

Daylight the next morning found Matthew well on his way. As before, he skirted the city of Atlanta and kept to the back roads. With luck, he would rejoin his regiment after being gone no more than ten days. After the horrendous fighting at Chickamauga, it would probably be no surprise that many of the other troops would be filtering in late. After riding hard all the way, a story of his capture and escape and an exaggerated tale of ill health would probably get him off with less than a spank on the hand.

Matthew arrived, suitably haggard looking, on Lookout Mountain where the Confederate army was holding onto the mountain like a bull dog. During the time he was away, little action had taken place. General Bragg's plan was to sit tight and try to starve out the Union forces. Matthew figured that the plan just might work. Their position was good, their fortifications strong and they had a bird's eye view of everything taking place below them.

Army life settled down for a while of peacefully waiting for the action to begin. Matthew slipped off once to check on Todd and found that under the care of the old woman, his wound had healed amazingly well and that he had left to rejoin his regiment. She had no idea exactly where that was and Matthew surmised that Todd had probably gone farther north.

Late in October, the peaceful holding of Lookout Mountain and

Missionary Ridge came to an end. The Union troops swarmed up the mountainsides like angry ants up an anthill and in spite of putting up a good fight, the Rebel forces were driven down. There was scant time to organize a plan to take any kind of concrete stand. The attack had taken them by surprise, under the cover of darkness. Part of the Rebels were driven into the hills, Matthew included, where they sought refuge and like dogs with their tails between their legs, stopped to lick their wounds. The remainder of Bragg's forces were driven into the heart of Georgia.

It was not until June, that Matthew was involved in any major battle. On the Twenty-seventh, they were attacked on Kennesaw Mountain by Union forces and succeeded in dealing a severe loss to General Sherman's troops.

Still, both the segments of the Confederate army were penned down, both farther north and in the south. Matthew, among others was beginning to see that any chance of the South becoming an independent nation was a lost cause. Their only hope was to hang on and keep the war going, until the North got tired of it.

In the month of July, the fighting centered in Atlanta and even though the South won a few victories, by early September, Atlanta had become occupied by Federal troops. News reached the ill-fed army of the South in Georgia of the taking of the Shenandoah Valley in Virginia. Times were hard for the South and Matthew, along with the others suffered from lack of nourishing food and worn out uniforms.

The situation became even worse in the month of November when a large part of Atlanta was burned and General Sherman's army, like fiends out of hell, destroyed a sixty-mile wide stretch of land, from Atlanta to the sea. It was during this time that Matthew was once again captured by the Yankees. This time, he was not successful in escaping and was sent to a Federal prison camp.

Bone tired and sick, Matthew, along with fifty other Rebel soldiers, was herded out of the boxcar that had hauled them into falling snow. Matthew's worn out boots and tattered uniform offered little protection from the bitter cold, as he marched with the other men into the confines of the prison. The former warehouse was little warmer than the air outside and the scene that met Matthew's eyes as he entered made his blood run even colder.

So many men were crowded into the room that there was hardly room to move. The enclosure more resembled a hospital, than a prison, for so many of the men were sick. The ragged scraps of humanity huddled in curled up balls on the floor, most of them without blankets and all of them were shivering in the cold. A single wood heater provided the only source of heat and the men were fighting among themselves for a chance to huddle around it.

Matthew was quickly finding out that the horrors of battle were nothing, compared to the degradations of prison life. His first meal consisted of a piece of rancid meat, no bigger than the palm of his hand and a cup of what was supposed to be coffee but tasted like nothing he had ever encountered before. Matthew refused to eat that first meal and his fellow prisoners fought for a chance to eat it in his place.

The state of health of the prisoners ranged from the fairly healthy new arrivals to men who were now reduced to the point of skeletal thinness. The men who had been there for a while were little more than animals. What little spirit they had left in them was concentrated on just staying alive. They talked of escape but other than scrounging for food, they were too lethargic to even try. Matthew counted eight dead men carried out that first day. The bodies were stripped of all clothing, their rags taken by the others. When he inquired about getting medical care, he was told that if he wished to live, the last thing he needed to do was see the so called prison doctor. The hospital was a tent behind the prison and the usual cause of death within it was freezing to death. The prisoners cared for each other as best they could and avoided the hospital tent at all costs.

By the end of the first week, Matthew began to feel the general lassitude and sickness of heart seeping into him. What was left of his ragged gray uniform hung off his body like moss from a tree. Hunger gnawed at him constantly. After the first couple of days, he had learned to eat the sorry rations that were given to him. Along with the others, he had begun trapping rats for food and had decided that they tasted a lot like squirrel.

His mind became a valuable refuge and for the first time, he began to understand his mother's retreat into the past. Though physical survival was a constant battle, mental survival was equally important. Matthew tried to avoid becoming too lost in the past. Part of his time was spent in devising means of escape, while at other times he occupied his mind with daydreams.

28

Though the men talked among themselves and often engaged in games of cards, boredom was as prominent among the prisoners as hunger. Any happening out of the ordinary was welcomed and the arrival of new prisoners was a ready source of excitement. They always had new stories to tell and sometimes had personal possessions on them that the Yankees had missed. Bartering for and even stealing such novelties had become a favorite pastime.

During the second week of Matthew's captivity a dozen more Rebel prisoners were brought in, accompanied by the usual excitement among the inmates.

The rumor had spread among them, that a new group of captives were coming in and they were eagerly watching and waiting for their arrival. When the new inmates at last arrived, a murmur arose from the men. As the first of them stumbled through the door, it was apparent that he had undergone a severe beating,. The ones who followed were bloody and bruised from head to foot. One man had recently lost an eye and another an ear. One thing that they all had in common was the bayonet wounds on their backs.

Matthew, who was sitting in a slumped position against the wall, sat bolt upright. The Yankee Sergeant that herded the men in ahead of him, like so many pigs, was the same one that had tormented him at Chickamauga. Matthew would have recognized that face anywhere. It remained in his mind's eye and haunted his dreams every day of his life.

The middle-aged Captain who sat against the wall next to Matthew, was so weak from hunger that he would not have been able to sit at all, without the wall to support him, spoke in a hoarse whisper, "Seen that one before, have you?" he asked. "Hear tell they call him the Butcher. They say he gets his kicks out of seeing the red of Southern blood. A nasty piece of work, that one. I hear the Union army threatened him with court martial for executing so many prisoners without authority. He's laid off killing so many, now he just tortures them."

"Yeah," replied Matthew. "I've seen him. I got the scars to prove it. I swore a long time ago I'd get that ill begotten piece of trash. Tell me, does filth like that have a name?"

The Captain had to wait for a fit of coughing to subside before he was able to answer. Matthew had to lean close in order to hear his words. "They say his name is John Saber. A fitting name for a butcher, I'd say."

Matthew repeated the name in his mind, fixing it firmly in his memory. If he lived to see freedom, he intended to hunt the man down. To spend weeks or months in this place would either see him dead or insane and he was determined to not end up either way.

Had not the will to live been so strong in Matthew, he would have never survived the next few months. He became nothing but a shadow of his former self. Sometimes, he found himself staring for an hour at a time at the bones of his hands and arms. His own body had become a stranger to him and he studied it curiously, wondering how something so skinny could still be alive.

The will to survive was growing weaker within him as each day passed and his mind was filled with strange visions. One of these was of water, so clear and deep, that a piece of tin could be seen on the bottom, sixty feet below the surface.

So emaciated and beaten down had Matthew become, that to survive another week seemed impossible. When freedom came, it was so unexpected that he considered it nothing more than another mental flight that his mind was taking in order to survive.

Chapter 6

Matthew lay listening to the sounds of shouting and gunfire going on just outside the prison walls. In his depressed state of mind, he only wished for the noise to cease, so that he could go back to sleep. After a time, the noise finally subsided and he thankfully closed his eyes. He was disturbed again almost immediately, when the prison doors burst open and he was beset with visions of gray clad soldiers. These soldiers were armed with flaming torches and guns and the dream seemed amazingly real. Matthew found the dream to be most entertaining. It was a very good dream, the best he had had in a long time. If only it was real, but of course it couldn't be. The vision of healthy Confederate soldiers carrying out their more unfortunate brothers from this hell on earth could only be a figment of his fevered mind.

Matthew decided that he must at least be dying for only in death could a man's mind play such tricks. He was even more convinced that he was dreaming when he felt himself being lifted up by a pair of strong arms. These arms were so brown that he could see the darkness even in the flickering torchlight. The dark face that went with the arms was filled with strength and determination to succeed.

It was a face that was strangely familiar, though a scanty beard had sprouted since Matthew had last seen it. Of course it couldn't be Todd. Todd was more than likely dead and this could only be his ghost. Matthew liked the dream and sought to stay in it. He weakly grasped a handful of a shirt that was Confederate gray and held onto it with what little strength was left in him. The dream was so real that he could actually feel the warm flesh of the man. Matthew suddenly felt compelled to speak to the vision that seemed so real. "Todd, you can't grow a beard worth a damn." he told the phantom.

In the state of mind that he was in, Matthew didn't find it at all strange when the dream phantom answered him. "Matthew? Good God in heaven!" it exclaimed. What he did find strange was the tears that gathered in the phantom's dark eyes. Surely, he had never heard of a ghost shedding tears.

Matthew drifted out of the dream and when he drifted back once more, he felt himself being loaded into an open wagon. Unseen hands, as gentle as those of a woman, wrapped him in a blanket and tucked it carefully around him. The dream was so real that he could actually see the outside of the prison. He could feel the presence of other prisoners around him and saw that even more were being brought out.

The dream was beginning to tire him, good though it was and he sensed an end to it in a grand finale. He dreamed that a cheer went up among the men, as the Federal prison went up in smoke. Matthew closed his eyes and went back to sleep.

Periodically, he continued to dream. As the wagon bumped along through the darkness, he could see stars and feel the clean fresh air upon his face. For the first time in months Matthew felt warm. He had to still be dreaming and he didn't want to wake up. If his mind was playing tricks on him, it was playing some very good ones.

Awareness came to Matthew once again with the light of day. At first he thought that he was still in the prison but the walls around him were made of canvas and he lay, blanket wrapped and warm upon a cot. Not trusting his senses, he fingered the blankets around him. The scratchy wool felt real enough and the cot he lay upon felt solid.

31

A pleasant looking woman wearing a nurse's apron came and bathed him from head to foot and he slept through most of the whole process. Later, the same woman fed him broth that was made with fresh vegetables and meat. Though he was able to consume only a little of it, his stomach felt full for the first time in months. Feeling as if he had died and gone to heaven, Matthew slept again, this time without dreams.

Matthew was awakened at mid-day at which time he was fed once more. A doctor came and treated the sores on his hips, elbows and knees and he was allowed to sleep once more.

Late in the afternoon, Matthew awakened on his own. His mind felt clearer than it had in weeks and he lay puzzling over the events of the night before. By now, he knew that the dream was truly real. He had indeed been rescued and though he had no idea where he was, he was glad to be there. Only one thing still puzzled him. The vision of Todd had seemed so real. Could it be possible that it had really been Todd who had carried him to freedom?

Matthew's eyes grew heavy once more and for a while, he dozed. He awoke from time to time to wonder if he had actually seen Todd, or only dreamed him. He emerged from yet another doze and found that the dream in it's entirety had indeed been real. Todd stood next to his cot and didn't disappear when he reached out a questioning hand to touch him. Matthew managed a weak smile for his friend and in a voice that hardly sounded like his own, inquired, "Where the heck am I?"

Todd pulled a chair up close to the side of the cot and sat down. "Virginia, back behind Confederate lines." he answered. "You look like hell, buddy." he concluded.

"You ain't too pretty yourself." Matthew replied. "We won the war yet?" he asked.

Todd shook his head in a gesture of futility. "Hell Matthew, the South's dead. It just ain't got the sense to lay down. I reckon it won't be long before this thing's all over."

"It's about time," Matthew said. "I sure would like to get my hands on those bastards that had us penned up like a bunch of animals. My Daddy's hogs got better treatment than we got." Matthew's gray eyes burned with the hatred that he felt within.

Todd scratched absently at his beard, what there was of it. "You look like getting a hold of somebody. Well I hate to spoil your plans for revenge, Matthew, but the truth is, there ain't a live Yankee left at that hellhole. You can lay there and stew and hate all you want to but I got a feelin' your days of killin' Yankees is about over, and mine too."

Matthew was silent for a moment, then looked Todd up and down. "Damn if you ain't a sight for sore eyes! What I want to know is, who the heck told you could grow a beard?" he asked.

Todd's laugh was rich and deep. "Too much Indian blood, I reckon. It ain't for looks no how. I lost my razor."

Matthew tried to laugh but ended up coughing instead. He held up an arm that was nothing more than skin wrapped bone. "Ain't that plumb pretty?" he asked. He let his arm drop back down onto the cot and turned his face away from Todd. "My God," he choked out, "Oh my God!"

"You'll be fat and sassy before long. I reckon you ought to be proud you're still alive." Todd reassured him.

When Matthew had once again regained his self-control, he agreed with Todd. "What little there is left of me. The Yankees may have got me down, but by God I ain't out yet."

"Now you're talkin'. Next time I see you, I better find you fit as a fiddle and rarin' to go." Todd said.

"You goin' somewhere?" Matthew asked.

"We're pullin' out in a few minutes." Todd replied. "I reckon by the time you're fit to travel, maybe this war'll be over."

Matthew reached for Todd's hand to shake it but ended up holding it instead. "You take care, I reckon I won't see you again for a while. If I ever get on my feet again, I'll look you up, even if I have to go clean to the Florida swamps to do it." he promised.

"That's one promise I intend to hold you to." Todd replied. For a moment his smooth forehead was marred by a flicker of a frown. He summoned up a smile and patted Matthew's painfully thin shoulder awkwardly in a gesture of reassurance. The chances of them both surviving until the war was over were slim indeed. He squeezed Matthew's hand and turning abruptly, left the hospital tent.

Matthew, not wanting to witness the departure of his friend, closed has eyes. He was tired, so very tired. With great effort, he opened his eyes and stared at the top of the hospital tent. It began to spin crazily and then disappeared into darkness.

It was a darkness that came and went for six long weeks.

Matthew drifted in and out of it like day into night. His body began to gain strength and after a time, he grew able to sit outside for hours at a time. Between the times of darkness, his mind drifted listlessly. His body, though still markedly thin, felt as heavy as a ton of bricks. To move at all was more trouble than it was worth.

Chapter 7

In April, the news of General Lee's surrender reached him. Mathew stood up, brushed himself off and began to walk. When he left the hospital tent, he had not planned to keep going, but one step led to another and then another. He had no horse, no gun and no food. All he had was the faded gray uniform that was now two sizes too big.

The further he walked, the stronger he felt, until his feet began a steady march that continued until sundown. Something inside of him was beginning to stir and come to life. The blueness of the spring sky became a thing of wonder and the songs of the birds in the tree tops took on an infinite sweetness. It was good to be alive and good to feel his feet walking over the good, clean ground.

Sometimes he traveled alone and at other times he joined up with other men dressed in gray and butternut brown. They ate when food was available and did without when it was not. They all had one goal in common, they were all going home. Home to try to rebuild all that was torn down and to begin a new way of life, built upon the ashes of the old.

The journey on foot took weeks. During that time Matthew's body took on strength if not weight. He became wiry though still too lean.

As his body gained health, so did his mind and spirit. For the first time in months, he began to think of the future. Silver Oaks beckoned to him, calling him home. He began to think of Elizabeth and their future together. For the first time, he let himself wonder if their last brief union had started another child. An ambition to raise many fine sons to help him carry on with the plantation began to form in his mind.

A feeling of apprehension began to come over him as he neared the city of Atlanta. Nothing near the city was left unscathed. The burnt out ruins of homes and farms littered the land. Most of the city was nothing but rubble and he was told that Sherman had considered nothing sacred in his reign of pillage and destruction. A dread filled his heart and Matthew somehow knew that Silver Oaks was no more than a memory.

The sight that met his eyes as he topped the hill overlooking his former home came as no surprise. Still, the sickness that he felt inside was overwhelming. The house had burned to the ground and the fields grew only crops of weeds. Not one of the slave houses stood intact and the whole place seemed deserted. He hoped against hope that Elizabeth had survived unharmed. The past four years had so hardened and numbed his emotions that he only felt an emptiness. He felt like a vessel that held nothing and would never be filled again. Along with the emptiness was a feeling of bitterness and hatred that ran as deep as the scars that covered the southern countryside.

With clinched fists and jaws Matthew wandered over the land that once was his home. His wandering footsteps at last led him to the family cemetery. What he found there came as no surprise. Unlike the old graves, marked with ornate granite markers, the two new ones were marked with wooden slabs. The names of his mother and Elizabeth were burned crudely but effectively onto them.

Matthew was filled with sudden rage, so strong that his whole body shook with it. He was beyond grief. He wanted to smash something but there was nothing left for him to vent his rage upon. Even the huge old oak that had shaded the graves was now split in two and lay dead upon the ground.

The breath in his body hissed in and out, like steam from a steam engine. He filled his lungs with air until it felt as if they would burst. It all came out in a scream that sounded like a cross between a Rebel yell and the scream of an enraged panther. It released some of the tension within him and left him suddenly weak in the knees, Matthew dropped down beside the graves and sat there trembling, staring at nothing. There was nothing left, nothing at all.

He was still sitting there when Lum found him. The big black man was light on his feet and Matthew hadn't heard him when he came up and touched him on the shoulder. Matthew came up swinging and would have struck his black friend, had not Lum seen it coming and restrained him. Matthew was wild eyed and fought against Lum's restricting hold. Only gradually did his eyes clear with the return of sanity as the restricting hold slowly changed to an embrace. Thus occurred a scene that would have warmed Lincoln's heart had he been there to see it. Former master and slave stood silently holding each other. They both wept bitter tears for what used to be and for what was now destroyed.

At last, with some degree of emotional control, Matthew drew away from Lum and stood back to look at him. Though Lum appeared to be in good health, there were signs that he too had suffered from the deprivations of war. Never, during the time of his servitude to the Kendall family, had Matthew ever seen his black friend so poorly dressed. Lum's clothes were as tattered as Matthew's own and he had no shoes at all.

To find Lum still there was a surprise and a pleasant one. The two men stood looking at one another for a while, neither of them had yet spoken and it seemed that there was little that could be said.

As for Matthew, the story was written in the lines on his face. A face that was too young to be so lined, and in his shaggy brown hair, now sprinkled with gray. Matthew's eyes, once so clear and full of life, now held only a deep sadness along with a steely hardness that they had never shown before. His body, which had once been slim of hip and broad of shoulder, was now a little stooped with defeat and stringy lean.

Lum shook his woolly head sadly and lowered his gaze. "It be sad times, Massa Matthew, sad times." he said.

Matthew's eyes met Lum's and spoke more eloquently than the words he said. "Wasn't it enough that they had us beat? Did they have to destroy everything? God help me, Lum, there ain't nothing left to build on. This is a God forsaken land."

Lum shuffled his bare feet in the dusty, red Georgia clay. "Massa, dey not be much I could be doin' to help. Dem Yankees, dey come and dey burn and tear ebberthin' down. Miz 'Lizabeth, she fought dem Yankees, she say ain't nobody gwine burn up de big house. Dem Yankees, dey cut down young Mizzus like she be nothin' mo' than weeds in de field. Old Mizzus, she not come out and dey burned de house down around her. Dey come in de night an' I be sleepin'. Time I wakes up, dem Yankees done be all ovah de place." Lum's dark eyes mirrored his misery.

Matthew walked over to Elizabeth's grave and placed his hand on the cold wooden marker. He looked at Lum and a flicker of pride flashed through the hardness in his Rebel gray eyes. "She fought them, Lum? Are you sayin' that Elizabeth actually tried to fight them, all by herself?" he asked.

"She sho" did." Lum replied. "I'se gwine miss Miz 'Lizabeth."

Matthew breathed in a sigh that shuddered from the depths of his heart. "I'll miss her too, Lum. Lord God, I'm going to miss all of them." His hand waved over the graves. "What do I do now Lum? What does a man do when he ain't got nothing left?" he asked, not really expecting an answer.

Lum's black eyes brightened a little. "You gots somethin' left Massa. You gots me an' you gots de gold."

"What gold, Lum?" Matthew asked incredulously.

"De gold yo' Daddy hab me bury. He say dem Yankees not gwine be gittin' dey hands on it." Lum replied.

A spark of warmth flashed through Matthew's eyes and he almost smiled. "Lum, do you mean to tell me there's gold buried on this place and you know where it is? You could have taken it and gone north. You could be livin' in style instead of staying with this burned out plantation." he said in amazement.

Lum's face registered hurt pride and hurt feelings. "Dat gold be yo's, not mine. I waits to see is you gwine come home."

Matthew was suitably chastened. "I'm sorry Lum." he apologized. "How have you been getting by?"

"I'se doin' jus' fine." Lum said with a grin. "I gots me a shack in de woods. Got me a garden and a ol' shotgun. Got me a mule too. I makes out."

"Well, Lum, you're a sight better off than I am right now. You reckon you could scratch up enough food to feed a hungry white man?" Matthew asked.

"Lawd Massa," Lum said with feeling. "You is de hungry'es' lookin' white man I done seen in a coon's age. I gots me a pot ob stew what'll put de meat back on yo' bones."

"You're better off than most of the white folks I saw when I came through Atlanta. How does it feel to be a free man?" Matthew asked.

Lum turned and began walking towards the woods and Matthew went with him. "It's gwine be a long time 'fore de black man be a free man." Lum replied.

"Kind of makes us even now, don't it Lum? Reckon that ought to

37

make them northern folks happy." Matthew didn't even try to hide the bitterness in his voice.

Lum stopped walking and turned to face Matthew. "We's all got a tough row to hoe, Massa. It look to me like de white folks and de black folks gotta stick, togetha' now dat de Nawth done won de wah." he said seriously.

Matthew clapped Lum's broad shoulder affectionately. "I reckon you're right Lum. Me and you, maybe we're freer than we've ever been. I'm not tied to this plantation and you're no man's slave. We can go where we please and do what we want to. We could start a new life with that gold my Daddy left." he said.

"Dat gold ain't got nothin' to do wid me." Lum started walking again. Massa, I'se done said dat gold be yo's."

"Lum," Matthew said seriously, "You and I have been friends for a long time. You ain't my slave any more. I never thought of you like that when you was. Don't you think it's about time you quit callin' me massa?"

"Yessuh, Massa." Lum agreed seriously.

The corners of Matthew's mouth twitched, softening the sadness for a moment. "Yessuh massa." he mocked. "Lum, you got to do better'n that!"

"Yessuh, Massa." Lum replied.

Chapter 8

In a few minutes, they reached Lum's place in the woods. It was little more than a shack but it had four walls, a roof and the promised pot of stew. Matthew ate heartily, which pleased Lum to no end. Matthew was very quiet and Lum let him be.

When the meal was finished and Matthew's stomach was full for the first time in weeks, he went outside to sit on the wooden steps of the shack. It was a peaceful place, no sign of the war was here. Along with the peace and quiet came a feeling of deep depression that filled Matthew's heart and soul. He had talked bravely to Lum about starting over but in truth, he had little will to begin. He felt like a jug that had been emptied of all that it was supposed to contain, and then refilled with something vile and bitter. There was still a burning rage in him that had no outlet. There was no peace in his heart, only a deep sadness that he felt would never cease.

Silver Oaks was no more and all of his family was dead and buried. In death, Elizabeth was more beloved to him than she had ever been in life. It came to him that he had never really known her, not the real Elizabeth. He had only known the woman her parents had molded to be, not the one she had become when push came to shove.

If she had survived, he felt that he could have loved the woman she had become. Elizabeth had grown strong and spirited under the duress of war. Matthew had developed a deep sense of admiration for her, along with a feeling of loss that hung over him like a black cloud.

Lum came and sat down beside him on the steps, offering companionship by just sitting quietly by his side. Silently, they watched as the Georgia sun went down in a fiery red ball. The air became cooler as the stars came out, one by one. A long way off a whippoorwill called its plaintive cry, echoing Matthew's feelings in a way that made his lean body shiver in response.

From out of the dark woods, there wandered a lanky bloodhound. Lum called the dog closer and began to stroke it's silky long ears.

"Dis dog done be figgerin' if it be a black man what feeds him, he jus' guesses he not gwine be trailin' down run away slaves no mo'. He sho' not gwine be bitin' de hand what feeds him." Lum said with a grin. The bloodhound licked Lum's hand and made friendly gestures to Matthew.

"Things sure have changed." Matthew said. "Time was, this dog would have been goin' for your throat, instead of licking your hand. I reckon this dog knows a good man when he sees one. Where 'd you get him Lum?" he asked.

"Same way I gots de mule." Lum replied. "He done got lost, when dem Yankees be runnin' ebberwhere. I jus' caught him up and feeds him."

"Lum, what do you think about Florida?" Matthew asked, out of the blue.

Lum scratched his woolly head and slapped at an offending mosquito. "Dat be where dey got dem wild Indians. Don't guesses I knows much 'bout de place." he admitted.

"How would you like to go there? Look the place over and see what it's like. I met up with a fellow from down there, he spoke mighty highly of the place." Matthew surprised Lum by saying.

39

Lum gave Matthew a startled look. "Lawd Massa, I gots no business down dat way. What you wants to go there for?" Lum asked in surprise.

Matthew sat quietly for a moment before replying. "The man I mentioned, that was telling me about Florida, saved my life a couple of times. We got to be as close as brothers. I reckon I just want to go see if he made it through the war all right. Besides that, I made him a promise that I would look him up. Other than that, I'm just plain curious about the place. Lord knows, there's nothing here worth staying for. I may as well drift around for a while. Some of the men I met up with on the way home figure on going out west but that's not for me. I figure the South will rise again and I want to be in it when it happens. I reckon a man couldn't get much farther south than Florida." Matthew concluded what for him was a very long speech.

Lum was skeptical about the whole idea. "Dat be a mighty long way to be trablin', 'less a man hab a horse an' a gun. You ain't got neitha'" he pointed out unnecessarily.

Matthew was quick to reply, showing that he had already given the matter a great deal of thought. "No, but I do have some gold and I reckon that even at today's prices, maybe there's enough to buy me what I need."

"Dey be mo'n enough, Massa. You bes' be lookin' out who you lets know you gots it. Dis ain't no time fo' a white man to be trablin 'round lookin' like he gots somethin' what anotha' be wantin'." Lum warned.

"I've done found that out Lum. I dang near got myself killed on the way home, over a pone of stale cornbread. There's people out there that would kill a man for the shirt off of his back, let alone some gold." Matthew replied.

Lum slapped his knee with the palm of his hand. "I knows where you can get you a hoss. There be a fambly neah heah what be on hard times. Dem folks got a purty good ol' nag dey sell you. Might be dey gots a gun too. Come moanin' we digs up dat gold and see what we can do."

The fifteen hundred dollars in gold that they dug up the next morning, was more than Matthew had ever dreamed it would be. There was some silver mixed in with the gold and Matthew turned it over to Lum, who went off to see about buying a horse and maybe even a gun. Both were in short supply since the war and he would probably have to pay twice what they were worth. Still, there was no other way.

Lum returned a few hours later, triumphantly leading an old brown mare and carrying a musket that looked to be even older than the horse. Both, however, looked to be serviceable and beggars couldn't be choosers.

After Matthew had inspected the horse and gun, Lum revealed some uneasiness on his part. "Dem folks be mighty suspicious ob a black man what got money. We gwine leabe dis place, we bes' hurry up. Dem folks come 'round an' rob us blind." he said uneasily.

Matthew agreed wholeheartedly. The ruins of the plantation depressed him and he was eager to put it all behind him.

They packed up as much food as they could carry and set off with Lum's bloodhound following behind. Matthew glanced over at Lum and thought that any man, black or white, would think twice before trying to rob him. Lum stood six-foot-six and had a sawed off shotgun hung around his neck. For a mild mannered black man, Lum had a face that could look as vicious as a bulldog's. He wasn't a man that Matthew would want for an enemy, that was for sure.

The first few days of their journey went without mishap. They stayed out of the way of other travelers as much as possible and the food they had with them lasted for quite some time. They saw less and less other travelers once they left Georgia. There was little difference in the land from that of south Georgia. High, dry piney woods was all that they had seen for miles and miles.

As they neared the central part of Florida, the lay of the land began to change. Piney woods became mixed with hammocks and oak thickets. Palm trees waved their bushy heads in the breeze and more and more wild flowers could be seen growing along the dirt track that passed for a road. Though Matthew had to admit that the countryside was pretty, he had yet to see the lush beauty that Todd had described to him so vividly. The land was flat, with only slight rises in the ground to pass for hills. Game seemed to be plentiful in the deserted stretches between settled areas. Some of the houses and farms that they passed seemed poor, while still others looked more affluent. The whole area seemed to be still only sparsely settled and much of it was only slightly touched by the hand of man. Once a clearing was passed by, the land reverted back to wilderness. There were few signs of any battles having gone on in these parts and only

41

an occasional burned out plantation or farm could be seen. Florida had escaped most of the fighting and had less visible scars to prove it.

The town of Gainesville was their last contact with civilization before they reached Ocala. They skirted the town without stopping, for Matthew had no desire to be around people for a while yet. His mind was still too preoccupied with memories of the war and his own tangled emotions.

There were times when Matthew rode for hours, without speaking a word. To Lum's observant eyes, he appeared to be lost in some private hell of his own. Lum looked sadly on at the man who had once been so alive and now seemed to be so dead inside. To Lum's way of thinking, his master had changed since the war. Matthew never laughed anymore and seldom smiled. Sometimes his eyes stared straight ahead and took on a glassiness like those of a blind man. Lum was tolerant of Matthew's moodiness and figured that he had earned the right to his periods of silent contemplation. Still, it pained Lum to see his friend so sad and disheartened. He missed the old Matthew and wanted him back.

They had not left the town of Gainesville far behind, when they reached an area where the dirt road crossed a long stretch of marsh. For acres and acres, there was nothing but tall, yellowish brown grass.

Matthew was deep in one of his moods and simply sat on the old brown horse, letting her follow the road at her own pace. He was lost in thought and was only vaguely aware of his surroundings. The mare was plodding along with a gait as comfortable as a rocking chair and the heat combined with the rocking motion further dulled his senses.

Lum, riding the slow paced mule, had dropped a hundred yards behind Matthew. Though the mare that Matthew rode was no ball of fire, he had come to depend on her placid nature. The bloodhound, tired and panting in the sapping heat, lagged along behind with Lum.

The last thing that Matthew would have expected to happen, came about. The slow moving mare that had carried him all the way from Georgia, suddenly let out a screaming whinny and began to buck like the wildest of stallions.

Matthew came out of his half stupor, sailing through the air and landed with a thud just inches from the marsh grasses that bordered the road. Shaken but unhurt, he sat up in surprise, wondering what had gotten into the mare. As he sat up, she passed him going the other way.

Before Matthew could gain his feet, he saw what had spooked her. The biggest rattlesnake he had ever seen lay coiled and ready to strike, only a few feet away! Without getting up, Matthew managed to scoot back up the road at record speed. He didn't get up until a safe distance lay between him and the evil looking serpent.

By this time, Lum had managed to catch the flying reins of the mare as she tried to bolt past him on the narrow road. Leading the mare, he rode up on the mule, just as Matthew regained his feet. The big black man gave an unnecessarily hard jerk on the reins of the mule and his eyes looked as big as saucers. "Lawd God!" he exclaimed and had the mule backing up the road, as pretty as you please.

They were at an impasse. The rattlesnake seemed to think that the road was it's own private property and had no inclination to get out of the way. Lum seemed to figure that anything less than fifty yards was entirely too close to the snake and stayed far up the road out of it's reach. Matthew was inclined to agree with him. The rattlesnake was as big as his thigh in the middle and he judged it to be at least eight or nine feet long.

Matthew finally regained enough control of his shaken nerves to take a shot at the serpent's ugly triangle shaped head. The old musket misfired the first time. He missed entirely the second time and finally got up enough nerve to get close enough to kill the big snake with Lum's sawed off shotgun.

Lum still wouldn't go anywhere near the rattler, even after it was dead. Once the snake had stopped writhing in it's death throes, Matthew cut off it's rattles. He counted eleven rattles and a button. It crossed his mind to skin the snake but he had no use for the hide and it was too hot to fool with it anyway. He kicked the body of the rattlesnake into the sawgrass and they continued on down the road.

By now, there was nothing dull about Matthew's thought processes. He alertly scanned every inch of the road ahead of him with great care. A strange track caught his interest and he called Lum to come take a look. Some creature had dragged itself across the road, leaving a brushed out area that was thirteen inches wide. Strange tracks bordered the brushed out area and they pondered the mystery for a while. Before they reached the end of the sawgrass marsh, the mystery solved itself.

What appeared to be a log stretched across the road in front of them, turned out to be an alligator that was at least seven feet long. Matthew had heard of the creatures but had never seen one before. He found the reptile rather fascinating but grew tired of waiting for it to get out of the way. He peppered it with Lum's shotgun and the pellets merely bounced off it's tough hide, without doing the least bit of damage. Apparently the pellets had at least been an annoyance to the alligator. It made a strange sound that was half blowing and half sighing and disappeared into the sawgrass at the side of the road.

Before they reached the end of the sawgrass, they saw several more snakes and quite a few turtles. The marsh ended rather suddenly and they were once more on ground that was high and dry.

Chapter 9

They spent the night camped beside the stagecoach road between Gainesville and Ocala in an area that was as wild as any Matthew had ever seen. As on many nights, he didn't sleep well and he listened long into the night to the sounds of the world around him. The Florida woods were alive with the hooting of owls, the chirping of frogs and the occasional woman-like scream of a panther. Sometime during the night, a black bear wandered through their camp, sniffed around and wandered on its way. It was nearly morning when Matthew fell asleep. He had awakened Lum shortly thereafter when he was beset with yet another nightmare.

"What it is you done be dreamin' now Massa Matthew?" Lum asked.

As usual, Matthew didn't want to talk about it but Lum insisted. Finally, after the fire was built to cook their breakfast, Matthew gave in. "It's all mixed up Lum. You know how nightmares always are. It starts out with me dreaming about that Yankee that tormented me with his bayonet and killed all those wounded men. Then I see the same man killing Elizabeth. It's so real Lum, I can see him piercing her through with his saber." Matthew stopped talking and got up to pace back and forth in front of the campfire. After some thought he asked the question that he had had dreaded asking. "Tell me something Lum. Was Elizabeth violated?"

Lum was a little shocked by the question. "Lawd God! No Massa, not dat."

The subject was dropped and they had continued their journey shortly thereafter.

They reached the town of Ocala later that day. The residents moved about their business slowly in the heat of the day. There was very little to the town itself. An unpretentious wooden courthouse was built upon the central square. The streets consisted of deep, dry sand and there were no sidewalks. There was a hotel, stores and a few private residences.

Matthew entered one of the stores to ask directions to the O'Mally plantation and was told by the owner that many of the local boys had returned from the war. As for young Todd, he didn't know as no one from out that way visited town in quite some time. The store keeper was friendly and talkative and it took Matthew a while to get away from him. At last, the old man gave him the directions he had asked for and Matthew left.

Though Matthew basically liked the small frontier town, he was glad to leave it behind. He found it hard to believe that a town so small was actually the county seat. He had nothing against the town, it was just that he was most content when riding slowly along the deeply rutted sand roads. He enjoyed the quiet and listening to the singing of the birds.

Dark caught them before they reached their destination and they once more camped for the night. The wilderness seemed to close in around them and the sounds of nocturnal birds and animals could be heard throughout the night. A whippoorwill called from a tree not far away and finally came to light in the branches of the oak tree, just over their heads. It's cry, which sounded so lonely and sad from a distance, took on a more agitated sound when heard close by. The bird sounded angry and Matthew could hear his own tangled emotions echoed in the cry of the small night bird. The whippoorwill flew away to another tree and called again, this time sadly. An owl, somewhere across the hammock seemed curious about the singer of such a sad song and called out in question, "Who?-Who?"

They lingered long that morning at the camp. Matthew was suddenly reluctant to find out whether Todd had yet made it home. He was beginning to feel like a fool for coming so far to see a man that might not even still be alive. When the early morning fog had cleared, the rest of the journey could be delayed no longer.

The dirt trek that branched off from the main road wound through a canopy of trees that met overhead and gave the impression that they were riding through a tunnel. Gray squirrels played in the trees over their heads and fussed and chattered as the two men passed below them. A fox-squirrel, as big as a common house cat clung to the side of a big pine and barked at them angrily. Their mounts stirred up a covey of quail and later still, another. On both sides of the narrow wagon road, the trees and underbrush grew thick and virtually impenetrable.

The trek twisted and wound it's way deeper into the wilderness and Matthew was beginning to wonder if they had taken the wrong road. A light, warm breeze found it's way through the thickets of trees and underbrush. It carried with it a scent so sweet as to rival the most expensive of French perfumes. They marveled over it, questioned it and for the most part breathed deeply and appreciatively of it.

They rounded a bend and a clearing sprang up suddenly in front of them. The weathered gray house that sat within the clearing was no mansion but was quite large. It was two storied and built in what looked to be two sections with a breezeway in between. There were several out-buildings, also of weathered silver-gray. The unpainted structures had a beauty all their own. The simple, clean lines of the buildings blended well with the primitive woodlands beyond the clearing. A well was placed so close to the house that the huge open front porch surrounded and covered it. One had simply to step out onto the porch to reach the well. The house itself was shaded by huge old oak trees and a half dozen orange trees that were covered in bloom. It was from these trees that the heavy perfume had originated. Above all the other trees towered a magnificent magnolia that rose high over the spreading limbs of the oaks. The entire yard was alive with color for flowering plants grew in profusion. Underlying the song of a mocking bird, perched high in the limbs of the magnolia, there was a peaceful silence.

A pack of hunting dogs that were sleeping under the porch came out barking, all at once. Matthew and Lum were hard put to keep the bloodhound from being attacked. A woman's voice called from inside the house for the dogs to be quiet and they immediately became still. An elderly Negro woman opened the door and peered cautiously around it.

"I'm looking for Todd O'Mally. Is he here?" Matthew inquired.

"Nosuh." the old woman replied. "Massa Todd still be gone off to de wah. Missy be out heppin' wid de hoein', she be de one you wants to see." She pointed a finger, gnarled with age and hard work, to indicate the direction.

The fields spread out behind the house for several acres. A good bit of the land was cultivated but the major portion of it lay unused.

Too far away to be seen clearly, three dark skinned people labored in the heat of the Florida sun, hoeing weeds from around the young cornstalks. The three were all dressed pretty much the same way, in baggy trousers and homespun shirts. Their heads were covered against the heat of the sun with identical woven hats, made from palmetto leaves.

As Matthew and Lum drew nearer, one of the three looked up and saw them coming. The hoe was laid down and the smaller of the trio ran across the field as gracefully and swiftly as a deer. The runner slowed to a walk as they came nearer. Now, Matthew could see that it was not a Negro as he had first thought, but what looked to be a young boy as Indian dark as Todd. The resemblance was remarkable but he found it strange that Todd had never mentioned having a brother.

The mystery was solved when the wide brimmed palmetto hat was removed and straight black hair, at least a yard long, spilled from beneath it. The girl eyed him curiously and used a slim brown hand to wipe the perspiration from her brow. She gave him a smile that was as bright as the Florida sun and laughed. "I saw the uniform and thought that it was my brother come home. What can I do for you?" she asked.

Matthew shrugged, "Nothing, I guess. I'm Matthew Kendall and I came here looking for Todd. I never figured I'd get here before he did. We met up north a ways, he saved my life a time or two." he explained.

The girl's dark eyes lit up and she gave him a sunny smile. "I'm Wynn O'Mally, Todd's twin. I haven't heard anything from him in a couple of years and I'm dying for some news. I'd really appreciate it if you'd come back up to the house and tell me what you know of him." she invited eagerly. Without waiting for an answer, she began walking towards the house as if she had no doubt that he would follow her.

47

Matthew observed the girl as she walked briskly ahead of him. Her walk was a tiny bit pidgin toed as was her brother's, but remained graceful in spite of her long strides. The curtain of jet black hair gleamed like a raven's wing in the hot Florida sun and her bare arms swung freely, exposed to the sun's burning rays.

Upon reaching the house, she accompanied Matthew inside, while Lum, as was fitting, waited on the porch.

It took a moment for Matthew's eyes to adjust to the dimmer light in the interior of the house. When he could see more clearly, he observed that the room he was in was high ceilinged and genteelly furnished. Matthew suddenly became aware of how ragged he must look in his worn out uniform and he wished that he had taken the time to purchase some better clothes.

Wynn, in spite of her rough boy's clothing, turned lady on him as fast as her brother could put on culture. "Would you please excuse me while I go and change into something more suitable for company. I'll have Granny prepare you something to drink and for your man as well. Please make yourself at home Mr. Kendall." she invited graciously.

She disappeared into the depths of the house and after a while, the old black woman brought him a glass of what tasted like a mixture of fruit juices. It was both tart and sweet at the same time and Matthew thought to himself that he had never tasted anything so good in all his life.

Wynn returned after a very few minutes had passed. She made no sound as she walked across the polished wood floor. Matthew was looking the other way and didn't hear her come into the room. She had a chance to study him before he knew that she was there.

She found it impossible to guess his age, though she guessed that he was probably younger than he looked. In spite of the gray in his hair and the lines on his face, she placed him as being just under thirty years old. His hair and beard were shaggy and she had a wild urge to take a pair of scissors to them both. His face seemed a bit pale, in spite of it's being darkly tanned but she liked the good clean lines of it. He appeared to be too thin but seemed strong enough. It was his eyes that had struck her the most. There was a hard, haunted look to them that hurt her to look at them.

He turned to look at her and she lowered her gaze lest he catch her staring. She had combed her hair and coiled it into a thick bun on the back of her head. The dress she wore was only homespun but was dyed a brilliant blue that set off the darkness of her skin. Wynn sat down gracefully and smoothed her skirts around her. "Now, tell me about that brother of mine. He'll be home any day now, I just know it." she said.

It crossed Matthew's mind once more that Todd might not even still be alive. However, he told her what he knew of Todd during the last two years and she was eager to hear all that he had to say.

When he had finished talking, it was as if she had read his mind. "I know he's alive. You see, I can feel whatever happens to him, no matter how far apart we are." she explained.

"How can that be?" Matthew asked.

"I don't know, it's just the way it is." Wynn explained. "I can see you don't believe me. Let me see if I can prove it to you. Something hurt his head once and a few days later, his arm." She indicated the exact spot on her own arm where the mini ball had pierced Todd's. "A day or two later, something burned like fire in the same spot. Am I right so far?" she challenged.

Matthew nodded disbelievingly. He had said nothing to her about the wounds Todd had received.

Wynn gave him a triumphant smile. "There's something more. Here," She reached down to indicate the calf of her leg. "It ached but didn't burn, so I think it must have been a break, not a wound. That was seven weeks ago, about the time that we heard about Lee's surrender. He ought to be able to come home soon."

Matthew was thoroughly astonished. "That's incredible." he stated. "Does he feel what happens to you?"

Wynn nodded. "Yes, if I'm hurt or afraid. I've felt the danger he was in many times. Thank God, the war's finally over."

"Yes, thank God!" Matthew repeated with feeling.

Wynn shifted on her chair and sat slightly forward. "So, Todd promised you hunting and fishing, did he? Well, since he's not here, suppose I take you instead. You will stay on until he gets back won't you Mr. Kendall?"

Matthew was hesitant about being penned down and it showed on his face. Once more, Wynn seemed to read his mind and he found it disconcerting. "Please, just for a few days, you don't have to stay forever." she insisted.

Though Matthew was still a bit reluctant, he at last nodded in

49

agreement, "A couple of days, maybe." he conceded. He was as tired as he had ever been in his life and the prospect of a few day's rest in this quiet place was beginning to appeal to him.

Wynn was openly pleased by his decision. Her dark eyes lit warmly, like coals that still held fire in their depths. She gave him a smile that was as warm and bright as the Florida sun. Matthew found himself responding to that smile. There was nothing false or flirty about it. Here was something that was real and tangible that the war had neither touched, nor destroyed.

Chapter 10

For two days, Matthew did little more than lie in the shade beneath the wide spread limbs of the oaks in the yard. By now, Lum had become acquainted with the three other ex-slaves and had found a place in their home. They had a small house of their own at the edge of the clearing as well as a good sized portion of land. Lum had told him that Missy Wynn had given them the house and land when they were given their freedom. It was out of a portion of her own inheritance. The old woman was the mother of the two younger blacks, a man and a woman. The younger two were once Todd and Wynn's personal servants, just as Lum was Matthew's.

A bond existed between these former slaves and their owners that went beyond loyalty into true friendship. Wynn and the three blacks on the plantation were a team, working together for the common good of them all. Under her direction they were totally self sufficient. Everything they could possibly need, if not want, was produced or made on the place. From the cotton that was spun on a wheel and woven into cloth for clothing to the wide brimmed hats that kept the hot sun off their heads. Matthew learned that Wynn worked alongside the two young blacks and supplemented their meat with wild game.

After two days of idleness, Matthew was beginning to grow restless. Wynn had refused to let him lift a finger to help out on the place. She had fed and pampered him, treating him as an honored guest. The past two days had felt like pure heaven to him, providing the homecoming he had not had in Georgia. Pleasant as it was, by the third day, Matthew could no longer be still.

Wynn sensed his restlessness and provided a cure. Since it was

Saturday, the family blacks had all gone fishing and Matthew and Wynn had the place to themselves. When Wynn suggested a ride to Silver Spring, Matthew was more than ready to take her up on it. He had long been curious about the place and was eager to see how much of what Todd had told him about it was true. Besides that, he had dreamed of the place in his sleep and wondered just how accurate his mental pictures were.

Matthew realized as he mounted the brown mare that he was at last gaining back some more of the weight he had lost. The ragged uniform was tight enough on him now, that when he raised his arm to reach for the saddle horn, the whole sleeve tore loose from the rest of the garment. He looked at the new rip, disgusted at himself once more for not buying new clothes.

Wynn, who had not yet mounted her own gray stallion, laughed at him without derision. "This is ridiculous." she said. "Let me see if I can find you something to wear that won't fall off of you before we get back. Todd's taller than you, I think but I believe he might have left something here that might just fit you." Without waiting for a reply, she dashed into the house to see what she could find.

Matthew felt like a fool. Here he was with gold in his saddlebags and wearing nothing but rags. He accepted the offer with as much grace as possible but it sure was a thing to sting a man's pride.

After a short delay while Matthew changed his clothes, they were on their way. Wynn led the way down a trail that wound it's way through the tropical jungle of the hammock. She was dressed once more in men's britches and her hair hung down her back in a long glossy braid. Matthew, riding in single file behind her, watched the braid swing on her slim back, to the motion of the horse. She rode astride, sitting as bolt upright as any cavalry officer he had ever seen.

Wynn looked back once and rode into a tree limb that hung over the trail. It left a reddened mark on her brown cheek and while it had done her little damage, it set off her otherwise unseen temper. She reached up and broke off the small limb viciously. "Damn!" she spat out, like an enraged wildcat. She realized what she had said and covered her mouth with her hand, blushing furiously.

Behind her, Matthew fairly roared with laughter. "Don't mind me." he told her, when he was able to stop laughing long enough to speak.

Wynn's laughter drifted back to him over her shoulder. "I reckon

51

you just found out that my Daddy didn't raise no lady when he raised me. Me and Todd sort of grew up wild out here along with the other varmints. Oh, I reckon he tried, he sent us to the academy in Ocala to teach us some manners but we didn't bring any home with us. He always said good manners ain't in how you talk or hold your fork, it's all in how you treat your fellow man." she explained.

"I think you're right. Now take my wife for example. She was raised from birth to be a lady but when the Yankees burned our plantation, she fought like a man to try to save it." Matthew replied.

Wynn turned around to look back at him and barely missed being swatted by another low hanging limb. She raised an eyebrow questioningly at him exactly as he had seen Todd do. "Your wife?" she asked.

"The Yankees killed her." Matthew replied. He grew quiet and the rest of the ride was taken in silence.

As they drew nearer to the spring, the vegetation grew so thickly that the horses could barely make it through them. At last, they emerged from the jungle-like tangle of underbrush at the very edge of the great spring,

Matthew was filled with awe, though he sat quietly on the mare and said nothing. The basin of the spring was perhaps a hundred feet wide or so and was as still as the surface of a mirror. It reflected the trees and foliage that grew around it, in an up side down mirror image.

Trees, flowering vegetation and a multitude of various colored birds surrounded the head of the great spring. It came up from the bowels of the earth and the Garden of Eden could not have rivaled it for it's beauty. Matthew drew in a slow deep breath of air. It was filled with the smell of wild growing things, rotting vegetation and clean fresh air. From where he sat atop the mare, the mirror-perfect reflection of the clear expanse of the water prevented him from seeing into its depths. He dismounted, tied the mare to a pine tree and walked as close to the edge of the spring as the soft, water soaked ground would allow. Opposite where he stood, on the other side of the great spring, a weathered dock extended into the water. A few Indian dugouts were tied alongside a couple of rowboats.

Gradually, Matthew became aware that Wynn had also dismounted and had come to stand beside him. "The dock is where the steamboats used to land. They brought cargo from up around

Palatka on the Ocklawaha River and up the Spring Run." she explained. "One of the boats was sunk a while back by the Yankees and I reckon it'll be a while before they start up again. They were the main carriers of supplies for Ocala. They ran keelboats for a while until the steamboats came along. The run," she pointed down the stream, "is about seven miles long and runs into the river." Wynn fell silent and looked up at Matthew to see if he had paid attention to what she said.

Matthew had indeed been listening, though his bitterness was somewhat softened by the beauty around him, it still came through. "The embargo! I heard about them destroying the salt works along the coast too. They couldn't beat us outright, so they proceeded to starve us to death. There was times that I craved salt so bad that I'd have gladly given my right arm for just a pinch of it." he exclaimed.

Wynn placed a hand on the sleeve of Matthew's borrowed shirt. "Matthew, you can't keep thinkin' like that. The war is over and Lee's surrendered." she said.

Matthew looked down at her with gray eyes turned as dark as thunder clouds. "Lee may have surrendered but I ain't. I reckon I'll hate Yankees as long as there's breath, in my body." he grated.

She tightened her hand to encircle the hardness of his arm. "Hate never solved anything, Matthew. We can't look on what they tore down, so much as what they didn't. Look at the spring Matthew, look all around you! There's life out there, just waiting to be lived. Captain Hart'll start his boat line again and people will keep farmin' whether they have servants or not. The South may be like a dog, whipped in a dog fight, but she'll shake the sand off herself and get up and go on. We'll scrape away the ashes that the Yankees left behind and build everything new, new and better than ever!" she insisted fervently.

Matthew drew his eyes away from the expanse of water before him to look down into the dark eyes of the girl by his side. She stared up at him intently and he felt the muscles in his face relax. In that moment, her resemblance to Todd was startling and he felt a closeness to her that was beyond his understanding. He put his arm around her in brotherly fashion and gave her shoulders a brief squeeze before letting go.

"Little friend." he said seriously. "You ain't been where I've been, nor seen what I've seen. I can hear the wisdom in your words but I reckon there's not enough grit left in my craw to think of building

53

anything. You know what I think? I think the Yankees killed me and I just ain't got the sense to lay down. I don't know what the heck or who the heck I am anymore." he said, without self-pity.

Wynn gave him a sunny smile. "I know who you are. You're Matthew, Todd's friend and mine. Grit in the craw may be fine if you're a chicken, but when you're a man, it just takes backbone." She ran a finger down his spine for emphasis.

Her finger, running down his spine tickled and a smile lit his clouded countenance. " So you think I've still got backbone. I hope to God, you're right." he said quietly.

"Backbone, smackbone!" Wynn said and laughed. "How about a boat ride across the spring? You ain't never seen nothin' like it."

She left his side and began untying a rowboat that he hadn't noticed, tied up among the grasses at the edge of the basin. "Me'n Todd built this boat the summer before the war started. We used heart cypress and worked on it for weeks. I reckon if nothin' don't happen, this'll still be a good boat when I'm an old gray haired woman." She gave him a look that contained pure mischief "By the way, in case we tip over, can you swim?" she asked.

"I can swim." he said flatly.

"Well, that's good to know." Wynn said with a grin. "You might better take your boots off just in case." The expression in her eyes was half-serious, half-teasing.

Matthew, suspicious of her intentions, took off his boots and climbed into the rowboat. When they were over the middle of the basin, Wynn dropped an anchor and leaned over the side of the boat. "If you put your shadow between you and the water, you can see down into it." she told him.

Matthew gave it a try and was amazed at what he could see. The water was so clear, that it was almost like looking through air. Grasses on the bottom were clothed in rainbow hues and fish swam around like they were floating in air. A catfish as long as his arm swam beneath the boat. He could see turtles and a variety of small fish as well as large silver ones. The big, silver fish seemed clothed in rainbows from the reflection of the sun shining down into the water. These were called mullet, Wynn told him. One of them jumped, disturbing the surface of the water, followed by another and yet another. Wynn produced a flat bottomed jar from the bottom of the boat, rinsed it clean in the water and filled it for a drink.

54

When their thirst was quenched by the cold clear water, she showed him another thing. She emptied the jar and held it bottom down in the water and instructed him to look down through it. The flat bottom of the jar clarified the scene below even better than his shadow had done. "Watch this." Wynn said, and produced a small chip of blue glass. She dropped it into the water next to the jar. The piece of glass, no bigger than his thumbnail, drifted slowly downward into the crystal clear depths, taking on the look of a bit of priceless opal. It settled on the bottom at least sixty feet below, still shining a brilliant blue and plainly visible.

Matthew could have spent the rest of the day just looking at the panorama below but Wynn was growing restless and tired of the heat. He too, was becoming aware of how hot and still it had become. The back of his shirt was soaked with sweat as it trickled down his back in small streams. It ran down his forehead and into his eyes, so that he was forced to abandon looking through the jar into the water.

He wiped the sweat from his eyes and looked over at Wynn. Her brown face fairly dripped with moisture. She gave him a mischievous grin that was sunny and almost boyish and began to rock the boat from side to side. "Somethin's wrong here, looks like we might have to abandon ship!" she said playfully. When Matthew still kept his seat, she dove at him, pushing him overboard.

The impact of the cold water on Matthew's overheated skin caused him to gasp and he came up sputtering and coughing. When he had caught his breath, he allowed his body to drift downward into the clear, cold depths. When his lungs felt as if they would burst, he fought his way to the surface.

Wynn floated on her back nearby. Her braid had come undone and her hair floated like black silk, around and below her. Matthew tried to float as she was doing but hadn't yet learned the trick of how to do it. He settled for treading water instead.

A sleek black animal, the size of a medium size dog, slid off the bank into the water. Matthew watched it in fascination as it's streamlined body frolicked and rolled in the water. It played with such joy and abandon that it made him smile just to see it. After a while, the otter grew tired of it's frolicking and disappeared.

Matthew was growing tired of treading water and swam over to the rowboat, where he could hold on and rest. Wynn dove beneath the surface and stayed under so long that he had begun to worry. Just as he had about decided to go in after her, she came up below him and startled him by grabbing his toe. She bobbed up out of the water in front of him like a cork, shaking water from her eyes exactly like a wet puppy.

"I feel like I've been here before." Matthew surprised her by saying. "I even knew how the water would feel."

"How could you possibly know that?" Wynn asked.

"I dreamed about it in a Yankee prison up north. I know this sounds strange but I saw it just the way it is." Matthew explained.

"It's strange, how you can dream like that, so real I mean. I've had dreams like that that before and it always took me a while to figure out that they weren't real. You about ready to get out? I'm getting waterlogged." Wynn said.

Chapter 11

They towed the rowboat back to shore and climbed out onto the bank, dripping wet. The hot air felt good to their cooled bodies. They led the horses down for a drink before Wynn led the way down a narrow trail that skirted the basin. The trail branched off into the hammock a few yards downstream.

"We'll come out at the back of the plantation on this trail." Wynn explained. "I need to check on my hog trap and see if I've caught that wild hog that's been rooting up my watermelon vines. I need to see how the melons are doing too, they ought to be ready to pick in another week. That is, if the hogs don't root them all up."

"What're you going to do with the hog if you catch him?' Matthew asked.

Wynn shrugged. "Just keep him penned up until after we get the cantaloupes and melons in. This time of year wild hog meat's too strong to be fit to eat." she answered.

Matthew was beginning to perspire again in the heat of the afternoon sun. He wiped his brow and stopped to listen to a rustling sound in the underbrush, next to the trail. A few feet away, the bushes began to wave ominously as if disturbed by some large animal. Matthew stood up in the stirrups in order to see better. A large turtle, as big around as a barrel, was making it's way along the black mucky ground beneath the palmetto bushes.

Matthew had never seen anything like it in his life! It's back was covered with green moss and it had an ugly serpent-like head. "What on earth is that thing?" he asked.

Wynn, who was a few feet ahead of him, rode back to take a look. When she was close enough to see, she too stood up in the stirrups for a better look. Her face lit up with pleased surprise when she saw the huge turtle. "That, Matthew, is tomorrow's dinner!" she exclaimed happily.

Matthew stayed on the mare while Wynn got down and waded through the black muck towards the turtle. "Dinner?" he asked incredulously. "You don't mean to tell me you'd actually eat something that looks like that!"

Wynn only laughed. "You ain't lived until you've eaten soft-shell turtle! Just wait till Granny gets through with this varmint, you'll think you've died and gone to heaven!" She had picked up a long stick from a dead sapling and was trying to turn the turtle over onto it's back. She wasn't having much success and when the stick broke, she fell down in the wet muck. "Don't just sit there! Get down and help me catch that booger." she insisted.

Matthew dismounted, wondering the whole time if an ugly critter like that could be worth so much trouble. The minute his feet hit the ground, they slid out from under him and he landed on his rear in the black muck.

Meanwhile, Wynn had regained her feet and was looking for another sapling. She couldn't find what she wanted and tried to turn the turtle over by hand. She couldn't get any traction in the slick mud and fell once more into the muck. Trying to brush her hair out of her eyes, she left a long streak of black mud across her face.

Matthew tried his hand at turning the turtle over and was doing pretty good until the turtle made a desperate lunge and he lost his grip. He sprawled face down in the mud and came up sputtering. He was sure by now that Wynn would be more than ready to give up on the turtle. Wiping the mud off his face and smearing it hopelessly, he looked at Wynn. She was holding her sides and laughing helplessly.

The humor of the situation suddenly hit Matthew and he doubled up with laughter. While they were both helpless with mirth, the turtle almost escaped.

Wynn was the first to recover and was up and after the turtle, slipping and sliding all the way. Matthew followed right behind her and together, they at last got it turned over on its back. They stood back panting and covered with muck and Wynn, at least, was triumphant.

The turtle, now that it was helpless, waved all four legs in the air and stretched its long serpentine neck out in an effort to right itself.

"Well, we've got him. Now what are we going to do with him?" Matthew asked.

"Why carry him home, what else?" Wynn's tone of voice suggested that her opinion of his mentality was as low as his was of hers.

Matthew looked from the upturned turtle to the horses, with open doubt in his eyes but figured he'd just have to humor her.

Wynn walked back to her horse with as much grace and dignity as the slick mud would allow and retrieved a hatchet from her saddle bag. She returned with the hatchet and a determined look on her face. "Now, Matthew, you get that piece of sapling over there and we'll see if we can't take some of the squirm out of this booger." she said.

Matthew obediently got the piece of sapling and approached the unfortunate turtle with a puzzled look on his face. He didn't know whether he was suppose to hit the turtle with the stick or what. He glanced over at Wynn for further directions. "Poke him in the face with it till he bites on real good." she instructed.

"Then what? Does it hold onto the stick and we can just lead it home, like a dog?" Matthew asked. He was still puzzled and more than half serious.

Wynn doubled up laughing at the idea. "No, silly! When it grabs hold, you pull its neck out farther and I'll chop off its head. It's about the only way to kill one of these critters." she explained.

Matthew raised both eyebrows at the same time, in a look of comprehension. "Shoot, I should'a known that." he said. When he aggravated the turtle with the stick, it grabbed on, just as she had said it would. Wynn efficiently decapitated it and stood back, obviously pleased with herself.

Matthew stood sweating in his already wet clothes. The headless turtle was bleeding profusely onto the mucky ground and gnats and flies were already gathering around it for a feast. A more unappetizing sight, he had never seen. "All right Wynn, it's time for you to tell me this is all a joke and you have no intentions of taking this thing home." he prompted.

Wynn gave him a look of wide-eyed innocence. "Now why on earth would I want to tell you a thing like that?" she asked. She returned the hatchet to her saddlebag and came back with a length of rope. After giving the matter some thought, she made a hole in the turtle's shell with her pocketknife. She ran the rope through the hole and stood back satisfied.

"Here, help me carry this thing." she told Matthew, in a voice that was all business. It was all that both of them could do to carry the huge turtle to the horses, neither of which wanted any part of it. They backed and shied until it became obvious that they wouldn't stand for any such nonsense.

"Wynn, these horses ain't going to stand for this. You might as well give up and leave this thing here." Matthew said, after they had struggled for a while, trying to load the turtle.

"What? Leave it here for the buzzards? If I come home without this turtle, Ned'll kill me deader than a doornail. I intend to get home with it if it hare lips the devil." Wynn said, with determination.

"Somehow or other, I just bet you will." Matthew said and laughed." Would you mind telling me just exactly how you intend to do it?" he asked.

Wynn gave him a haughty look and proceeded to show him. Much to the consternation of her horse, she tied the rope to her saddle horn and proceeded to drag the turtle home.

Matthew watched her take off ahead of him and followed at a safe distance. Wynn was covered from head to foot with black muck and the turtle bounced along behind her. It was covered with dust and pine straw, mixed liberally with oak leaves. Matthew was hard put to decide which of the two was the dirtiest.

Chapter 12

They emerged in due time out of the hammock at the back side of the plantation. A small field of watermelons and a field of cantaloupes lay before them in neat rows. Just looking at the watermelons made Matthew's mouth water. Wynn left her horse at the edge of the field and bent to examine the melons. "Another week and they'll be ready. I sure hope I catch that hog before he ruins any more of them." she told Matthew.

Matthew was busy thumping watermelons in an effort to find one that was ripe enough to eat. He could see fairly fresh signs of where a hog had raided the field. Vines were rooted up and melons bitten into. "This hog ain't a he, it's a she. The tracks look like a sow with pigs to me." he said. He found a watermelon that looked to be almost ripe when he thumped it and pulled it from the vine. He took it to the edge of the field, near a big oak tree and cut it open with Wynn's pocketknife.

The melon wasn't ripe enough to suit Wynn and she only ate a small amount of it. Matthew, on the other hand ate three slices before he was satisfied. He had a craving for fresh fruit and vegetables that seemed as if it would never be satisfied. By the time they had finished, they had watermelon juice dripping down their chins and were both sticky all over.

After eating the melon, they went to check on the hog trap. It consisted of a pen built in the woods and baited, so that if a hog entered to eat the bait, a door slid shut behind it, leaving it trapped. They were in luck, for they could hear the hog's angry squeals long before the pen came in sight. When they got there, they found that the pen contained not only a sow but five pigs as well. Three other pigs were left outside when the trap door had slid shut.

"You can't beat that for luck." Wynn exclaimed happily. "I'll just keep the sow penned up until the crops are in but the pigs will do to fatten up for meat. It looks like we're gonna have smoked pork and bacon for a long time to come." she said, with a pleased smile.

Wynn took off after one of the pigs, dove after it in a flying leap and just barely missed it. She went after it again and finally caught it.

Meanwhile, Matthew had caught the second pig and they carried them to the pen to the accompaniment of high-pitched squeals. The sow went into a frenzy and began leaping at the sides of the pen but calmed down once the two pigs were inside.

The third pig proved to be more of a problem and it turned into a wild chase. A half a dozen times, they almost had it in their clutches, only to dive for it and miss at the last possible moment.

By the time they finally caught the pig, they were both covered with dirt. It stuck to the watermelon juice, their still wet clothes and sweaty bodies. They were so covered with dirt, muck and sand, that it was almost impossible to tell if they were black or white.

In high spirits, they left the sow and her pigs in the pen and went off laughing and out of breath. Matthew could not remember ever having laughed so much in his life.

Catching wild pigs might be a practical thing to do but he had never dreamed that it could be so much fun. Plantation raised as he was, getting this dirty had never been encouraged by his straight-laced mother. Even in childhood, he had never been engaged in play that was as hilarious as the pig chase. Matthew had become aware that his face was actually aching from so much laughter.

He risked a glance at Wynn, knowing that it would set him off again and not caring. There she was, covered in leaves, dirt and muck and still soaking wet. Her hair was a tangled mess and coated with leaves and twigs. Wynn looked like some wild boy sitting ramrod straight in the saddle, not caring one whit if she was dirtier than the pigs they had caught. The grisly looking turtle dragging behind her, was even dirtier than she was.

The expected fit of laughter came and his sides fairly ached with it. Wynn gave him a look that was as haughty as that of any duchess and looked him up and down. She stuck her nose in the air and gave a snort that was as expressive as that of a pompous English lord and looked down her nose at him. He let out a whoop of laughter and almost lost his seat on the saddle.

Wynn dissolved into helpless fits of giggles and when she had calmed down enough to talk, she said "If you think I look a sight, you ought to see yourself. Didn't your Mama teach you better than to go around looking like that? Matthew, you're the dirtiest one man I ever seen in my life!"

"Well if that ain't a case of the pot calling the kettle black, I don't know what is. Are you sure your mother was Cherokee? You look more like one of them wild Seminoles to me." Matthew teased.

"Humm, so you think I look wild, do you? Just wait until that big, mean looking watchdog of yours sees you. He's liable to blow your head off before he figures out that it's you under all that dirt." she warned.

"You mean Lum? Why Lum ain't got a mean bone in his body. You're right about one thing though. I'd hate to be on the receiving end of that shotgun if he ever got riled up enough to use it." Matthew said, with a grin.

"Well, we'll see soon enough. It looks like they're back from fishing. I can't hardly wait to see their faces when they see us. Let's act like nothing's happened and see what they do." Wynn suggested.

With straight faces and great dignity, they rode calmly down to the small spring where Ned, Lum and Pearl were gathered. They too, were wet but none of them was as dirty as Matthew and Wynn. The spring was a small one and a shallow stream ran out of it.

Lum and Ned stood knee deep in the neck of the stream, driving stakes into it's sandy bottom. "What are they doing?" Matthew asked.

"Penning up catfish." Wynn replied. "Ned catches them and pens them up to keep until I go to Jacksonville to sell them for him. That's where I take my produce to sell it. I ought to do pretty good this year, now that the Yankees aren't occupying it anymore. The ship Captains usually pay pretty good for watermelons and oranges." Wynn explained.

Three black faces turned to look at them as they rode up and three pairs of black eyes sparkled with suppressed mirth. Not one of the three dared to crack a smile. Long years of slavery had taught them never to laugh at the expense of white people.

Ned was the first to overcome his surprise at seeing white people in such disarray, perhaps because he had seen it before. "Missy, dat be what I think it be?" he called out.

"Ain't he pretty? If you'll dress him out for me, we'll cook him for dinner tomorrow. You got a mess of catfish to go with him?" Wynn asked.

Ned grinned good-naturedly. "We sho' does. Jus' you come look at what we done caught." he invited.

The three blacks had done well indeed. They had driven the smaller of the two farm wagons down to the river that morning before daylight. In the back of the wagon bed sat a tub made from half of a large barrel. In it were a couple of dozen large red-bellies, a bunch of speckled perch and several large-mouthed bass. Another tub was used strictly for catfish and it was these that they were penning up in the spring.

The stake fence across the stream was now mended. Lum and Ned carried the tub full of catfish down and dumped them into the spring. There were a number of catfish already swimming around, from previous catches. Ned was a little upset that some of them had escaped due to the gaps in the fence.

Matthew couldn't get over the size of the catfish. Some of them were as long as his arm and would go ten or twelve pounds. He complimented the Negroes on their catch and an unbearable urge to go fishing was born in him.

He stood at the edge of the spring with Wynn, while Lum and Ned went to get the turtle. The two strong black men lugged the heavy turtle down to the spring and proceeded to wash the dirt and trash from it. Lum was as skeptical as Matthew was about the idea of eating the turtle but Ned assured him that there was no better meat on the face of the earth. Judging from the amount of trouble that Wynn had gone to get it, Matthew figured that there might just be some truth in what Ned had said. He still had his doubts though.

The rusty remains of a moonshine still stood beside the spring and it looked to have been several years since it had seen any use. "My Daddy used to run off a batch once a year, for home use. He never was too big on drinking though." Wynn explained.

Lum and Ned were still in the spring, washing on the turtle. They overheard Lum whisper to Ned, "What you reckon dem white folks done been up to? Dey looks like dey done fought de wah and lost."

Matthew and Wynn glanced at each other and although they tried valiantly to keep their faces straight, they both ended up laughing helplessly. Over their laughter they managed to hear Ned say to Lum, "Dem folks done be gwine crazy."

As if to prove the two black men right, Matthew attempted to throw Wynn in the spring but she tripped him and they both tumbled in together. Pearl, who was sitting quietly, watching the whole thing and secretly watching Lum, lost all control and fairly shrieked with laughter.

Matthew came up out of the water in time to catch Lum looking at Pearl with a look in his eyes like a moon struck teen-ager. Wynn saw it too and they exchanged a knowing look.

It took several minutes of scrubbing themselves and their clothes in the spring to remove all the dirt and muck. They emerged, wet and dripping but cool and refreshed. Pearl still sat by the spring and she shook her head in amazement at their behavior.

When all of them got back to the house, they found that Granny was impatiently waiting supper on them. She scolded them all soundly, black and white alike. "What you mean comin' in heah like dat? You chillen gwine track up de clean flo'. I'se a good mind to gits me a switch to you young 'uns!" she threatened.

63

Wynn soothed the old black woman's ruffled feathers as best she could. " Don't fuss so, Granny. We brought you a mess of fish and a big soft-shelled turtle. Maybe you can get Ned to go cut us a mess of cabbage to go with them. "Now, won't that taste good?" she asked.

"Yassum Missy. Now you gits you some dry clothes on 'fore you catches yo' death ob 'newmonie. What yo' Mammy say, she be heah to see you like dis?" Granny continued to scold.

Wynn gave a small laugh, "Plenty, the best I can remember." she said and went inside to change her clothes.

Chapter 13

Matthew smiled as he changed into dry clothes. It felt good to be clean and dry again and to be dressed in clothing that was not rags. After he had dressed, he took a long look at himself in the mirror. He decided that now that he was well on the road to regaining his health, if he were to shave and get a haircut, he wouldn't look half bad.

Wynn must have been thinking along much the same lines, for when she met him in the upstairs hallway she was carrying a pair of scissors. She had changed into a dress that was a soft, lemon yellow and her hair was neatly braided to hang over one shoulder. It was hard for Matthew to believe that this ladylike creature was the same girl that he had rode, swam and frolicked with all day. Could this be the same girl that had scrambled in the muck after a turtle and chased pigs in the dirt? She looked like some exotic princess, with her dark hair and eyes and she had pinned a white gardenia over her right ear.

A feeling swept over him that he had never felt before and he quickly stuffed it back down deep inside himself. He would be moving on before long and thoughts like the one he had just had were utterly foolish. Besides, she was Todd's sister.

Wynn gave him an impish grin and led him outside. She sat him down in a straight chair beneath the shade of the oak tree and proceeded to give him a haircut. Granny, who was busy putting platters and bowls on the picnic table by the porch, clucked over the pile of hair that was fast collecting on the ground.

Matthew exulted in a feeling of contentment and drowsiness. The day of fast paced fun, the heat and the dip in the cold spring had left him feeling relaxed and mellow. For a while, he had actually managed to forget about the war and all that it had taken from him. He almost dozed in spite of the clicking scissors that were coming dangerously close to his ears. His chin drifted towards his chest and Wynn scolded him.

"If you don't hold your head still, I'm going to mess this up. You're not falling asleep are you?" she asked.

"Of course not." Matthew denied, but he was soon nodding again. The hot evening air seeped into him like a potent drug. It was scented with the sweet smell of gardenias, magnolias and orange blossoms. Blending with all this was the smell of dry sand, the hammock and good clean air.

He came out of his near stupor when Wynn tapped him on the back of the head with her scissors. "Now, sleepyhead, that's done. Do you want your beard cut too?" she asked.

"Needs it don't it?" Matthew mumbled lazily.

Matthew sat up straighter in the chair as she walked around in front of him. She tilted her head this way and that, looking at him, then began snipping at his beard. He was suddenly painfully aware of her. She was standing close to him and leaning even closer. He ventured a glance at her face and the expression it held was nothing more than one of intent concentration and seriousness.

In desperation, he shut his eyes to avoid the sight of the warm body that was tantalizingly too close for comfort.

"Darn it Matthew, wake up! Oh well. I'm finished anyway." Wynn fussed good-naturedly. She began to brush the loose hair off of him without a hint of self-consciousness. If she felt one drop of the awareness that he was feeling, she showed no signs of it.

Matthew went off to shave the remainder of his beard and chalked the whole thing up to the fact that he was way too long without a woman.

The face that emerged from beneath the beard came as a surprise to him. The face in the mirror was almost that of a stranger, even to himself. It amazed him that four years, even war years could make that much difference in a man.

He'd been twenty-four when the war between the States began and now at twenty eight, he looked like a man of thirty five. His newly cut brown hair was sprinkled with gray and his forehead had developed grooves that weren't there before. The years spent mostly out in the open had etched lines like crow's feet around his eyes. Even the civilian clothes seemed strange to him. It was a very long time since he had worn anything but Confederate gray. The weight he had lost in the Union prison had not fully returned and even the lanky thinness of his body seemed strange to him. His face felt naked without the beard but he figured he'd get used to it. He shrugged his shoulders at his reflection in the mirror and went to see if supper was ready.

The picnic table in the yard was laden with food and Matthew became aware of how hungry he was. Wynn was helping Granny put the last of the food on the table and the Negroes had finished dressing out the turtle. They all sat down at the table, black and white together. Matthew thought of the time, not long in the past, when such a thing would never have occurred.

The Saturday evening meal was as big as a typical Sunday dinner and Matthew delighted in the variety of food. Only a man who was forced to do without as he had in times past, could fully appreciate it. Bowls of green beans, candied sweet potatoes and okra stewed with tomatoes and bacon was served as well as a variety of meat. Since white flour was still almost impossible to obtain, corn bread was served with every meal.

For a while there was little conversation as everyone was too busy eating to talk. When the worst of their hunger was appeased, conversation began.

Wynn sat directly opposite Matthew and was the first to notice that while he had sampled everything on the table, he hadn't touched the fried squirrel. Her curiosity got the better of her and she asked, "What's the matter, Matthew? Don't you like squirrel?"

"No." Matthew replied shortly.

"You really ought to try some of this. Granny cooks it better than average." Wynn encouraged.

"I'm sure she does." Matthew replied politely.

"Then why don't you try some?" Wynn persisted.

Matthew gave up all pretense of tact and good manners. "There was a time when I liked squirrel as well as anybody. That was before I spent time in that Yankee prison. Cooked squirrel looks too much like rat to suit me." he said.

Wynn hung her head. "Matthew, I'm sorry. I wish I hadn't brought it up." she said apologetically.

"Don't worry about it. You didn't know." he said.

66

After supper, Wynn helped Granny with the dishes and Matthew went along with the Negroes to cut a cabbage. His curiosity had gotten the better of him when he had seen them taking off with an axe to chop it down. He was bound and determined to find out what kind of a cabbage was so big that it had to be chopped down with an axe. He figured that it must be one hell of a cabbage.

He stood back totally baffled when Ned began to chop down, not a cabbage but a tree. A palm tree to be exact. "I thought he was going after cabbage. What's he doing cutting down a tree?" Matthew asked Lum.

Lum was equally puzzled. "Beats me, Massa." he replied.

After a time, the mystery was solved when Ned proceeded to cut the heart out of the palm tree. This apparently was the "cabbage" they were talking about. Matthew thought that it was a strange place indeed, where people ate ugly turtles and trees.

Dark was long in coming this time of year and the Negroes took off in the wagon to set green limb sets on the river. Matthew wasn't clear on just what this consisted of but felt reasonably sure that it had something to do with fishing. He determined that if he was still around the next time they went, he'd go with them and find out.

Wynn came out of the house carrying a half a pone of corn bread. "I'm going down to the spring and feed the catfish. You want to come along?" she asked.

It seemed a good time for a walk and he decided to join her. The sun was hanging low over the hammock and the evening was still and quiet. It was pleasant just to walk unhurriedly through the soft sand and watch the sun go down.

When they reached the small spring where the catfish were corralled, Wynn crumbled the corn bread into little pieces. They watched as the catfish came eagerly to eat it. When the last of the bread was fed to the fish, Wynn sat down beside the spring and Matthew joined her. The western sky over the hammock was blazing with color and a few black clouds were silhouetted against the brilliance of the setting sun.

"Black clouds in front of the sunset means we'll get rain. We sure do need it." Wynn commented.

"It looks like you've done well here. You work as hard as the field hands do. How've you managed to keep up with all of this?" he asked.

Wynn sighed, "It hasn't been easy. I don't know what I would have done if Ned and Pearl and Granny had left me like the others did." She slapped at a mosquito.

"How many slaves did you run?" he asked.

"Only fifty. Daddy was planning on expanding but the war came along and he never got to it."

Matthew picked up a pebble and tossed it into the spring. "The war interrupted a lot of plans." he said.

"How big was your plantation, Matthew?" Wynn asked.

"We ran about a hundred and fifty blacks." Matthew replied. "We raised mostly cotton. The only thing left when I got back from the war was Lum and the land. I was real glad to see Lum but the land is worthless without blacks to work it."

"I know what you mean. We're doing pretty good here, all considered. We don't make much profit but we've managed to raise or make everything we need. White flour and white sugar has been impossible to get and dress goods and soap can be got but they're sky high. I made some money on my cane last year. Syrup sold real high. I got fifteen dollars a barrel for it. The money really came in handy."

"You don't raise much cotton." Matthew observed.

"Just enough to spin for cloth for all of us. I haven't fooled with any more than that. We need what land we can keep under cultivation in food crops." Wynn explained.

"You eat a lot of game and fish I noticed. I like wild meat too, but is it really necessary that you eat turtles and trees?" Matthew asked, only half teasing.

Wynn laughed. "Those trees are swamp cabbage and they taste better than real cabbage by a long shot. And turtle's better than beef any day. Especially the beef we raise here, it's tougher than whit leather at best."

"Yeah, I got a hold of some like that in the army. We didn't know whether to try to eat it or make shoes out of it. We needed something to eat as bad as we needed shoes, so we flipped a coin to decide." Matthew gave a wry smile. He was surprised that he could joke about it at all.

In spite of Matthew's joking manner, Wynn was able to see through to the hardships he must have faced. "It must have been mighty hard on you. You weren't used to having to do without, were you?"

"No, I can't say that I was. I'd like to be able to say that it was all worth it but sometimes I wonder." Matthew said quietly.

"I reckon, you've got a right to wonder. It must have been terrible for you." Wynn said sympathetically.

Matthew sat silently for a moment, just staring at the sun, which seemed balanced on the treetops. Finally he spoke. "While I was gone, my father died of a fever but I kind of figured that he just didn't have the will to fight it. My son died of the same fever and my mother lost her mind. She didn't even have sense enough to leave the house and the Yankees burned it down around her. Elizabeth died trying to keep the Yankees from burning the house." Matthew's voice betrayed little emotion.

Wynn looked at Matthew, his face was still and empty and his gray eyes still stared unblinkingly into the setting sun. She wanted to say something, anything that might give him comfort. But what could she say to a man who had lost so much? Her pity for his losses was a helpless thing and she doubted that he would want it.

As the sun dropped down behind the trees, the mosquitoes came out in droves. Wynn stood up, bracing herself with a hand on Matthew's shoulder. She allowed it to linger a moment longer than was necessary. "We'd best go back now. The mosquitoes are eating me alive and the night air isn't good for us." she said.

Matthew looked at her a little blankly, as if he were pulling himself back from a world of his own. Vivid blue images of the sun were imprinted on his vision, blocking his view of her. It was a moment before he realized that she was holding out a hand to help him up. He took the offered hand, accepting it's assistance, though he didn't need it. "You're strong." he said.

Wynn shook her head. "No, Matthew, I don't think so. I just do what I have to do and keep on living until I die. That's all any of us can do." With that, she turned and began walking back toward the house.

Matthew followed a few steps behind her, lost in thought. To keep on living, yes, that was it. To keep on living until one died. There was nothing else a body could do. It was what he had been doing for four long years and the question in his mind was, "Now what?" He had to live until he died, except he had no idea how or where.

Chapter 14

Wynn, who was walking in front of him, stopped without warning. Matthew, still lost in thought walked into her. He automatically put out his hands to steady her before looking to see what had caused her to stop so abruptly. A brilliantly colored snake with black and orange rings was crawling lazily across their path. "It's only a king snake." he said.

"Yes," Wynn agreed. "Black ring first. I thought for a second, it was a coral."

Matthew realized that he still had his hands on her shoulders and removed them abruptly. He had his mind half on the snake and half on the fact that Wynn stood no taller than his chin.

"You can't take a step in this country, without looking where you're putting your feet." Wynn said.

"I found that out. Lum and I ran up on a big rattler when we crossed that long stretch of grassy swamp, between here and Gainesville. It was eight or nine feet long and had eleven rattles and a button. I cut off the rattles, remind me to show them to you some time." Matthew replied.

"Did you skin it?" she asked.

"What for?" Matthew asked. "It was hot as heck out there and I didn't have any use for the hide."

"You could have sold it for good money in Ocala." Wynn replied.

By now the king snake had crawled off and they continued on their way. This time, side by side, with Matthew paying more attention to the ground in front of him. "You folks don't waste much around here" Matthew observed.

"Nature's a good provider. A person could live off the land here if they were of a mind to. The Seminoles did until the army drove them back into the swamps." Wynn explained.

"That war hasn't been over long, has it? Did your folks ever have any trouble with them?" Matthew asked.

"Some, they didn't bother us too much. Maybe Daddy having an Indian wife made them a little soft towards us. I sort of doubt it though. No Seminole would ever marry a white person." Wynn replied.

"How did your father come to marry your mother?" he asked.

Wynn gave him a companionable smile. It was a question that

was asked of her many times before. "My Daddy came from Georgia, just like you did. Before the government sent the Cherokee people out west, they had a town that was like any white man's town. It was called New Echota. They had their own constitution and even printed their own newspapers. When my Daddy was a young man, he had a lot of dealings with the schoolmaster there. The school is where he met my mother. He married her and carried her off to settle here in the Florida territory. It wasn't even a state then." she told him.

"I've heard of that town before." Matthew replied. "From what I understand, they figured that if they couldn't lick the white people, the best plan was to join them and live the same way they did."

"Yes, but it didn't make much difference when the government decided that they wanted their land." There was a touch of bitterness in Wynn's voice.

Matthew glanced over at her, with a grim look on his face. "That's Yankee politics for you. It's just too bad they can't learn to mind their own business." he said.

By now, they had reached the house just as full darkness fell over the hammock like a curtain. After a long, full day and they soon parted to go to bed.

It was too hot to sleep and Matthew lay awake and thoughtful for quite some time. There was something about this place that seeped into a man's soul and he was beginning to understand Todd's love of it. The fact that Todd hadn't come home yet worried him. If his friend was dead, he didn't want to know about it. He thought that he should be moving on soon, before this place really got into his blood. Perhaps it had already, for he felt reluctant to go. Still, it wasn't proper for him to stay here alone in the house with a woman, his best friend's sister.

Wynn was an enigma to him, for he'd never known another woman like her. The coddled ladies he had grown up with, he could understand. They were like hothouse flowers, with their magnolia white skin and genteel ways. The women he was accustomed to were taught from the cradle how to charm and flirt with a man. They could promise a man heaven with a look in their eyes that was as hot and sultry as the southern sun. Elizabeth was that way, with eyes that spoke of untold delights but never delivered. Without meaning to, Matthew found himself comparing the two women. Wynn never flirted or pretended about anything and her eyes, as dark and mysterious as midnight promised nothing. She treated him like a brother and was as comfortable as an old shoe to be around. He had found her to be a female version of Todd and he had felt the same, almost instant friendship for her that he felt for her brother. He could remember Todd saying that his sister was the best buddy he had ever had. Now that he had met her, he could understand why. In the one day that he had spent, almost exclusively in her company, he had enjoyed more fun than he had in the last ten years put together.

He'd have to tread softly where she was concerned and make his departure soon. Though she didn't always behave like a lady, he'd have to treat her like one. She considered him her friend and so did Todd. These sudden attacks of physical desire that she sometimes evoked in him had best be ignored. It wasn't worth risking her friendship and Todd's just to satisfy his woman-starved body. More than that, he didn't want to stay around long enough to care too much about her. He had learned the hard way that if a man cared too much about anything, it was taken away. He had no intention of letting this happen to him again.

Lightning and a sudden clap of thunder signaled the beginning of a summer rainstorm and cooled the air. The rain pattering on the cedar shake shingles of the roof soothed Matthew's mind and he was soon asleep.

He awakened early the next morning, while Wynn still slept and Granny had not yet arrived to cook their breakfast. Matthew dressed quietly and washed his face and hands in the china basin on the washstand. His newly cut hair fell down over his forehead and he tamed it down with a splash of water. He slipped quietly out of the bedroom and tiptoed down the stairs.

Everything was clean and fresh after the rain. The heat of the day had not yet descended over the hammock. A cardinal splashed happily in a puddle of water and a mockingbird sang as sweetly as a nightingale in the high branches of the magnolia. The flowers in the yard were blooming in a riot of color after the rain of the night before. Some of the plants were unfamiliar to him and he would have to ask Wynn what they were called. A blue jay lit in the puddle next to the cardinal and the contrast of red and blue was vivid against the white, clean swept sand of the yard. The difference between this place and the war-scarred countryside of Georgia was as different as heaven and hell.

The Negroes were the first to emerge into the early morning air. They had already eaten their breakfast and said that they were going to hitch up the wagon and go check on their catfish sets. Matthew, who was full of restless energy, decided to go with them. He could skip breakfast and make do with a handful of oranges from one of the trees in the yard. His craving for fresh fruit was amazing and he had eaten great quantities of oranges since he his arrival. They seemed to give a strength to his deprived body as nothing else could.

The Negroes were in exceedingly high spirits and they broke into song as they drove the wagon through the tunnel of trees that covered the road. Matthew sat on the seat of the wagon, along with Ned and before long he found himself joining in their singing.

Lum and Pearl rode in the back of the wagon, seated on a bale of hay. If their seat was a bit crowded, neither of them seemed to mind in the least. The jostling of the wagon over the bumpy, rutted road, continuously made them sway into each other. Matthew could see that Lum was perfectly happy with the situation. If he was reading the signs right, there was a good chance that when he left here, Lum might just have good reason to want to stay behind. Matthew didn't want to part from Lum but Lum was a free man and could do as he pleased.

In no time at all, they emerged onto the main road that led to the Ocklawaha. As they neared the river, the land grew more tropical and jungle like. Strange exotic birds flew among the trees and their songs filled the air. As the sun climbed higher in the eastern sky, the heat increased until streams of sweat trickled down Matthew's back and down the ebony faces of the Negroes.

When they reached the bank of the river, they walked down to where a large rowboat was tied up to a cypress tree. They got into the boat and the two strong black men began rowing upstream against the current. For the most part they ignored the swarms of mosquitoes and deer flies that fed on their bodies. After a while, Matthew grew tired of slapping at the insects and ignored them as best he could. Trying to keep them driven off was a losing battle.

A few yards upstream, they came to the first green limb set. It was a simple but effective means of catching fish. A long length of heavy cord was tied to the springy limb of a tree that hung out over the murky brown water. To the end of this was attached a heavy lead weight and a large fish hook. The hooks were baited with the entrails

73

of the turtle he and Wynn had caught the day before. When the first line was pulled from the water, the bait was gone but there was no fish. Ned said that a gator had probably stolen it. The next line held a catfish that would go ten or twelve pounds and Matthew thought to himself that it was as bigger than anything he had seen in Georgia. Ned dropped the big catfish into the tub of fresh water that sat on the bottom of the boat. He re-baited the hook and dropped the line back into the water. "Ain't gwine ketch many in de day time but we picks up a few." he explained.

When they reached the next green limb set, Matthew reached to pull the line out of the water. He removed the catfish, being careful of the spines and dropped it into the tub. Now that he understood how it was done, he was having the time of his life. The Negroes were catching the fish to sell but to him it was sport.

Once all the green limb sets were checked and baited, they had a tub full of catfish and had only to drift back to where they had left the wagon. Now that Matthew wasn't distracted by the fishing, he had a chance to observe the river. It was enclosed on both sides with dense tropical jungle. During the drift back to the wagon, he saw several alligators, both in the water and on the bank. They came in all sizes, from a mere foot long to ten or twelve feet. Herons, cranes and wild ducks were plentiful along the water's edge and flying overhead. A bald eagle swooped down gracefully on it's immense wingspread and landed on a nest atop a tall dead cypress tree. The cypress trees were fascinating with their strange roots growing out of the ground and water in odd shapes. The river itself had a musky fertile odor of plants, trees and rotting vegetation. It ran snake-like through the jungle in a contrary direction, the opposite way of any river Matthew had ever seen. A variety of turtles sunned themselves on logs that had fallen into the river, perhaps due to storms in the past.

All too soon, they were back at the landing. Lum and Ned carried the heavy tub up the bank and loaded it into the bed of the wagon. When they had counted them up, they had a total of fifteen big catfish to haul to the spring.

On the way back, they startled a doe deer that was feeding near the road. She took off like a flash of lightning with her white tail in the air, like a flag of truce. They came upon the tracks of a black bear and Ned said, "Missy done said she gwine shoot us a bear dis winter. Dem skeestahs sho' does make fine eatin'."

"Ned, you mean to tell me that that girl hunts bears?" Matthew asked incredulously.

Ned only grinned, knowing that it was so but enjoying seeing Matthew's bewilderment. "Sho' 'nuff Missa Matthew, las' yeah she done kill a pantha'. Ain't nothin' much dat gal be 'fraid ob. She take on de ol' debbil hisself, he gits in her way."

Matthew sat quietly for a while, digesting this piece of information. He knew that Wynn had spunk but wasn't hunting bears and panthers going a bit too far? He wondered if they ate panther meat in Florida but was afraid to ask.

When they arrived back at the plantation, Wynn ran out to see what they had caught. She was wearing the yellow dress again and Matthew still found it strange that she could look so ladylike and still hunt bears and panthers. She exclaimed over their catch and seemed as pleased as if she had caught them herself. "They sure were biting good last night, Ned. Y'all keep this up and I won't have room left in the wagon for my watermelons." she said with a grin.

Ned, pleased with her complement, returned her grin, "Don't you be worryin' none Missy. If we ketches mo'n we needs we jus' keeps dem in de spring an' fatten dem suckahs up jus' like you gwine fatten dem pigs." he reassured her.

Wynn laughed, "Ned, have you ever seen a fat catfish?" she asked.

"Yassum." Ned replied seriously. "Me'n Massa Todd ketched us one what be so fat he look like he done eat up all de feed in de ribber."

"You and Todd, huh." Wynn laughed skeptically.

"How come I never saw it?" she asked.

"It be got away." Ned explained, with a grin.

Wynn laughed, "It got away, huh? You don't reckon you might just be pulling my leg do you Ned?" she asked still laughing.

"We ketched it Missy, Sho' 'nuff," Ned insisted.

Chapter 15

When the catfish were all hauled to the spring, Matthew returned to the house to see what Wynn was doing. He found her sitting in a rocking chair on the porch, mending mosquito netting. He took a seat on the porch swing and sat rocking it back and forth contentedly. Wynn was a little too quiet and after a while, he asked her if something was bothering her.

Wynn stopped rocking and let her mending fall to her lap. She gave him a small smile and shook her head. "No, not really," she said. "I reckon Ned talking about Todd got me thinking about him. It worries me that he's not home yet. Four years is a mighty long time to be gone. Do you reckon he's changed much?"

"That would be hard for me to say, since I didn't know him before the war." Matthew replied.

"What about you? Did the war change you any Matthew?" she asked.

This question took a little thought to answer and he took his time, more or less speaking his thoughts out loud. "I guess you could say that it did. It changed everything around me and I reckon I changed right along with it. I don't know...everything is different now." He fell silent, it was a difficult question to answer. He knew that he was not the same man who had gone to war.

Wynn's smooth brow creased slightly and she began to rock slowly in her chair, as if she too was thinking out loud. "I reckon the war changed all of us here in the South. It changed me, I know. Before the war I was perfectly content to let Daddy and Todd run the plantation. I figured that it was about time for me to get married and start my own home and family. I never thought the day would come, when I had this place to run by myself, especially without servants. If the war had never happened I'd probably be an old married woman with a couple of children by now." She smiled wryly at the thought.

Matthew spoke before he thought, "Somehow, it's hard to imagine you in that role." he said.

Rather than being offended, Wynn only laughed. "Yeah, I reckon it is. I'm not too sure I could ever be a typical settled housewife. I was young then and it was the thing to do. If you were a girl, you got married as soon as you got out of school and started raising children. That's what was expected of me." She shrugged her shoulders.

"How come you didn't?" he asked.

"Like I said, the war changed everything. I was seeing a young man from one of the plantations near here. I'm sure I would have married him if it hadn't been for the war. He went off with the rest of the young men from around here. He was one of Marion County's first to die."

"That's too bad, I'm sorry it had to happen that way." Matthew said sympathetically.

Wynn shrugged her shoulders. "I'm sorry that he died but I can't say that I'm sorry about the rest. I realize now, that he wasn't what I wanted in a husband and I know now that I wasn't ready to settle down. I guess I was just doing what was expected of me. Strangely enough I like things the way they are now. I like running the plantation, even without servants. I like the way we all work together to make ends meet. I'm glad I'm not married with a bunch of children. I like being able to be myself."

"Don't you ever want to get married?" Matthew asked.

"Sure, some day. I even want children but next time it's going to be my idea. It may be a long time in coming, if ever. Society has a way of making molds and expecting a person to fit into them. Well, I just don't seem to fit any of those molds and I don't think that I ever will." Wynn replied.

Matthew was silent, remembering what Todd had said about her, "That girl's too wild for any man to tame." he had said. It was true, there was a wildness to Wynn. But there was more to her than that. She was a free spirit and any man that could tame her would destroy her. Indeed it would take one hell of a man to be man enough for her.

That man would be a lucky man indeed. One thing was for certain, it wouldn't be him. He stood up abruptly. "I'm going to go find Lum, I need to talk to him." he said.

Wynn raised a black winged eyebrow at Matthew's departing back. She wasn't surprised at his sudden departure from her. He was no different from most men. She had a way of scaring them away. Most men were looking for doormats, not partners. Well, that was fine with her, she wouldn't be a doormat for any man.

Matthew found Lum sitting beside the spring, watching the catfish swim around. He dropped down beside him and they sat for a while in companionable silence. Finally, Matthew spoke. "I reckon we ought to leave here tomorrow." he said.

Lum looked at him with first a look of surprise, then one of sadness. "Massa, what you say if I say I not gwine go with you?"

"You're a free man Lum." Matthew said. "You can go or stay as you please."

"Massa, I goes with you if you say so. You knows dat." Lum said humbly.

Matthew shook his head. "We've been together a long time Lum, but you've got your own life to lead. This wouldn't have anything to do with Pearl, would it?" he asked.

Lum looked embarrassed. "It sho' do." he admitted. "Dat gal done gone an' got me all tied up in knots. I be plumb crazy 'bout dat gal."

"Looks like you're thinkin' about jumping the broom, Lum."

"Yessuh, I guesses I be thinkin' like dat'. Dat is if she'll hab me."

Matthew looked at Lum in surprise. "You mean you haven't asked her yet!"

Lum shook his head. "I jus' ain't be foun' de right time."

"Well, Lum," Matthew said. "You'd better not wait around too long. She seems like a real good catch."

"Massa,, I sho' does hate to see you leab heah. I'se sho' gwine miss you." Lum said sadly.

Matthew looked a little sad too. "I'll miss you too Lum." he said sincerely. "I came here to see Todd and he's not here so I have no reason to stay on. I can't live off Miss O'Mally's hospitality forever, you know."

"I guesses not. Dis sho' be a fine place, I likes it heah." Lum replied.

"Me too Lum, but it's not my place and I reckon I'd best be moving on."

"You tell Missy Wynn you gwine go?" Lum asked.

Matthew shook his head. "No, I wanted to talk to you first."

"Massa Matthew, If I be you, I think twice 'fore I leabe dat gal." Lum advised.

"Lum, it ain't that easy for white folks. She probably wouldn't have me if she won me on a bet and I'm not too sure I want to get involved right now. I haven't been a widower long and she's not like the women I'm used to. I just don't need anything like that in my life right now. Besides, what have I got to offer a woman? Some worn-out land in Georgia and a little bit of gold. I'll admit that the idea crossed my mind but it ain't nothing but foolishness."

"White folks worry too much." Lum said.

"I reckon so Lum. I admit that girl tempts me sometimes but you know how it is. I've been without a woman for a long time and it makes it hard for me to think straight. I can't afford to think that way. She's Todd's sister and besides, if I acted like I wanted to court her,

78

she'd probably run me off with a shotgun."

Lum laughed heartily. "Dat gal jus' might."

"You're dang right, she might. It sure would be a joke on me to live through four years of war and then get done in by some wild Florida swamp girl." Matthew said and joined in Lum's laughter.

"She be different all right." Lum conceded.

Their conversation was interrupted by the ringing of the dinner bell at the house. Hungry as a bear, as usual, Matthew along with Lum wasted no time in getting back. The handful of oranges he'd eaten for breakfast were long gone and his stomach was growling in protest.

The Sunday dinner was served outside and there looked to be enough food to feed an army. Granny had stewed the turtle on a slow fire overnight and then coated it with meal and fried it along with the fish. Matthew found out that it was indeed better than beef. The swamp cabbage looked strange to him but he took a small helping and tasted it hesitantly. Wynn was right, it was better than regular cabbage. The turtle was fried to a golden brown and was juicy and tender. Matthew ate until he felt as if his stomach would burst. By the time Granny served the blackberry pie, he was too full to eat more than one slice of it.

"I never ate so much in my life." Matthew said. "I can see now why Ned would want to kill you if you hadn't brought home the turtle. I never thought an ugly critter like that could taste so good. Tree ain't bad either." Matthew said, with a laugh.

Wynn joined in his laughter. "If you think turtle and swamp cabbage is good, just wait until you taste alligator tail! You ain't seen nothing yet."

Matthew was sure that she was joking. "Alligator tail? Next you're going to tell me that panther meat's good to eat." he said, with a grin.

"Of course not." Wynn said, with a twinkle in her eyes. "Cat meat's way too stringy."

When the meal was finished, Wynn suggested that they walk down to the pen trap and feed the pigs. Matthew was nearly too full to move, but decided that the walk would do him good.

Once they were out of earshot of the house, he asked, "Has Pearl said anything to you about her and Lum?"

Wynn giggled. "I'll say she has! That big black buck is all she can talk about."

"Lum's talking about jumping the broom, it looks like they've got it bad." Matthew said, with a laugh.

"It sure does." Wynn agreed. "Has he asked her yet?"

"No, but he's going to." Matthew replied.

Wynn looked pleased. "That ought'a make Pearl happy. You reckon they'll want to stay here, or start out new somewhere?"

"I kind 'a think they'll want to stay here. I guess another pair of hands on the place wouldn't hurt. I reckon I'll be leaving tomorrow. I've enjoyed my stay here but it's time I was moving on." Matthew said.

Wynn stopped in her tracks and confronted him. "Matthew, you can't leave until Lum and Pearl get hitched!" she exclaimed. Her brown face took on a pleading look. "I was sort of counting on you staying, at least long enough to help me take my produce to Jacksonville. Besides, what if Todd gets home and you've just left? Couldn't you just stay at least another week and help me get my melon crop in. We've got enough work here for ten people."

Matthew spoke what was on his mind. "What're your neighbors going to say about me staying in your house? What about your reputation? Have you thought about that?" he asked.

Wynn only laughed. "Matthew, you ought'a know me well enough by now to know that I don't worry about stuff like that. Besides, we don't have company much out here. No one even knows you're here." she argued.

In truth, Matthew didn't really want to leave, so he agreed. "I suppose I do owe you some help for your hospitality. I'll stay for Lum's wedding and the trip to Jacksonville but I'll be leaving as soon as we get back."

Wynn rewarded him with a pleased smile. "I was hoping you'd agree to stay, I've made the trip to Jacksonville a few times with just Ned and Pearl but I felt mighty uneasy."

"I didn't think you'd be afraid of anything." Matthew said skeptically.

Wynn cut her eyes at him. "Hah! That shows what you know. A body that ain't afraid of anything is a fool or crazy one." she said.

By now, they had reached the watermelon field and they stopped to cut a couple of culls to feed to the hogs. When they had carried them to the pen they found the ground around it littered with tracks.

Two of the pigs were missing and the sow had claw marks down her back. "A panther!" Wynn exclaimed. "That varmint'll be back! Free pork chops is too good to pass up."

"Yeah," Matthew agreed. "Looks like a big one to me. Look at the size of those tracks!"

"It's a big one all right. I've got plans for those pigs. I don't intend to let that cat have them for supper." Wynn said.

"What do you intend to do?" Matthew asked.

Wynn looked up into his eyes. "How do you feel about sitting up tonight and waiting for that varmint to come back?" she asked in return.

"I suppose it might work." Matthew said, nodding seriously. "Like you said, it'll be back for another pig and it sure wouldn't hurt to be waiting when it gets here." Though it hurt his pride, he had to say it. "I'll have to borrow a gun though, that old musket of mine's bad to misfire. I reckon I could get Lum or Ned to set down here with me."

Wynn raised an eyebrow at him. "Matthew, I ain't seen a black man yet that would set up at night waiting for a panther. I don't know about Lum but Ned's way too spooky."

Matthew was inclined to agree with her. "Yeah, I guess you're right. When it comes to something like that, Lum's as spooky as anybody. I can't say as I blame him though. It won't be the first time I've hunted at night by myself."

Wynn looked at him in surprise. "Who said anything about you going by yourself? she asked. "I reckon I can hunt panthers as good as any man."

Matthew would have argued with any other woman he knew, before allowing her to take on such a dangerous undertaking. However he knew that Wynn could handle the situation. Todd had once told him that his sister could out-shoot most men. He couldn't think of anyone he'd rather have along on the venture, unless it was her brother.

"I just bet you can." he agreed. "That sow looks pretty scratched up."

Wynn took a closer look at the sow. "I'll get Ned to doctor her. I'd hate to see her get screw-worms in those scratches. Granny makes up some kind of stuff that will heal them up in no time."

"What does she put in it?" Matthew asked.

81

"I don't know for sure." Wynn replied. "Some kind of black smelly stuff."

"Could be creosote. I think that's what my overseer used to put in the stuff he made up." Matthew threw the cull watermelons over the fence to the hogs.

"Now that you mention it, I think that may be what she uses. If we're going to stay up hunting that cat tonight, I reckon we'd better go back to the house. We need to check the guns and I for one, want a nap. We sure won't get much sleep tonight and tomorrow's a busy day."

Chapter 16

Walking beside Wynn back to the house, it was hard for Matthew to imagine her shooting a panther. There was nothing about the way she looked in her yellow dress to suggest that she was a tomboy. He decided that he was a lot more comfortable with her when she was dressed in the loose britches she wore for work. At least, then he wasn't constantly tempted to make a fool of himself.

Matthew found himself looking forward to the night; it was a long time since he had hunted anything besides Yankees. It galled him to have to borrow a gun though. Never in his life, had he ever shot anything but the best and to be reduced to carrying a worn out musket went down hard. One of these days, he'd get him a really good gun, if it took all the gold that he had. He wanted a Spencer rifle but would rather have a good pistol if at all possible. He was used to wearing one and felt lost without it.

The afternoon was spent in cleaning guns and taking a nap. Wynn had two good muskets, one of which was once her father's. Still, Matthew borrowed Lum's sawed-off shotgun to use as a backup in case anything went wrong. Muskets were deadly weapons but after using a repeating rifle in the war for a while, he found muskets aggravating to reload. Seven shots were a lot better than one any day.

Darkness fell over the hammock like a veil and the night was lit only by stars until the moon came out. It rose round and full over the treetops and Matthew and Wynn settled themselves more firmly in the branches of a great live oak tree, whose branches over-hung the hog pen. They sat not three feet apart on their separate branches and absorbed the stillness of the night. The stillness was broken only by the orchestra of the frogs that occupied the spring and the occasional inquisitive hoot of an owl. A whippoorwill a half a mile away began its lonely calling. "Jack married a widow." it proclaimed to the stillness of the night.

The region of the hog pen was lit almost as bright as day by the full moon, so that anything that approached it could be readily seen. A prowling raccoon passed on it's way to the spring and paid little attention to the sow or her brood.

After a time the sow became restless, pacing back and forth within the confines of the pen. Matthew became instantly more alert, his eyes scanning the area as far as the moonlight would allow. He became aware of the fact the sounds of the night birds had stilled. Even the faint breeze that had stirred the treetops had stopped. There was a feeling of anticipation in the air. It was as if the hammock and its inhabitants were holding their breath in silent waiting.

Matthew looked briefly away from the scene below but it was impossible to see Wynn in the shadows of the oak limbs. He could feel her presence and fancied that he could hear her soft breathing. He adjusted the shotgun on it's strap around his neck and checked to make sure that the musket was primed. Other than the continual chorus of the frogs the night was deathly quiet. So quiet that he was able to hear the whisper of sound that Wynn made as she shifted slightly against the small limb she was using as a backrest. A familiar sense of danger filtered into his senses and he drew his eyes back quickly to the moonlit scene below.

A lean, graceful form slunk from out of the thicket and Matthew found himself holding his breath. The long sinewy form crept silently in the moonlight. It circled the hog pen, keeping low to the ground. Lying almost flat on it's belly, the great cat crept in a straight line towards the helpless sow and her pigs. The sow saw the cat coming and bravely placed herself between it and her pigs. The panther crept to within a few yards of its victims and crouched even lower, preparing to spring. The big cat was totally unaware of the two people perched in the oak tree over it's head. The sights of two muskets were trained on it's lanky form, with deadly intent.

Wynn was the first to fire and the stillness of the night was shattered. The bark of the musket sounded as loud as cannon fire and was followed almost immediately by the sound of cracking wood.

The small limb, on which she was resting her back, snapped off from the recoil of the gun. To her credit, she made no sound as she fell to the ground below, hitting hard on her back. During the time it had taken her to fall to the ground, the wounded panther leapt high into the air with a blood-curdling scream. It hit the ground spinning in tight circles and biting at it's injured side.

Matthew aimed and fired a second shot at the writhing cat, succeeding in wounding it a second time. The panther, crazed by the pain of its injuries, ran instinctively towards the sounds from which it's pain had come. It was heading straight for Wynn, who lay helpless on the ground.

There was no time for Matthew to think, only to act. He jumped feet first to the ground, placing himself between the charging cat and Wynn. She tried to sit up, just as his feet touched the ground, just in time to see the approaching danger and cringe face down on the ground. Both barrels of the sawed off shotgun went off point blank into the panther's face. Momentum carried the body of the great cat head on into Matthew, sending him sprawling. He found himself lying in a tangle of dead cat, blood and gore.

He pushed the body of the dead cat off of him and turned his attention to Wynn. His hands found her body in the darkness beneath the tree and he ran his hands over her seeking signs of injury. She made no sound and a sense of dread came over him such as he never had felt before. Her shirt was sticky with blood and he had no way of knowing whether it was the cat's or her own. "Wynn! Are you hurt?" he questioned frantically.

Wynn didn't answer him, she only pulled herself into a sitting position by clutching a handful of his shirt. She tried to speak but only a strangled sob escaped from her aching chest. "Knocked the breath out 'a me." she finally gasped.

"Is that all? Are you sure?" Matthew implored, still running his hands over her feeling for injuries.

"I'm sure. Oh God, Matthew. I was so scared!" Her voice was wobbly and she still had a death grip on his shirt. She drew a long quivering breath and began to cry.

Now that Matthew was fairly sure that she was uninjured, his own reaction set in. No battle that he had ever fought in had left him shaking as he was shaking now. Blindly he reached for the sobbing girl and held her. Huddled together, beside the dead cat, they simply held each other. As they grew calmer and Wynn's quiet crying came to an end, Matthew became aware of other feelings. Wynn's body, pressed closely against him, was warm and firm and definitely all woman. The long thick braid of her hair lay under his hand and felt as smooth as silk and her scent reminded him of cinnamon and cloves. The very feel of her body fascinated him. She was firm, where other women were as soft as pillows. Her satin smooth skin covered a body that was well toned, shaped by hard work and hard play. The thought of how that magnificent body would feel against his own in a more intimate setting, sent a wave of desire through him that was so strong and sudden that he groaned out loud.

Wynn drew away from him at the sound, trying to see his face in the darkness. "You're not hurt are you Matthew?" she asked in sudden concern.

He drew in a slow breath, trying to calm the sudden storm of emotion that had assailed him. To act on his desire would be sheer insanity. It was a matter of honor and of personal pride. This was his best friend's sister, not some common trollop. He had nothing to offer her and he owed it to himself and to Todd to do her no wrong.

"I'm fine." he said. "Are you sure you're all right? You hit the ground mighty hard."

Wynn managed a small laugh. "Yeah, I did hit hard. I guess I'll be a little stiff and sore tomorrow but nothing's broken. We manage to get into the worst messes, don't we? I never figured we'd end up covered in panther blood, before the night was over."

She was right, they were both liberally spattered with the big cat's blood. "We do have talent for getting in a mess." Matthew agreed.

They got up and began to brush the leaves and twigs off of their clothes. Wynn became suddenly still and quiet. "What is it?" Matthew asked.

"Nothing, I just thought about Todd, that's all." Wynn answered.

"What about him?" Matthew asked.

"He'll worry. He senses when something happens to me. I know it sounds strange but he'll know that I was in some kind of danger and that I had a fall." Wynn explained.

A frown crossed Matthew's brow under the cover of the darkness and he spoke his own worries aloud. "Wynn..., how can you be so sure that Todd's still alive? He should have been home a long time ago."

Wynn laughed a small laugh in the quiet of the night. "Matthew," she said softly. "you just don't understand about us, Todd and me. If he was to die, I'd know the minute it happened." There was not even the slightest bit of doubt in her voice as she spoke.

Matthew picked up the two muskets. "You're right, I don't understand." he said. "We can deal with the dead cat in the morning. I don't know about you but I sure could use some sleep." he continued.

Wynn took her musket from him and began walking towards the spring. "Yeah, and a bath too. I'm going to wash the cat blood off of me before I go back to the house."

Matthew followed her. He too wanted a bath but wondered just how she intended to go about it. He'd been skinny dipping before, but never with a woman. The thought was certainly intriguing but he wasn't too sure that now was a good time to try it. There was definitely a limit to what a man could stand and still remain a gentleman.

When they reached the spring, Wynn sat down and calmly began to remove her shoes. Matthew stood back, waiting to see what she would do next. He didn't know whether to be disappointed or pleased when she calmly walked into the spring, still fully dressed. Matthew took off his boots and joined her in the spring.

The night was hot and the water cold and refreshing. It was no more than three feet deep in the center of the pool and they knelt down in order to fully submerge themselves. The moon was hidden behind a cover of clouds but suddenly came out, lighting up the night with it's silver glow.

Wynn stood up next to him and began to wring water out of her hair. The moonlight glistened on the beads of water clinging to her skin. Her wet shirt clung to her upper body, like a second skin , revealing the outline of her small breasts to him. She seemed to be totally unconscious of the fact and while Matthew fought down yet another bout of desire, he realized that she seemed to be feeling nothing of the same. There was nothing purposely seductive about anything that she was doing. She was as comfortable here with him, as she would have been with her brother, and as trusting. If she had given him even the slightest hint that she might feel otherwise, Matthew would have lost all control. It was obvious that she thought of him as a second brother and expected him to behave as if he was. He had best learn to think of her in the same way, he had no other choice.

When they returned to the house, they went to their bedrooms to change into dry clothes. Matthew was just pulling back the covers on his bed to climb in when she knocked on his door. He quickly climbed back into his pants and went to see what she wanted.

She stood in the doorway, looking almost shy. She carried a candle and was covered modestly from neck to feet in a long white cotton nightgown and wrapper." I forgot to thank you for saving my life." She said softly. "In all the excitement, it never crossed my mind."

The thought hadn't crossed Matthew's mind either. "Forget it. You'd have done the same thing if it was me. You don't have to thank me." he said.

"Of course I do. I just wish I'd thought to do it sooner. That was a very brave thing you did out there. That cat could have clawed you to pieces." she insisted.

Matthew felt uncomfortable under her praise. "Look, forget it. It was nothing." Wynn stepped closer to him and stood on tiptoe to kiss his cheek. "It wasn't nothing and I'll never forget it." She stepped back from him and gave him a sunny smile. "Good night Matthew." she said and walked back down the hall to her own bedroom.

Matthew closed the door quietly as she walked away. His hand went involuntarily to his cheek and he suddenly regretted his promise to stay on for a while longer. While behaving in complete innocence, Wynn had a way of continuously tempting him. He vowed to himself that as soon as the trip to Jacksonville was over, he would leave. His every instinct told him to go now, but he had promised to accompany her. If he had known then, what he knew now, he would never have made that promise.

Chapter 17

The next day was a busy one. Matthew, Lum and Ned spent the biggest part of it getting the wagons in shape for the coming trip to Jacksonville. They packed the wheels with grease and added new boards as needed to the wagon beds. Matthew felt a strange kind of pride, that he was able to hold his own doing this kind of work alongside the two black men. Although as a boy growing up he had protested having to learn such skills, he could now see the wisdom his father had shown in making him learn them. It had always been the belief of the senior Mr. Kendall that any plantation owner worth his salt would know how to do any task that he required his blacks to do. So it was that Matthew's father had insisted that he learn the workings of a large plantation, literally from the bottom up.

Lum had finally popped the question to Pearl the day before. Ned, riding one of the mules went out late that afternoon to make arrangements for his sister's wedding.

Word would spread quickly among the local black population and they would come in from miles around to attend the shindig.

For the next couple of days, Wynn was occupied a great deal of the time with Granny and Pearl, making plans for the wedding. Matthew busied himself about the place and avoided being alone with Wynn as much as possible.

He worked in the fields and helped Lum and Ned with their various chores.

Lum and Pearl's wedding was to take place on Sunday night and early Saturday morning they butchered a steer to cook for the wedding party. That afternoon, he and Lum went to Ocala to purchase new clothes. Matthew bought a new suit for himself and made Lum a present of new clothes as a wedding gift. He'd had to insist but he had persuaded Lum to take enough gold to insure him and Pearl a good start.

By Sunday night, all was in readiness for the wedding. A bonfire was lit in the yard to light the proceedings and a crowd of blacks had come in from all directions. They had arrived in wagons, on mule back, and on foot to attend the festivities. Everyone that came had brought with them a dish of this or that, so that the barbecued steer was the family's only contribution to the meal.

A band of Negro musicians played various instruments and the yard was soon filled with singing people.

The time came at last for the ceremony to begin. The black preacher called the couple forward. Pearl was dressed all in white and looked happy enough to burst. The preacher said the traditional words over the couple and the ceremony was concluded with the black custom of jumping the broom.

The wedding feast followed and then the dancing began. The

Negro musicians played one lively tune after another and the spirits of the whole crowd began to run high.

Matthew and Wynn were the only non blacks attending the wedding. At Wynn's insistence, Matthew tried out some of the dances with her. It was a far cry from the ballroom dancing that he was used to but as much or more fun. Matthew found his spirits running as high as those of the blacks. He was happy for Lum and Pearl and wished them the best. It felt good to be dressed in his new clothes. They were not of the quality he had worn before the war, however they fit him well and he felt that he looked more like the man he had once been. Wynn had also dressed for the occasion and was looking extremely lovely.

Later in the evening, a group of the Negro women started up a dance of their own. They swayed and twisted to the primitive beat of a tune that held the sounds of their African ancestry. To Matthew's surprise, Wynn joined in with them. She had on a dress made of some light material and wore no hoops beneath the skirt. The turquoise colored cloth twisted and turned around her legs as she moved to the primitive tempo of the music. One of the black musicians was playing a drum and as the beat of the music increased the dance became even more wild and sensual. Wynn's hair came loose from it's pins and tumbled down her back. Her body, moving to the primitive rhythm was as graceful and liquid in movement as the black women's and Matthew couldn't take his eyes off of her.

When the dance ended, she went to help Granny clear away some of the food from the table. Matthew wandered off down toward the spring to be alone. As he got farther away from the yard, the music became muted but it's rhythm still beat in his blood. He walked alone in the night air until his passion cooled and he wandered back to the party. The hour was late and the Negroes who had come for the wedding were making their departures. Matthew went into the house and after a while all was quiet as the last wagon pulled away.

Wynn came into the house to find him sitting alone in the parlor. She sat down in a chair across from him and pulled off her shoes with a sigh of relief. "That was some shindig." she commented.

Matthew nodded in agreement. "I never attended a finer wedding." he said.

"And a very long one." Wynn continued. "I'm worn out." she said suppressing a yawn. "We've got to start loading melons in the morning. I offered to let Lum and Pearl take a few days off for a honeymoon but they insisted that there was too much work to do." She yawned again. "We should be ready to go by Tuesday"

Matthew stood up and stretched his arms over his head. "I'm going to bed, tomorrow is another day." He told her good night and left her sitting alone in the parlor.

Wynn watched his departing back as he left the room. She stood up tiredly, retrieved her shoes from the floor and blew out the lamp. She was hot and tired and she thought wistfully of going down to the spring. Instead, she climbed the stairs to her room and undressed in the dark. As tired as she was, sleep wouldn't come. She was too angry with herself to sleep. What must Matthew think of her, dancing like that with the Negro women? Well, there was no way that she would ever be able to impress him anyway. He was used to ladies and she just didn't fit the category. Sure, she could play the part and do it quite well but it would only be an act. She was simply who she was and could be nothing else. She tossed and turned for a while longer, before finally falling asleep.

The next day was unusually hot and the work was hard. Throughout the day, they all worked frantically, harvesting the watermelons and loading them in the wagons. The largest of the two wagons was piled high with watermelons and cantaloupes packed between layers of Spanish moss. The second wagon contained yet more watermelons and the tubs of catfish. There were still a few bushels of oranges left that had to be fitted in somewhere.

At last everything was loaded and they went back to the house for a late supper. They were all too tired to eat very much and Wynn especially ate very little. Granny chided her for it, "What be th' mattah with you chil'? Why you not be eatin' yo suppah?"

"My stomach's a little queasy Granny." Wynn explained. "Lawd chil' you not gwine get sick is you?" Granny asked.

Wynn shook her head. "Not me, Granny. Todd's the one that's sick. I just feel it, that's all."

"How you knows dat?" Granny asked.

"I just do Granny. I reckon it ain't nothin' serious." Wynn replied.

Matthew wondered about it but said nothing. Wynn didn't look sick, only tired. She, like the rest of them, was dirty from head to toe.

"Maybe I just got too much sun. I think I'll go down to the spring and cool off. You want to come with me Matthew?" Wynn invited.

Against his better judgement, Matthew joined her for a dip in the spring. Neither of them had much to say and they soon returned to the house.

The night was hot and sultry and not a breath of air was stirring. As dark fell, it began to rain, a softly falling rain that didn't last long and only made the heat more oppressive.

Some time before dawn, Matthew was awakened by one of his nightmares. The heat in the up-stairs bedroom was stifling and he wandered to the bedroom window, hoping to catch a breath of cool air. It was raining again and flashes of lightning lit up the yard below his window as bright as day. A slight breeze began to stir and he stood still enjoying the play of it on his overheated body.

Suddenly he caught a glimpse of a movement on the ground below, it was only a flash of white and then it was gone. He stood staring,, trying to figure out what he had seen. Another flash of lightning lit up the sky and for an instant the scene below him was lit up as bright as day. It was Wynn that he saw, she was dressed in her white nightgown and standing in the rain. Another flash of lightning followed a moment after the first and Matthew caught his breath in wonder. The girl below had shed her nightgown and stood naked beneath the curtain of falling rain. She had her arms raised toward the sky like some primitive goddess in her ancestry. Matthew knew that he should move away from the window, he had no right to be watching her like this. However, he felt helpless to do otherwise. He remained where he was, holding his breath and waiting for the next flash of lightning. As if it were a wish come true, another bolt lit up the sky, followed by another and yet another. Never in his life had he seen anything so beautiful. Wynn was dancing and whirling to the beat of some primitive drummer that only she could hear. Her body was perfection in every detail and he was surprised to see that she was not as brown all over as he had thought. Although her face and arms were Indian dark, the rest of her was markedly lighter.

The rain began to fall harder and yet another flash of lightning lit up the night. This bolt was much closer and he began to fear that she was in danger of getting struck.

A moment later, he heard the front door being closed quietly and heard the creaking of the floorboards as she crossed them and ascended the stairs. He held his breath, not daring to move as he sensed her passing his room. When he heard the faint click of her

91

bedroom door closing, he let out his breath in a long sigh.

He suddenly became aware that his fingernails were digging into the window sill and he loosened his grip. It was all that he could do to remain where he was and not go to the room down the hall. He had never dreamed that anything could exist that was as beautiful as what he had just witnessed. His desire was a physical pain and he felt as if he was on fire with it. There was nothing he could do about it but grit his teeth and hope that it would pass.

The frustration in him began to turn to anger. He was angry with Wynn and with himself. Angry at her for making him feel this way and angry at himself because he couldn't help it. He clinched his fists and thought savagely, "Honor be damned!" He had almost reached the door when reason once again took over. There were some things in life that a man could not have and she was one of them. With more will power than he thought he possessed, he returned to his own bed.

Chapter 18

The morning dawned bright and clear after the rain of the night before. They had eaten breakfast before dawn in order to get an early start and they left as soon as it was light. Wynn was in good spirits and didn't seem to notice Matthew's more somber mood. Lum, with Pearl at his side, drove the smaller wagon and Ned rode on the tailgate. That left the larger wagon to Matthew and Wynn. The mules splashed through the puddles that still stood in the low places along the road. The Negroes in the wagon behind them were carrying on a lively conversation. As they pulled out onto the main road, Matthew made an effort to shake himself out of the mood he was in. "Are we going to cross the river?" he asked.

Wynn glanced over at him. "No, the Yankees burned the bridge at Sharpes Ferry. We'll take the Baseline road to Orange Springs and then take the Fannin road on to Palatka. We ought to make good time, if the road ain't washed out and we don't get stuck in a mud hole somewhere." she told him.

"I didn't realize that there was that much action in this part of the country." Matthew said.

"There wasn't a lot." Wynn explained. "We heard a lot of rumors but that's mostly all that they were. Gainesville and Palatka were occupied for a while. There was a company of black soldiers that came in from Palatka and burned a plantation near here. It went down real hard on the woman that owns it, she's a widow but was doing pretty good until they burned her place. They took all of her servants captive but one of them escaped. He ran to Ocala to get help but by the time he got back with the home guard they were leaving. Four of our local men got killed and the Yankees got away by crossing the river and burning the bridge behind them. I heard that they raided a plantation across the river and captured one of the boys that was still at home but he got away."

Matthew listened to her story with interest, then asked. "Were you ever in any danger?"

Wynn smiled a little and shook her head. "Believe it or not, I never saw one Yankee the whole time. I guess I was lucky."

"You were lucky! If I never see another Yankee, it'll be too soon. I've seen enough of them to last me a lifetime!" Matthew said bitterly.

Wynn nodded in understanding. "I ain't got any use for them either. Matthew, what you and Todd went through, it must have been pure hell."

Matthew didn't answer, he only nodded and grew quiet.

It was dark by the time they reached Fort Brooks at Orange Springs. The weather was good, with no sign of rain so they decided against staying in the boarding house.

Matthew helped Lum and Ned unhitch the mules, while Wynn and Pearl cooked supper over an open fire. Soon the air was filled with the good smell of frying bacon and hoecakes baking in the coals. The only thing lacking was coffee and Matthew, though he was used to doing without it, still missed it.

The simple meal seemed extra good after the long day of traveling and it was good just to sit by the fire and rest. A gentle breeze, along with the smoke from the campfire helped to keep away the hungry swarms of mosquitoes and sand gnats.

Lum and Pearl soon took off by themselves to sleep under a canvas lean-to some distance from where the wagons were parked. Ned left soon after to bed down under the smaller wagon, leaving Matthew and Wynn alone at the campfire.

For a time, neither of them spoke, being lost in their own thoughts. They sat in companionable silence, listening to the sounds of the night. There was only the call of a whippoorwill and the occasional call of a screech owl. Wynn shivered in spite of the heat of the fire and the humid summer night.

Matthew saw her shudder and asked, "What's wrong? Did a mouse run over your grave?"

Wynn smiled at him in the firelight. "Something like that." she said. "They say when you hear a screech owl that somebody's going to die. It gives me shivers, even though I've never seen it to come true."

"Me either." Matthew replied. "I've never been one to believe in superstitions."

Wynn shrugged. "I guess I don't either." She yawned widely, behind a slender brown hand. "I think I'll turn in. I've got a backache from sitting on the wagon seat all day."

Matthew gave her a look of concern. "Are you sure you didn't hurt yourself, when you fell out of that tree?" he asked.

Wynn stood up and pressing her hands to the small of her back arched like a cat. "Yeah, I'm sure. I always get a backache when I sit too long." she said.

Matthew stayed by the fire a while longer, after Wynn had gone to sleep under the largest of the two wagons. Although, he felt some small interest in seeing the town of Jacksonville, he also was longing for the journey to be over. He was beginning to feel the strain in his friendship with Wynn. They had talked very little that day and the journey had seemed to go on forever. The easy, joking and playful teasing that had seemed so natural between them was now missing. It was all his fault, he had to admit, but he couldn't seem to help it.

Wynn had tried more than once that day to engage him in conversation. She had pointed out landmarks along the way and told interesting stories about their history.

He had listened attentively as she told about such places as Coa-Hadjo's town and Fort Mackay. He had tried to keep up his end of the conversation but had failed miserably.

He was, in a way, only reverting back to what for him was a natural quietness. In truth, there were few people in this world that he felt anywhere near being talkative around. He and Lum had always shared an easy companionship. It was the same way with Todd and later with Wynn. He found that easy to understand because the two were so much alike in so many ways. Wynn's sense of fun and

94

adventure appealed to him as well as her easy, friendly manner and common sense. Early in their relationship, when he was still able to look on her like a sister, everything was just fine. In the short time he had known her, he had discovered the other side of her. Behind the tomboy was a woman of such primitive sensuality as to make his blood run like fire through his veins. Someday some man would come along who had the ability to unleash that other side of her and he envied the man who could do it. As for him, he was helplessly besotted with her, while she thought of him as no more than Todd's friend and her own.

Matthew sat thinking this all over, until the campfire burned to ashes, then went to join Ned under the other farm wagon. After a while, he slept.

Morning came all too soon after his restless night. They ate a hurried breakfast, hitched up the mules and were once more on their way.

Later in the day, they passed Port Lawson, near Palatka. The journey was uneventful and they at last came to Jacksonville, with just enough daylight left to conduct their business.

They avoided the main part of town and went immediately to the docks, which even in the late afternoon were still bustling with activity. Wynn's destination was the open-air farmer's market that supplied both the local population and the incoming ships.

The area along the docks was swarming with humanity. The crowd consisted of local people who had come to shop or sell their goods. Many sailors from off the docked ships wandered about and there was a smattering of Negroes and even a few Yankee soldiers still in evidence.

The local white population ranged from back woods crackers to fine ladies and elegantly dressed gentlemen. As Wynn left the wagon to conduct her business, Matthew couldn't help but notice the attention she drew. A group of sailors stopped to stare at the dark beauty, dressed in lemon yellow. They made a move to approach her but Matthew and Lum headed them off. Matthew took Wynn's arm in a proprietary way and Lum stood right behind them scowling like a bulldog. The big black man's mean look combined with the wicked looking shotgun hanging around his neck gave the sailors second thoughts. A black man with a gun was not a common sight and certainly not one who stood six-foot-six. If anyone who saw him thought that a black man had no business with a gun, no one seemed to have the nerve to try to take it away from him.

Wynn knew exactly where she was going and soon found the man who usually bought her produce. He was a fat, jolly, bald headed fellow and he greeted her by name.

"Miss O'Mally! I haven't seen you in a long time. Reckon now that the embargo's been lifted, we can all get back to business. What you got to sell, Miss O'Mally? I sure have been looking forward to some more of that good cane syrup." The man stopped to let Wynn get a word in edge-wise.

"I'll have some corn later on and a new batch of syrup this fall. I've got a load of watermelons and cantaloupes. I have some oranges too, good sweet ones from grafted trees." she told him.

Wynn haggled with the man for a good thirty minutes before they agreed on a price. In the end, she sold him everything but the catfish. By the time the wagons were unloaded of all but the barrels of fish, it was almost dark.

They drove the wagons away from the town and made camp for the night beneath a grove of oak trees. They would return to the docks early the next morning and try to sell the catfish and then go into the town proper to shop.

The next morning, after yet another unsuccessful attempt to sell the fish, they went to the shops in the main part of town. Lum, Pearl and Ned stayed behind with the wagons.

Wynn was as delighted as a child at Christmas as she splurged on white sugar and a fifty-pound sack of flour. Unable to resist, she paid too much for a length of sky blue cloth for a new dress. She also bought seeds for the fall garden. "Well, that about does me. I've spent too much already. You got any shopping to do?" she asked.

"Yeah, a few things. We'll take this stuff back to the wagons and then I'll come back." Matthew replied.

He shouldered the sack of flour and Wynn carried the lighter packages. When her packages were safely stored in the wagon, Wynn and Matthew went back for yet more shopping. Matthew had hidden away all of the gold, except a couple of twenty dollar gold pieces.

As they walked along the wooden sidewalk, a Yankee soldier bumped into Matthew, seemingly on purpose. If it hadn't been for Wynn being along, a fight would have occurred. As it was, he pretended to ignore the whole thing but his eyes burned with suppressed rage.

After some careful shopping and a lot of haggling over prices, Matthew at last purchased a new .44 revolver and a pair of new boots. He had paid high for the pistol but was pleased with it.

By early afternoon, their shopping was complete and they had found a buyer for the catfish. They had sold them to the owner of a boarding house that featured a restaurant.

Chapter 19

As they neared the docks, news was being spread that a ship was coming in from the Virginia coast. Matthew, Wynn and Lum went down to the end of the pier to watch it come in.

The big sailing vessel was a magnificent sight, with it's white sails shining in the sun. They waited until it dropped anchor and the passengers began to disembark. Among the ordinary passengers was a group of Rebel soldiers returning from up north. They were a ragged looking lot but Wynn watched them closely, thinking about Todd. The last of the ragged looking veterans had already walked down the gangplank when yet another one appeared. This last tired Rebel made his way down the gangplank with difficulty. He was using a cane and limping on his right leg.

Wynn had ceased to watch the passengers and she and Matthew were looking the other way when the soldier broke into a limping run and headed straight for Wynn. She cried out in surprise as he clutched her shoulder, spinning her around.

Lum, who was watching the whole thing, sprang into action. Before he knew what was happening, the soldier was lifted off his feet as Lum grabbed a handful of his shirt, just below the collar.

Wynn let out a squeal of pure delight, restrained Lum with one hand and Matthew with the other, seconds before she flew into the arms of the ragged young soldier. Lum stepped back and so did Matthew. Matthew's heart leapt with joy as he recognized who it was. Todd O'Mally was not dead, as he had feared!

Matthew's eyes grew hot and he had to blink away unmanly tears as he stood watching the reunion of brother and sister. The pair stood just holding each other for what seemed like a long time, before they drew back to look at each other. Wynn was crying from pure happiness but was laughing through her tears.

Todd was the first to speak. "My God, Wynn! Where'd you get that big watchdog? He like to a scared me to death."

Wynn wiped the happy tears from her cheeks. "That's only Lum. He came with Matthew." Wynn explained.

Todd's eyes suddenly fell on the clean-shaven man standing off to the side. He stared at him for a moment, trying to remember where he had seen him before. Todd suddenly let out a whoop. "Matthew! You son of a gun. That ain't really you, is it? How'd you beat me home?" he exclaimed.

"It's me all right." Matthew replied. "What took you so long?"

The two men embraced and stood back looking at each other. Wynn ducked her head under her brother's arm and stood holding him with both her own.

"I can't believe it." Todd said. "Here I was wondering how the heck I was gonna get home from here. Next thing I know, here's Wynn waiting for me like she knowed I was coming. And Matthew. I swear to God, buddy I thought I'd never see you again, you looked like death warmed over the last time I seen you."

"I almost didn't make it." Matthew replied.

Wynn stood back to look at Todd once more, her black eyes sparkling with happiness. "What took you so long Todd?" she asked.

Todd shrugged and looked a little sheepish. "I was at Appomattox when Lee surrendered. Hell, a bunch of us boys got drunk and I fell off my horse, or something, I ain't sure just what. Anyway, I broke my fool leg. I've been laid up with it for a while, then it took a while to get enough money together to pay my ship passage. I wasn't up to walking home all the way from Virginia. I'd a been better off walkin'. I was seasick most of the time. I don't care if I never see the deck of another ship as long as I live."

Wynn gave Matthew a triumphant smile. "What'd I tell you Matthew? I knew he had done something to his leg. I bet now, you'll believe me when I tell you he's alive." Wynn's musical laugh rang out. "I knew you were seasick too." she told Todd.

Todd hugged his sister tight to his side. "You don't miss much, do you? What I want to know is what kind of scrape you got yourself into a week or so ago. I woke up in the middle of the night and thought I'd fell out of bed. I see you survived whatever it was." he

98

said with a grin.

"I fell out of a tree." Wynn said, without elaborating. Todd gave her a skeptical look. "In the middle of the night? Now that one's gonna take some explaining." he laughed.

Wynn laughed with him. "We've got a lot to catch up on but right now; what do you say we go home?"

Todd looked down into Wynn's eyes solemnly. "You ain't got no idea how good that sounds." he said. "I can't wait to hear all the news. Have you seen Sarah lately?" he asked.

Wynn gave Todd a knowing look and tugged playfully at his scraggly beard. "She was fine last time I saw her. She'll have a fit when she finds out you're home. She's worried about you and missed you almost as much as I have."

Todd looked pleased but teased Wynn back by pulling her hair. "Lay off the beard will you, it took me a long time to grow it." he said.

She couldn't resist pulling it again. "Todd, who the heck told you you could grow a beard?" she asked.

"That's what Matthew wanted to know. Truth is I still ain't found my razor."

They began walking back toward the wagons with Wynn and Todd still arm in arm. "When did Matthew ask you that?" Wynn wanted to know.

Matthew answered her. "Todd carried me out of that Yankee prison more dead than alive. I was about half out of my head at the time but I remember thinking that was the most moth eaten looking beard I'd ever seen."

"You never told me about that." Wynn accused.

Todd turned to Matthew. "I thought you'd be back at your plantation in Georgia. I figured if you lived, you might come to Florida eventually but I never thought I'd find you here when I got here."

"Silver Oaks was burnt to the ground when Sherman went through. There wasn't anything left there to keep me. I couldn't stay there, so me and Lum headed down this way. I thought I'd come and look you up." Matthew explained.

Todd's smooth brow creased with a concerned frown. "What about your wife and son? Did they get out all right?"

Matthew shook his head. "The boy died of a fever and the

Yankees killed Elizabeth." he answered in a voice devoid of emotion.

Todd put a hand on Matthew's shoulder. "My God. I don't know what to say."

"There's nothing can be said." Matthew replied.

The journey back to the O'Mally plantation seemed to fly by. There was a lot of news to be caught up on and a million things to be discussed.

Todd laughed so hard that he almost fell off of the wagon seat when he heard Matthew's version of the story of catching the turtle. When he heard about them killing the panther and Wynn's near escape when she fell from the tree, Todd grew serious. "Now that I'm home, maybe you can leave such things to me. No woman ought'a have to deal with that kind of thing." he told Wynn.

Wynn only laughed at him. "Why should men have all the fun? You never used to object to me going hunting with you." she reminded him.

"No, and I reckon I still wouldn't but I figured you'd be out of the notion to do all that stuff by now." Todd argued.

Wynn grew serious. "There's been nobody but me to do it for a long time now since Daddy died. I couldn't very well sit around while the varmints wiped us out. There wasn't any man there to do it for me or to keep meat on the table. I guess all of that's beside the point though. I just plain love to hunt and fish."

Todd gave his sister an affectionate hug. "It's been hard on you, running the place by yourself, ain't it?" he said regretfully.

"No harder for me than for the rest of the women in Marion County. I wasn't alone, I had Granny and Pearl and Ned. I don't reckon I'd have made it without them. I've been all right Todd." Wynn assured him.

"Still, I hate it that you had it to do." Todd said.

"Well, now that you're home you can take over. To tell the truth I got mighty tired of being responsible for everything all the time." Wynn told him, then smiled. "It sure is good to have you home." she said.

"It's good to be home." Todd said with feeling. "I can't hardly wait to see the plantation again and I want to go swimming in Silver Spring. I intend to eat up everything in the house for a while. There was times when all I could think about was Granny's cookin'." Todd said wistfully.

"Looks like you could use a dose of it." Wynn said and poked him in his lean ribs. "Granny's done put a good ten pounds on Matthew and he's only been here a couple of weeks. We may be low on money but one thing we've got plenty of is something to eat." she assured him.

"Army rations weren't nothin' to brag about at best. I reckon all us boys got mighty lean and stringy before it was done with. We were a lot better off than the ones of us that got sent off to those Federal prisons. The last time I seen Matthew, he wouldn't have weighed ninety pounds in a wet overcoat and that's no exaggeration. Good God, Matthew, that wasn't but six months ago. Sometimes it seems like a hundred years." Todd said.

Matthew nodded. "At least that long." he agreed. "There still ain't enough of me to fill out the clothes I wore when I was at my best. I reckon I could still stand to put on another twenty or thirty pounds. I've eat more in the last two weeks than I did in the last two months put together." he told Todd.

"I can't imagine Matthew weighing ninety pounds." Wynn said. "But then I never thought I'd see Todd looking as thin as a rail either. I thought that times got a little hard around here but we never lacked for food on the table. We did get so hungry for salt though that we boiled it out of the dirt from the smokehouse floor. Granny will have you boys fattened up in no time Todd. I bet as soon as Sarah finds out you're home she'll have a hand in it too."

Todd's black eyes lit up at the mention of Sarah. "You think she really has been waiting for me all this time? I was worried about her finding another man while I was gone." Todd said apprehensively.

Wynn laughed. "Now why would she want another man when she had you?" she asked.

"I guess a girl like Sarah could do a lot better than the likes of me." Todd said. "But what about you Wynn? I'd have thought you'd be married by now and have a couple of kids."

Wynn cut her eyes at her brother sharply. "And just where was I suppose to find a husband? There ain't been a man over fourteen or under sixty in Marion County in the last four years."

"I never thought of that." Todd's eyes began to twinkle mischievously. "I would a figured that you and Matthew would have something going by now." he said.

Matthew, who was sleepily listening to the conversation and

101

driving the wagon suddenly choked. He turned beet red and bent double coughing. Wynn sitting between the two men, rescued the reins and gave Matthew a sharp slap on the back.

"Now look what you've done Todd! No use to get all choked up about it Matthew. If I had my sights set on you, you'd know it by now." Wynn said in exasperation.

Todd laughed long and hard at the havoc he'd created. When he finally stopped laughing he said, "Good God you two, don't wreck the wagon!"

Matthew wiped the sweat from his brow and choked out, "I just swallowed a gnat, that's all, no need to make such a big deal out of it."

"Sure you did." Todd teased.

Chapter 20

The trip home from Jacksonville was made in less time than it had taken to go. Everyone was glad to be home. Todd, of course was especially happy and after being greeted enthusiastically by Granny, the first thing he did was to take a walk over the plantation. Matthew and Wynn stayed behind to unload the wagons while Ned and Lum unhitched the mules.

By the time they were finished, Todd had returned from his walk and he praised his sister profusely. "You've done good Wynn. I never figured I'd come home and find crops in the fields and a full smokehouse. Folks on farther north ain't faring nearly so well." he told her.

Wynn made light of it but looked pleased. "I just done what I had to do." she said.

Todd gave his sister an enthusiastic hug. "I'm one lucky son of a gun, you know that. I'm home. I'm alive, and this leg ought to be as good as new before long. You've saved the plantation for me and short of having a couple of fingers that don't work right. I'm still in one piece. I'm a heck of a lot better off than most of the men I went to war with." he said.

Wynn's eyes turned to see Matthew standing off to the side. His face was devoid of expression but his eyes held a hard, haunted look.

"Yes, Todd, you are lucky." she said softly. Her heart ached for Matthew, who had come home to nothing.

Todd, seeming to read her thoughts, bent down to whisper in her ear. "Don't worry, a man like Matthew may get stomped down but he won't stay that way long."

Wynn looked up at her brother and nodded. Matthew, sensing a private moment between the two had gone inside.

"You're right Todd." she said quietly. "He's got guts."

"I know I'm right." Todd said confidently. "A lesser man would be dead by now. You know, Wynn, I think he feels like he owes me for getting him out of that Yankee prison. But when he saved you from getting clawed up by that panther, he paid me back in full. Maybe more. I didn't know he was there when we raided that Yankee hell hole but Matthew knew exactly what he was doing when he got between you and that panther."

Wynn leaned her head on her brother's shoulder and nodded. She hadn't missed the real affection and admiration in his voice. "Yes, he did know. I guess I owe him a lot myself." she said.

Todd spent the next day resting, eating and sleeping. He shaved off his scraggly beard and Wynn cut his hair. Dressed in civilian clothes once more, he felt like a new man. Wynn smiled fondly at him when he came down for supper that night. "Now you look like the brother I remember." she said. "I think it's about time we had us a celebration. You reckon we could get together enough fish and frog legs to have a fish fry here next Saturday night? All the neighbors will be anxious to welcome you home and this place ain't had a good frolic in years. We could get Old Man Johnson to bring his fiddle and we could maybe have a dance. I could send Ned around to all the neighbors to let them know." Wynn's black eyes sparkled with enthusiasm. It was obvious that she had already put considerable thought into the matter.

Todd was as enthusiastic as Wynn. "Now you're talking. I don't know which is the most fun, having a fish fry or getting ready for one. It'll be a good excuse to get together with Sarah. I'm way behind on my courting." he said with a grin.

"I'll say you are." Wynn laughed. "I'd have thought you'd have been over there to see her by now. But if you're looking for an excuse, you could ride my horse over there and tell her about the fish fry." she suggested.

103

Todd slapped the table with the palm of his hand. "I'll do just that. In fact I think I'll ride over there tonight. I don't reckon a fellow's got to have an excuse to go see his girl though."

"Now you're talking sense little brother!" Wynn exclaimed.

Todd pretended to be offended. "Now look 'a here, just because you're three minutes older than I am don't give you no right to refer to me as little brother." he argued.

"Yes it does." Wynn insisted.

As soon as supper was over, Todd went to see Sarah. Matthew, sitting on the porch with Wynn, watched as he rode off. Wynn paced the length of the porch and back. "I'm too restless to sit still." she complained. "If Todd didn't have my horse, we could take a ride down to Silver Spring."

Matthew was restless too and he allowed his restlessness to override his better judgment. "I reckon that nag of mine could carry both of us if we don't push her too hard." he said.

"Then let's go! I'll change into some pants and we'll be on our way." Wynn said with enthusiasm.

By the time she came back out, Matthew had the mare saddled and was waiting for her. He helped her up first, then got on behind her. He had to reach around her to reach the reins and she sat stiffly for a time but soon leaned back, in order to give him more room. Matthew was intensely aware of the slim young body pressed so closely against him. Wynn, on the other hand, seemed totally relaxed and chattered on about the fish fry they were planning and about how happy she was that Todd had come home. She kept up the amiable chatter until they reached the spring and he helped her down. "You're mighty quiet Matthew." she observed.

"It's my nature." he replied.

Wynn shook her head. "No. I don't think so. Something's bothering you." she insisted.

"I'm just restless, that's all. I think I'll stay a day or two more and visit with Todd, maybe until after the fish fry and then be moving on. I reckon I'll go down to the southern end of the state and look around, then maybe go back to Georgia." he said.

Wynn turned to him and frowned. "You know you're welcome to stay here as long as you like."

"I can't sponge off your hospitality forever." he said.

"But Matthew, I wish..." she paused. "Well I suppose if you feel you have to go, then you'll go no matter what I say." There was a note of defeat in her voice.

A feeling of tenderness swept over Matthew and he spoke to her sincerely. "You've been good to me Wynn. You gave me the homecoming I never had in Georgia. I'll miss you but I really do have to move on." He gave her shoulder a brotherly squeeze.

They rode back to the house in silence for Wynn was now as quiet as Matthew.

Todd returned later that night and woke up Matthew and Wynn by riding into the yard at a full gallop and letting out a Rebel yell.

Matthew and Wynn collided at the head of the stairs on their way to see what all the commotion was about. "Lord Matthew! What do you reckon's got into Todd? You don't reckon he's drunk do you?"

Matthew shrugged and took the lamp from her, letting her precede him down the stairs. They got to the front door just as Todd came in, grinning ear to ear. "Hey Wynn." he said. "You don't reckon you could turn that fish fry into a wedding party do you?" he asked.

Wynn stood there gaping at him then asked, "Todd, are you drunk? What're you talking about?"

Todd threw back his head and laughed heartily. When he could talk, he said, "No, I ain't drunk. Sarah allowed that she had waited for me long enough and the next thing I knew, we'd decided that Saturday night was a perfect time to get married."

Matthew recovered from the surprise first. "Well, you son of a gun, you don't waste no time, do you? Let me be the first to congratulate you then!" he said and reached out to shake Todd's hand. Todd was too happy to settle for a mere handshake and hugged him instead.

"Me too!" Wynn exclaimed and gave her brother an affectionate hug. "You could do a lot worse than Sarah. She'll make you a good wife."

"She will, won't she." Todd agreed happily.

Wynn's eyes lit up and she snapped her fingers as if she had just remembered something. "This calls for something special and I think I know just the thing! You boys go sit in the parlor and I'll be right back." she said.

Wynn lit another lamp and went off to the kitchen. She joined them in the parlor a few minutes later carrying a tray with a crystal decanter and three delicate long stemmed glasses.

"Is that what I think it is?" Todd asked, with a grin.

Wynn smiled back at him and poured the three glasses full. "It sure is. Daddy's prize bottle of Kentucky bourbon. I've been saving it for something special and I guess this is it." She handed each of them a glass and took one for herself. She raised her glass in salute and said, "To Todd and the future Mrs. O'Mally." The fragile glasses rang like bells as they touched them together, before they each sipped the amber liquid.

Matthew then raised his glass to propose another toast. "May all your troubles be small ones." he said gravely.

Todd caught the joke and laughed heartily. "Watch it Matthew," he said. "I just might name my first small trouble after you." By the look on his face, Todd was dead serious.

Matthew's face and eyes betrayed his feelings. "I think I'd like that." he said solemnly.

"You might want to use the name for one of your own someday." Wynn pointed out.

Matthew shook his head and gave her a sad smile. "I already named a son of mine for myself. I'll never have another by that name but it would be an honor to me if Todd were to use it someday."

Wynn sat down her glass and reached for Matthew's hand as a tear slid slowly down her cheek. "I'm sorry I said that. I didn't know. Forgive me Matthew."

Matthew squeezed her hand reassuringly. "Wynn, don't cry for me. There's nothing to forgive. This is a happy time." He picked up her glass and replaced it in her hand and raised his own in another toast. "To the future." he said.

Chapter 21

Early the next morning, Wynn sent Ned out to spread the word about the wedding and fish fry. By necessity, they spent the day working in the fields and catching up on other neglected chores. That evening at supper, Todd suggested that they go down to Silver Spring Run and gig some mullet to smoke for the fish fry. Wynn agreed enthusiastically. Matthew said that he had never used a gig before but thought he'd like to try it.

By dark, they had launched the rowboat at the head of the spring and began drifting down the run. Wynn sat in the bow of the boat, holding a lit lantern out over the water on a pole. The light from the lantern penetrated the crystal clear water and showed up the mullet as silver flashes darting beneath the surface. The Silver River, or run as it was called, was like another world at night. The clear sky above it was lit by a million stars and the jungle on either side of it seemed to stand sentinel over the run. The light from the lantern reflected in the eyes of a deer that had come to drink at the edge of the stream. An occasional alligator could be seen in the dim light, looking like a log along the bank. The eyes of the alligators glowed in the lantern light, like those of some prehistoric monster.

Before they had drifted far, Todd stood up in the boat and raised the shaft of the gig up over the water. He held it suspended with the four sharp prongs just above the surface. At just the right moment, he plunged it beneath the water as fast as lightning. When he pulled it back up, a streamlined silver fish, some fourteen inches long was impaled on the gig. Matthew removed the mullet from the gig and placed it in a crocus bag at his feet. In no time at all, Todd had gigged three more of the silver fish. He turned the gig over to Matthew. "Here, you try it." he said.

They changed places and Matthew stood in the center of the boat and held the gig up over the water as he had seen Todd do. He missed the first couple of times but soon got the hang of it. He found that he seemed to have a knack for the sport and he soon was handling the gig as competently as Todd. After a time, he offered the gig back to Todd but he refused. "I've been on my feet too much today and standing in the boat hurts my leg." Todd said.

Matthew was having the time of his life and before long the crocus bag was nearly filled. He thrust the gig into the water once more and came up with, not a mullet, but a large-mouthed bass. It looked as if it would weigh at least ten pounds. Wynn whistled in admiration of the big fish. "Let's see you do that again." she challenged.

Matthew raised the gig up over the water once more. The bass had appeared darker in the water than the mullet, so he aimed for the next dark shape that swam by. To his surprise, he came up with not another bass but a baby alligator! It was speared through the tail and was making high-pitched sounds of distress.

"Now you've done it!" Todd exclaimed. He grabbed both paddles and began rowing up stream as hard as he could. Matthew sat down hastily to keep from falling out of the boat and Wynn hurriedly put out the lantern and came to help him get the alligator off the gig. The moon was up now and they could see mama alligator slide off the bank and head straight for the rowboat. Matthew forgot that he was ever a gentleman and that a lady was on board. "Oh shit!" he exclaimed.

The alligator was gaining on the boat rapidly. Todd made an effort to paddle even harder. "For God's sake Matthew, get your pistol and shoot that thing before she sinks us!" he shouted.

Matthew had forgotten that he had the pistol in all the excitement. He drew it from its holster on his hip and emptied it at the gator. He never knew if he killed the alligator or not but it submerged and they never saw it again.

Matthew wiped his brow and breathed a sign of relief. "Whew, I'd rather have a Yankee after me any day than one of those boogers!" he exclaimed.

Now that the danger was over, Todd joked about it. "Shoot Matthew, that little ol' gator wouldn't hurt you." he said.

Matthew gave Todd a dirty look. "That little ol' gator was as long as a freight wagon and she sure as heck wasn't chasing us for the fun of it." he argued.

"Matthew's right." Wynn said. "That gator could have sunk us easy. I sure wouldn't want to be breakfast for one of those boogers."

Todd figured that he was outnumbered and shut up.

They returned home without further incident and stayed up until midnight to clean the fish and put them to smoking in the smokehouse. The night was too hot for it to wait until the next day.

Wynn went to bed and left the two men sitting on the porch.

"I've had more fun since I've been here, than I had in my whole life up until now." Matthew confided to Todd.

"I guess you see now, why I love it here so much," Todd said. "Wynn told me you plan to leave right after the wedding. I don't understand why you want to leave, if you like it here so much. You know you're welcome."

Matthew gave Todd the same excuse he had given Wynn. "I guess I'm just restless."

Todd was silent for a moment, then spoke. "You don't seem restless to me, as a matter of fact I'd say you was way too quiet. I'd say you was a man with something bothering him. You want to talk about it?" he invited.

Matthew was silent too for a moment, then he just simply said, "No."

Todd was more perceptive than Matthew thought him to be. "It wouldn't have anything to do with that half wild sister of mine, would it?" he asked.

Matthew gave up making excuses. "Yeah, I guess it does." he admitted.

"What's she done now?" Todd asked.

"Nothing." Matthew said. He was still reluctant to tell Todd how he felt. Todd surprised him once again with the depth of his perception. "Okay, let me see if I've got this thing figured out." he said. "You're plumb crazy about her and she won't give you the time of day."

"That's about the size of it." Matthew admitted. "How did you know?" he asked.

"Shoot Matthew. Any fool can see the way you look at her. As for Wynn, well, just give her a little more time." Todd replied.

Matthew sat quietly for a moment, thinking things over. Todd's immediate grasp of the situation amazed him and he wondered if it was as obvious to everyone else. Todd's attitude about the whole thing indicated that he not only understood how he felt, he seemed to harbor no disapproval. Matthew seldom expressed his innermost feelings to anyone, except perhaps to Lum. At this time he felt the need to talk and decided to take a chance on baring his soul. "Todd, you ought to know how it is. I've been married and got used to having a woman regularly, then I went off to war. I realize this is not a fitting thing to say about a man's sister but that girl's driving me crazy. Not on purpose, you understand. She doesn't feel about me the way I feel about her. The thing is, I can't stay here feeling the way I do and be able to stand it." Matthew fell silent, wondering if he had said too much.

As it turned out, he needn't have worried. "I see what you mean," Todd said. "In fact I know exactly how you feel. When I came home I didn't know if Sarah even still felt the same way about me as when I left. But once I saw her again I knew that waiting was plumb out of the question. Hell, Matthew I know I ought'a wait a month or two at least before I even think about getting married. It didn't take long for me to find out I couldn't stand to wait that long. As for Wynn, who can say how that girl feels. That sister of mine is a law unto herself. I guess I'll understand if you leave but I wish you'd give it some more time."

Matthew shrugged in the darkness. "It's either leave, or make a complete ass of myself. It don't leave me much choice does it?" he asked.

"I reckon not." Todd agreed.

The next two days were busy ones, along with the usual work, they were all busy preparing for the wedding and fish fry. Ned and Lum provided the fish and cut down enough swamp cabbage to fill a small wash pot. By Friday evening, they had enough fish to fry and a good supply of smoked mullet. All that remained was to gig enough frogs to have an adequate supply of frog legs.

Wynn, Pearl and Granny had spent a big part of the day baking cakes and pies. Wynn had sat up half the night before sewing the sky blue length of cloth she had bought into a new dress to wear to the wedding. Though she wasn't overly fond of sewing, she did it well and was pleased with the results. The dress was trimmed in lace that she had salvaged from an old ball gown and had a daringly low neckline.

Matthew, Wynn and Todd set out just at dusk dark to go frog gigging along the stream that ran from the catfish spring. Wynn carried the lantern while Todd and Matthew gigged the frogs. They waded barefoot down the shallow stream and kept a sharp eye out for water moccasins along the way. They didn't have as much luck as they had hoped but with all the other stuff they had to cook, it didn't make much difference.

Matthew and Todd rode the horses to Ocala the next day, more to get out of the way of the women, than anything else.

During the course of the day Granny got Wynn alone in the kitchen and gave her a motherly dressing down. "What be de mattah wid you chil"? You is s'pose to be happy now dat Massa Todd done be home. Heah you is lookin' like you done be los' yo' bes' friend!" she said sternly.

"Maybe I have Granny. Matthew's gonna leave tomorrow." Wynn said.

"What it is you done be talkin' chil'? You's not gwine let dat man git away is you?" Granny asked impatiently.

110

Wynn made a minute study of the floor in front of her. "Ain't much I can do about it Granny." she said sadly.

"Lawd hab mercy chil'! What you mean?" Granny asked sharply.

Wynn shrugged her shoulders. "I mean...he's a gentleman Granny, he ain't going to stay here for the likes of me." Wynn argued.

Granny paused in the middle of putting a strip of piecrust over the pie she was making and wiped her hands on her apron. "Lawd chil' de way dat man look at you, it done be wrote all ovah his face." She shook a floury finger at Wynn for emphasis. "You wants dat man, you bes' be lettin' him knows you wants him, heah!"

Wynn looked suitably chastened but argued nevertheless. "But Granny, what if he's not interested? I'd feel like a fool flirting with a man that didn't care."

Granny picked up another strip of piecrust. "He be innested chil'. You wants dat man you bettah be steppin' lively else he done be gits away!"

When Todd and Matthew got back from Ocala late that evening, Todd cornered his sister on much the same subject.

"But Todd," Wynn argued. "he don't care anything about me. He's not showed one sign of it."

Todd didn't cut any corners, he was exasperated with her and didn't mind letting it show. "The hell he don't!" he said emphatically. "If you don't want him leaving here, you'd best be letting him know it! What's the matter with you anyhow? How do you expect to capture a man's interest if you're gonna run around in britches all the time. Hell Wynn, you used to flirt with that boy at the academy, you was so sweet on. Don't tell me you've forgot how." he snapped.

Wynn blinked her eye's rapidly. Her brother's scolding hurt and she was near tears. "Maybe I have Todd." she admitted wistfully. "It just never seemed right to flirt with Matthew. It just didn't seem like there was any use to try." A tear ran down her cheek in spite of her efforts to stop it. "Oh Todd...I don't want him to leave."

Todd was still too exasperated to have very much sympathy. "Well, if you don't want him to leave, you'd better be thinking about how you're gonna stop him. I sure as hell ain't got what it takes to keep him here." Todd turned and walked away.

111

Chapter 22

Wynn bit her lip and watched as her brother walked away. There wasn't time to think about all that now, it was time to get dressed for the wedding. The guests would be arriving soon and she was the hostess. Nevertheless, she spent more time dressing and fixing her hair than she had in years.

Once the guests began to arrive, her duties as hostess kept her busy throughout most of the evening. There was no time for anything else.

The wedding of course was the main event of the evening. With the men off to war there were very few weddings in the past four years. Sarah's parents had wanted the wedding to be held in one of the churches in Ocala but Todd and Sarah had decided against it. The preacher from the Baptist church had agreed to come out and conduct the ceremony and he had brought along the church choir to sing. The wedding was a simple one compared to those that used to be held before the war. Still, it was as traditional as the circumstances would allow.

Sarah's father gave the bride away. She was dressed in a flowing gown of white satin and lace and Wynn knew for a fact that she had bought the material for it before the war began. Wynn grew misty eyed as her brother stepped up to take his place beside his bride. Sarah was as blond and fair of skin as Todd was dark and they made a striking couple. One of Sarah's cousins acted as maid of honor and Matthew, of course was Todd's best man. Old Man Johnson played the wedding march on his fiddle and the church choir sang Oh Promise Me. Wynn wept openly as Todd and Sarah repeated their vows.

As soon as the wedding was over, the dancing began. It was sad to see how many of the young girls had no partners and that there were so many widows among the crowd. Marion County had lost so many of her men and boys to the cause of the Confederacy.

Matthew came once to claim her for a dance but other than that, she saw very little of him. As was typical of many such gatherings, the men and boys tended to stay in one group and the women and children in another.

After the dancing began, the men and boys were kept busy dancing with all the women and girls for they were outnumbered two to one. Matthew, being both young and single was kept busy trying to dance with them all. Wynn found herself suddenly seething with jealousy, everything in skirts from thirteen to forty, seemed to be not only flirting with Matthew, but competing for his attention.

After what seemed like forever, the festivities ended. Sarah stood blushing prettily with Todd on the front porch and threw her bridal bouquet into the crowd of hopeful girls and women. Wynn, standing near the back of the crowd was surprised when she found the bouquet in her hands. She looked at Sarah in surprise and Sarah winked at her before going into the house with Todd. The crowd gave a cheer and began to disburse.

Wynn held the bouquet of orange blossoms beneath her nose and sniffed thoughtfully. Sarah had weighted down the bouquet with a small rock to make it easier to throw and had tossed it to her on purpose.

Some of the neighbors who lived nearby left for their own homes accompanied by others who lived farther away who would spend the night. A couple of the families would spend the night on the plantation before leaving the next morning.

Wynn at last got them all settled and was finally able to retreat to the privacy of her own room but not to sleep. She blew out the lamp by her bed and waited for what she knew was yet to come. Once the last light in the house was extinguished, the expected banging on the front door began.

The shivalree had begun. The bride and groom were now expected to rise from their bed, if they had gotten that far, and serve drinks and refreshments to those who had come to their door. Wynn knew they had not yet gone to bed, she was listening for the cow bells she had tied to the bed springs.

Wynn waited a suitable time for Todd and Sarah to go down and answer the banging on the door. She heard them descend the stairs, together, followed soon by the house quests.

She met Matthew in the hallway and they went down the stairs together. The shivalree continued until daybreak, with much drinking of hard spirits and hilarious laughter. Sarah and Todd put up with the shivalree in the spirit of fun in which it was intended.

Soon after daybreak, the guests finally left, including those who had stayed overnight. Wynn had helped Sarah cook a huge breakfast for them all, before sending them on their way. The sun was up over the hammock by the time the bride and groom were finally left alone. Wynn and Matthew were still sitting at the kitchen table when the couple ascended the stairs to the master bedroom.

Wynn gave Matthew a mischievous grin. "Be quiet and listen." she said.

In a few minutes the quiet of the early morning was broken by the clanging of cowbells coming from the region of the upstairs bedrooms.

Wynn giggled, "Todd's going to kill me."

Matthew laughed with her. "Yeah, and I'd say you deserved it too." he said.

Wynn gave Matthew a sunny smile. "I know but I'd give anything to have seen his face when those cow bells started clanking. I bet he's under the bed right now, trying to get them untied." She dissolved into yet another fit of giggles.

Matthew laughed heartily at the idea and then grew quiet.

The silence that prevailed over the house grew to be almost deafening, after the hilarity of the night. Matthew broke the silence at last. "It's been a long night and it's been fun. Todd and Sarah will probably sleep all day and I don't reckon I'll wait to tell them goodbye."

Wynn looked at him in shocked surprise. "Matthew, surely you're not still planning to leave this morning. You haven't had a wink of sleep all night."

"Losing a night's sleep doesn't bother me much. I need to be on my way." Matthew said. "My saddle bags are already packed and all I need to do is saddle my horse and be on my way."

"But Matthew, you can't go without saying good bye to Todd and what about Lum?" Wynn argued.

Matthew shrugged and seemed unconcerned. "I'll see Lum before I go and Todd will understand."

Wynn watched helplessly as he walked out the door to go saddle the mare. She blinked back tears and after a while went outside to wait for him at the stable door.

When he came out of the stable, he wasn't leading the mare as she had expected. Wynn couldn't look at him, she stood there staring at a patch of sandy soil immediately in front of her feet."

"My horse has gone lame." he stated flatly.

Wynn raised her face to look at him and this dislodged the tears

114

that were balanced precariously on her lower lashes. She paid no heed to them as they slipped unnoticed down her cheeks.

Matthew came closer to stare down at her in bewilderment. "Hey, it's only a horse and it's lame, not dead." He reached out and brushed the tears from her cheeks with his fingertips.

Wynn's lips trembled and two more tears escaped down her cheeks. She reached out to fiddle with a button on his shirt. "I don't want you to go." she said in a quivery little voice.

"I can't go." he said obtusely. "My horse is lame."

Tired from the long night, Wynn suddenly lost her temper. Her black eyes flashed and she hit him squarely in the chest with her clenched fist. "Damn you, Matthew Kendall! If you think I'm gonna beg you to stay, you've got another think coming!" she snapped.

"I'm not going anywhere." he said, his gray eyes twinkling with amusement.

His amusement was more than Wynn could take with good grace. "Dad gum you, Matthew! Don't you laugh at me!" she snapped.

"I'm not laughing." Matthew denied. The twinkle had gone out of his eyes and they were suddenly dark and serious.

Wynn glared at him for a moment longer, her dark eyes mirroring anger and hurt. At last, unable to bear seeing that look Matthew reached out and pulled her head gently against his shoulder. He gave her a warm hug and stood, swaying, rocking her as if she were a child.

She drew back from him after a while and looked up at him through wet black lashes. "What's wrong with your horse?" she asked.

Matthew laughed. "Old age mostly. She's got a swollen left foreleg. I'm surprised that the old nag lasted this long"

Wynn began to fiddle with a button on his shirt once again. "I heard old man Johnson say that someone's got a couple of horses for sale at Fort MacKay." she told him

Matthew smiled in pleased amusement. "You don't want me to go but you're helping me to find a horse so I can. Make up your mind Wynn." he teased.

She gave his shirt button a sharp tug. "It is made up. I think I told you once, that if I ever set my sights on you, you'd know it."

"Tell me something Wynn." he said seriously. "Are you going to pull the button off my shirt or give me a kiss?"

Wynn continued to pull on the shirt button, drawing him closer. "In broad daylight?" she asked.

"In broad daylight." he repeated. He put a hand on either side of her face and drew her closer still. Slowly, he lowered his lips to hers. He was unprepared for her response and his own reaction. She melted into his arms with a soft whimper as a jolt of physical awareness shot through them both like a lightning bolt. Her lips opened of their own free will, giving admittance to his seeking tongue. His arms tightened around her, pulling her close against his aroused body. She pushed away from him and looked up at him. There was fear and wonder in her dark eyes. He drew her back into his arms and held her until his own passion cooled and her trembling had stilled. At last they drew apart.

Chapter 23

"What do you think about us taking the wagon to Fort MacKay to see about those horses and leave the house to Todd and Sarah? Or are you too sleepy?" Matthew asked.

"I'm not too sleepy." Wynn replied. "Besides, if we leave, Todd and Sarah can be alone and maybe then Todd won't kill me over the cow bells."

Wynn slipped quietly up the stairs to freshen up, while Matthew hitched up the team of mules to the wagon.

They were soon on their way and to Wynn's surprise, Matthew was behaving as if nothing had happened between them. They discussed the wedding and frolic of the night before and Matthew asked questions about the new people he had met.

When they were a couple of miles from home, Wynn indicated a wagon road leading off to the side. "Would you mind if we took a little side trip? she asked. "Widow Marlow lives down that way and I haven't had a chance to check on her lately. She lost her husband in battle of Gettysburg and she's been having a rough time of it ever since."

Matthew shrugged, "Sure, if you'd like. We've got plenty of time." he said, agreeably.

The Widow Marlow's farm was located less than half a mile

down the dirt trek. The once productive fields were choked with weeds and only an acre or which was set aside for the house garden was cultivated. The house and outbuildings were built to last but they too showed signs of neglect.

The widow was standing beside a wagon, which was pulled up close to the open porch. As Matthew and Wynn came into the yard, a boy of ten came out of the house lugging a crate that was as big as he was. "That's her oldest." Wynn said. "She has six more."

The harassed looking, middle-aged mother helped the boy set the crate in the wagon, before greeting her guests. She wiped her sweating face on her apron and gave Wynn a tired smile. "Wynn, it's good to see you." she said. "I'm sorry I missed Todd's wedding but I've been getting ready to move and I was too tired to go. Me'n the young'uns are goin' back to Alabama, I got people there. I just ain't got the heart to try to keep this place goin' on my own no more. Who is that you got there with you?"

Wynn introduced Matthew and the two shook hands. "Have you sold the farm then?" Wynn asked.

The widow wiped her brow once more and dropped down wearily onto the porch steps. "Who'd buy it?" she asked. "I don't know of a soul that's got enough cash money to buy a place now-a-days. I got a man comin' from Ocala to look at my stock. Maybe I can get enough out of my animals to stake us on the trip back home to Alabama." she said tiredly.

"You mean to say, you're going to abandon the farm, after all the years of hard work that's gone into it?" Wynn asked.

"I don't have no choice. With my man gone, I can't do it by myself since the servants all took off to God knows where." the widow said, disheartedly.

"How many acres have you got here Mrs. Marlow?" Matthew asked.

"Sixty, a third of it's good hammock land and a third's mixed acres. The rest of it's still in timber. I hate to let it go, it's a good farm. We got good water here, we was doin' good 'til the war came along." the widow replied.

"What do you figure the place is worth?" Matthew asked.

Widow Marlow gave a bitter laugh. "Not a hill of beans, unless somebody was to come along that's got some cash money. Hard cash is scarcer than hen's teeth. If a body ain't got a way of gettin' a hold of

117

some Yankee dollars, they ain't got nothin'. Confederate money ain't worth th' paper it's printed on."

"Just suppose somebody had some cash. What would it take to buy this place?" Matthew asked.

The widow scratched her head. "I'd settle for enough to get me'n th' young'uns back to Alabama. It's probably worth six hundred by pre-war standards but I'd take a lot less. I just wanna go back home."

Matthew grew silent and Wynn and the widow talked for a few minutes more before they took their leave. "Let us know if we can help in any way." Wynn called over her shoulder as they left the yard.

When they had gone down the road a ways, Wynn said, "You were awfully interested in what she wants for the farm. I can't help but wonder why."

Matthew shrugged. "I felt kind of sorry for her. I thought maybe we might run across someone that would buy it." he explained.

At Fort MacKay, they had little difficulty in locating the man with the horses. He led them to a fenced in corral and pointed out the two he wanted to sell. "I really hate to part with them, they're a matched pair." the man explained, indicating the two dapple-gray horses. "They'll pull a buggy or make good riding horses either one. I don't really want to sell them but I'm in need of some cash and something has to go."

Matthew opened the gate of the corral and examined the two horses at length. They were both in fine shape, deep chested and strong. "What'll you take for them?" he asked.

The man didn't blink an eye. "A hundred and eighty dollars a piece or preferably three-fifty for the pair. I hate to break up a good set."

"That's a little steep isn't it?" Matthew asked.

The man shrugged. "Good horse flesh is hard to find." he said.

"So is cash money." Matthew replied. "I'll give you a hundred and twenty five for one of them and not a penny more."

The man scratched thoughtfully at the whiskers on his chin. "Make that a hundred and thirty, cash money and you've got yourself a deal."

"I'll have to think about it." Matthew replied.

Wynn was tugging at his sleeve and he allowed her to lead him off to the side. "I've got seventy five dollars left from the melons, if you need it Matthew." she told him quietly.

Matthew gave her a smile. "I don't need it but thank you for the offer. If you really want to spend it though, I'll go half on the other horse for a wedding present to Todd."

Wynn turned her back on the man who owned the horses and nodded enthusiastically.

Matthew returned to bargain with the man once again. "I'll give you two-fifty for the pair." he offered.

The man looked undecided. "Cash?" he asked.

"Gold." Matthew replied.

The man's beady eyes lit up like candles. "Mister, you just bought yourself a pair of fine horses." he announced.

Matthew and Wynn returned home late in the day They managed to unhitch the mules and hide the horses in the stable before any signs of life were seen from the house.

They found Todd, Sarah and Granny in the kitchen. Todd was sitting at the kitchen table, looking drowsy when they came in the door. "Where'd you two get off to?" he asked, stifling a yawn.

"We've been to Fort MacKay." Wynn replied.

"Fort MacKay? What on earth did you want to go there for?" Sarah asked.

"Matthew's horse went lame and we want to see about buying another one." Wynn explained.

"Did you find anything interesting?" Todd asked.

"I bought myself a good dapple gray." Matthew replied.

Sarah waved a hand at the table. "Sit down you two, supper's ready." she said. When they were seated, she continued. "I always liked a dapple gray. My Daddy had one before the war. He was one of the best horses I ever seen." She yawned delicately behind her hand and began passing bowls of food around the table.

"I'll have to take a look at him after supper." Todd said. "I've gotta get me another horse as soon as I can get the cash together. Maybe after the cane comes in." He stifled another yawn.

Matthew and Wynn looked at each other and grinned. As if on cue, they both yawned at the same time and they all began to laugh.

After doing justice to the supper Sarah had prepared, they complemented her on her cooking. "I don't think none of us will be up much longer, let's go take a look at that horse, Matthew." Todd said.

The horse was duly admired and Todd made the comment that

he'd like to find one just like it. Wynn led the other horse out of it's hiding place and grinning ear to ear, she placed the reins in her brother's hand. "It's a wedding present from Matthew and me." she said.

Todd and Sarah were both delighted with the horse. They went back to the kitchen, still talking about it and Granny sent them all to bed, saying she would take care of the kitchen.

After being kept up by the shivalree the night before, they all slept late the next morning. Granny, who had gotten up early and was waiting to cook their breakfast, scolded them soundly. "What be de mattah heah, I'se 'bout 'cided you chillen gwine sleep de lib long day."

"We're up now Granny, don't fuss so." Wynn soothed.

Granny was still inclined to fuss. "Where Missa Matthew be? How come he ain't heah?" she fumed.

"Take it easy Granny, I'll go call him." Wynn offered.

She came back down the stairs a moment later. "He's not in his room. Y'all reckon he's outside somewhere?"

Todd went out to look but came back a few minutes later alone. "He's not out there. His horse is gone too." Todd told them.

Wynn's eyes widened in alarm. "Todd, did he take his saddlebags with him?" she asked fearfully.

"If they're not in his room, I guess he did." Todd replied. "Surely you don't think he left without saying goodbye do you?"

By the look on Wynn's face, it was obvious that that was exactly what she thought. "They're not there, Todd. If he just went out to ride his new horse, he wouldn't take them with him." She bit her lip and blinked rapidly.

Todd thought that Wynn was going to cry but he underestimated the O'Mally pride. She squared her shoulders and lifted her chin. "Well, there's no use standing around, let's get breakfast going." she managed to say in a steady voice.

By the time they had breakfast ready to serve, they had all come to pretty much the same conclusion as Wynn. Their usual hearty appetites were missing and the conversation around the table had dwindled to almost none.

They were just about to get up from the table, when hoof beats sounded in the yard. Granny was the one who went to the door to see who was there. They all breathed a sigh of relief when they heard her berating Matthew.

"What you mean Missa Matthew, gwine off dis time a day an' not be eat yo' breakfast? It done be cold."

"Don't fuss so Granny. It won't be the first time I ever eat a cold breakfast." Matthew was heard saying.

Matthew came into the kitchen, to find them all sitting in front of barely touched plates of food. "What's the matter with y'all?" he asked. He sat down at the table and began helping his plate. Everyone remained silent and he looked around at them expectantly.

Todd finally answered for them all. "Well...to tell the truth, we got up and you weren't here so we thought you'd left for good without saying good bye."

"Left? Not me. Whatever gave you that idea?" he asked innocently.

"Well, you do have to admit it did look strange. You were gone, your horse was gone and so was your saddlebags." Todd said.

Matthew laughed. "So y'all decided I'd run out on you, did you? Well, I guess y'all will have to put up with me for a long time to come. I just bought Widow Marlow's farm, lock, stock and barrel." he said with a grin.

Wynn, who had managed to hold onto her composure up until now, let out a squeal. Her chair fell over backwards as she jumped up. She dashed around the table and landed in the lap of a very startled Matthew. She hugged him and gave him a kiss on the mouth before she realized what she was doing. Once she realized, she blushed beet red, covered her face with both hands and left the room.

Todd, who was sitting across the table from Matthew, raised one dark eyebrow at him and asked, "Now what ails her?"

Matthew only shrugged and gave Todd a silly grin.

"Good Lord!" Todd cried. "They've both gone crazy, let's me and you get out of here!" Todd took his new bride by the hand and led her out of the house.

Matthew found himself sitting at the table alone. Granny made an effort to keep her face straight but failed miserably. "I ain't nevah gwine get dem chillen raised." she lamented.

Matthew gave the old black woman a smile that endeared him to her forever. "I reckon there's such a thing as getting too raised Granny. I was more of an old man at twenty than I am now." he told her thoughtfully.

121

Granny eyed him shrewdly, the wisdom of her years was shining in her black eyes. "Missa Matthew, you done learnt yo'sef a thing. Dis life don't go 'round but once. Man what fo'gets how to play be bettah off daid."

Matthew finished his breakfast and lingered a while hoping that Wynn would return. He was anxious to talk to her about his plans for the farm he had bought. He gave up on her after a while and went outside to see what was going on.

Chapter 24

Lum, Pearl and Ned had come to admire the new horses and get on with the day's work. They spent the day hoeing weeds from around the corn and sugarcane. The four men worked in the fields, while the women occupied themselves at more womanly tasks about the house. Pearl and Granny did the weekly wash, while Wynn and Sarah made soap.

They stopped long enough to eat a simple noon meal of black-eyed peas and corn bread and take an hour's rest in the heat of the day. Lum and Pearl took their break at their own house and Todd and Sarah had gone up the stairs together. Granny went to take a nap and Matthew and Wynn found themselves alone under the magnolia tree in the yard.

Lulled by the heat of the day and their full stomachs, both of them were drowsy and content. Matthew sat leaning against the trunk of the tree with his eyes half closed. Wynn lay on her back, staring up into the limbs of the huge old tree. Lazily, Wynn turned on one side and propped her head on one hand. "Matthew?" she said drowsily.

"Umm?" he grunted.

"Never mind." she said.

Matthew sat up straighter against the tree trunk. "Go ahead and ask." he said. "You're wondering where I got the money to buy the farm, aren't you?"

"Well, yeah, I was wondering. You showed up here on a worn out horse, wearing what was left of ragged uniform. I would have thought you didn't have two cents to rub together." Wynn admitted.

Matthew smiled, "That's the impression I wanted to make. I'm not rich by a long shot. My Daddy had the foresight to bury what gold he had, to keep it out of the hands of the Yankees. I've got just about enough left to make some improvements on the farm and start a new life. I didn't dare travel around looking like I had anything. There are people out there who'd kill a man at the drop of a hat, if he looks like he's got something worth stealing." Matthew explained.

"It hasn't been that bad here. At least not yet." Wynn said. "What have you got in mind for the farm?"

Matthew shrugged. "I wish I could answer that but the truth is I haven't got that far. Buying the farm was a spur of the moment thing. I'd just made up my mind to stay here and there was the farm, about to be abandoned. I needed a place to live and the widow needed the money, so there you are. I couldn't afford to pay her what the place is worth but at least she won't have to go back to Alabama empty handed. A woman alone, with seven children to raise, it's a sad thing."

"When do you plan to move in?" Wynn asked.

"She'll probably be there two or three more days. I'm going with her to Ocala tomorrow to transfer the deed. I reckon as soon as she moves out, I'll move in. By the way, the man never showed up to look at her stock, so she made them part of the deal. I'll have to be there to tend the stock as soon as she leaves." Matthew answered.

The discussion probably could have gone on for much longer but the noon respite had come to an end. They continued to work in the fields and at various other tasks for the remainder of the day.

It was after dark by the time the Negroes returned to their own places, leaving Todd, Sarah, Matthew and Wynn alone at the house. Finding it too hot to stay inside, they went to sit on the porch. The air was heavy with the promise of coming rain and the mosquitoes and yellow flies were out in droves. Wynn lit a smudge pot to keep them at bay.

Matthew watched her curiously, wondering what she was doing. The smudge pot consisted of an old tin dishpan, half filled with sand and the other half dried cow chips. When burned, the cow chips gave off a thick, white smoke, with no flames. The smoke served to keep the insects away. A wind came up, preceding the thunderstorm and further dispelled the insects, as well as somewhat cooling the air.

They were all tired from the hard day's work and they sat quietly, for the most part. Todd sat leaning against one of the posts that supported the porch roof, with Sarah sitting between his legs, reclining against him. Matthew and Wynn shared the porch swing and sat rocking contentedly back and forth.

Somewhere off in the distance, a bull gator bellowed and the screams of a big cat could be heard coming from the far side of the hammock. The chirruping of insects blended with the music of the frogs down by the spring. The frogs' voices ranged from the deep bass of the bullfrogs to the bell-like notes of the rain frogs. Silence in the Florida woods was nothing more than an illusion, for the land was never still.

Flashes of lightning and the sound of distant thunder heralded the summer rainstorm, long before the sheet of falling water reached the house. It could be heard pelting the trees and palmettos with drops the size of dimes as it came sweeping across the hammock. The whisper of sound grew in intensity as it swept closer. Like a living thing, the curtain of rain crossed the fields and eventually the yard, to fall musically upon the cedar shake shingles of the roof of the house.

Todd and Sarah scrambled from the edge of the porch to escape being wet by the rain. They soon went inside, leaving Matthew and Wynn alone on the porch swing.

The swing was located at the end of the porch farthest away from the worst of the blowing rain. It was pleasantly cool, after the intense heat of the day and a joy just to sit and watch the storm. The worst of it lasted only a moment before tapering off.

The sound of the light rain, pattering on the roof and dripping to the ground filled Matthew with a deep feeling of peace. He could remember no time in his life when he had ever had a deeper feeling of contentment.

Awareness of the girl sitting quietly by his side filled his being and he reached for her hand in the darkness. Her dark head came to rest on his shoulder and brought with it the scent of her that was like cinnamon and spice. He had to warn himself to tread softly, for the very touch of her was like touching flame to tinder. The kiss they had shared the day before had shaken him to the very core of his being. Wynn was innocence and fire. Matthew hadn't known that such strong emotion could exist. What he had to remember was, that while he was a little shaken and a little overwhelmed, Wynn was very openly frightened.

Her smooth cheek moved caressingly against his shoulder and she tilted her head, as if trying to see his face in the darkness. His

124

eyes sought her in return but so complete was the darkness, that he could no more than imagine her face. Drawn by a desire that was at the moment, stronger than his sense of honor, he reached for and found her in the darkness. She went into his embrace without reserve, pressing her body against him. His name came from her lips in a soft murmur as her hands slid up his back. As a man dying of thirst seeks water, his mouth sought for and found hers. She met him more than half way. Her lips and tongue sent spears of flame darting through his body and filled him with an aching need. With a groan, he broke the kiss and held her away from him, his breath coming in short gasps.

In her bewilderment Wynn's hands came to rest on his chest, just over his pounding heart. "Matthew, what is it?" she asked softly.

"Honey, you have no idea what you're doing to me." he replied huskily.

"I think it's called kissing, Matthew." Wynn said, with a smile in her voice.

He laughed in spite of himself, breaking the tension. "Yes, I believe you're right and if you do it like that one more time, I won't be responsible for what happens next." he warned.

"What happens next?" she asked mischievously.

Matthew laughed once more, but couldn't have been more serious. "What happens next is you find out I'm not a gentleman and I'll probably get my face slapped."

Wynn tugged at his shirt button. "Surely you wouldn't take advantage of a lady." she teased.

"I don't know. I've never had a lady pull the buttons off my shirt before." he replied.

"And you still haven't, so behave yourself!" Wynn laughed and gave the button one last tug.

"It's stopped raining." Matthew said.

"Uh-huh, are you changing the subject Matthew?"

"What subject? I believe I was told to behave myself." Matthew said with a chuckle.

"Do you always do what you're told?" she asked.

"No, so I suggest you watch it."

The conversation continued on in this manner for quite some minutes before they went back inside.

Matthew was gone for much of the following day. After escorting the widow Marlow into Ocala to transfer the deed, he lingered at the farm to help her in loading the last of her belongings into the wagon.

He returned to the O'Mally plantation just in time for supper. There was just enough time to unbridle the gray and wash his hands before going inside to join the family around the table.

"Well, how'd it go?" Todd asked.

"Fine." Matthew replied. He helped himself from the heaping platter of fried, smoked venison that Sarah passed to him and went on. "There was ten dollars back taxes owed on the farm, that had to be caught up. The place is mine now, free and clear."

"Did you hear any news?" Wynn asked.

"Not much, there's talk about getting the mail service improved. It should be running at least once a week before long. They're trying to get the academy going again but they're not having much luck finding teachers." Matthew replied.

"I reckon it'll be a while before everything gets going again." Todd said.

"Is Mrs. Marlow leaving in the morning?" Sarah asked.

"She's all set. She's got a cousin going with her. It relieves my mind. By the way, before I forget it, Mr. Blake down at the tannery said to tell you he's got a market for alligator hides. He said he'd give you a good price for all you could bring him." Matthew replied.

Todd perked up instantly. "Now there's an idea! It ain't often a man can combine good sport, and earn extra money at the same time." he said enthusiastically.

"I don't reckon I need money bad enough to go out hunting gators but if you want to try it Todd, go ahead." Matthew replied

"Shoot Matthew, there ain't nothin' to it. Me and Wynn used to do pretty good at it before the war." Todd said.

"You and Wynn. I might have known she'd be in on it. Do you gator hunt too, Sarah?" Matthew asked.

Sarah looked at him as if he had just grown a second head. "Not on your life!" she stated firmly.

"Well, I wouldn't miss it for the world." Wynn said. "Not only is it good fun, but it's a good way to earn some extra money. You don't know what you've been missing until you try it Matthew."

The general opinion left Matthew little choice in the matter. He could hardly refuse to be involved in anything that Wynn considered fun. "Well, when you get ready let me know. I guess I'll try anything once." he replied.

Wynn gave him a pleased smile and changed the subject. "How much stuff is Widow Marlow taking with her? You reckon you'll have all you need to start out with?" she asked.

Matthew shrugged. "As far as I can tell. She's just taking the personal stuff. Everything else goes with the farm. Why don't you ride over there with me tomorrow and look things over." he suggested.

"I'd like that." Wynn said with a smile.

Chapter 25

By mid morning the next day, Matthew riding the gray and leading the mare, set out for his new home. Wynn, as they had planned, went with him. Today, she was wearing a dress. He probably would have thought nothing of it, except for the fact that he had never seen her on a horse in anything but britches.

Soon after they arrived they began a tour of the yard and out-buildings. The stable was stocked with the usual assortment of harnesses, hay and implements. The widow had left behind two mules that looked to have plenty of work left in them. There was a buggy and one farm wagon, as well as the usual plows and farm implements.

From the stable, their next stop was the smokehouse, which they found to their surprise was nearly full. There was a chicken house, with a closed-in chicken yard, that contained two dozen hens and a couple of roosters. The hog pen had fallen down and a half dozen hogs were roaming freely about the yard. The hogs had apparently run free for quite some time for all the flowerbeds were rooted up. They were a good domestic breed, with no sign of having been crossed with the wild hogs that roamed the surrounding woods. A herd of half wild, part long horn cattle and one dried up milk cow ranged as free as the hogs. In the backyard, just far enough away to be inconvenient, was an open well. The water was good and the supply adequate.

The once productive fields, where cotton and sugar cane had grown, now lay fallow and choked with weeds. The surrounding woods were already trying to reclaim them. The acre or so of ground set aside for the kitchen garden was planted in corn, peas, squash, beans and potatoes.

The house was one-storied and rambling. It was built in two sections, one side consisting of the house proper and the other side containing the huge kitchen and pantry. The two sections of the house were joined by an open breezeway, which one had to cross in order to go from one section to the other. They found the kitchen to be well stocked with pots and pans, canning equipment and a few mismatched dishes. The pantry was over half full of home canned vegetables, meal and rendered lard.

The main part of the house was big and rambling and the high ceilinged rooms were left completely furnished. The big front room, too informal to be called a parlor, was a little shabby but comfortable looking. By all appearances, the bedrooms had been added on as the size of the family increased. They stretched like dormitories along a long hall and were five in number.

When the tour was finished, Wynn summed up her general impression. "For the time being, it looks like you have about all you need."

"Yes, I think so too." Matthew agreed. "I've got a lot of work to do here though. The roofs all leak and I'll need to rebuild the hog pen, I don't expect to do much with the fields right now, except maybe burn off the weeds a little later in the year. The house and out buildings look pretty solid but I'll need to replace a few boards here and there. I want to put up fences too, I don't much like the idea of my stock running loose. I notice everyone here seems to go for open range but I'm not that sold on the idea." What sounded so simple when said, would amount to a tremendous amount of work for one man to accomplish.

Wynn looked thoughtful. "Matthew, this place must not seem like much to you, after what you had in Georgia." she said.

"The South we knew is dead." Matthew said, in way of reply.

Wynn hadn't missed the note of pain in his voice. The lifestyle he must have led before the war was hard for her to imagine. "Tell me about your plantation, Matthew." she invited.

To please her, he described it in glowing detail, from the white-columned mansion, to the vast holdings of slaves, land and equipment. When he was done, Wynn reached to take his hand.

"It must have been beautiful Matthew. I know you must miss it." she said sympathetically.

Matthew became silent and thoughtful for a moment, looking into the dark depths of her eyes. "I miss some things." he said at last. "I miss my family, my son especially. I had such high hopes for that boy."

"What was she like, Matthew? Your wife, she must have been very lovely." Wynn felt compelled to ask.

Matthew's eyes turned away from Wynn's face to stare across the room. She squeezed his hand. "I'm sorry Matthew. I shouldn't have asked." she said.

Matthew's gaze met Wynn's once more. "No Wynn, it's all right. You have every right to ask. Yeah, she was lovely and in the end, braver than I gave her credit for being. I think I hesitate to talk about her more from guilt than grief." He stopped talking, surprised at himself for admitting to Wynn, what he had hardly been able to admit to himself.

Wynn, for once, held her tongue but the question was there in her eyes.

"It was a marriage of convenience our parents set up so that the two plantations would be joined. There was nothing wrong with Elizabeth, no man could have asked for a better wife. She certainly deserved better than she got. I never loved her until it was too late." Matthew said sadly.

Touched by the sadness in his voice, Wynn wrapped her arms around him and rested her head on his shoulder. She was filled with a sadness of her own, for she felt she could never compete with the fine lady who once had once been his wife and the mother of his son.

After a time, he eased her away and with a finger under her chin, raised her face so that he could look into her troubled eyes. "What's past is past." he said. He dropped a quick kiss on her forehead and took her hand to lead her outside.

"Now, tell me, do you think I should rebuild the hog pen where it is or move it up yonder, farther away from the house?" he asked, indicating with a pointing finger the location he meant.

Wynn gave him a smile, pleased that he had asked her opinion. "Up yonder would be better. I never did think hogs ought to be kept too close to the house."

"I was thinking, maybe under that oak, it'd give shade in the summer and they could still get in the sun in the winter, if I put it half way under." he said.

Wynn nodded her agreement. Not long after, she returned home, leaving Matthew alone on his own place.

Later in the day, Todd and Sarah came by and still later Lum and Pearl. It was not until night that he realized that for the first time in ages, he was totally alone.

The more he had looked the place over, the more he had found that needed done. He had eaten a simple evening meal from the basket of cooked food that Sarah had brought over and went out to sit on the porch. While he sat, he thought over the things he had to do and how best to accomplish them. The prospect seemed overwhelming and he found his thoughts drifting to other things.

Since his relationship with Wynn had changed, he had had little time to think about it. Now that he was alone, with nothing more than the sounds of the night to disturb him, he found that he could think of nothing else.

Wynn's questions about his former life and Elizabeth had started him thinking about how things were now, and how they were in the past. In spite of himself, he found that he couldn't help comparing the two women. Elizabeth, so soft, blond and fragile, with her genteel ways and practiced manner of flirting. Wynn, on the other hand was dark, strong and as beautiful as some long gone Indian princess in her ancestry. Not once had Wynn been flirtatious, though she had a way of teasing that was charming. Her eyes, so dark as to be often unreadable, promised him nothing but when he had at last held her in his arms, she had come to him without reserve or reticence. Her uninhibited response to him had the effect of driving him almost wild. She was the kind of woman every man, including himself, dreamed about but never hoped to find.

In Wynn, he had found a woman that he knew he could love. The thought, rather than warming him, sent ice water running through his veins. Hadn't life taught him that to care for anything was to lose it? He realized now that the greater his feelings had grown for her, the greater his fear had grown. Matthew clinched his fists and his jaw tightened with determination. This thing that was happening between them had to end! He couldn't bear to lose anything else. Life had taken enough from him already. With this decision made, he arose from his seat on the porch and went to his lonely bed.

During the week, he spent his time working on the farm. From daybreak to sunset, he drove himself to the limit of his physical endurance. The pace he had set for himself was designed to leave him

130

too tired at night to do anything but fall into the deep sleep of exhaustion. His determination remained strong, kept so by the icy fear of seeing her dead if he ever came to love her. Still, in spite of himself, he found that he often looked up the wagon road that led to the farm, half expecting to see her coming.

Wynn too, at this time was struggling with a new way of thinking. Todd had quite naturally taken over the responsibility of running the plantation and Sarah was now the mistress of the house. Wynn was no longer the mistress of all that she surveyed. She had become only the sister, living with her brother and his wife. The adjustment was hard for her to make and left her feeling empty inside. She was finding that there were times when she felt like a visitor in her own home. Todd and Sarah, quite naturally, were wrapped up in themselves as was normal for newlyweds. Sometimes Wynn felt like an outsider looking on. She kept herself busy, alternating between helping Sarah with the house and the men in the fields. She missed Matthew being there, it left an ache inside her and often left her staring into space.

It was now a week since she had last seen him. Each day, she had expected him to come but he remained noticeably absent. At first, she hadn't been overly concerned but as time went on and she still hadn't seen him, her uneasiness grew. By the end of the week, she made up her mind to go and see him. She probably would have done it before now but it was improper for a lady to seek out a man. Wynn was making an effort to behave more like a lady. She had it in her mind that that was what Matthew would want from her. She had spent more time at household chores and less time in the fields. Well, lady or not she knew that she had to see him. She baked a couple of blackberry pies and some loaves of bread to take to him. They would serve as a good excuse to go and she really was worried about him getting enough to eat. As she rode out to take them to him, Todd gave her yet another excuse to go. "Tell Matthew that if he wants to, we could go gator hunting tonight." he said.

Armed with proper excuses and dressed in her favorite yellow dress, Wynn set out. She hummed a tune as she rode along carrying the basket of food.

Matthew, overworked and in a fowl mood from hitting his thumb with a hammer, was just climbing down from the stable roof when she arrived. His greeting to her was cordial but lacking in enthusiasm.

He thanked her politely for the pies and bread and took the time to show her what he had gotten done around the place. She could just as well have been Lum or Ned, for all the attention he paid her. Wynn didn't stay long. She delivered her brother's message and feeling hurt and uncomfortable, soon left.

As she rode off Matthew said for her to tell Todd that he would see him that night.

Wynn rode home slowly, feeling utterly bewildered. She couldn't understand why Matthew had behaved toward her as he had. He had made his interest in her plain enough in the past and she wondered what she had done to change his mind. Her hurt soon turned to anger, as the O'Mally pride began to take over. If Matthew thought that she wasn't good enough for him,, then to heck with him. She'd not make a fool of herself for any man! Her newly found determination to behave more like a lady fled as quickly as it had come. She had decided against going gator hunting with him and Todd. Ladies didn't hunt alligators. Now, she changed her mind. She was who she was and wouldn't pretend to be anything else.

Matthew, who was still in a foul mood, knocked off early from his work and made a simple meal from what he had on hand. He knew that he would be welcome and probably even expected at Todd's for supper. Feeling contrary, he delayed his arrival until after meal time. He, himself couldn't understand the mood he was in.

Chapter 26

Matthew arrived just as Todd and Wynn were loading a couple of lanterns and a specially constructed gig into the wagon. Along with these was a hatchet that had a longer than average handle. He hadn't put much thought into what kind of equipment they would be using but somehow or other, he had expected a little something more than a hatchet and gig.

Todd shed a little more light on the subject. "Since you've got your pistol, I reckon I won't need to take a gun. You about ready to go?" he asked.

"Yeah, I guess." Matthew replied.

They drove the smallest of the two farm wagons down to the river to where the big boat that the Negroes used for fishing was tied up. Along the way, Todd tried to engage Matthew in a conversation about gator hunting. As it turned out, Todd talked a lot and Matthew listened. Meanwhile, Wynn sat quietly between the two of them. Her chin was raised a good inch higher than normal and her lips were pressed into a tight line. Todd didn't seem to notice that either one of them was behaving in any way other than normal.

Once they were on the river, Matthew's mood seemed to lift. Wynn took over and paddled the boat just enough to keep it on even keel as it drifted downstream.

The Ocklawaha at night seemed an alien and enchanted world. The vast jungle that bordered it dissolved into the blackness of the night, so that they seemed to be drifting between the lantern lit water below and the star-studded sky above. As they drifted along, the light from the lanterns startled the birds along the shore and they rose up with flapping wings alongside the boat.

Spotting something near the bank, Todd stood up in the boat and signaled for Wynn to bring them in closer to shore. As they drew nearer, the eyes of an alligator lit up in the lantern light. The distance between the gator's eyes seemed to be at least the length of a hammer handle. Matthew was having trouble believing that Todd was actually going to try to gig anything that big. However, as Todd raised the gig in readiness, Matthew drew his pistol. The tines of the gig sank in to the hilt as Todd thrust it at the great reptile. He pulled back immediately, leaving the head of the gig with rope attached firmly embedded in the gator's thick hide. The alligator sank immediately and Todd reared back on the rope. It began almost instantly to thrash and twang as the bull gator began to roll. When the gator broke the surface once more, Matthew aimed carefully for the exact spot, he figured an alligator's ear would be and pulled the trigger. The alligator stopped thrashing and Matthew moved forward to help Todd with the rope.

"Looks like you got him, first shot but you can't ever tell with these boogers." Todd said.

They maneuvered the gator until it lay in the water alongside the boat. It was all the two strong men could do to keep the huge reptile from sinking.

"You sure it's dead?" Wynn asked.

"I ain't never sure about one of these critters. We got our hands full, you get up here with that hatchet and make sure." Todd replied.

Wynn had just managed to reach the side of the boat when the big gator came suddenly to life. It's huge tail lashed out, hitting the side of the boat so hard that it felt as if it had been struck by a cannonball! Wynn lost her balance and had to grab onto Matthew's shoulder to keep from falling out of the boat. At the same time, she raised the hatchet up over her head and brought it down. It made a satisfying thunk as it sank into the gator just behind its head, severing its backbone.

The gator once more lay still in the water. "Good going! We got 'im now." Todd said in praise of her.

"Yeah, but what are we gonna do with him? That thing's bigger than the boat!" Matthew said.

"He'll fit." Wynn assured him.

Matthew eyed her skeptically, thinking all the while that he'd have to see it to believe it.

Fifteen minutes later Matthew, bathed in sweat, found himself sitting astride the alligator's broad back. Wynn, in the bow shared a seat with it's head and Todd shared the stern with it's tail. It was time to begin the laborious chore of paddling the heavily loaded boat back upstream against the current.

It was all the three of them put together could do to get the big gator up the bank and slide it up a plank and into the wagon.

"Well, that's one." Todd said. "Y'all want to try for another one?"

Matthew, who was beginning to enjoy the whole thing, forgot his weariness. "Might as well." he replied.

Two hours later, they returned with still another gator. This one was a good bit smaller than the first one. They loaded it into the wagon and set out for home.

Half way home, Wynn fell asleep sitting up on the wagon seat and her head drifted onto Matthew's shoulder. He couldn't very well let her fall off, so he put his arm around her to steady her. There was no getting away from the feelings that she inspired in him. Not with her firm young body resting against his side. She never ceased to amaze him. This girl dressed in rough boys clothing and smelling of alligator, was the same one who had delivered perfectly baked pies to him earlier in the day. The same girl who had dressed in dainty lemon yellow and smelled of cinnamon and spice. He could sit there and lie to himself, that he only held her to keep her from falling, but his body knew different.

Todd looked over at his sister and smiled fondly. "Plumb give out ain't she?" he commented.

"I reckon." Matthew replied. "It's been a long day." The wagon hit a pothole, throwing Wynn's limp body closer to him still.

"Some little gal ain't she?" Todd asked, not really requiring an answer.

Matthew said nothing but be couldn't have agreed with him more.

When they pulled up into the yard at Todd's house, Wynn didn't stir. Todd got down and held out his arms. "Hand her down here, once she goes to sleep like that, she's out like a light." he said.

Matthew handed Wynn down into her brother's waiting arms and climbed down to stand beside them. To his surprise, Todd handed her back to him. "Here, you take her upstairs. My leg still ain't up to climbing those stairs carrying a load. She's heavy as a chunk of lead." With that, he went to unhitch the mules, leaving Matthew to deal with Wynn.

She half awakened as he was struggling to hang onto her and open the front door at the same time, just enough to mumble something unintelligible and wrap her arms around his neck. Fortunately, Sarah had thought to leave a lamp burning at the head of the stairs and he was able to make his way up them with very little trouble. The girl in his arms was heavy but not overly so. He would have guessed her weight at no more than a hundred and thirty pounds at most. He managed to locate the door to her room in the darkened hall and fumbled in the dark until he found her bed. He deposited her on top of the covers and went to retrieve the lamp from the head of the stairs.

When he returned to her room, he looked around curiously, as he had never been in it before. Her bed was strictly feminine with a pink canopy of pure linen. Beside it, on the floor was a deerskin rug. On her dresser, along with the usual feminine clutter, was a pocket knife and a pair of wire cutters. The walls were papered in delicate pink roses, yet somehow the rack made of deer horns that held her musket didn't seem out of place. A small section of wallpaper was missing in one corner of the room, as if a foot wide square of it had been cut out and purposely removed.

Matthew turned his attention back to Wynn. He placed the lamp on her bedside stand and carefully removed her shoes before tucking

135

her under the covers. He opened the window and carefully arranged the mosquito netting around the bed. As he picked up the lamp and turned to leave the room he heard her murmur sleepily, "Night, Matthew." He turned to smile down at her. "Night, Wynn." he replied softly and left the room.

By the time he got back downstairs, Todd had the mules unhitched and was leading them into the stable.

"Get her to bed all right?" Todd asked.

"Yeah." Matthew replied. "You want me to come back in the morning and help you skin the gators?"

"Nah, I'll get Ned to help me. You might as well spend the night though, beings it's so late, no use to go home at this hour." Todd offered.

The offer was tempting, but Matthew refused. "If you don't need me to help with the gators, I've got plenty I need to do tomorrow. I've got to get started on the hog pen. Those damn hogs are keeping me awake at night. They keep bumping around under the floor and they've nearly rooted up a couple of the supports under the front porch."

Todd closed the stable door and yawned noisily. "Yeah, hogs can be a pain in the ass all right. You need Lum to come help you?"

"If he don't mind." Matthew said, as he mounted the gray. "There's enough work on that place for three men. I'm going to have to see about getting some full time help one of these days."

"Well, that shouldn't be hard, there's plenty of black folks around here that ain't got nothing to do. I reckon I'll see you soon." Todd said.

"Yeah, well get some sleep, tomorrow's another day." Matthew said as he rode away.

"Good night buddy." Todd called after him.

Chapter 27

Matthew returned home and went immediately to bed, feeling tired enough to sleep for a week. As soon as his head hit the pillow, the usual nightly grunting and bumping beneath the house began. He lay there, tired and miserable, listening to the commotion the hogs were making and trying not to think about Wynn.

It was almost dawn when he finally fell asleep, only to be awakened by a nightmare. It was the same dream that had haunted him for weeks but this time it had taken on a new twist. It had started out pretty much the same, he saw a troop of Yankee soldiers that had come to loot and burn Silver Oaks. As if he had actually been there, he could see Elizabeth as she struggled with them. As usual, the face of her killer was as clear as day. It was the evil face of the Yankee devil, Sergeant Saber.

Only in a nightmare could anything seem as real as when the sword had pierced Elizabeth's heart. It was at this time that the dream took on a horrible new twist. Matthew saw himself standing by, helpless to move or interfere as Elizabeth fell to the ground but when he looked it was not Elizabeth, it was Wynn. Matthew's scream of horror woke him up and he scrambled from the sweat soaked bed to pace the floor. The nightmare was nothing more than the result of his own fear.

Lum arrived early that morning and they spent the day working on the hog pen. By late evening, it was done and it took them a good hour and a half to get the six hogs rounded up and inside it. Lum said that he had best be getting home, as Pearl would be waiting supper on him.

Matthew stood in the red glow of the setting sun and looked with satisfaction on the well-built hog pen.

He had done a good day's work and he was pleased with it. It was pleasant to spend the day with Lum, sharing the work and enjoying the companionship. It pleased him to know that Lum was happy with Pearl and with his place on the O'Mally plantation.

When Matthew got back to the house, he made a quick trip to the kitchen and went to sit on the porch. In his hand was a whole blackberry pie and a fork. He had to admit that it wasn't a very conventional supper but it sure beat cooking. The few times that he had tried to prepare his own meals had turned out to be miserable failures. He had done pretty well at heating up canned goods but invariably burned any kind of meat that he tried to cook.

As full dark fell, a whippoorwill began its lonely calling and the sounds of the Florida night descended on the clearing. Matthew let the loneliness seep into his soul. He felt that he was no better off than before deciding to stay in Marion County. He was trapped now, obligated to the farm he had bought. Now, he wished that he had followed his first instincts and left soon after he had arrived. He didn't want to want Wynn, but he did and it scared the hell out of him.

His morose thoughts were interrupted by the sound of running footsteps coming up the road. Matthew put down the now empty pie tin and stood up to see who was coming. As he stood watching, a young black girl, dressed in a shabby cotton dress ran into the yard. She stopped when she saw him and held out her hands beseechingly. "Missa, I don't know what I'se gwine do. My man done got snake bit down de road!" she cried out breathlessly.

"Where's he at?" Matthew asked, as he came down the steps.

The black girl pointed up the road and waved her arms. "He be up by dem oaks what grows all in a bunch. He be mighty bad off Missa. I gots to hab hep or dat man gwine die on me fo' sho!" Her voice rose to a wail at the end.

"Alright, calm down girl. I'll hitch up the buggy and go get him." Matthew told the frightened black girl.

He found the young black man in the oak grove, just as she had said. They had apparently set up camp for the night when the man had gotten snake bit.

A scrawny looking hound dog had apparently stirred up the rattlesnake and been bitten in the neck. The dog was already dead and the young black man was unconscious.

Matthew loaded the sick man into the buggy and the girl supported him on the seat.

"How'd he manage to get bit?" Matthew asked, as he snapped the reins to start the gray.

"Dat dog done be carryin' on somethin' awful an' Willy he go runnin' in de dark. Po' Willy not see dat skeestah an' he step on it. Oh Lawd! Oh Lawd!"

Matthew figured the best course of action was to distract her. "What were you doing out camping this time of night?" he asked.

"We's been huntin' work. Me an' Willy, we jus' be startin' out. We jus' jump de broom las' week an' we gots to find us a place to lib an' Willy, he need work." the girl explained.

"Well, we'll take Willy up to the house and see what we can do for him. What's your name girl?" Matthew asked.

"My name be Lissa. I sho' hates to botha you like dis Missa." she replied.

"Don't you worry Lissa." Matthew reassured her. "I reckon if that snake bite was going to kill Willy, he'd be dead by now. The chances are, the dog got most of the poison.

"Oh Lawdy, I sho' hope so Missa." Lissa replied.

Matthew finally got Willy to the house and laid him down on the front room floor. The calf of the black man's left leg was badly swollen and he was burning up with fever. He was obviously a very sick man but Matthew figured that he would most likely survive. He considered going for a doctor but decided that by the time he got back with one, Willy would either be dead or better on his own.

He and Lissa wrapped up Willy's leg with wet rags and when this was done, Matthew turned his attention to Lissa. "When did you eat last?" he asked.

Lissa shrugged her shoulders. "I disrembah, yestiddy or the day befo' I guesses. He been habin' a time sho' 'nuff. Don't know now why us wants to be free. Free be jus' anotha way to starb to death. We be way yondah betta off 'fore 'mancipation." Lissa lamented.

"Well, the kitchen's that way." Matthew said and pointed to the door that led to the breezeway. "Go help yourself. I'll stay here with Willy."

Lissa started toward the kitchen but turned back with a puzzled look on her face. "Missa, why you botha to hep us?" she asked.

"My name is Matthew," he said. "I don't know of a living thing, man nor beast that ought to be left hurt and hungry with no one to help them. I've been both and it ain't no fun." he replied.

Lissa continued to look puzzled. "Missa Matthew, I can't pay you." she said worriedly.

Matthew smiled at her. "Don't worry about that Lissa. Go get something to eat." he said.

Lissa was worried about it and still hesitated. Kindness from a white man usually came at a price and she doubted that this one was any different. "Willy be mighty sick, Missa. It be a long time 'fore he be able to work but I'se a good cook an' I makes a purty good housemaid too. I be willin' to work hard fo' you Missa. I pays you back someways." She finally went off to the kitchen, leaving him alone with Willy.

The young black man, who was unconscious up until now, began to awaken by degrees. He rolled his eyes fearfully at Matthew and said. "Massa I'se sick. I can't cut no cane today. Please don't whup me no mo'."

Matthew looked on Willy with pity. He'd never held with the idea of whipping blacks, slave or not. "Rest easy boy, you're not going to get whipped." he said kindly.

"I works tomorrer." Willy mumbled.

The smell of bacon frying came from the kitchen and after a while Lissa came back. "How Willy be?" she asked worriedly.

"I reckon he'll be all right. He woke up for a minute a while ago." Matthew told her.

By the next day Willy was still sick and his leg was still badly swollen but he showed no signs of being near death. Matthew had awakened to the smell of bacon frying as Lissa cooked his breakfast. True to her word, she worked all day in the house, cooking and cleaning.

The evening after the fourth day since the black couple's arrival, Matthew came in from working and caught Willy out by the stable. He was sitting on a chopping block and had what looked like every hoe, axe and knife on the place sharpening them. He was pedaling the grinder with his right leg and had the other one propped up on a milking stool. The pile of implements beside him was sharpened to a razor's edge and sweat was rolling off Willy's black face in streams. He was frowning in concentration as well as from a good bit of pain.

Matthew examined the newly sharpened implements and said, "Willy, you have no business trying to do this, you're still sick. I'll admit that everything on the place was dull but you could'a waited until you got better."

Willy nodded and wiped the sweat off his brow. "I knows it Missa Matthew but I jus' gots to be busy. No use me settin' 'round heah worryin' 'bout how bad dis leg be hurtin'. Jus' make it seem wuss." he said with a white-toothed grin. Matthew shook his head. "'Yeah, I reckon but don't over do it. A snake bite's nothing to play around with." he warned.

"I knows dat Missa Matthew. I guesses dis leg can res' jus' as good propped up heah as it can in de bed." Willy argued good-naturedly. "We gots to earn our keep." he said with a grin.

"Well, you're doing all right so far. If you and Lissa want to stay on, there's plenty of work for y'all to do. I can let you stay in one of the shacks and you can have all the food you can eat. I can't afford to pay much but I'll give y'all a little along." Matthew offered.

Willy's eyes, still a little bright from fever, lit up even brighter.

"Missa Matthew, dat be mo' dan fair. Me an' Lissa sho' 'preciates it. All me'n dat gal wants be a way to make us a libbin' an' a roof ovah our heads." he said sincerely.

By the end of the week, Willy and Lissa had set up housekeeping in one of the abandoned slave cabins and Matthew was pleased with the whole setup. Lissa was doing a fine job in the house and Willy was busy at whatever work he was able to do. So far, the couple had proven to be trustworthy and willing to work

Chapter 28

It was now a week since Matthew had visited the O'Mally plantation, so he rode over there after supper on Sunday night. Todd and Sarah had come to see him in the middle of the week but Wynn hadn't been with them. He had wondered why she hadn't come but had refrained from asking.

When he arrived, he found Todd and Sarah sitting on the porch but Wynn was nowhere to be seen. Todd inquired about the couple he had hired and the discussion ran from the usual topics of farming and the weather, to making plans for another alligator hunt. Finally, curiosity got the better of Matthew and he inquired about Wynn.

"She's gone to a box social across the river but she ought to be back any time now." Sarah told him.

This bothered Matthew more than he let on and he lingered on the porch talking for a much longer time than he had intended, waiting for her return.

Wynn came home just after dark had fallen. Someone had seen her home from the social, for they could hear him call good night as he rode away. She rode up to the hitching post and dismounted with a swish of silken petticoats and an enticing glimpse of leg. After securing the stallion to the hitching post, she gave them all a general hello.

They returned her greeting and Sarah asked, "Well, did you have fun and who was that, who brought you home?"

Wynn sat down on the porch steps and arranged the skirt of her ruffled white dress around her. "Yes, it was fun. The Delaney boys are back from the war and so is John Marsh. You know how the Delaney boys are, they sure know how to liven up a gathering. I ended up sharing my box with James, that was him that brought me home. I wouldn't be surprised it he comes courting before long. There's a peanut boiling at the Milford plantation next Saturday and everyone's invited." she replied.

Todd looked at Sarah. "Well, I reckon we can't miss that. The Milfords always did put on a good shindig." He turned to Matthew. "You're going ain't you?" he asked.

"I wouldn't miss it." Matthew replied. "I think I could eat my weight in boiled peanuts."

Wynn yawned behind her white-gloved hand. "Todd, you reckon you could put my horse away? I think I'll go on up to bed, it's been a long day."

"Yeah, I'll see to him." Todd replied.

Wynn went up to bed and Matthew left soon after she had told them all good night. He should have felt relieved that backing off from her had worked so well but it only left him feeling as it a mule had kicked him in the gut. Here he was, working himself into a state of near exhaustion in order to keep his mind off of her and she seemed totally unaffected. While he suffered, she was blithely going off to box socials and talking about some man coming to court her. It made him wonder if she had felt anything for him in the first place, perhaps he had only imagined the fiery responses she had given to his advances. He tried to convince himself that it was all for the best but the knot in his gut didn't get any looser at the thought. How could she forget so easily? Thinking back on it, she hadn't paid any attention to the fact that he had even been there. Judging from the amount of attention she had showed, he could just as well have been one of the dogs for all she cared. As he rode along towards home, he clinched his jaw until his teeth ached. Granted, he had wanted to end what was between them but he sure would have felt better about it if she had seemed at least a little bit bothered. Matthew was utterly miserable but could see no help for it.

During the next few days, he continued to work long hours on the farm. The pace he had set for himself was grueling and the heat was unusually oppressive. He found himself watching the sky for signs of rain but saw none. Not one drop of rain had fallen in the past two weeks. The heat wave and his own emotions continued to drag him down.

Toward the end of the week, Lum came by with a message from

Todd. "Missa Todd say you bes' be watchin' out, he done kilt a mad fox, right in de yard." he told him.

"When was that Lum?" Matthew asked.

Lum looked a little excited. "Jus' dis mawnin'! Dat fox done be walkin' 'round like he not be one bit 'fraid. He growl at Miz Sarah an' 'bout scare her to death!" he exclaimed.

"Good God Lum! She didn't get bit did she?" Matthew asked in alarm.

Lum shook his head. "Nawsuh, she jus' screech like de wil' cat an' Missa Todd, he come runnin' an' shoots de skeestah."

"Did it get to the dogs?" Matthew asked.

Again, Lum shook his head. "Dey'd a been right in de middle ob dat fox 'cept I be skinnin' catfish at my place. Dey all be wid me. Missa Todd done pen up ebber one ob dem suckahs."

"Well, it's a good thing. He would've had to shoot every dog on the place if they'd tangled with that fox." Matthew said.

"Dat's de truth." Lum agreed. "He say he still gwine go gatah huntin' tonight if you still wants to go."

This suited Matthew just fine, he had done nothing all week but work and was ready to do something else.

"I still want to. You tell him I said I'd be there and that I said thank you for the warning. I'll keep a close eye out for anything that don't act right." Matthew replied.

"Yassuh Massa, I tells him. Dat Missy Wynn, she gwine go too?" Lum asked.

"I don't know. I guess so, you know how she is about hunting." Matthew replied.

Lum grinned. "Dat Missy Wynn be some gal, when you gwine get hitched?" he asked.

Matthew's eyes snapped open in surprise. "I don't know as I'm going to. Whatever gave you that idea Lum?" he asked incredulously.

Lum eyed Matthew shrewdly and began to count of reasons on his fingers, "Massa gwine leab heah but Massa he stay." Lum held up one finger. "Massa done bought dis good house an' farm." Up went another finger. "Massa, be get dat look in he eyes, what looks like my ol' houn' dog when he see de coan bread comin'." Lum held up another finger. "Missy Wynn, she done be took up lookin' 'cross de hammock like she done see clear to tomorrer." Up went a forth finger. "Missy Wynn, she can't set still. She be off heah an' yondah

143

like de mule what's got de burr unner he saddle." Lum stuck out his thumb.

Matthew held up a hand for Lum to stop. "Look Lum, just because I decided to stay here and bought this farm don't mean I'm planning to get married. And what does Wynn being restless have to do with anything? She ain't never been one to sit still." Matthew argued.

"Mebby so." Lum agreed. "Dat don't change de way dat gal run one way an' you runs de otha' like you both 'fraid you's gwine get caught."

Matthew gave Lum an exasperated look. "Lum, you'd better save you philosophy to use on Pearl. I'm not about to get hitched and Miss Wynn's too busy thinking about some fellow from across the river to even think about me." he stated flatly.

Lum just shook his head. "White folks jus' don't know what it is dey be wantin'."

By now, Matthew was more exasperated than ever. "Well Lum, I reckon I'll know it if I ever decide I want to get married again. I'm not near as dumb as you seem to think I am." he argued.

Lum just shook his head and gave Matthew a sympathetic grin. "I'se glad to hear it Massa but you gwine be a gray haired ol' man 'fore you makes up yo' mind."

Matthew threw up his hands in a gesture of surrender and his gray eyes grew bleak and hopeless. "Lum, I learned the hard way that if a man cares too much for anything or anyone, it gets taken away. I'm not going to let myself get into a position where it'll matter any more."

Lum put his hand on Matthew's shoulder. "Massa Matthew, what be de wuss, habin' somethin' den losin' it or nebber habin' it in de firs' place?" he asked.

Matthew turned his back on Lum for a minute, then turned to face him. "Lum, if I could answer that, I could tell you why the sun rises in the east and sets in the west. I could tell you why innocent women get murdered and children have to die before they ever really live. I could tell you why old women lose their minds and old men die of broken hearts. I could maybe even explain to you, why men fight when there's nothing left to fight for." he paused. "I reckon when I have an answer to all that, I'll be just about as smart as God, for only He knows."

144

Lum shook his woolly head sadly. "Massa, you builds dat wall 'round you high 'nough, you finds out you as much a prisoner as you be in dat Nawthun prison."

Matthew had no answer for this and he changed the subject. "When do you reckon it'll rain?" he asked. "My corn's drying up,"

Lum scratched his head thoughtfully. "Fo' long I guesses. You get yo'sef a daid chicken snake an' hang dat skeestah in de foak ob a tree, you gets rain. We done gots one ober at Missa Todd's. Ned an' Pearl say dat do de trick ebber time." he replied seriously.

"Now where did they get a crazy idea like that?" Matthew asked.

"It works Massa, you tries it an' you see." Lum insisted.

Matthew had little faith in such things but when he ran across a chicken snake later that day, he killed it and hung it up in a tree, just in case.

It was with mixed feelings, that he set out later that evening to go gator hunting. He was looking forward to the hunt but was dreading another encounter with Wynn.

When he arrived at the O'Mally plantation, he found to his surprise that it would only be him and Todd going on the hunt. In spite of himself, he couldn't help asking, "Where's Wynn?"

Todd gave him a half smile and shook his head. "I don't know what's got into that girl. She's been gone off somewhere every day this week. She went to some doings in Ocala and said she'd be gone overnight. It just ain't like her to miss out on a hunting trip. When she ain't off somewhere, she just sits around and stares off into nothin'. I ain't never seen her like this." Todd said in bewilderment.

This puzzled Matthew too but he thought that he might have something of an answer. "She's had total responsibility for the plantation for a couple of years now. Maybe she's just blowing off a little steam, now that you're back to take over." he suggested.

Todd nodded. "Yeah, that crossed my mind too but she's doing more than blowing off steam. Something's eating that girl and I'll be damned if I know what it is. I take that back, I reckon I do." Todd said thoughtfully.

Matthew raised an eyebrow at Todd inquiringly.

Todd snapped the reins to get the mules going and turned to look Matthew in the eyes. "I'll be damned if I know what ails either one of you! I kind of thought for a while there that you might just end up being my brother-in-law. What the hell happened, buddy, you and her have a fight?" he asked.

Matthew was the first to break eye contact. "No, nothing like that." he answered.

Todd was getting exasperated with him and it showed in his voice. "Well if you two didn't have a fight, then what the hell's the matter?" he asked bluntly.

"What makes you think anything's the matter?" Matthew asked.

At this point, Todd lost his temper. "Any fool can see that you're working yourself ragged from can-see to can't-see and you hardly ever come around. Wynn's running around all over the country like something wild and changes the subject every time your name gets mentioned. Now, what the hell's going on?" Todd snapped.

"Todd, I'm a damn fool. I should'a left a long time ago and I would have if that old nag of mine hadn't gone lame. I should have anyway when I bought the gray. But no, what do I do? I up and buy a damn farm just like I had good sense! Now I'm trapped here and can't go nowhere." Matthew's voice held. a note of desperation.

"Matthew, you ain't makin' a damn bit of sense. Why'd you buy the farm if you didn't want to stay here and what's that sister of mine got to do with all this?" Todd asked in exasperation.

"Everything and nothing." Matthew said vaguely.

Todd jerked the reins, bringing the mules to a halt. When he turned to look Matthew in the eyes once more, his own were shooting daggers as sharp as bayonets. "Damn it Matthew, this is me you're talkin' to. Are you going to tell me what's bothering you, or am I gonna have to beat it out of you?" I've had a damn 'nough of this!" By now, Todd was almost yelling.

Matthew gave in. "All right, it ain't worth me and you fighting about it. We've been friends too long to start that. You're right, there was something happening between Wynn and me but I put a stop to it."

"What the hell for?" Todd snapped.

At this point, Matthew gave up completely. When Todd wanted to know something, there was no getting around him. "Look Todd, everything I ever loved is dead and gone. If I let myself fall for Wynn, it'd be the same as giving her a death sentence. Is that what you want for your sister?" Matthew asked and turned away.

Todd blew out a long breath in a near whistle and he was no longer angry. "So that's it! Matthew, I never figured you for a fool,

146

but that beats all I ever heard. Are you gonna stand by until she finds herself some other man? There's more than one way of losing, buddy and that's one of them! You could board a ship and sail clean to China and run from what you feel, or you could stay here and take a chance. You ought'a know that this life don't offer no guarantees. Me or you could die this very night but more than likely, we'll live to be old gray haired men. You've had more than your share of losses but not one of them was your doing. Now, if you turn your back on Wynn you can't blame nobody but yourself when you lose her."

"Todd, I'm scared. I have nightmares where I see her dead and God help me, it makes my blood run like ice water. The whole damn war didn't scare me as bad as this does." Matthew admitted desperately.

Todd put his hand on Matthew's shoulder. "Turn it around Matthew. What if it were me who lost everything? Would you have advised me not to marry Sarah because I might lose her too?" he asked kindly.

Matthew's answer was given instantly and without thought. "Of course not." he admitted.

Todd gave him a triumphant smile. "There you have it! Let's get to the river and get us a couple of them big lizards." He snapped the reins and they were once more on their way.

By midnight, they had four good sized alligators loaded in the wagon and were on their way home. By that time, Matthew had come to the conclusion that even though the hunt was fun with Todd, it just wasn't the same without Wynn.

After two days of soul searching, Matthew had decided that Lum and Todd were right. There was more than one way to lose something you loved. So it was, that he was looking forward to the peanut boiling with growing excitement. It was time for him to begin some serious courting.

Chapter 29

The four of them went together in Todd's wagon and by the time, they arrived at the Milford's, Matthew had learned a thing or two about the O'Mally pride. Every effort he had made along the way to engage Wynn in conversation had failed. She didn't seem to want to be friends any more much less anything else. As soon as they arrived, Wynn went off on her own, leaving him with Todd and Sarah.

This was a large gathering and spirits, especially among the men were running high. Jugs of home brew were secreted in the barn and the men were slipping off at regular intervals to take a nip. The dancing had not yet begun and the raw green peanuts boiling in a washpot full of salted water, were not yet ready. Another washpot was filled with corn on the cob and the air was filled with the good scent of burning wood and the contents of the pots.

Sarah went off with a group of ladies and Todd, along with Matthew slipped off to the barn. The home brew was hundred proof and plentiful. It was passed around and each man drank straight from the jug. When Todd's turn came, Matthew looked on in amazement. With a thumb hooked through the handle of the jug. Todd upended it and took several big swallows without blinking an eye, before handing the jug over to him.

Matthew accepted the jug with good will, though he had never developed a taste for the stuff. His idea of drinking was a glass of fine brandy or perhaps a hot toddy before the parlor fire at night. In imitation of Todd, he upended the jug and let the raw corn liquor trickle down his throat. By the third cautious swallow, his eyes began to water and he lowered the jug and passed it on to the next man.

The old man who took the jug from Matthew had apparently been sampling it's contents for quite some time and he was already red cheeked and bright eyed. He expertly upended the jug and his bush of white whiskers bobbed up and down with the rhythm of his swallows. He at last, reluctantly lowered the jug and after wiping his lips on his sleeve, passed the jug on. He turned to Matthew and Todd, ready to talk. "You boys been doin' some gator huntin' I hear. Y'all doing any good at it?" he asked.

"Yeah." Todd answered. "We ain't had time to go much but I reckon we're doing all right."

"I used to hunt gators a right smart when I was young but it got to be too much work. I been huntin' rattlesnakes for their skins lately, it's a whole lot easier." the old man said, with a good-natured grin.

Matthew saw Todd's eyes light up with interest and cut him off before he could voice the suggestion that the two of them should do the same. "Rattlesnake hunting is where I draw the line, you want to go snake hunting, you'll have to do it with somebody else." he told

148

Todd firmly.

Todd shrugged. "I reckon I ain't got time right now, no way." He turned to the old man. "You seen any sign of rabies out your way Mr. Turner?"

The old man scratched at his whiskers thoughtfully. "No, I ain't seen nothin'. I heard tell that Jake Clement had to shoot one of his best coon dogs last week, when it tangled with a mad wildcat down around Sharpes Ferry. Shame, it was a good dog, the wildcat got clean away. I hear tell, he hunted that cat for three days and ain't found it yet. I seen a man die one time that got bit by a rabid dog, there ain't no worse way to die. They had to tie him up to a pine tree at the last to keep him from biting his wife and young'uns. Poor soul snarled and foamed at the mouth somethin' awful." the old man concluded.

Todd finally got a word in edgewise. "I killed a rabid fox at my place the other day. It was right in the front yard in broad daylight. It nearly scared my wife to death."

"She better be scared! Rabies ain't no joke." Old Man Turner said.

By then the jug had made a full circle and had come back to Todd. Todd tilted the jug and took a long drink before handing it to Matthew. The sounds of a fiddle and a banjo signaled the beginning of the dancing. Matthew put on a show of upending the jug before passing it on to Old Man Turner. He had actually consumed very little of it's contents. He and Todd stayed talking with the old man for a while longer before going outside to join in the dancing.

The white sand and gray dirt of the yard sent up small clouds of dust around the feet of the dancing couples. The whole yard was lit up with fat lightered torches and a blazing bonfire. Here and there an occasional lantern hung from the branches of an oak or magnolia tree, making the open yard seem as festive as the ballroom at Silver Oaks had once been. Matthew stood for a moment watching the dancers but his mind had drifted back to the now long gone ballroom at Silver Oaks.

As if it had only been yesterday, he could see the ladies in their ball gowns, drifting across the polished floor in the arms of the elegantly dressed gentlemen. The twanging and screeching of the banjo and fiddle seemed to fade away and he could hear the orchestra playing. In his mind, he could hear the stately waltzes of the not too distant past. Across the crowded floor he could see Elizabeth gliding toward him, her feet seemed not to be moving at all beneath the voluminous skirts of her gown. In his mind's eye, he could see himself guiding her effortlessly through the steps of the dance as she looked up into his face. How clearly he could remember how her blue eyes had sparkled in the light of the hundreds of candles that lit the room. She had pouted and flirted with him with such art that he had taken her out to the rose garden and voiced the proposal that was expected of him. She had shyly said yes and offered him her pouty red lips for a kiss to seal the agreement. He had drawn her into his arms and she had allowed him only the briefest of kisses before pulling away. "It's not proper." she had said. He had accepted this statement without much thought. Even though her lips had given him little, her blue eyes had promised him the world and heaven all rolled into one.

Matthew was shaken out of his thoughts of the past, when someone bumped into him from behind. He turned to see who it was and found Wynn playfully retreating from a young man who had obviously been hitting the jug a little too heavily. "I can't dance with you now." she told him as she took Matthew's arm. "I promised this one to Matthew."

She had done no such thing but he played along with her. The musicians were playing a badly done version of a waltz and he led her away to join the other dancing couples.

"Was he bothering you?" Matthew asked.

Wynn shook her head. "He was just a little obnoxious, nothing I couldn't have handled but it was just easier this way." She looked up at him but didn't smile.

She said nothing more and Matthew became aware of the feel of her slim uncorseted body beneath his hand. He made an effort to draw her closer but she refused to comply.

The waltz ended an another began. Wynn attempted to slip away but Matthew detained her. "I believe you owe me one for helping you get rid of that drunken Romeo." he said. Wynn shrugged and went back into his arms.

"I missed you the other night. It just wasn't the same hunting without you." he said and gave her a tentative smile.

Wynn raised her chin and set her mouth in a stubborn line. "I'm sure you and Todd did just fine without me." she said.

Matthew shrugged. "Not as good as if you'd been there." he assured her.

Wynn's black eyes flashed in a fit of temper and her shoe came down hard on his instep in what he was sure was no accident. He used the opportunity to pull her closer as he pretended to stumble. Her head came to rest on his shoulder with a little bump and he realized he was being a little rough with her but didn't care. She pulled away enough to glare up at him angrily. "If you want a hunting partner you can damn well go with Todd." she spat out like an angry kitten.

Matthew's eyes twinkled and he grinned down at her angry face. "Todd ain't as pretty as you." he said.

Wynn blinked and continued to look up at him with an angry expression on her face but her eyes had softened. "Hunting partners don't have to be pretty." she snapped.

Matthew winked at her and grinned a teasing grin. "No, but it sure does make it a lot more fun if they are." he insisted.

The waltz ended and Wynn stepped quickly away from him. She raised her chin once more in a fit of pride and temper and stood with one hand on her hip and used the other one to shake a finger in his face. "Now you listen here Matthew Kendall! If you think you can treat me like dirt one minute and make it all up with a silly complement the next, you got another think coming! You're not the only fish in the sea. I can do very well without you!" She turned sharply on her heel and walked away, leaving him standing there.

Matthew wandered back to the barn and when the jug was passed he drank long and deep of it before passing it on. The first session with the jug was a little more than he was used to and this second session was pure insanity. It was funny though, how much easier the stuff went down, once you got used to it.

By the time the peanuts and corn were done, Matthew was getting a little unsteady on his feet. Like everyone else, he ate his fill of the salty peanuts and corn on the cob dipped in butter. The food sobered him up somewhat and he would have probably been alright. However, Todd led him off for one last drink for the road.

The last drink from the jug turned out to be a big one and by the time they were all loaded in the wagon Todd was more talkative than ever and a little wobbly on his feet. By then, Matthew was down-right staggering and his mood was decidedly morose.

Wynn ignored him completely and wouldn't even speak. Todd talked enough for all of them, though nobody answered him. Wynn and Sarah were too mad to talk and Matthew was too sick. The jolting of the wagon was pure torture to his rolling stomach and spinning head. Half way home, he was sick over the side of the wagon. That served to sober him up just enough to make him ashamed of himself. It soothed his pride somewhat when Todd was in the same fix a few minutes later. At least he wasn't the only one that couldn't hold his liquor.

At this point, Sarah took over. "Get in the back with Matthew." she commanded. "I'll drive the wagon." Todd stumbled from the seat into the bed of the wagon and fell face first when she gave him a little shove. He raised up long enough to rub his smarting nose and mumble, "Aw, Honey." before he either went to sleep or passed out.

When they got to Matthew's farm, he managed to get himself out of the wagon. He called it stepping down but it was more like falling. He ended up on his knees in the dust in the yard and had just about managed to get up by himself when Wynn came to help him. She pulled him up by one arm. "Come on Matthew." she commanded. He gave her a silly grin and obediently leaned on her shoulders with one arm.

Looking thoroughly disgusted, she led him to his bedroom and turned down the covers before helping him to sit down on the side of the bed He sat there without moving while she stumbled around in the dark and finally found some matches and a candle. Once the candle was lit, she came to pull off his boots and push him down onto the bed. Instead of settling down quietly as she had expected, Matthew pulled her down on the bed with him. She tried to get away but he rolled on top of her, pinning her down. She continued to struggle and finally got a hand free to slap him sharply across the face.

By the time his ears quit ringing, Matthew was cold sober. He blinked at her as if he were awakening from a dream and rolled off her onto his back. He threw an arm over his eyes, ashamed to look at her. "I'm sorry Honey. I wouldn't hurt you for the world. I'm just drunk, that's all." he apologized.

Matthew's bed was up against the wall on one side and Wynn would have to climb over him to get out. "Is that why you did it? Just because you're drunk?" she asked.

"No, not because of that. You drive me crazy woman, now get

out of here, you ain't safe. I want you entirely too much to behave myself." Matthew warned her.

Wynn started to climb over him but lay on top of him instead. "I am safe, in another minute, Sarah will be in here to see why I'm not out yet."

Matthew clutched blindly at what little integrity he had left and tried to push her off. "If you don't get out of here right now, she may just get an eyeful. In another minute, I won't let you go." he warned once more.

Wynn gave him a quick but passionate kiss on the mouth, letting her body melt against him. She was up in an instant, blew out the candle and was out the door. "Go to sleep Matthew." she said softly on her way out.

Chapter 30

Matthew awakened the next morning with a raging headache. The bright morning sun coming through his window stabbed into his bloodshot eyes and cut into his head with all the force of a hatchet blow. To make matters worse, the morning was already stiflingly hot and showed every sign of getting hotter. He kicked his feet free of the tangled sheets and rolled over with a groan. It took him a minute to remember what had happened to make him feel so bad.

When he remembered, he rolled over and groaned again, burying his face in his pillow. One thing about it, when he made an ass out of himself, he didn't do it half way. Not only had he made a fool of himself, which was bad enough; before it was done with, he had mistreated Wynn. How could he expect her to forgive him when he couldn't forgive himself? As if she wasn't mad enough at him already, he'd behaved like a cad. She'd probably never speak to him again and at this point, he couldn't say that he blamed her.

Matthew finally dragged himself out of bed, longing for a cup of coffee which he didn't have. At least he wouldn't have to worry about facing breakfast, being Sunday, it was Lissa's day off. Dragging his feet all the way, he went to the front porch wash shelf and upended the bucket of water over his head. This helped some, but not much. He toweled most of the water from his hair and combed it as he looked into the cracked mirror over the shelf. He frowned at himself disgustedly and went out barefooted to feed the stock.

Long before he reached the hog pen, he could hear their agitated squeals. He reached automatically for his pistol, before remembering that he didn't have it on him. A black bear was wandering dazedly around the hog pen but making no attempt to get at the hogs. A clump of white foam hung from the bear's snout and he was ambling along, growling and grumbling to himself.

Matthew took off back to the house on the run and dashed inside to get his pistol, hoping that the bear would still be there when he got back.

He needn't have worried, the bear was still there, just ambling along in a daze. Matthew walked to within ten yards of the bear and aimed carefully before pulling the trigger. The bear fell to the ground and lay still. Matthew wasn't taking any chances, he fired three more shots into the bear before he was satisfied that it was dead. He walked carefully around it a couple of times, looking it over and trying to decide what to do with it.

This rabies epidemic was getting out of hand. He couldn't take any chances on any other animal getting into the carcass and maybe spreading the disease. He decided to let the bear lay, while he went back to the house to put on his boots and figure out what his best course of action would be.

Just as he reached the house, Willy came running into the yard. "I hears you shootin' up heah. What be de mattah?" he asked excitedly.

"Morning, Willy. Everything's all right. I just shot a rabid bear up by the hog pen. I'm glad you're here, maybe you can help me figure out what to do with the carcass."

"Lawd hab mercy, Missa Matthew. What's we gwine do 'round heah? Ebberthin' in de country be comin' down wid dat stuff. I'se not seed de likes ob it in all my boan days." Willy said, looking worried.

"Me either, Willy. Just let me go get my boots on and we'll see about getting rid of the thing. I can't just leave it laying around, something might get into it." Matthew said.

"Yassuh, I be thinkin' on it while you be gone." Willy replied agreeably.

Matthew went into the house to get his boots, thinking all the while that this was just what he needed. As if the day hadn't started out bad enough with the headache he had awakened with, now he had this to deal with. Only a damn fool would have gone traipsing out to feed the stock in his bare feet and he should have known better than to go out without his pistol. The trouble was, his head hurt too bad to let him do much rational thinking at all.

The thought occurred to him that he needed to let Todd know about the bear but the very thought of having to face Wynn after last night was something he dreaded. He decided that if he were given a choice of getting a beating or facing her wrath, he'd just as soon take the beating.

No matter how hard he tried, he could only remember bits and pieces of what had happened. He remembered Wynn slapping his face but couldn't remember how she had gotten into his bed or why she had slapped him. Suddenly the memory of what had happened next became clear to him. Intentionally or not, Wynn had teased him with her body. Perhaps she wasn't as mad at him as he had thought but still he dreaded facing her. He had never been that drunk in his whole life before and had never behaved in a less than gentlemanly way towards a lady.

Well, enough about that, he had other problems to deal with at the moment. He still hadn't finished feeding the stock and he had to figure out what to do with the dead bear. He pulled on his boots and went to join Willy, who had already gone up to the hog pen to see the bear.

"Dat be one big skeestah, Missa Matthew." Willy commented as he walked up.

Matthew massaged his aching forehead and fought down the nausea the sight of the bloody bear inspired in his queasy stomach. "Yeah, you reckon it'd be safe to bury it?" he asked Willy.

Willy looked Matthew over thoughtfully. "Nosuh, I gots a bettah idea. Dat ol' sink hole back up yondah be jus' de place. Dat be wheah dem folks use'ta lib heah pile up all dem rocks from out ob de field." he suggested.

"Sounds fine to me Willy. I guess we could drag it up there with the mule and something would be less likely to dig it up if it was covered up with rocks."

Matthew dawdled around the farm as long as possible. He fed the stock and Willy helped him dispose of the dead bear. His head was still aching and he dreaded the ride over to Todd's in the heat and with the horse's gait jarring his head.

It was mid-morning by the time he got there and he found Wynn

155

rocking slowly back and forth in the porch swing. He dismounted with care, trying not to jar his aching head and tied the gray to the hitching post, before meeting her eyes. She sat there with her face so expressionless, that it was impossible to guess what mood she was in. She had not said so much as a good morning to him.

"I just killed a rabid bear over at the farm. It was up by the hog pen just wandering around in a daze." he told her.

Wynn stopped rocking and said thoughtfully, "It's the heat. I never seen it so hot or so many cases of rabies around here before. It's not even dog days yet." She still didn't smile and her voice sounded listless. She began to rock back and forth once more.

"Where's Todd?" Matthew asked.

The corners of Wynn's lips tilted up slightly and there was a ghost of a twinkle in her eyes. "Sarah got him up at the crack of dawn and made him go to church." she answered.

Matthew sat down on the porch steps and rubbed absent mindedly at his aching head. "Guess she's mad at him." he ventured to say.

"That's an understatement if I ever heard one." Wynn replied.

Matthew could put off his apology no longer. "Look Wynn, I'm sorry about last night. I usually don't get drunk and make a fool of myself." he said humbly. If he thought that this was enough to get him off the hook with her, he was wrong.

"What you do is your business Matthew, not mine." she said tersely.

Matthew turned around so that he could look her in the eyes. "It's your business when what I do causes you to be offended." he replied.

Wynn's black eyes flashed fire. "You're not the first drunk man I ever had to fight off and I reckon you won't be the last." she snapped.

Matthew was at a loss for words, so he sat there silently. He knew that he deserved all that he was getting from her. He wondered which offence had made her the maddest, his neglecting her or his getting drunk and making an ass of himself. He kept hoping she would say something but she remained as silent as he was.

At last, not knowing what else to do, Matthew got up to leave. Wynn waited until he had mounted the gray before walking to the edge of the porch. She stood there looking slim and regal in her simple dress of light blue homespun. Her hair was arranged crown-like on the top of her head and her haughty expression added to her

156

queenliness. Suddenly she smiled and it was as if the sun had come out from behind a cloud. "Take care of your headache Matthew." she said.

He grinned back at her, feeling a great sense of relief wash over him. "I think I'll ride down to Silver Spring and make a point of falling in head first. I don't suppose you'd like to come along?" he asked, hopefully.

"I'd like to but I don't feel well today." she answered.

Now that he thought about it, she did look pale beneath her tan and there were dark circles beneath her eyes.

He recalled now, having seen her rubbing her lower belly as if it hurt. "You're not coming down with something are you?" he asked in concern.

Wynn gave him a wane smile and shook her head. "It's...nothing. I'm not sick Matthew." Her pale face suddenly flushed under her tan and she looked away.

It was suddenly clear to Matthew, that her ill health was strictly a female complaint. She looked utterly miserable and was obviously in pain. He was torn between wanting to comfort her and leaving her in peace. As he watched, her face lost it's flush and she bit her lip.

Matthew couldn't stand it. He got down off the gray and walked up the porch steps to stand in front of her. "You sure you're all right?" he asked, and gently brushed a damp strand of hair off her forehead.

Wynn's lower lip quivered and her eyes were suspiciously bright. "I feel like hell." she said, as a tear rolled down her cheek.

Matthew smiled slightly at her choice of words and slowly pulled her head down onto his shoulder. She stood a little stiffly at first but relaxed after a moment and leaned into him with her arms around his waist. He massaged the small of her back with one hand and stroked her hair with the other.

"That feels good." she murmured.

He said nothing but continued to rub her back. He'd done the same for Elizabeth at such times and she had sworn that it worked wonders.

After a time, she patted his back in a gesture of dismissal and drew back slightly to look up at him. "How'd you know to do that?" she asked bluntly.

Matthew shook his head as if to say he didn't know and said nothing. He didn't think she would want to know that he had learned it from Elizabeth.

She searched his eyes for a moment, then buried her face in the crook of his neck. "She must have been so special Matthew." Her voice was muffled but he still understood her.

"Not as special as you." he said softly. He kissed the top of her head and held her closer.

Wynn pulled away once more to look into his eyes. "I don't understand you Matthew." she said, looking troubled.

He raised an eyebrow at her inquiringly but she only shook her head and hid her face against him once more.

Matthew continued to rub her back and she pressed against him as if the pressure relieved her pain. The results were inevitable and he knew that she could feel the effect she was having on him. An ache began in his own body and he slid his hand down her back, drawing her tighter against him. She offered no resistance but drew away in a moment to look up at him with troubled, half-frightened eyes. He stroked her cheek reassuringly and gave her a brief kiss on the lips. "Go take a nap Honey, you'll feel better." he said gently.

"You going home?" she asked.

Matthew shook his head. "Swimming" he answered.

"Come for supper. Granny and Sarah are going to cook a mess of quail Todd brought in. Sarah stuffs them like little turkeys with dressing, they're really good."

"I'll be here." he agreed,

The swim in the cold spring water relieved Matthew's aching head and the other ache along with it. He took the trail back that led around behind the O'Mally plantation. He halfway hoped to run across another turtle but didn't and rode over to see Lum and Pearl before going home. The heat was so intense that his clothes had nearly dried on him before he got there.

When he left Lum's, he took his time riding home. He was enjoying the feel of the gray beneath him and he kept a sharp eye out for snakes and any animal that might have rabies. Puffs of dust rose up beneath the hooves of the gray with every step and the moss hung from the trees like the beards of old gray men. Not a breath of air stirred to disturb the palmettos and gallberry bushes that grew along the road. It was the kind of restless heat that sapped both man and beast of all energy.

Before going to the house, Matthew stopped by to check on Willy

158

and Lissa. They had settled in happily, contented with the cabin and the small wage he was able to pay them. Willy's leg was still sore and not quite healed but he was managing to do a full day's work in spite of it. With Willy's help, and working long hours himself, Matthew had come a long way toward getting the farm in shape.

The buildings had all been repaired and at least half of the fences were up. Lissa had kept busy canning vegetables from the house garden and the pantry was once more completely full. One of the sows had given birth to a litter of nine healthy pigs. Matthew was pleased with the progress. He had given some serious thought to the idea of raising stock instead of produce. He already had a good start with the hogs and was considering buying a quality bull to breed with the herd of half wild cattle that still roamed free.

Matthew arrived back at the house with time to spare, before going to Todd's for supper. He found himself wandering through the house as if he had never seen it before. He realized that he was looking at it, not with the eyes of a bachelor but with the eyes of a man who intended to marry and live with a wife.

It was a good house, though not at all luxurious and he looked at it now with an eye for improving it's interior. The bedroom he had chosen for himself was not the largest, or master bedroom and he considered moving into the larger room. The master bedroom was furnished with a big, four poster bed and a couple of wardrobes.

A sudden vision of himself and Wynn together on the feather mattress crossed his mind, causing him to gasp out loud. Perhaps Wynn wouldn't like the bed at all. Maybe she would want to move in her canopied bed, with the ruffles. He smiled at the thought. She had told him once that she didn't fit the mold society tried to put her into. It was true, she was a free spirit, a unique combination of toughness and femininity. He couldn't imagine her ever being tied to a house and children as most women were. Whatever her man was involved in, she would be right in the middle of. He liked the idea of that. He wanted more than a housekeeper and brood mare. He wanted a woman that would be his partner, friend and lover, not some drudge who thought only in terms of house and children.

Matthew realized that he was only day dreaming. Just because his mind was made up certainly didn't mean that hers was. It was pure arrogance to assume that she would even have him if he were to ask. She seemed fond of him and she responded to him with a fire that scorched him. However she had proven that she could take him or leave him and proved it by seeing other men. In a fit of self-doubt, he wondered if he was even man enough for her. She was more woman than he had ever encountered and it would take one hell of a man to match her.

With a shake of his head, he came out of the spell of deep thought that had possessed him. He was still standing in the middle of the floor in the master bedroom, staring at the bed. With an ironic grin, he left the room, shutting the door behind him. A few minutes later, he had changed his clothes and was on his way to Todd's.

Chapter 31

Todd was out in the yard when he rode up. "What's this I hear about you killing a mad bear at your place?" he asked in way of a greeting.

Matthew gave him a detailed account of the event and then asked with a mischievous grin, "How was church?"

Todd blew out his breath in a half whistle. "Whew, I would'a never guessed that that sweet little blond headed wife of mine had such a temper! I may have to sleep by myself for the next month. I always figured that a man had the right to tie one on once in a while but you never seen such a fit as she pitched. You know I ain't never been one to go to church but I had to do something to smooth her ruffled feathers." he said, looking a little sheepish.

Matthew gave Todd a sympathetic grin. "Don't feel too bad, Wynn wasn't very impressed with me either. She was mad enough at me all ready, then I had to go and make an ass out of myself." he said.

"She must not be too mad if she asked you to come to supper, you and her get things patched up?" Todd asked.

Matthew shrugged. "I guess, she didn't seem mad when I left her this morning at any rate."

"Well, I'm glad to hear it buddy. I was beginning to have serious doubts about you two." Todd said with a grin.

"Hell, I still don't know where I'm at with her. She's got me all mixed up." Matthew admitted.

"Now what's she done?" Todd asked.

160

Matthew shook his head. "I came over here this morning to tell you about the bear and she wouldn't even smile at me. I tried to apologize but she acted like she didn't want to accept it. She finally softened up a little when I started to leave and I asked her if she wanted to go swimming at Silver Spring."

"Why didn't she go?" Todd asked.

"She told me she didn't feel good. She did look kind of peaked. It worried me, so I got down off my horse to see if she was all right. It turned out, it was just her woman's time of month and I guess she really was hurting. She ended up crying a little and I petted her some." Matthew explained.

Todd gave him a look of sodden comprehension, "No wonder my belly hurt! I thought it was from drinking too much liquor last night. Damn Matthew, I'm gonna be in one hell of a fix, if she ever has a baby. How'd you know that's what it was?"

Matthew's jaw dropped comically at Todd's statement. "The hell you say! You don't mean to tell me that every time she gets cramps, you feel it. Do you really mean to tell me, you feel everything that she does?" He was thinking that it would be down right embarrassing if Todd knew everything his sister felt.

Todd laughed heartily at Matthew's expression. "Only if something hurts her and then only if the pain is severe. I can tell when she's in danger, like when the panther almost got her, I felt that. When we're far off from each other, we can only sense the big troubles, like when I got shot in the arm, hers burned a little. When I broke my leg, hers just ached a little, kind'a like when the weather changes. If she stumped her toe or hurt her finger, I wouldn't feel it unless we were in the same room." he explained.

"I still think it's the damnedest thing I ever heard of. It must be a pain in the ass sometimes." Matthew said.

Todd laughed again. "Only if she falls on it. You still never said how it was you knew what ailed her. Surely she didn't tell you."

It was Matthew's turn to laugh. "Not hardly! I was married to Elizabeth long enough to recognize the symptoms. Haven't you been through it with Sarah yet?" he asked.

Todd thought a minute. "No, come to think about it I haven't." Todd replied.

At that moment, Sarah came to call them to supper. They washed their hands at the porch wash shelf and went inside to eat. Granny was absent from the kitchen and Matthew asked where she was.

Sarah answered him. "I told Granny to take the day off, it's too hot for her to be cooking at her age. She's going to eat with Lum and Pearl. Now that Pearl's got her own household to look after, they eat at their own place most of the time. Pearl still helps me some with the heavy cleaning but with me and Wynn both here, we don't really need that much help." she explained.

"You can say that again." Wynn agreed. "I used to wonder how on earth I'd ever get it all done and now I find myself hunting something to do."

"You've done enough here already. It's about time you had some time for yourself." Todd said to Wynn.

Wynn gave her brother a fond smile. "I guess I'm having a little trouble getting used to it. You won't let me help with the field work and with four women on the place the rest of it gets done in a hurry."

"Getting bored Wynn?" Matthew asked.

Wynn passed him the platter of baked quail and said, "I suppose I am."

"Me too sometimes." Sarah admitted. "You know what I'd like to do?" She waited for someone to ask what.

Todd obliged her. "What's that?" he asked.

I've got a terrible craving for some good old crabs from Salt Springs. I'd like to go over there and camp for two or three days and eat crab until I start to walk like one." Sarah said wistfully.

Todd thought for a minute. "I guess we could take off enough time for that. Come to think of it, I ain't had no crab since before the war. I'm kind'a hungry for some myself." he replied.

Sarah's eyes lit up with enthusiasm at the prospect. "Oh Todd, could we? It would be such fun. Matthew, could you get loose from the farm long enough to go with us? I know Wynn'll want to go."

Matthew thought for a moment. "I guess I don't have anything going that won't wait for a few days. Willy and Lissa can take care of things while I'm gone. I don't know if I like to eat crabs or not though. I seen some at the docks in Charleston once but I never thought about eating them." Matthew answered.

"You never had turtle or swamp cabbage before either but you liked that." Wynn reminded him. "Just wait till you eat boiled crab! They're fun to catch too." she said.

Matthew laughed. "If you say it's good, I believe you. I still haven't tried alligator tail though." he said.

"And whose fault is that? Y'all have been out gatoring twice and still ain't brought in one young enough to eat." said Sarah.

"Well, we been more concerned with the size of their hides than their meat. Old Man Blake pays by the foot." Todd said in the way of an excuse.

"When do y'all want to go?" Matthew asked.

"How about Friday?" Todd suggested. "That'll give us time to make sure everything's caught up before we leave."

"That sounds fine to me." Matthew replied.

Throughout the rest of the meal they talked of other things. Foremost on their minds was the continuing heat and drought and of course the rabies epidemic. They considered delaying the trip to Salt Springs until the epidemic was over but decided that as long as they were cautious, there was nothing to worry about.

Matthew and Todd stayed in the kitchen until Sarah and Wynn had the dishes done and the food put away. When this was done, they all retired to the porch, which was the usual for a summer evening.

The air outside was very little cooler than inside the house. The blue of the evening sky was dotted with billowy white clouds and showed no promise of rain. Todd and Sarah, their first quarrel obviously over, sat together in the porch swing and Matthew and Wynn sat on the steps. As the sun set, the mosquitoes and yellow flies began to swarm, the smudge pots were lit and conversation became sporadic. It was good just to sit quietly at the end of the day, watching the sunset and listening to the sounds of the evening.

Matthew shifted his position until he could lean back against the post nearest the steps. Wynn looked over at him and gave him a smile that was as affectionate as the ones she reserved for Todd. He smiled back at her and held out his hand and she came over to him and sat down between his legs, so that she could lean back against him. He wrapped his arms around her waist and rested his cheek on her hair. A glance at Todd and Sarah told him that they were doing the same thing, for Todd had turned around sideways on the swing. Todd gave them a wink over the top of Sarah's blond curls.

Wynn sat so still and breathed so shallowly that Matthew was beginning to wonder if she had fallen asleep.

A movement in the semi-darkness at the bottom of the steps caught Matthew's eye and he finally made out the shape of a large toad that was almost the same color as the gray sand of the yard. The toad made a hop and landed on the bottom step. It paused for a second, then hopped up on the next one and then the next, until it sat on the edge of the porch next to his out-stretched legs. In a move as fast as lightning, the toad's tongue shot out and an unfortunate yellow fly disappeared down it's throat as quick as a flash.

"Pretty smart, ain't he?" Wynn asked quietly. "The bugs come to eat us up and he comes every night to eat the bugs."

"Yeah, look at that, he just got another one." Matthew replied.

"There was one that used to come up on the porch when me and Todd was little. We used to roll bird shot at him and he'd swallow them until he got so heavy, he couldn't even hop." Wynn said.

"And then Wynn would make me hold it up by it's hind legs and shake it until all the shot came out." Todd laughed at the memory.

"We used to think that he came up on the porch just to see us, we didn't know he was just after the bugs." Wynn added. "Did you do stuff like that when you was little, Matthew?"

"Not much," Matthew replied. "My mother wouldn't let me get dirty. I used to sneak around and do things though, especially after my Daddy gave me Lum for a birthday present one year. We were both about twelve that year and Lum knew more about having fun than I did. We used to sneak off and go swimming and when we got older, hunting and fishing. We didn't get into too much. The worst thing we ever done was steal some of my Daddy's tobacco and whiskey." At this point Matthew stopped to laugh. "I don't know which one made us the sickest, the whiskey or the tobacco. I never cared much for either one since then." he concluded.

Wynn gave a small giggle. "You wouldn't have known it last night." she teased.

"It's the truth." Matthew insisted. "Last night was the second time I was ever drunk in my life. The first time was when me and Lum got into my Daddy's whiskey. I guess I wasn't cut out to be a drinking man. I ain't too good at it."

"You hit the nail on the head that time! And Todd ain't no better. It was all me and Sarah could do to get him in the house last night. We thought about leaving him in the wagon. The time before that, he fell off his horse and broke his leg." Wynn said.

"It ain't as much fun as it's cracked up to be." Todd admitted.

"So you're just now figuring that out, are you?" Sarah asked, without malice.

"Lay off woman." Todd said gruffly, but he kissed his wife's cheek as he said it.

Conversation came to an end once more and they remained sitting on the porch in companionable silence. Matthew let the feeling of contentment wash over him. It was good to be here, in this place with Todd and Sarah and with Wynn in his arms.

The night became suddenly dark as a drifting cloud covered the moon. The opportunity was too good to resist and Matthew sought Wynn's lips in the darkness. She must have been thinking the same thing, for she met him half way. Aware of Todd and Sarah so close by, Matthew had meant to keep the kiss brief but Wynn had other ideas. When he would have drawn away, she had flicked his lower lip with her tongue. Matthew forgot all about Todd and Sarah and lost himself in the taste of her mouth on his. The light of the moon coming out from behind the cloud, penetrated his closed eyelids and he drew back instantly.

The porch swing was empty and Matthew wondered how Todd and Sarah had managed to go inside without making a sound. Maybe Todd wanted to be alone with Sarah as much as he wanted to be alone with Wynn. He lowered his head once more to her waiting mouth and hoped that she had enough sense to halt things before they went too far. He didn't have the strength to even try. He let himself go, taking possession of her mouth, as he wanted to do with her body. He wouldn't have cared if that kiss had gone on forever.

She drew away at last, her breath coming in little gasps. She turned to face him and hid her face against his neck. It was impossible for him to tell where the trembling in his body left off and the trembling in hers began. In that moment, he knew that she wanted him as badly as he wanted her. Wynn's lips pressed against his neck and began to move in a series of tiny wet kisses, causing him to gasp out loud. His hand went between them to cover her small firm breast. She drew in a sharp breath and let it out in a rush of warm air against his neck. Driven by a need that was stronger than logical thought, he sought her lips again. Her passionate response was almost more than he could bear and the need to feel her body against his own was nearly out of control. She offered no resistance when he lowered her to the porch floor and lay on top of her. Not until his hand began to work it's way up under her skirt, did she call a halt. "Matthew, I can't,

I can't, not now." she said.

He realized that it was true. She was refusing him not because she wanted to but because she had to. He rolled off of her and lay panting, tortured by the ache in his loins. Her warm hand touched his thigh and he gasped out loud. "Honey, don't touch me, I can't take any more," he said between clinched teeth.

Wynn sounded near tears. "Matthew, I'm sorry, I would you know. I want to. I don't know what to do."

"Just let me calm down a minute, that's all. It's been a long time and wanting you makes me hurt." he explained.

Wynn reached for his hand in the darkness. "Matthew, I didn't mean to. I don't want you to hurt." she said and pressed his hand against her wet cheek.

Matthew squeezed her hand in an effort to reassure her. "I know Honey, it'll pass, it's just different for a man that's all. I didn't expect you to know that."

"There's a lot I don't know." Wynn said dejectedly.

Matthew stood up and reached for her hand to pull her up beside him. She stood there with downcast eyes, unable to look at him.

"Wynn, Honey, it's all right, really it is." he said.

She raised her eyes, trying to see his face in the moonlight. "Matthew, it can't keep being this way. I may be a fool but I'm not stupid." she said quietly.

Matthew drew in a deep breath and let it out slowly, "Wynn, will you marry me?" he asked simply and without preamble.

"Is it that simple Matthew? If the time had been right, you'd have had what you wanted anyway. Do you think you have to marry me to get what you want?" Wynn asked seriously.

Her words hit Matthew like a slap in the face, wounding him more surely than a knife in his heart would have done. "Is that your way of telling me no?" he asked.

Wynn turned her back to him and stood leaning against a post. She stared out across the darkened yard for a long time before she answered him. "There has to be more reason than that Matthew. Just because we want to do something we're not supposed to do, is not enough reason to get married. No Matthew, I won't marry you for that." she said quietly.

"Do you really think that low of me Wynn? That I'd marry you just to get you into my bed?" Matthew asked through throat muscles

166

that were nearly too tight for him to speak at all.

"I don't know what to think, Matthew. I'm all mixed up. It was a lot easier when we were just friends." Wynn answered.

Matthew took two steps down the steps and turned to look at her, straining to see her face in the shadows. "We could never be just friends Wynn, not for long. With us it has to be all or nothing and to be honest with you I can never accept the idea that it's nothing."

She had no answer for that and he mounted the gray and rode away.

Chapter 32

The hooves of the gray made almost no sound as Matthew rode home slowly that night. The roadbed was bone dry and three inches deep in soft sand, A slight breeze sprang up, softly rattling the palmettos and whispering through the tops of the oak and pine forest. The breeze served to dry the sweat on his brow, cooling him somewhat but holding no coolness of it's own. The pain caused by Wynn's rejection of his proposal sat upon his shoulders like a heavy weight. Todd and Lum were right, there was more than one way to lose someone.

Matthew sat up straighter in the saddle. "No, by God! I can't accept that!" he exclaimed out loud. Wynn was wrong about him and he'd have to find a way to prove it to her. It was true, he wanted her body almost to the point of obsession but there was more to it than that. He wanted her love and her sense of fun and laughter as well as her strength. He wanted her stubbornness and pride, her temper and her tears. He wanted the easygoing companionship and rowdy play that they had shared at first. As he had told her, it was all or nothing and he wanted it all.

Her accusation still stung. How could she possibly believe that he wanted only her body. After a little honest thought, he could see how she might. With them, a formal courtship had not been possible from the start. How was a man supposed to make formal calls on a woman, when they lived in the same house? In a formal courtship, there was a slow progression of events, following a set pattern. A series of chaste meetings in which a little flirting occurred, was followed by holding hands and when the proposal was accepted, there was a brief kiss to seal the agreement. With them there was no slow progression of events, only a consuming flame that began with their first encounter.

Still, normal progression or not, it was more than Matthew could understand. Her rejection had cut him to the quick. She had as much as told him that she was willing to give him her body but not her hand in marriage. She was wrong about what he wanted from her and he was beginning to wonder just what it was that she wanted from him.

Before he knew it, he was back home and he went to bed only to toss and turn but not to sleep.

The next day dawned as hot and dry as the one before. Matthew was tired from lack of sleep and weighted down with his problems with Wynn. He spent the morning stringing barbed wire and putting in posts for yet another section of fence. He worked harder than necessary in an effort not to think. Needing to be alone, he had set Willy to cutting wood in another section of the farm. He'd had Lissa pack him a lunch that morning, as he didn't plan on being back at the house at noon.

By midday, his hair and clothes were as wet with sweat as they would have been if he had worn them swimming in the spring. He had abandoned his shirt earlier that morning and left it hanging on a fence post a good ways back.

At high noon, he stopped work to rest in the shade of an oak tree. He had no appetite for the food he had brought along but drank deeply from the jar of tepid water. After a while he laid down on his back to rest. Not far away, a mourning dove called softly to it's mate and a locust buzzed monotonously in the branches over his head. Matthew had not intended to sleep but his eyes had drifted shut of their own accord.

Tired from the sleepless night before, he slept deeply and soundly and did not awaken until mid afternoon. He had turned over in his sleep and lay flat on his stomach, with his head resting on one arm. The dry oak leaves on the ground behind him crackled as someone walked across them. Coming awake instantly, Matthew acted by instinct alone, in one lightning quick motion, he rolled to a sitting position and drew his pistol at the same time.

He lowered it instantly when he saw that it was only Wynn.

"Damn, I almost shot you! Don't ever sneak up on me like that!" he exclaimed. His voice was sharper than he had intended.

Wynn sat down on the ground nearby and wiped sweat from her

brow with the back of her hand. "Lord, Matthew, you scared the life out of me. I never saw anyone move so fast in my life. I didn't mean to sneak up on you." She was dressed in baggy pants and her hair was hidden beneath the wide brim of a palmetto hat. A black smudge of dirt ran across one cheek and down to her chin and her feet were bare.

Matthew grinned at her in affectionate amusement. "What on earth have you been up to?" he asked. He had just now noticed that she was carrying an axe and a tin can.

"I've been grunting up fish worms. You've got the best place for it down by that low place in the southeast corner. I never figured on getting almost shot for trespassing." she answered him with a sunny smile.

"Now you've got me. How do you grunt up fish worms?" Matthew asked.

"It's easy, first you have to know where to find them. Then you drive a stake in the ground and vibrate it with the blade of an axe. The worms can't stand it and come up out of the ground and all you have to do is pick them up." she explained.

"You planning on going fishing." Matthew's grin still showed amusement.

Wynn wiped at her face self-consciously, causing yet another streak of dirt. "What's the matter Matthew, is my face dirty or something?" she asked innocently.

Matthew laughed. "You look like a little boy that's been playing in the dirt " he told her.

She gave him a grin that was indeed boyish. "You ain't the cleanest man I ever seen either. I've got enough worms for both of us if you want to go with me. I'm going to ride down to the river and do some bank fishing. Sarah got up this morning saying she'd kill for a mess of red bellies. I figured that if she wanted them that bad, I'd go catch her some."

Matthew brushed at the leaves stuck to his sweaty chest. "So Sarah's craving red bellies, is she. Yesterday it was crabs." he said with a grin.

Wynn returned his grin and began brushing the leaves off of his back. "Sounds suspicious doesn't it?" she agreed. Her hand on his back became suddenly still. "Matthew?" she said questioningly.

"Hum?" he murmured, enjoying the feel of her hand on his back.

"What made these scars?" she asked, tracing them one after the

169

other with her fingertip. There were more than a dozen of the small white scars and they stood out starkly against the tanned skin of his back and shoulders.

A Yankee with a bayonet. I got knocked out at Chickamauga and ended up captured. I was so dizzy, I kept falling down and every time I went to my knees, that son of a...um, stuck me in the back. That's where I met Todd, you know." Matthew explained.

"No, I didn't know. Was he captured too?" Wynn asked.

"Yeah, that's when he saved my life the first time. I fell down and couldn't get up even with that Yankee using my back for a pincushion. They killed the prisoners that couldn't keep going and I didn't think I could walk another step. Todd helped me up and ordered me to walk and I made it with his help. I'd have never made it on my own, I was so dizzy I couldn't see straight and I'd lost a lot of blood from a gash on my arm. We both managed to escape, that's how Todd got shot through the arm."

"You said that was the first time. When was the second?" Wynn asked.

Matthew's gray eyes became haunted and hard. When he carried me out of that Yankee prison. I was nearly dead and nothing more than a rack of bones. I owe your brother more than I can ever repay." he said quietly.

"I don't think Todd sees it that way." Wynn replied.

Matthew changed the subject. "If we're going to get Sarah a mess of fish, we'd better hurry. The afternoon is half gone." He stood up and went to get his shirt and tools.

Wynn had left her horse tied up in Matthew's yard and her fishing pole was leaned up against the porch. Matthew saddled the gray and found an old fishing pole that the widow's oldest boy had left behind. He stuffed his shirt and some extra line and hooks in his saddlebag and they were ready to go. The ride to the river was pleasant in spite of the heat. It seemed a long time since Matthew had been anywhere like this with Wynn. Today seemed set apart, not confused by the wild emotions that had clouded their thinking the night before.

When they reached the river, they tied the horses and walked down a trail left by other fishermen. Wynn stopped and sniffed the air delicately. "That's either a fish bed or a gator hole. I'm not sure which." she said.

Matthew had smelled nothing out of the ordinary and he came to stand near her. He too sniffed the air and was able to pick out the slightly sweet, slightly fishy smell. "Yeah, I smell it. I've noticed that smell before when we were out gator hunting but I didn't think nothing of it." he said.

"I bet it's over there by those cypress knees. If we can catch them bedding, we'll have a mess in no time." Wynn said. She began to unwrap her line from around her pole. Matthew did the same and they soon had their hooks baited and in the water. "The river's down." Wynn commented.

"It's lower than it was the first time I saw it." Matthew agreed. The tip of the pole began to twitch and soon he pulled in a red belly the size of his two hands put together. At almost the same instant, Wynn did the same.

"I bet I catch the most." she challenged. The race was on. Matthew won it by one fish and they rode home with their catch.

"If I hurry, these can be ready in time for supper. Want to come help us eat them Matthew?" Wynn asked.

Matthew declined, using work to be done as an excuse. The day was much too pleasant to be complicated with another session like the night before. It was as if they had declared a truce, putting their relationship on the shelf for the time being. Perhaps Wynn had decided that if being friends was more comfortable, then that's what they would be.

The respite helped but it was no answer. The next few days were busy ones and Matthew saw no more of Wynn during the remainder of the week. His work on the new fence was progressing and in spite of the intense heat, he managed to get a lot done. Though he had kept on the lookout for any more rabid animals, he had neither seen nor heard of any more incidents in the area.

Friday morning dawned clear and hot, with still no sign of rain. The blue of the sky was unbroken and not a cloud was in sight. The crops in the fields were dry but not yet hurting and a fine layer of dust dulled the vegetation along each side of the road. Todd and Sarah along with Wynn, met him at the end of the road to begin their trip to Salt Springs.

Chapter 33

Todd, with Sarah at his side, drove the farm wagon. It was loaded

171

with the rowboat that was usually tied up at the river and with a tent and other paraphernalia that would be needed on the outing. Wynn, like Matthew had chosen to make the journey on horseback and they rode along ahead of the wagon to avoid the cloud of dust stirred up by its wheels.

Soon after they crossed the river, the road was bordered by a forest of mostly pines. The ground was flat, with only slight rises that passed for hills. Once past the Cedar Creek bridge, the pine forest and gallberry flats became more dominant.

"How far is it?" Matthew asked.

"Fifteen miles." Wynn answered. "It's mostly scrub from here on out."

Matthew raised his eyebrows questioningly. "What's scrub?" he asked.

Wynn grinned. "Mostly high dry pine woods. It's poor land where nothing much will grow." she explained.

The road continued to wind it's way through the forest and the land began to rise and fall like ocean waves. It went up and down lazily and was higher and dryer than the rich hammock land from which they had come.

When they at last arrived at Salt Springs, Matthew found it fascinating. Though much smaller than Silver Spring, it was still impressive. He still found it a thing of wonder that water could come from the earth in such amounts as to make a river, or run as it was called.

The head of the spring was surrounded by cypress, oaks and palm tress. Beneath one of the spreading oak trees, they set up their camp in a place used by others before them.

When the camp was set up to their satisfaction, Todd slapped irritatedly at a horse fly and wiped his brow. "I don't know about the rest of you, but. I'm gonna get in that water and cool off." he announced. As he talked, he stripped off his shirt and boots. He took off running down the hill and dove headfirst into the main boil of the spring.

Matthew followed suite and jumped into the spring with a splash a few feet away from Todd. The water seemed icy cold to his overheated body and he came up sputtering and shaking the water from his head. He quickly became used to the temperature of the water and cupped his hand to take a drink. "Ugh, this stuff tastes

172

funny, smells kind 'a funny too." he observed.

"It's got a lot of salt in it." Todd explained.

"Wonder where the women got off to?" Matthew wondered out loud.

"Probably went in the tent to change into their swim dresses." Todd answered.

A moment later, Wynn and Sarah came down the hill, dressed for swimming. Matthew thought that women's swim dresses were the most ridiculous looking things he'd ever seen but refrained from comment.

Wynn jumped in as had Todd and Matthew but Sarah had to be coaxed.

"It's easier if you just jump right in." Todd said.

Sarah would have none of it and waded in slowly a bit at a time, getting used to the icy water by degrees. Once she was fully wet, she swam over to Todd and clung around his neck to keep her feet out of the grass.

Wynn made a game of swimming under water and grabbing Matthew's toes or pulling his feet out from under him.

He retaliated by dunking her repeatedly until she gave up pestering him. She finally settled for hanging around his neck as Sarah was doing with Todd. "Whew, I'm getting cold." she said. She snuggled against him for a moment as if to keep warm but before he could really start to enjoy it, she began to tickle him in the ribs. He dissolved into helpless laughter and finally in self-defense, slung her over his shoulder and hauled her out of the spring. He carried her half way up the hill, before depositing her unceremoniously on her feet. She kicked and screamed all the way but her eyes were sparkling with fun when he set her down.

Grinning mischievously, she tweaked the hair on his chest and earned herself a playful slap on the backside. "You about ready to start catching crabs?" she asked.

Todd and Sarah came out of the water right behind them and they went to launch the rowboat. When the boat was launched and safely tied up to a cypress tree, Matthew and Wynn went looking for something to use for bait. They soon returned with a couple of long-legged water birds, which they plucked and cut up into pieces. "Pieces of the neck work best but any part will do." Wynn explained.

The four of them boarded the rowboat and allowed it to drift down the run with the current. The water was amazingly clear, just as the water at Silver Spring was. As Wynn had said, catching crabs was easy. One simply tied a piece of bait on the end of a stout cord and trailed it along in the water. When a crab got a hold of the bait, the line was brought in slowly, hand over hand and the crab was picked up in a net, just before it let go of the bait. The blue crabs were then dropped into a tub.

Matthew was torn between paying attention to what he was doing and looking at the scenery. Several bald eagles made their homes in the tops of dead cypress trees along the run and he found the great birds magnificent. Whooping cranes also were plentiful along the run and their white feathers shone like silver in the sun.

In no time at all, they had what Todd proclaimed was enough for a mess and they paddled back up the run to their camp.

Once there, Sarah and Wynn made a fire under a wash pot and filled it with water, to which was added salt and other spices. Cleaning the crabs for cooking wasn't difficult. One had only to remove a small portion from underneath the belly of the crab and it was ready to cook.

Matthew had learned early how to avoid being pinched by the sharp claws. What he had thought were two heads were really arms. These arms could pinch like crazy and he had a sore thumb to prove it.

He learned that he was in for yet another surprise, for when the blue crabs were cooked, they turned coral red. When the crabs were done, they sat down for a long feast. It took a long time to get full eating crabs, for the delicate white meat had to be picked out of the shell. A pair of pliers was used to break open the arms and to Matthew's way of thinking, these contained the best meat, though Todd said he preferred the body meat best.

"Did you notice they have a woman on their back?" Wynn asked Matthew at one point.

He shook his head and Wynn pointed out the shape of a woman dressed in a puffy sleeved dress with a small waist and gathered skirt. "Well I'll be darned." he said. "It sure does."

They were still eating crabs as the sun began to go down and the pleasant evening was marred by a swarm of sand gnats. The tiny insects were too small to be seen but soon had them all itching all over. Todd built a smudge out of damp oak leaves and this helped to

174

dispel them somewhat, as did the slight breeze that sprang up just at sundown.

In spite of the breeze, it was still hot after dark and they went for another swim to cool the sand gnat bites and themselves before changing clothes for the night.

Full, tired and contented after the long day of fun and travel, they settled around the campfire. The light of the fire seemed to be no more than an oasis in the middle of a tropical jungle. One could almost imagine that this was Africa or some other far-away place. The cat-like call of the limpkins blended with the hooting of owls and the calls of whippoorwills. The frogs added their chorus to the symphony of night sounds and an occasional bull gator or great cat gave their voices for emphasis.

Cool and comfortable after the heat of the day, it was pleasant just to sit staring into the flickering flames of the campfire and think one's own thoughts. Todd sat cuddling Sarah and it struck Matthew how perfect the two of them looked together, Sarah's blondness against Todd's Indian darkness.

Matthew sat holding hands with Wynn, reluctant to do anything more. It was easier not to start something that couldn't be finished. He grew drowsy watching the flames and yawned widely. After a moment, he laid down on the ground and rested his head on Wynn's lap. She ran her fingers through his hair and it was both soothing and stimulating.

After a little while, Todd and Sarah went to the tent and Matthew was alone with Wynn once again. He settled his head more comfortably on her lap, determined not to start anything. Not only would hanging onto his control avoid frustration, but it might serve to show Wynn that he wanted more than her body.

Her hand in his hair soothed him until he fell asleep and she woke him up to go to bed. He stood up lazily and reached a hand to help her up. She put her arms around his waist and stood for a moment with her head on his shoulder. Holding onto his resolve, he held her closely for a while and then planting a kiss on the top of her still wet head, sent her into the tent to go to bed.

He followed a few minutes later and lay down beside her on the pallet to sleep.

He could hear Todd softly snoring and Sarah's quiet breathing. He was intensely aware of Wynn so close to him in the crowded tent.

He reached out for her hand in the darkness and lay holding it a long time after her breathing had become light and shallow with sleep.

The morning sun shining through the canvas of the tent awakened him. Wynn was in his arms asleep, with her head on his shoulder and one leg thrown across him. Todd and Sarah had already gotten up and left the tent, a fact he was grateful for as the position they were in could prove embarrassing. He didn't want to move or wake her up. She felt so right, just where she was, as if she was where she belonged. Her hair half covered her face and lay across his chest like a mantle of black silk. It felt like silk beneath his callused fingers as he lay playing with a strand of it in utter contentment.

He gradually became aware that she was awake and lay looking at him. He met her eyes and gave her a lazy smile. The corners of her lips turned up slightly and the look in her eyes was soft and warm. They were lit with a glow from within, that spoke of an emotion that he couldn't name.

His lazy smile gradually widened into a grin. "Get up from there and quit looking at me like that, before it gets you into trouble." he warned.

Wynn pretended to pout but sat up, pushing her hair out of her face with one hand. "Where's Todd and Sarah got off to?" she asked.

"I don't know, they were gone when I woke up." Matthew answered.

"Um, probably slipped off to catch something for breakfast." Wynn said. She was already fully dressed, having slept in her clothes. She put on her shoes and left the tent ahead of him.

Matthew lay there a minute more, before putting on his shirt and boots. When he stepped outside the tent, the morning sun shone brightly, quickly burning off the last of the thick morning fog. Wynn had walked down to the main spring and stood watching the fish swim around in the clear water as she combed out her hair. Matthew washed his face and combed his own hair before joining her at the spring.

He stood behind her for a moment, with his hands on her slim shoulders, then unable to resist, he began to braid her hair. It felt soft and warm and alive under his hands as he fashioned the thick strands into a long rope down her back.

When he was done, she put an arm affectionately around his waist and stood beside him. "Look at those baby turtles down there.

176

Aren't they cute? I might try to catch me one later for a pet." she said.

"Yeah, they are cute. I been thinking about getting me a couple of puppies to train to hunt. It seems funny not to have a dog on the place." Matthew replied.

"I suppose it does. I can't remember ever not having dogs around. What kind do you want to get?" she asked.

"I don't know. A mix maybe, something that will hunt but make good company too. It gets lonely on the farm of an evening when the work's done and Willy and Lissa go back to their cabin." Matthew said wistfully.

Wynn looked up at him intently with her soft black eyes. "You get lonesome, Matthew?" she asked.

He nodded but didn't hold her gaze. "Well, yeah. I asked a pretty little girl to marry me but she turned me down. I guess I'll just have to get me a dog for company." He said it with an ironic grin, but sounded serious enough.

"Lonely ain't a good enough reason to get married, Matthew." she said.

Frustrated and a little stung by her words, he looked down into her eyes. "Then what the heck is a good enough reason?" he snapped.

Wynn soothed his temper with a quick hug. "When you hit on the right reason, I'll let you know." she promised. It was encouragement of a sort and Matthew hugged her back, wondering what reason she thought was good enough.

Just then, Todd and Sarah returned in the rowboat with a mess of fish and a large turtle. They ate the fish for breakfast along with some hush puppies and put the turtle on to cook for later. They spent the rest of the day catching crabs and fishing. They swam when they got hot and took a nap when they grew sleepy in the middle of the afternoon.

By Sunday morning, they had had enough of eating crabs and fish and loaded up to go home. They had a couple of tubs full of live crabs to take back for the Negroes. On the way back, they ran across a couple of big rattlesnakes, which Matthew shot but left the skins to Todd.

Chapter 34

They arrived home to find the Negroes in a minor uproar. In their absence, a pack of wolves had raided both the O'Mally plantation and Matthew's farm. Lum, armed with his sawed off shotgun, had managed to run them off the plantation but they had gotten into Matthew's flock of chickens and wiped out half of them before Willy finally drove them off by banging on a tin pan. "That's the first I've ever heard of there being any wolves around here." Matthew said.

"There's still a few packs left, especially in the scrub but there hasn't been many around here since the army was in this area during the Seminole war." Wynn explained. "How many were there?" she asked Lum.

Lum scratched his woolly head thoughtfully. "Eight or ten I guesses, I'se too busy shootin' to be countin'." he answered. "It be too dark to be seein' much." he added.

"Well, maybe it's a one time thing. I reckon if they come back, me and you'll have to go on us a wolf hunt, Matthew." Todd said.

"Yeah, I suppose so, this time of year with rabies in the area is a bad time for a pack of wolves to move in." Matthew replied.

"Well, we'll just have to keep our eyes and ears open and hope that they don't come back. I got enough to do right now without worrying about them boogers. My corn will be ready by the end of the month." Todd said.

Matthew helped them unload the wagon and then mounted the gray. "I guess I'd better be getting home. I think I'll work my old musket over. I'd feel better if I could get a hold of a decent rifle. A pistol's all right for close range but I sure would like to find me a good repeating rifle." he said.

"Yeah, you and me both. Good guns are scarcer than hen's teeth since the war. The one I brought home with me served me well but I sure would like to get my hands on one of those Spencer's. Maybe when I sell my corn I can get me a good pistol at least." Todd agreed.

Wynn and Sarah, who were inside, came back out, just as Matthew was leaving and stood together on the porch. He looked at the two women standing side by side and thought that they looked like sugar and spice. Amused at the thought, he gave the two a broad grin and waved them goodbye. "I'll see y'all in a couple of days, if not sooner." he said as he rode away.

As it turned out, he saw them sooner. That very night, the wolves came again. Matthew killed two before they got away but sought out Todd early the next morning to plan on a wolf hunt. "Yeah, I heard them howling last night." Todd said. "Did they get any more of your chickens?"

"No, not this time. Did they come on your place?" he asked.

"They came through here but I ain't found any sign of them getting into my stock. I haven't had time to search the woods yet to see if they've been at my cattle. I guess the best thing to do is hunt them at night, they probably den up in the day time." Todd said.

"Yeah, I guess so. I'll meet you here at dark and we'll prowl around for a while. I had Willy bury the two wolves I killed in the sink hole and cover them up with rocks. If they were carrying rabies, I didn't want to take any chances of it getting spread around." Matthew said, with a frown.

Todd scratched his head. "I don't know if it can even be spread that way but I don't believe I'd chance it either. Well, I'll see you tonight. I'll get Ned to fix us up a bunch of torches to take with us. By the way, you know that Wynn's gonna want to go. I'm against it but you know how she is."

"I don't much like the idea either but I guess she'll be alright. She's a better hunter than most men I know." Matthew replied.

Todd grinned. "Yeah, she is at that, she can match me shot for shot in a shooting match, or at least she could before the war. I doubt if she's lost her touch. I'm kind'a glad Sarah's not like that but then Wynn's Wynn and I wouldn't have her any other way." he said.

Matthew grinned in agreement. "Me either." he said.

"Where is she this morning anyway?"

"She went to help one of the women over at Conner cut out a new dress. She said she wanted to go early before it got too hot." Todd replied.

"That's just like her, sewing dresses in the morning and going wolf hunting at night." Matthew said with a laugh.

"Know her pretty good don't you? Tell me something buddy. When are you gonna get around to asking her to marry you?" Todd asked.

"I already did." Matthew informed him. "She turned me down."

Todd looked at him in open surprise. "You're kidding." he stated flatly.

Matthew shook his head. "I'm afraid not."

"What the hell ails that girl?" Todd asked.

"You got me." Matthew said. "I'll see you tonight." He rode off shaking his head.

Todd seriously considered confronting his sister on the subject but decided against it. The two of them would be better off working things out for themselves.

They met that night just after dark and rode through the hammock under the light of a nearly full moon and blazing torches.

In the woods, halfway between the two houses, they stopped in an open space near an oak grove. "The best I can figure," Todd said, "is that they've got them up a regular run. They'll cross my place first, then head up to yours for another crack at them chickens."

"Yeah, kind of looks like it. They ought to come through right around here somewhere. You reckon we'd do better if we put out the torches? I hear wolves won't come in close to where there's fire." Matthew said.

"I think you may be right." Wynn said. "What bothers me is wolves can see better than we can in the dark. It sort of puts us at a disadvantage."

"The moon'll be up good in another hour. We ought to have pretty good light by then." Todd said.

"Why don't we hide in the edge of the hammock, near that abandoned cane field on my place. That way, we have a chance of catching them in the open and we can take better advantage of what moonlight there is." Matthew suggested.

This plan met with both Todd and Wynn's approval. A half-hour later, after picking their way through a thicket, they reached the edge of the hammock and put out the torches. It was a good location. The trees hid them in deep shadow but they were able to look out onto the empty cane field with a fairly good view.

"When I followed their tracks earlier today, they came out just to the right of here." Todd said.

"It's a still night. If they don't catch wind of us or change their habits, we might just get them. I guess there's a chance they might go off to a different area after losing a couple of members of their pack last night." Matthew replied.

"Well, all we can do is settle in and wait and see what happens." put in Todd.

Once the talk had ended, the silence seemed oppressive. Even the usual calls of the night birds seemed subdued and any small sound made by the three waiting hunters seemed magnified. The slightest movement caused the leather in their saddles to creak and any movement of the horses' hooves caused the dry leaves to crackle in a way that sounded explosive in the silence.

The two horses ridden by Matthew and Todd suddenly became restless. Matthew's horse blew noisily and stamped at the ground with a restless front hoof. He reached down to pet the gray's neck soothingly and strained his ears, trying to hear the slightest sound that might be the cause of the horses' alarm. Todd's horse sidestepped and uttered a soft whinny that was answered by Wynn's stallion.

The hair on the back of Matthew's neck prickled, as if he were being watched from behind and he turned carefully in the saddle to look behind him, reaching automatically for the pistol on his hip. His eyes strained to penetrate the darkness but he could see nothing.

Of their own accord, the three horses crowded closer together. The three hunters became aware at the same time of small shuffling sounds in the leaves and bushes in the underbrush that surrounded them.

"Light a torch Wynn!" Matthew hissed.

He had no sooner said it than a match flared in the darkness. The fat lightered torch hissed and flared up, revealing a circle of glowing eyes. The wolves had them surrounded on all sides. They drew back slightly at the sight of fire but kept circling.

Wynn held the torch up high over her head and Todd aimed and fired his musket at a pair of glowing eyes. A wolf dropped with a yelp of pain and lay thrashing on the ground a few seconds, before it was still. Matthew picked off two more with his pistol and the remaining four wolves retreated into the darkness but soon returned. Todd's musket once more boomed, picking off yet another wolf.

Todd's horse suddenly reared up as one of the remaining three ran in to bite at its heels. Todd was caught off balance in the midst of reloading his musket and hit the ground with a thud. Wynn was off her horse in a flash to stand over her brother, holding the torch over him and in front of herself like a shield. Two of the wolves ran off into the night, but the one that had tried to attack Todd's horse came boldly closer. The normal fear of fire seeded to be absent in this one and it sent chills up Matthew's spine. The remaining wolf crouched to

181

spring, and Matthew emptied his pistol at it. He hit the wolf three out of the four times he shot and the wolf lay still a scant four yards from where Todd lay half stunned on the ground.

Wynn knelt beside her brother, just as he was sitting up. "You all right Todd?" she asked.

"Yeah, I'm all right, I landed on my head didn't I? Looks like we're even Matthew, that was some pretty good shooting. Never mind me, Wynn. Get that torch over there and see if that booger broke the skin on my horse." Todd got up and rubbing the back of his head with one hand, went to examine the horse. They looked it over carefully but found no sign of even a scratch.

"That was close." Todd said, with a sigh of relief.

"I'd sure hate to have to shoot her."

"Now ain't you something? You come within an ace of being wolf bait yourself and here you are worrying about the horse." Wynn chided him.

"Well shoot, Wynn, I know I'm all right but if that horse had got one scratch, it'd have to be destroyed. I'd bet my last dollar that that wolf was coming down with rabies." Todd said.

"He's right, Wynn. I'd say the whole pack was behaving a little out of character. I just wish we'd been able to get all of them." Matthew said.

"Well, I doubt if we'll see any more of the other two tonight, I guess we might as well go home." Wynn rubbed the back of her head absently as she said it.

Todd's soft chuckle broke the last of the tension in the air. "What's the matter Wynn, got a headache?" he asked.

She gave him a dirty look. "Yeah, but I bet it's nothing compared with yours." She grinned a little at the last.

"You can say that again." Todd agreed. "We've got enough coffee at the house to make a pot. Sarah's folks brought us a pound they got from Gainesville and I've been saving the last of it for something special. I guess this'll do. Come on home with us and have some, Matthew."

"Good Lord, Todd, if I'd known you had coffee at your place I would have been over there breaking the door down to get at it! I haven't had a good cup of coffee in so long, I've about forgot what it tastes like." Matthew replied.

"Well what are we waiting for? Let's go." Wynn said with

182

enthusiasm.

Chapter 35

When they got back, they found Sarah waiting for them. She'd heard the shots and was anxiously pacing the floor with worry. She hugged Todd with a sigh of relief as he came in the door. "I was worried sick! No wonder Wynn always wants to go along when you go hunting. It sure beats staying home worrying, at least she knows what's happening." Sarah observed.

"You worry too much, woman. How about making us a pot of coffee and we'll tell you all about it." Todd said, rumpling Sarah's blond curls affectionately.

"I can hardly wait." she said. "I've got some blueberry pie to go along with the coffee." She led the way to the kitchen and they followed her gladly.

In a few minutes, the kitchen was filled with the good smell of coffee brewing and Sarah listened with interest as they each gave their own version of the wolf hunt.

When the coffee was done, they each had two cups of it along with a piece of Sarah's blueberry pie. The main topic of conversation of course was the wolf hunt and talk of wolves in general.

Matthew drained his coffee cup to the last drop. "I don't know when I ever enjoyed anything so much. Of all the things that's been in short supply since the war, I reckon I've missed coffee the most." he said.

"Me too." Todd agreed. "It may keep us up all night though, since we're not used to drinking it anymore."

"I don't even care." Matthew stated. "I reckon I'd better go home though and give it a try. Tomorrow's another day." He stood up to leave. "Thanks again for the coffee and pie." he said.

"I'll walk you to the door." Wynn said and followed him to the porch.

As soon as the door was shut behind them, Wynn reached for his hand. "Thank you Matthew." she said softly.

"For what?" he asked.

"For saving me and Todd from that wolf." she answered.

Matthew gave her hand a tug and pulled her into his arms. "I just shot a wolf, that's all. What was I supposed to do? Let it get at the two people I care the most for in this world?" he asked.

She gave him a hard tug and moved back a little to look up at him. She reached up to trace the line of his jaw with her finger. "Do you care for me, Matthew?" she asked softly.

"Don't you know that by now?" he asked. She shook her head and teased his lips with her fingertips.

"What will it take to convince you?" Matthew asked. He pulled her tight against him, resting his cheek against her soft hair. He felt her shake her head mutely against his shoulder.

Matthew breathed a long sigh. "Honey, I want to marry you and I think you know that I would gladly die for you. I don't know what it is you want from me." he said a little sadly.

Wynn made a soft sound in her throat that was a little like a laugh. "You're talking all around it Matthew but you're getting close."

He rested his chin on her head and stared off into the night for a moment, puzzled by her words. "I don't know any other way to tell you that I love you." he said at last.

Her arms tightened around him. "There, was that so hard?" she asked.

Matthew drew back to look down at her. "Is that what you wanted to hear? That I love you. I thought you knew that." He was still more than a little bewildered.

"I needed to hear you say it." Wynn replied.

"It doesn't come easy for me Wynn. I never said those words to another living soul in my entire life." Matthew admitted.

"Not even your wife?" Wynn asked incredulously.

"No, never." he answered.

"But Matthew, don't you see? That's the only good reason there is for getting married. I told you that when you hit on the right reason I'd let you know. It's so simple, you love me and I love you. That's the only reason there can be." Wynn said seriously.

A trembling set in that shook his body from head to toe at her words and his voice quaked with it when he spoke. "No one ever said those words to me either Wynn. I'd like to hear you say them again."

Wynn hugged him tight and repeated the words over and over as she rained kisses on his face. She stopped at last at his lips, kissing them long and passionately. She drew back and repeated them once again. "I love you Matthew Kendall." she said with feeling.

Matthew's trembling hadn't stopped. "Then you will marry me?" he asked.

"I will." she replied simply.

"Tomorrow?" he asked.

Wynn's sweet laughter rang out in the night. "Yes tomorrow. Right now if I could. The sooner the better."

"Be ready the first thing in the morning. I don't want to wait for a big ceremony and I certainly don't want a shivalree. Woman, I've waited for you to be mine about as long as I can stand." Matthew stated honestly.

"I don't care about the frills either Matthew. I just want you." Wynn said softly.

Her words set him on fire and he kissed her passionately. Her slim body trembled as she pressed more closely against him. In spite of their mutual need, she at last drew away from him. "We've waited this long." she said breathlessly. "I guess we can wait just a little longer."

"I guess we'll have to." Matthew replied.

"Will you go in with me to tell Todd and Sarah? I'd like for them to be our witnesses. We don't dare just elope. Todd would kill both of us." Wynn said.

"I'll go with you, just give me a minute though, I can't go in there like this." Matthew said with a laugh.

Wynn blushed scarlet in the darkness but gave him the time he needed.

Todd and Sarah were still seated at the kitchen table when they came back inside, hand in hand, "I thought you'd done gone." Todd said to Matthew.

"Not quite." Matthew said, with a grin. "I figured I'd better come back in and tell you that your sister and I are running away to Ocala first thing in the morning. She's consented to be my wife."

Todd's eyes lit up and the fact that he was pleased with the news showed in his smile. "Hell, it's about dog-gone time. I'd about given up on you two." he exclaimed.

Sarah gave a squeal of surprise and was across the room in a flash to give them both a hug. "People don't usually tell it, if they're planning to run away but I'm glad you did." she said happily.

"We'd like for you two to come along, it won't be a fancy

185

wedding but I'd like for you to be there." Wynn said.

Todd slapped Matthew on the back in a gesture of brotherly affection. "If someone's going to marry my sister, then I'm real glad it's going to be you." he said sincerely.

Matthew laughed as a wave of pure happiness swept over him. "I bet when you were sitting with me in that holding pen in Georgia, you never figured, I'd ever be your brother-in-law." he said.

"No, I can't say that I did. If I recall, it seems like I told you that my sister was too wild for any man to tame." Todd answered and laughed.

Wynn shot her brother a look but Matthew only grinned and gave her an affectionate hug. "I don't want to tame her. The South will rise again but it's going to be a long haul. I need a woman that will pull with me, not against me." he said sincerely.

Wynn looked up at him, obviously pleased by his words. "I'm just me, Matthew." she said simply.

"That's why I love you." he replied.

It was not until much later as Matthew rode home, that he noticed the change in the atmosphere. The night had become more oppressively hot and there was a sultry stillness to the air, making it seem heavy and hard to breathe. The three-quarter moon hung low over the hammock and was encircled by a ring of white light. The sky overhead seemed to be lit from behind with a greenish glow. Only a few hours ago when they were hunting, the sky was clear, except for a few drifting clouds.

Matthew felt a growing tension within himself that had nothing to do with his plans to marry Wynn. He shook the feeling off literally, with a shake of his body in the way that a dog shakes off water. The feeling of oppression fled from him as quickly as it had come and he felt a lightness in his heart. Tomorrow, no today, for it was past midnight, would be his wedding day. A feeling of utter elation swept through him and he kicked the gray into a trot.

In spite of the two cups of coffee and his high running emotions, Matthew slept. He awakened before daylight and went out to feed the stock and hitch up the wagon. By the time these tasks were completed, he was hot and sticky and went to draw water from the well.

It would be at least another hour before Willy and Lissa would be arriving to start their day's work. This would give him ample time and privacy to bathe and get ready go. He stripped naked on the open porch and lathered his body from head to foot and rinsed by pouring a whole bucket of water over himself. He allowed his body to dry by itself as he lathered his face and shaved with more care than usual. He threw the dirty water into the yard and gathered up the clothes he had taken off. A sudden gust of wind swept over his body. It felt fresh and almost cold as it rattled the leaves in the top of the palm trees and whispered through the pines with a hiss. It was gone as quickly as it had come, leaving behind it a stillness in the air. Matthew shrugged and went into the house to dress.

He arrived at Todd's just as the sun rose over the tops of the trees in the hammock. Small black clouds drifted swiftly across the sky as if driven by a high wind, while everything below remained deathly still.

Todd met him in the front yard as he drove up in the wagon. "Mornin' Matthew. It's a good thing we're getting an early start. From the looks of that sky, I'd say we're in for one hell of a big blow. I sure hope we make it back before it hits." Todd's voice held a note of apprehension.

Matthew got down from the wagon. "Good morning to you too." he said and laughed. "You think it's going to storm?" he asked.

"Yeah, it's bound to. It's a little early in the season but I can feel it coming. I just hope it doesn't flatten my cane and it'll be another week before the corn's ready. "

Matthew could hear the worry in Todd's voice. "Surely it won't be that bad." he said.

"You ain't never been in one of our Florida storms before. They can get mean and from the looks of things, this one's gonna be a big one." Todd eyed the sky with a worried look.

"Well, there's nothing we can do about the weather." Matthew said philosophically.

"I guess not." Todd said and a grin brightened his face. "You sure as hell picked a good time to get married, what with a blow coming and all. But then since it's Wynn you're marryin', I guess I shouldn't be surprised. Nothing much that girl does is ordinary." he said with a laugh.

Matthew returned Todd's grin. "That's the truth. You reckon you could hurry those two up? If we're in for a storm I'd like to get back home before it starts."

Todd gave Matthew a knowing look. "Sometimes these things last for three days at a time. Maybe you didn't pick such a bad time to get married after all. There's a lot to be said for being penned up in a cozy house during a storm, with the right person." He grinned and gave Matthew a wink.

"Now you're talking." Matthew said with a grin.

"Yeah." said Todd. "It is an interesting idea at that but if them two don't come on, we'll be spending three days paying rent in a room at the Ocala House. I'll go see if I can find out what's keeping them."

"Maybe you'd better." Matthew agreed.

Todd went inside to see what was keeping Sarah and Wynn, while Matthew stayed behind to restlessly pace the yard. He'd crossed the yard no more than twice, when Lum, Pearl and Ned arrived. Pearl and Ned gave him a curious once over when they told him good morning but went on about their business. Lum lingered.

"Lawsy Massa, where it is you gwine off to dis time ob de day?" You done dress up like it be mighty 'portant. Mus' be you gwine go and it gwine stoam." Lum looked him up and down as he spoke.

"You've got that right Lum, it is mighty important. I'm on my way to Ocala to get married. Miss Wynn has finally accepted my proposal." Matthew answered.

Lum's eyes, along with his whole face lit up. "Glory be!" he exclaimed.

Before Matthew even knew what was happening, the big black man had him in a bear hug and was laughing with delight. Matthew returned Lum's hug with equal enthusiasm. Careful Lum, you hug me any harder and Miss Wynn'll have to get her someone else to marry." he said, with a laugh.

Lum stepped back but left his hands on Matthew's shoulders in a gesture of brotherly affection. He gave Matthew a good-natured shaking, laughing all the while.

"Massa, you done be de slowes' one white man I ebber see. 'Bout time you gets yo' mind made up."

"It was her mind that took getting made up Lum. I wish there was some way you could go along with us but you know how it is. We didn't decide on all this until late last night and then we decided to make it simple." Matthew explained.

"Las' night? I thought you done be gone huntin' dem wolves."

"We did Lum. There's about six of them that won't be bothering

188

us anymore. That reminds me, something's got to be done with them. I forgot all about them with the excitement going on about getting married."

"I takes care dem suckahs Massa, what you want done?" Lum asked.

"Lord, that's something else I forgot. Willy and Lissa don't know a thing about all this. I tell you what. Go over to my place and tell them where I've gone and Willy knows what to do with the wolves. They're in the woods next to that empty cane field."

"I do jus' dat." Lum agreed.

Chapter 36

At that moment Wynn and Sarah came out of the house. Matthew couldn't take his eyes off Wynn. The dress she wore was white, though not a wedding dress. The full skirt of the dress emphasized her tiny waist and the plunging neckline showed off her neck and shoulders to perfection. She wore a matching hat with a tiny veil that covered no more than her forehead and it was set at a saucy angle atop her elaborately arranged hair.

She seemed to drift across the weathered boards of the porch as effortlessly as the patches of white clouds were drifting across the Florida sky. Without realizing that he had moved, Matthew walked across the yard to meet her. She held out a white gloved hand to him and when he took it, she lowered her eyes for a moment, then looked straight into his own. The smile in her eyes was slowly matched with the one on her lips. It began with a slow tilting up at the corners of her mouth and grew into the familiar warm grin. For a few seconds, Matthew stood transfixed by her beauty, before giving her assistance that she really didn't need down the porch steps. For a moment in time, no one existed but the two of them. Matthew gradually became aware of Todd and Sarah, who stood hand in hand, looking on in pleased amusement. Todd met his eyes and laughed. "If you two want to tie the knot before the storm hits, we'd better get a move on." he said.

Soon, they were in the wagon and on their way.

They reached Ocala in time to have dinner before going to seek out the preacher. The Ocala House was a two storied wooden building with wide columned verandas. The meal was served at a large table laden with the finest food available. Though the meal was delicious and the conversation around the table lively, they didn't linger any longer than necessary.

Leaving the hotel, they stepped out into the dusty street and paused for a quick look at the weather. While they were inside, the ominous green glow in the sky had darkened and was gradually being replaced by a solid grayness that stretched from horizon to horizon. "I don't like the looks of that sky." Wynn said. "I'd say the storm will hit just before dark."

"I think you're right." Todd agreed. I don't want to try to run your business, but if I was you. I'd go right across the street to the courthouse and find me a Justice of the Peace. By the time we find the preacher, we'll have used up a good bit of time."

"What do you think, Wynn?" Matthew asked.

"Todd's right." she replied. "I sort of had my heart set on the preacher, he's a fine man with a good sense of humor, but he does tend to get a bit long winded. The way he likes to talk, we'd be a couple of hours getting away from him and it could get us caught in the storm."

Matthew grinned good-naturedly. "Then the Justice of the Peace it is." he said. Wynn took his arm and they crossed the street to the courthouse.

The ceremony was brief and in less than half an hour, Matthew and Wynn left the courthouse accompanied by Todd and Sarah.

"Well, how does it feel to be a married man again?" Todd asked.

Matthew grinned. "I guess it hasn't sunk in yet." he replied.

Wynn laughed. "Do you suppose we just dreamed it? It doesn't seem possible that something that important could be accomplished with just a few words and a piece of paper."

"Yeah, I know the feeling." Todd said. His face grew serious and he reached to shake Matthew's hand. "Congratulations buddy." he said sincerely. He gave his sister a warm hug and she smiled at him happily.

Sarah hugged them both and Todd for good measure. "If you two are as happy as me and Todd, you'll do fine." she said.

Even as they stood in front of the courthouse talking, the sky was darkening. Although it was still early afternoon. it was almost as dim as evening. Matthew glanced up at the sky and gave Wynn's shoulders a brief squeeze. "Let's go home." he said simply.

In spite of the darkening sky overhead and the eerie stillness, the trip home was made in record time and their spirits ran high. Not only because of the happy occasion but from something bred of the atmosphere itself. The impending storm generated a feeling of excitement, so that even while dreading it they felt an intense sense of anticipation. The approaching hurricane seemed to have a strange effect on every living creature and the mules pulled the wagon with unaccustomed speed as if they were in a hurry to reach the shelter of the stable. On the short trip from Ocala to Silver Spring, they saw at least half a dozen snakes crossing the road. Even the birds seemed restless and were behaving abnormally. Blue jays, usually only seen in pairs, flocked together and flew back and forth between the trees.

"Look at them Matthew, they know a storm's coming. I don't believe it, there's a bat in broad day light!" Wynn exclaimed.

"Strange, isn't it?" Matthew replied. "I've never seen anything like it."

"I reckon not." Todd said. "I guess these storms didn't reach up into Georgia where you come from. Look up yonder." He pointed to the sky. "That's sea birds up there. They usually don't come this far inland. It's a sign of some really bad weather." Todd cracked the whip over the heads of the mules to hurry them along.

When they reached the O'Mally plantation, the sky was covered with black clouds. There was a strange brightness that came not from the sun but from a kind of eerie green glow. Lum and Ned had all the windows boarded up and everything loose in the yard had either been put up or tied down.

Todd and Sarah got quickly down from the wagon and Sarah dashed immediately into the house. "I'll bring your bag, Wynn. You two better hurry, you can get the rest of your things later." She called over her shoulder as she ran. She returned a few minutes later and handed Wynn's bag up to her, "I threw in a few more things I thought you might need. It may be a couple of days before you get back here, if this blow turns out to be as bad as it looks like it could." she said.

"Thanks Sarah. Y'all take care now." Wynn said.

As they drove out of the yard they heard a bull gator bellowing. Matthew's rooster was crowing in the false twilight and could easily be heard from two miles away. Driven by a sense of urgency, Matthew cracked the whip over the mules' heads and they broke into

191

an unaccustomed trot.

The first gust of wind came just as they entered the lane that led to Matthew's house. It began with a muffled roaring far across the hammock and increased in sound as it drew nearer. Where Matthew and Wynn sat on the seat of the wagon, the air was still but a half-mile away, the palm trees and pines were bending half way to the ground with the force of the wind. Matthew cracked the whip over the mules once more as the roar grew louder. In spite of his effort to hurry, the roaring northeast wind caught them. It hissed through the pine trees and tore limbs off the oaks as it passed. Dirt from the road stung their faces and hands. The mules lowered their heads against the force of the wind but kept going. The gust of wind was gone as quickly as it had come and left behind it an even greater stillness than before.

Moments later, they reached the yard and Matthew was down off the wagon in a flash reaching up to help Wynn. "Get in the house." he commanded. "I'll be in as soon as I put up the team."

Wynn ran into the house long enough to put her bag away but was right back out. She helped him unhitch the wagon and put up the team in spite of her white dress and his protests.

"It looks like Willy done a good job of getting ready for the storm. I see he got the windows boarded up. I wonder if he thought to get your hogs out from under that oak tree," Wynn said, as they shut the stable door.

"Oh Lord, the hogs. Run see while I find something to nail up across this door!" Matthew said.

Wynn ran around the house and up the trail to the hog pen, her white skirt billowed around her as she ran.

"They're still in the pen and the chickens too." she told him when she got back.

"It'll take us three hours to get all of those hogs and chickens caught up. I don't think we've got that long." Matthew said grimly.

"Matthew, we gotta try. Those hogs are worth a lot of money."

Matthew finished nailing the board up across the stable door. "Yeah, I guess we'll have to. Go change clothes and we'll see what we can do."

"What about you? You can't round up hogs and chickens in your good suit." Wynn pointed out.

"I got a better idea. I'm just gonna turn them loose. The chickens can do the best they can and the hogs'll go straight under the house." Matthew said with a grin.

Wynn laughed. "Why didn't I think of that? I don't need to change clothes to open up a couple of pens. I wonder if there's plenty of fire wood and extra water drawed up."

"You go check on the water, I know there's plenty of firewood. I'll go let the hogs and chickens out." Matthew said.

The water buckets as well as the dishpan and several big pots were also filled. Wynn ran back outside to see if Matthew needed any help. He was just coming back from the hog pen and she met him half way to open the gate on the chicken pen. Is there anything else we need to do?" he asked.

"Not that I can think of." she replied. "I guess we're about as secure as we're gonna get. We might as well go on in. Lissa made supper for us."

They walked hand in hand to the front porch and stopped to watch the weather. As they watched, a great roaring began once more in the northeast. The mighty wind carried the rain with it this time as it swept across the hammock. While they watched, it topped a great oak and bent the pines halfway over and scattered palm trees in it's path. The rain, driven along with it, slanted at an acute angle, like a lace curtain in a high gale.

Before the storm reached the yard, they hurried inside and shut the door behind them. Just as Matthew fastened the latch the wind hit the house. It shuddered and seemed to sigh but was built to last.

"I bet we lost some shingles then." Wynn said, matter-of-factly.

The house was almost as dark as night with the windows boarded up but Wynn could still make out Matthew's smile. "Yeah, I bet *we* did." he said, with emphasis on the 'we'.

Wynn realized the significance of the word 'we' and came into his arms. Matthew held her tight, savoring the feel of her warm body in his arms. She drew away enough to raise her lips for a kiss and he eagerly obliged her. The storm outside was forgotten as a storm began to rage within himself. His senses were filled with the feel of her firm young body dressed in satin and lace and with a scent of her that was like cinnamon and cloves.

A gust of wind slammed against the door on which Matthew was leaning, so hard that he felt the pressure against his back. He raised his head, startled at the intensity of tumult going on outside. The

193

drumming of the rain on the cedar shingles of the roof made a sound that filled his head, seeming to make thinking difficult. He became aware of the rattling of the windows and the banging of a loose board somewhere on the other side of the house. He stood listening, with his head cocked to one side. The tumult of the wind and rain drowned out the rumble of the thunder so that he heard it as no more than a muffled booming. It was not unlike the sound of far off cannon fire.

Wynn moved away from him restlessly and went to peek out through a gap in the boards that covered the window. Matthew came to join her and bent to look also. The world outside was transformed as if it was gripped in the hands of an angry god. A solid curtain of rain, driven by the raging winds seemed to scour the earth. Trees and bushes leaned and bent with the force of it and whipped about as if shaken by a mighty hand. Matthew was fascinated and the immense power of the great storm filled him with a sense of excitement. A rush of adrenaline swept into his system as in the face of great danger, accelerating his heartbeat and sharpening his senses. He found the feeling familiar. It was the same as the feeling that had gripped him each time he had gone into battle.

Wynn left his side and went to light a lamp. Even inside, the air seemed restless and disturbed. The flame in the lamp wavered on the wick as if it were dancing to the rhythm of the storm outside. It dispelled the darkness in the room and caused shadows to dance on the walls and ceiling.

"Come to the kitchen, Matthew. I'll warm up supper." Wynn said.

"I'm not really hungry but I suppose since Lissa's already got it cooked, it'd be a shame to waste it. I wonder if she and Willy are alright. That shack's not built as strong as this house." Matthew said, with concern.

"I wouldn't worry too much, Matthew. We build things here in Florida with the hurricanes in mind. This place has been through a couple of big blows already and stood it all right. We had one here a couple of years ago that was worse than this one." Wynn removed the hat pins from her small white hat as she talked and laid it aside.

"You reckon this'll destroy Todd's crop?" Matthew asked.

"He'll probably have to harvest the corn as soon as this is over but it should be alright. The cane's what's in danger but if it don't get flattened to the ground it may be all right too. We lost our cane two years ago. At any rate there's nothing we can do." Wynn shrugged and gave him an optimistic smile.

She blew out the lamp and Matthew went to open the door that led to the breezeway. He paused with his hand on the knob. "You ready?" he asked.

"As I'll ever be." she replied.

Chapter 37

The force of the wind caught the door as he opened it, almost tearing it from his grasp. They stepped out onto the covered breezeway and Matthew closed the door behind him with great difficulty. Wynn preceded him, crossing the breezeway. She was bent against the force of the wind and pelted by the blowing rain. He dashed across the open space to open the kitchen door ahead of her, feeling the pull of the wind against his body with every step. The kitchen door was pulled out of his hands as he turned the knob. It swung inward and slammed into the wall with a bang. They stepped quickly inside and Matthew closed the door by putting his whole weight against it.

The room was almost as dark as night and he lit a lamp and set it down on the kitchen table. The blowing rain had dampened their clothing and Wynn wiped beads of moisture from her face. The elaborate coils of her hair had loosened in the wind and wet tendrils stuck to her face and neck. Matthew located the kitchen towel and handed it to her. She dried her face and arms and instead of handing the towel back to him, she carefully dried his face herself. Pleased by her care, Matthew captured her hand and kissed it before pulling her warm, damp body into his arms.

She melted against him, hugging him almost fiercely and returned his kisses with a passion that matched his own. Her tongue met his half way, sending liquid fire through his veins and setting his heart to pounding. The familiar ache began in his loins and he slid his hands down her satin clad back, pulling her closer still. A small moan of pleasure began deep in his chest and escaped half muffled by her mouth on his. To his disappointment, she broke the kiss and looked up at him with eyes that held both desire and fear. "If you keep that up, we never will get around to supper." she warned.

"Right now, supper isn't what's on my mind. But if you're hungry, we'll eat." he said. Matthew released her and went to build up the fire in the stove, ignoring as best he could the fire in his body. He doubted that Wynn was any hungrier than he was. Her insistence on having supper was nothing more than an excuse to delay going to bed. There was no doubt in his mind that she wanted him but her desire was dampened by her fear of the unknown. He'd waited for her so long that he felt he could hardly wait any longer. Drawing in a deep breath, he released it slowly. He too was beginning to feel nervous; he wanted their wedding night to be perfect for her, yet worried that his self-control was up to the amount of patience that she needed and deserved.

He closed the door of the firebox and adjusted the damper before turning to face Wynn. She was standing beside the table twisting her hands but dropped them quickly to her sides. She seemed to give herself a little shake and went to the stove, where she began lifting pot lids.

"Look at this Matthew. Lissa must have gone to an awful lot of trouble. She even fried a chicken. And did you notice, she put flowers on the table?" Wynn said, a little too brightly.

"Yes, that's nice." Matthew answered.

He crossed the room to stare out the window at the storm. Her nervousness was beginning to rub off on him and he sought for something to say that would get their minds off of the night to come. He suddenly felt awkward and tongue-tied. It was a feeling he had never experienced in Wynn's company before.

True night was beginning to fall and as it grew darker, the storm seemed to lessen somewhat in intensity. Matthew turned away from the window and just to keep himself busy, he lit another lamp and a couple of candles. He moved the two lamps to different locations to better light the big kitchen and arranged the two candles next to the bouquet Lissa had arranged on the table.

Wordlessly, Wynn gave him a shy smile and began setting the table. Among his scant supply of dinnerware, not two plates matched but she placed them on the table as carefully as if they were the finest of china. She arranged the plates on opposite sides of the table and Matthew waited until her back was turned to arrange them side by side. She emptied the pots on the stove into bowls and as she came to set them on the table, she noticed what he had done. Her pleased smile quickly grew into a laugh. "Whoever heard of having a wedding supper in the middle of a hurricane?" she giggled.

"Maybe we'll start a new trend. Next time I run of to get married, I think I'll do it the same way." Matthew said with a laugh.

Wynn placed her hands on her hips and glared at him in pretended outrage. "Next time? Matthew Kendall, there ain't going to be a next time, so you'd better eat your supper!"

Matthew laughed. "Giving me orders are you? I'm beginning to feel like a married man already." he said with a grin.

"You're darn right." Wynn laughed but turned serious almost immediately. "Call it a request Matthew, there's no giving or taking of orders in a partnership."

Matthew pulled a chair away from the table and held it for her while she sat down. "In that case, I shall honor your request as stated and suggest that you dine as well." He purposely made his voice as courtly and formal as possible.

Wynn laughed but continued the game. "Why thank you sir. I would be pleased to."

Matthew took the chair beside her, laughing heartily as he sat down. "Madam, would you do me the honor of passing the beans?" he asked.

"Of course sir." Wynn replied formally but found it impossible to keep a straight face. She passed the bowl of beans to him as one would pass a royal dish.

Matthew helped himself to the beans and passed them back to her. She in turn passed him the corn bread.

"There was a time when such talk was all I heard. I can't believe that I spent so much of my time being so formal." Matthew said.

"Matthew, you didn't actually talk that way, did you?" Wynn asked incredulously.

He reached for a piece of chicken and shrugged. "No, of course not. Not that bad anyway but I did talk a lot different. My mother would've had a case of the vapors if she'd heard me use the word ain't."

"Why and when did you stop talking that way?" Wynn asked.

"The war." he stated flatly. "There wasn't any room for such formality. We were in too dire straits to worry about sounding like gentlemen. Out of it all, there was one good thing. It was the first time in my life I'd ever been allowed to be myself. It doesn't take

197

very many nights of sleeping in the mud to make a man realize that he's no different than any other man."

"I don't think I'd have liked you very much before the war." Wynn said honestly.

"I don't either but I didn't know any other way." Matthew replied.

Wynn smiled and reached to cover his hand with hers. "I love you just the way you are."

Matthew squeezed her hand and leaned to kiss her check. "I'm just a man." he said simply.

"My man." she corrected.

Neither of them ate very much and the meal was soon finished. Wynn washed the dishes after tying on an apron over her dress. When she was finished, Matthew untied the apron and hung it on a peg. "Time to brave the storm again." he said. He blew out both the lamps and the candles and they crossed the breezeway once more.

As soon as the lamp was lit in the front room, Wynn stood awkwardly for a few seconds. She brushed at the beads of water on her skirt self-consciously. "I...suppose I should get ready for bed." she said in a small voice.

Matthew gave her an indulgent smile and kissed her lightly on the forehead. "Take your time, I'll be along in a little while."

Wynn lit a candle to light her way to the bedroom and Matthew heard the door close quietly behind her. He paced the room a couple of times as restlessly as a caged animal, then sat down tensely on the settee to wait. In a few minutes, he heard the bedroom door open once more and Wynn softly called his name.

She stood half way in and half out of the bedroom door and gave him a sheepish grin. "I'm stuck Matthew. There's about a hundred buttons down the back of this dress and I can't reach them."

"Here, I'll do it. Turn around." he said. The buttons were indeed small and tedious and unbuttoning the dress was easier said than done. "Move closer to the light, I can't see what I'm doing." he complained.

Wynn moved out of the doorway and went to stand with her back to the candle. With unsteady hands, Matthew struggled with the row of tiny buttons until they were at last all undone. The gap left between the buttons and holes left bare only a strip of skin on her shoulders. The rest was hidden by her lacy undergarment. Unable to resist, Matthew parted the dress an inch more and kissed the back of her neck. She gave a small gasp and stepped away from him as if he had burned her and turned to look at him with frightened eyes. In her loosened dress and with her disheveled hair, she looked more like a frightened child than grown woman. The fear in her eyes hurt Matthew and he held out his hands to her.

"Wynn, come here. Don't be afraid of me." he pleaded softly.

Seeing the pain in his eyes, Wynn came quickly to take his outstretched hand. Her eyes sought a spot over his head and she refused to meet his gaze.

"I...I might not please you." she stammered.

Matthew let go of her hands to hold her face gently between his palms and forced her to look into his eyes. "Honey, there's no way you couldn't please me." he said sincerely.

"But Matthew," she started to say.

"Shh-hush." he commanded. One by one, he removed the long pins from her hair until it tumbled down her back like a curtain of black silk. He held her face in his hands once more and gently pressed his lips to hers.

Her soft mouth seemed to quiver against his own and she raised a hand to cup his cheek. As the kiss deepened, Matthew felt the tension drain from her body. Her hand slid down to caress his neck and drew from him a gasp of pleasure. For a second the kiss was broken but he reclaimed her lips instantly and pulled her tighter against him. His hands eagerly sought the bare skin on her back as he plunged his tongue more deeply into her mouth.

He became aware of her fingers tugging at the buttons of his shirt and leaned back to give her room Shyly, she undid the first two buttons and then another. Her hand sought the skin on his chest and she softly ran her fingers through the mat of hair that covered it. She looked into his eyes with no trace of fear.

With hands that trembled, Matthew eased her dress off her shoulders and once past them, it dropped to the floor. The lacy chemise that still covered her upper body was closed with a series of tiny pink ribbons and he untied them one by one. Reverently, he slid the garment from her shoulders, reveling in the sight of her bare breasts. Before he could touch her again, she reached to slide his shirt from him and let it drop to the floor. In wonder, he caressed her, feeling her softness responding to his touch. She gasped with pleasure and with one hand untied two tiny ribbons at her waist. She stood before him naked and unashamed.

"You are so beautiful." he exclaimed. He filled his eyes with the sight of her before turning to blow out the candle. He quickly removed his pants and shoes and joined her on the bed.

She came into his arms eagerly but grew tense and afraid when he pulled her close to his aroused body. Drawing on patience that he didn't know that he had, Matthew slowly stroked and soothed her until she was once more relaxed and unafraid. He caressed her more intimately until her body began to tremble beneath his hands. By now, Matthew ached with need and was dangerously close to the point of no return. When her hand came to rest on his thigh, there was no way out. His need was great and the time without was too long. He knew that if she touched him, he would explode and at this point, he didn't care. He needed her touch and the release it would bring, with a desperation that was beyond shame. As if she had read his mind, her hand crept higher and her tentative touch brought a cry from him that startled her. She started to move her hand away but he captured it pressing her fingers hard against him. She touched him hesitantly at first, then more boldly. Wynn felt it happening a split second before it began and her fingers tightened instinctively around him. Matthew heard his own cry of pleasure as if it had come from some throat other than his own. In a few precious seconds his body grew limp with relief.

He felt Wynn move beside him as she propped her head up on one hand. "Matthew?" she whispered questioningly.

He reached for her in the darkness, drawing her close to his side. "I did something wrong." she whispered apologetically.

Matthew laughed softly and hugged her tightly. "You did something very right. I know you don't understand all this but you just gave me something very special. I can't love you the way I want to if I'm too far gone to wait for you "

Wynn kissed his shoulder softly. "You're right, I don't understand, but you'll teach me won't you." she said.

"We'll teach each other." Matthew replied. He got up from the bed and fumbled in the darkness for a match to light the candle.

"Where are you going?" Wynn asked.

Matthew gave a small laugh as the match flared. "If you must know, I'm sticky. I'm going to go wash."

Wynn giggled. "I didn't get to bathe either. We could go wash in the rain." she suggested.

"Woman, you're crazy! Whoever heard of taking a bath in a hurricane?"' Matthew asked incredulously.

"Listen Matthew. The wind's died down, it shouldn't be that bad out there now." Wynn argued.

Matthew stood for a moment listening. "I believe you're right. Let's go before it picks up again." His mind was suddenly filled with the memory of another stormy night when he had watched awe-struck from an upstairs window as Wynn danced in the rain. He felt his body responding to the memory and the sight of Wynn rising naked from the bed. He held the candle with one hand and took hers with the other. They made their way through the darkened house to the breezeway and stepped out into the brisk wind.

The candle was blown out instantly and they stepped out into the heavily falling rain. The yard was ankle deep in water and the wind driven rain was cold on their skin. Wynn had picked up a bar of soap from the washstand on the way out and they lathered each other leisurely under the shelter of the breezeway, before stepping back out into the rain to rinse. They hugged each other against the chill of the wind. "I'm freezing." Wynn complained.

They went back inside and made their way to the bedroom in the darkness. Matthew dried Wynn's body carefully with the towel from the washstand. He lingered over the task, enjoying it to the fullest. When he was done, Wynn returned the favor, caressing his body as she dried him. Still slightly chilled from the wind and rain they returned to the bed and snuggled close for warmth.

Chapter 38

Matthew explored Wynn's body slowly, caressing every inch of her and showering her with kisses. Her response was like wildfire as she returned his caresses. As their passion built, he touched her more intimately and she responded to his touch with a moan of pleasure. He continued until she pulled him over her with a whimper of need. Carefully, he lowered himself to her, not yet seeking entry. He kissed her and as his tongue entered her mouth, she thrust her hips against him. Their bodies came naturally into perfect alignment and he pressed slowly into her, until he was stopped by the barrier of her

201

virginity. Fearful of hurting her, he paused. Wynn's hands slid down his back and she moaned, breaking the kiss as her fingernails dug into his hips. "Now!" she insisted, between clinched teeth. He drew back a little and in a split second, their union was complete. "You all right?" he asked.

"Um huh. Don't stop." Wynn moved restlessly against him. Matthew began to move, slowly at first, then faster as he began to sense that her need matched his own. She suddenly stiffened and the waves of her pleasure surrounded him. She cried out his name and went limp for a second. He began to move once more and she gasped with renewed pleasure. Her arms tightened around him and he felt himself exploding, merging with her as their very essences united into one. He collapsed on top of her but when he would have rolled away, she held him fast.

"Did I hurt you?" he asked.

"Not much. Matthew, I never dreamed it was like that." Wynn replied in awe.

Matthew rolled off her then and drew her head onto his shoulder. "Me either." he admitted.

"But you've done it before." Wynn said, without thinking.

"Never was it ever like tonight." he said, with feeling.

Wynn settled herself more comfortably against his side. "The wind's stopped, the eye of the storm must be over us." she said with a yawn. Matthew didn't answer and with a contented sigh, she too fell asleep.

The returning fury of the storm, once the eye had passed over, awakened Matthew. He had not slept overly long but very deeply, so that he awakened gradually. In spite of the storm that raged outside, he felt filled with an inner peace. A sense of deep joy swept over him as he became aware of the girl that slept at his side. She had rolled away from him and lay on her back. For the time being, he was content to simply lay quietly beside her, just knowing that she was there and that she belonged to him.

All along, almost from the first time he had seen her, he had sensed the fire in her. Yet nothing had prepared him for the reality of it. It was wrong for him to compare her with Elizabeth but in the privacy of his own thoughts, he found it impossible not to. They were as different as fire and ice, these two women. Elizabeth had given herself to him out of nothing more than a sense of duty. Wynn, on the other hand, once her fears were overcome, had given herself without reserve. She possessed a sensuality that was beyond his wildest dreams.

Matthew drew in a long breath as his body responded to his heated thoughts. Though the sharpest edge was taken from his long years of pent up desire, he found himself needing her again with an intensity that surprised him. He wondered if he would ever get his fill of her firm young body.

Turning on his side, he threw back the tangled covers and reached for her in the darkness. Leisurely, he explored the plains and curves of her sleeping body, lingering over her small but shapely breasts. Even in her sleep, they responded to his touch. She stirred slightly but didn't awaken as he pressed a palm against the flat hard plain of her stomach. Suddenly hungry for the taste of her, he lowered his head to her breast, drinking in the sweetness of her. She awakened with a soft moan of pleasure and her arms reached to encircle him. Her fingers twined in his hair, pressing his head more firmly against her. He abandoned her breast for the greater sweetness of her mouth. Without breaking the kiss, he rolled over on his back, taking her with him so that she lay half on top of him.

Wynn nipped his lips with her teeth, almost painfully, drawing a groan from deep in his chest. Matthew gasped as her hands began to move over his body, leaving trails of fire. She abandoned his lips entirely as she explored his body. Matthew lay still, wanting only to savor her touch. He was hungry for this, the feel of her loving hands on his flesh. The need was more than physical for her hands on his body expressed her love for him more eloquently than words. With her touch, she worshiped and adored every inch of him, until the one part of him she had left untouched ached for the feel of her hand. Unable to bear the wanting, he guided her hand with his own. She touched him hesitantly at first, then almost curiously, stroking him, loving him.

Unable to lay passive any longer, he reached for her, letting his hand give back the pleasure that she gave him. The time came, when their bodies caught each other in a frenzy of mutual need. Giving, taking, the one driving against the other in desperate abandon, until their two bodies melted into one.

Matthew lay panting, with still pounding heart and rested his cheek against the softness of her breasts.

"I love you." he murmured huskily.

"And I love you." she replied.

Her voice was shaky, as with tears and he reached to touch her cheek in the darkness. He found it wet and raised up in alarm. "Wynn?" he questioned, fearing that he had hurt her.

"I'm only happy, Matthew." she explained. Then overcome with emotion, she hugged him fiercely, crying out his name in pure joy. "Matthew! Matthew! My darling, my darling!" She held him to her as if she would never let him go, sobbing softly and rocking him in her arms. The intensity of her love overcame him and his happy tears mingled with hers.

Wynn's arms slowly loosened from around him and her breathing, soft and slow, told him that she slept. Almost too tired to move, Matthew settled her close to his side, pillowing her head on his shoulder. Sleep overcame him almost instantly.

By morning, the full fury of the hurricane had passed, taking the wind with it and leaving the rain. It pounded steadily on the roof and ran in small waterfalls from the gutters.

Matthew and Wynn were awakened by a pounding on the front door. Still half asleep, Matthew pulled on his pants and ran his fingers through his rumpled hair. Though the house was still dark, the gray light of dawn showed through the cracks in the boarded-up windows. Half stumbling in the darkness, Matthew made his way to the front door. He opened it and squinted as his eyes adjusted to the comparative brightness outside the house.

Willy stood on the porch with his hat in his hand. Rain dripped off his soaked clothes onto the porch floor.

"Y'all all right?" Matthew asked, stifling a yawn.

"Yassuh." Willy answered quickly. "I'se jus' been checkin' up on de place. You done los' yo' chicken pen an de hawgs be out. I guesses dis place not be bad off. Me'n Lissa los' half de shingles on de house an' we done gone to de nex' house ovah. De windows done be broke outta dat one but de roof be still on it."

Matthew stifled another yawn. "Well Willy, we'll see about getting your roof fixed when the rain stops. You and Lissa dry enough where you're at?" he asked.

"We be jus' fine. We good an' dry where we's at." Willy assured him.

"Then I guess there's no use for you to try to do any more work until the weather clears. Have you already fed the stock." he asked.

"Yassuh." Willy replied.

"Go on home and get dry then. Tell Lissa not to worry about the housework until the rain stops. Y'all done a good job looking after the place while I was gone, you might as well take off an extra day or so." Matthew said.

Willy beamed at the prospect of time off and looked pleased at the complement. "Yassuh, you de boss." he agreed good-naturedly. He jammed his wet, floppy hat back on his head and loped off across the yard at an awkward trot.

Matthew turned to Wynn, who had come to stand beside him in the open doorway. "That boy's still limping from the snakebite." he commented.

"It probably hasn't healed yet. He seems like a pretty good hand to work, I reckon you could have done worse. Some of these blacks around here ain't worth the powder it'd take to blow them away." Wynn walked past him to the edge of the porch to look out at the storm-washed yard.

From what they could see, there was little damage. Limbs littered the ground and a few shingles were missing from the stable roof. From the far end of the porch, they could see that the chicken pen lay in shambles.

"I wonder if Todd had any damage at his place." Matthew said.

Wynn nodded. "Probably a little more than here. The way the fields are situated, there's less to break the wind and his place sets on lower ground. Water usually stands in the yard for a day or two after a big blow. If I know Todd, he's probably got Lum and Ned and gone out already to get the corn in."

"Maybe I should go see if they need any help over there." Matthew said.

Wynn shook her head. "The three of them can handle it. If there was any major problem over there, they would have let us know by now. He may need some help with the cane, if it's not flattened. But that'll be after the first frost if the storm didn't hurt it too bad." As she talked, she was running a hand up and down his bare back.

Matthew reached to pull her into his arms. "Can't keep your hands off me, can you woman?" he teased.

Wynn giggled, but didn't bother to deny the accusation. She merely shook her head in silent agreement and raised her lips for a

205

kiss. Matthew smiled down at her, drawing pleasure from the sight of her. Her lips were red and a little swollen from his kisses and her cheeks were pink from contact with his beard. She looked sleepy-eyed and well loved.

"What are you smiling about?" she asked. "You." he replied. "You look exactly like a woman that just spent the night in bed with a man."

Wynn blushed scarlet under her tan but only laughed. "How else could I possibly look?" she asked. "I did spend the night in bed with a man."

"So you did, you brazen hussy." Matthew teased.

"Hussy, am I?" Wynn said in pretended outrage. She pulled the hair on his chest sharply in retaliation. "And you're just a dirty old man." she accused.

Matthew laughed and pulled her tight against him. "Does that feel like an old man?" he asked, moving against her suggestively.

"Umm, well, let me think about it." she said. She rotated her hips against him experimentally. "Definitely not over the hill." she proclaimed with a laugh.

In a sudden move, Matthew lifted her off her feet and carried her across the porch floor. She let out a shriek but wrapped her arms around his neck. "What are you doing?" she gasped.

"Carrying my bride over the threshold. I believe we never got around to it yesterday." He carried her through the front door and kicked it shut behind him. Instead of putting her down, he carried her to the bedroom and dropped her unceremoniously in the middle of the rumpled bed. She landed with a bounce and lay laughing up at him. Her dressing gown had come untied, exposing an enticing strip of bare flesh. She reached out her arms to him and Matthew unbuttoned his pants, letting them drop to the floor. He stepped out of them and leapt at her with a growl. The bedsprings squeaked in protest as he landed on top of her. She tickled his ribs and with a burst of helpless laughter, he tickled her in return. Laughing uproariously, they tumbled together across the bed. "Enough! Enough!" Wynn cried out in surrender. She continued to laugh until he silenced her with a kiss. Playfully, she poked him in the ribs and he rolled onto his back, pulling her on top of him.

He captured both her hands in one of his, holding them fast. Her eyes sparkled with mischief and something more, as she moved her

206

body over him teasingly. The teasing light in her eyes faded, changing to one of pure passion as she settled herself onto him. He gasped with pleasure as her warmth closed over him and he released her hands. She moved awkwardly at first, then found a rhythm and his hips rose and fell to meet her. She cried out in ecstasy a moment ahead of him and he followed her closely with a cry of his own. She rolled away and they slept once more.

Chapter 39

It was nearly noon when they awakened. The rain still pattered on the roof and it felt good just to lie in each others' arms. Wynn's hand crept up his thigh but Matthew pushed it away with an indulgent laugh. "I think the dirty old man is at least temporarily over the hill." he joked.

"And the brazen hussy is getting hungry." Wynn laughed contentedly. "Are we supposed to eat breakfast or dinner?" she asked.

"Whatever you feel like fixing. I could eat a horse." Matthew proclaimed.

"One horse coming right up!" Wynn laughed as she climbed over him to get out of bed.

Matthew laughed, eyeing her appreciatively as she crossed the floor and began digging around in her bag for clothes. "It wouldn't be the first horse I ever ate." he said with a grin.

Wynn turned to look over her shoulder at him, raising one eyebrow and reminding him of her brother. He chuckled at the thought, for right now the similarity of facial expression was the only resemblance that was apparent.

She responded to his laugh with a grin and began digging around once more in the bag that held her clothes. The light in the room was dim and she apparently was having trouble locating what she was looking for. She extracted from the bag, what resembled a thick pink rope, with knots tied in it. She held it out in one hand, looking at it with a disgusted frown, before tossing it to Matthew. "My nightgown." she explained, with a laugh.

"I guess this is Sarah's way of getting even for the cow bells."

"Well, as it turned out, you didn't need it anyway." Matthew said with a grin.

Wynn crossed the room and dumped the contents of the bag out onto the bed. "I wonder what else she put in here." she said and began sorting through the small pile of clothing. She pulled out a dress and a pair of stockings and broke into a fit of giggles. "I don't believe it!" she exclaimed.

Matthew sat up in bed, to better view the contents of the bag. "What?" he asked.

"She took out all my underwear." Wynn explained. "I'd have never figured on straight laced Sarah doing such a thing."

"I can't imagine her staying straight laced for long, married to your brother." Matthew said with a grin.

Wynn laughed and good-naturedly sought out the underwear she had worn the day before. In a matter of minutes, she was dressed and sat down to comb out her hair. It was hopelessly tangled and she tugged at it impatiently with the comb.

Matthew arose lazily from the bed and took the comb out of her hand. "Here, let me do it. You're about to snatch yourself bald headed." She surrendered the comb to him without protest and sat still as he began to comb the tangles from her hair.

"I was beginning to wonder if you were going to get up, or if I was going to have to bring you your breakfast in bed." Wynn teased.

"Now there's an idea," Matthew replied.

"Oh no you don't! If I have to get up and cook, the least you can do is get up to eat it." Wynn stated flatly.

"And get the boards off the windows and see for myself how bad the storm messed up the place." Matthew finished for her. He combed the last of the tangles from her hair and began to braid it down her back.

"You do that very well," Wynn commented.

"It gives me a good excuse to get a hold of it." Matthew explained. "Do you remember the first time I ever saw you?" he asked.

"Of course." Wynn replied. "I was working in the field and when I saw your uniform, I thought you were Todd coming home."

"And I thought at first you were a field hand and then a boy. I saw your resemblance to Todd right away and was puzzled because Todd had never mentioned having a brother." Matthew continued.

Wynn looked up at him in surprise. "Surely not! You thought I was a boy?" she exclaimed incredulously.

Matthew laughed. "Until you took your hat off and all that hair came tumbling down." he explained.

Wynn smiled at the memory. "I was embarrassed for a stranger to find me looking like that." she confided. "I suppose I'll never forget how you looked either."

Matthew stopped in the middle of tucking his shirttail into his pants. "And how was that?" he asked.

Wynn's smile was tender as she answered him. "Half starved and ragged, and the look in your eyes was the most heartbreaking thing I'd ever seen."

Matthew tilted his head questioningly and she went on to explain. "So sad and kind of hard and haunted. It hurt me just to look at them."

"You cared that much, to hurt for me. You didn't know me from Adam's house cat." Matthew said quietly.

Wynn shrugged and reached for his hand. "A person would have to be totally heartless not to care. If you could have seen yourself, you'd know what I mean." she told him softly.

"It's a wonder you didn't run me off. I hadn't had a haircut and shave or a bath in a very long time and to be honest, I didn't much care." Matthew said laconically.

"You're not the first man I had seen, just back from the war. They all looked like that. Remember how Todd looked when he got off that ship? He wasn't quite as starved looking as you but he sure did look ragged. You know what Matthew?" she asked.

Matthew shook his head.

"I kind of liked the beard, at least I did after I trimmed it. Have you ever thought of growing it back?"

Matthew shrugged. "No. I never thought much about it either way. I remember looking in the mirror after you cut my hair and thinking that I looked as old as the hills. At the rate I'm going, I'll be completely gray headed by the time I'm thirty."

"How old are you?" Wynn asked.

He chuckled wryly. "Twenty eight, going on a hundred and eight." he replied.

"Only six years older than me and Todd. I like the gray in your hair." Wynn stated flatly.

"Yeah, well I'm glad you do but I sure as heck didn't figure on my hair getting gray before I was at least forty. I didn't have one thread of gray before the war." Matthew replied.

Wynn hugged him tenderly and kissed his whiskered cheek. "It must have been pure hell, Matthew." she said sympathetically.

He pulled her close and kissed the top of her head. "It was hell." he agreed. "But it was worth it in the long run. I ended up in heaven here with you."

Wynn laughed softly. "A while ago, I was a shameless hussy. Are you implying now that I'm an angel?"

"My angel." he said fiercely and hugged her tight. "But there's a little of the devil in you and I love that too."

Wynn swatted him play fully on the backside. "You have your moments of being devilish yourself Matthew." she said cheerfully.

Matthew sat on the side of the bed and pulled on his socks and boots. "Take your time cooking breakfast. I have to shave and the chores will take a while." he said.

When they emerged onto the open breezeway, they found that the rain had slackened to no more than a steady drizzle. The sky overhead was still gray but seemed less threatening. They went their separate ways, Wynn to the kitchen and Matthew to check on the storm damage. Matthew's boots were soon thoroughly soaked as he splashed through the puddles in the yard.

Willy was right about the damage, there was very little. The chicken pen Matthew considered to be no great loss. He could only find one rooster and a couple of hens and for no more than that, the pen wasn't worth replacing. The hogs had come out from under the house to wallow in the mud hole that completely blocked access to the out house. They were all present and accounted for, as well as the pigs. A couple of settings of eggs would replenish his flock of chickens but he would have hated to lose even one of the hogs.

With the help of a crowbar, Matthew made short work of removing the boards from the windows. By now, he was thoroughly wet from the drizzling rain and actually felt a little chilled. Because his feet were muddy, he removed his boots on the porch and as he bent to unlace them, he was startled by the flapping of wings and the loud quacking of a duck.

He looked up in time to see a large white, domestic drake settle on the wash shelf on the end of the porch. It was joined almost immediately by its mate. The two ducks flapped their wings and began to busily oil their feathers. "Now, where did you two come from?" Matthew asked, expecting no reply. The drake cocked his head and quacked loudly. "Well, I obviously don't understand duck talk but you might as well make yourselves at home." Matthew said.

To his pleased surprise, Wynn had filled the wash basin with hot water for him to shave. He usually didn't bother heating it himself but hot water was definitely better for shaving than cold.

The two ducks continued to sit on the wash stand as he shaved and combed his hair. They watched him with great interest but flew off as he lifted the basin to toss the water into the yard.

Matthew's stomach rumbled with hunger as the scent of frying bacon reached him and he hurried to the kitchen to find Wynn. She stood bare-footed in front of the stove scooping eggs from a pan onto a plate. She turned as he closed the door behind him. "You're as wet as a drownded rat Matthew." she said.

Matthew shrugged out of his wet shirt and hung it near the stove to dry. "So's your dress tail. Have you been out?" he asked.

"Yeah, there's a lake between here and the outhouse. The hogs seem to think it's their private swimming hole." Wynn said, with a grin.

"I noticed. The wind blew most of my...our chickens away. I couldn't find but one rooster and a couple of hens. We gained two ducks though." Matthew replied.

"Ducks!" Wynn exclaimed. "Where'd they come from?"

"I don't know. They just flew up on the wash shelf on the front porch when I went to shave." Matthew replied.

Wynn began setting the plates of eggs and another of bacon on the table. "On the porch! Do you know how big a mess ducks make? To my way of thinking, they're way yonder nastier than hogs." she said.

Matthew shrugged good-naturedly as he helped himself to the bacon. Wynn poured gravy in a bowl and set a pan of hot biscuits on the table. "Well, it's not like I went out and bought them. They just sort of came free with the storm. I reckon it's Mother Nature's way of paying us back for the chickens. I have to admit, I kind of like them." he told her as she sat down to eat.

Wynn had cooked a very large meal for only two people but they were both hungry and did it justice. Matthew grinned at her in approval as she stood up to clear the table. "One part angel, one part devil and one part good cook. What more could a man ask for?" he stated in way of complementing her on the meal.

"Wynn shrugged. "I guess I do alright but cooking sure ain't my favorite activity." she admitted.

"And what is?" Matthew asked.

She gave him a wicked grin. "Besides hunting and fishing?" she asked

Matthew laughed. "I can guess that one." he replied.

"Oh, can you now?" Wynn asked. There was a slight hint of her Irish father's accent in the way she asked it.

"Yeah. Do you want to ride over to Todd's in a little while, to get the rest of your things? I'm kind of anxious to know how they made it through the storm, " Matthew suggested.

"I'd like that." Wynn said. "But do you reckon we could take the buggy instead?"

"Sure, I don't see why not. I suppose it would be easier to bring your things back that way than on horseback." Matthew replied.

Wynn blushed. "It's not so much that, though it would be easier with the buggy. The truth is, I'm too sore to sit on a horse."

Matthew looked at her with sudden comprehension. "Why didn't you say something sooner?" he asked.

"It's not that big a deal. I'm just not up to riding a horse right now is all. You look surprised. Didn't Elizabeth get sore?" she asked.

Matthew felt the muscles in his jaw tightening. For the first time, he was angry with Wynn. He didn't want her to question him about Elizabeth, especially about something so personal. However, he had overlooked her questions up until now. He took in a deep breath and let it out slowly before answering her.

"Look Wynn, I know you're curious about Elizabeth and me and maybe you have a right to be. I'm going to answer you this time but please don't question me about it again. We never loved each other and there was no passion between us. Going to bed with me was a duty she had to perform. I've learned more about loving in the last few hours with you than I did in the entire time I was with her. I was fond of her, I respected her, I might even have loved her given enough time. She's dead Wynn, and in her dying, she left me free to love you. Let her rest in peace."

In spite of his anger, Matthew had spoken softly. He hadn't intended to hurt Wynn with his words but he knew that he had. She kept her back to him, still slowly putting dishes into the hot water to be washed. Although he couldn't see her face, he could tell by the droop of her shoulders and her lowered head. He put his arms around her from behind and hugged her close. "I'm sorry Matthew." she whispered.

"It's all right. You didn't mean anything by it and I shouldn't have gotten angry." Matthew apologized in return.

Wynn turned in his arms to bury her face against his neck. "I'm not so much sorry about that Matthew. I'm more sorry that she died without knowing the kind of love that we have." she said softly.

Matthew hugged her closely, realizing just how big her heart was. "I'm sorry about that too Honey, more than you'll ever know. But a man has little choice in whether he feels love or not." he replied.

Wynn gave him an affectionate squeeze and kissed him briefly on the chin. "I guess I'd better get these dishes done." she said brightly. "I'm a little anxious to see how Todd and Sarah are doing."

"Fine, I'll hitch up the gray and we can go as soon as you're through here." he replied.

Chapter 40

A half-hour later, they were on their way. Matthew had to stop a half dozen times in the two short miles to Todd's to remove fallen branches and once even a small tree that had fallen across the road. In some places, the puddles were so deep as to cause even the strong gray difficulty in crossing them.

When they arrived, Matthew looked around in amazement. The entire yard was standing four inches deep in water. The house sat on somewhat higher ground and resembled an island, as it was on the only dry ground around. From the looks of things, the house and out-buildings had survived the storm well. A large oak tree had fallen on the outhouse and it lay in shambles beneath it.

Matthew drove the buggy right up to the edge of the porch, so that they could get to the house without wading. Todd came out on the porch, just as they stopped. "Get that horse away from the edge of the house Matthew! Every snake in the county's moved in under there." he called out in warning.

Matthew gave Todd an astonished look but heeded the warning instantly. When they were a safe distance from the house, Matthew

213

took off his still wet boots and rolled his pants legs up to his knees. Wynn also removed her shoes and stockings and they searched the ground around them carefully, before jumping down from the buggy. "Don't worry." Todd called out. "There ain't none in the yard, they're all under the house."

In spite of Todd's assurance that there were no snakes in the yard, Matthew and Wynn crossed the yard with extreme caution. Once on the porch, Matthew breathed a sigh of relief. "The only thing I hate worse than a Yankee is a snake." he told Todd, with a touch of irony in his voice. "How'd your crops make out?" he asked.

Todd shrugged. "I can save the corn, we've done got half of it in. I reckon the cane just might make it. I'm gonna try leaving it lay on the ground and letting it put out runners. It might make it that way and I can trim it up when we harvest it." Todd replied optimistically.

"I didn't know cane would do that!" Wynn exclaimed. "I lost a crop here two years ago because I figured there was no use in letting it lay."

"Well, you can't win 'em all." Todd said philosophically. "How's things at your place?"

"We lost most of the chickens and half the roof blew off the cabin Willy and Lissa were using. I guess we made out pretty good, we even gained two ducks." Matthew replied.

"Well how about that! Y'all come on in. I've got to get back out to the corn field, I just came in to see about Sarah." Todd said.

"What's wrong with Sarah?" Wynn asked in alarm.

Todd laughed a little but became instantly serious. "It's funny but it ain't. She's scared to death of the snakes and refuses to come out of the bedroom until they're gone. She's up there sitting in the middle of the bed with the door and both windows shut." he explained.

"Oh no! Poor Sarah." Wynn exclaimed.

"I can't say as I blame her. I'm kind of tempted to do the same thing myself." Matthew said, only half joking.

"Shoot buddy. I was hoping to get you to go under the house with me and shoot them with your pistol. I can't have Sarah shut up in the bedroom like a hermit until the water goes down." Todd said.

"Todd, old buddy, I'd do about anything for you. But crawling under a house with a bunch of snakes is where I draw the line. You're welcome to use my pistol all you want to but I'm not going under that house." Matthew said firmly.

Wynn said nothing but the gleam in her eyes told Matthew all that he wanted to know. "Oh no you don't! No wife of mine is going under a house with a bunch of snakes. You can just forget it right now!" he ordered.

Wynn tilted her chin in a show of stubbornness but wisely kept quiet. "I'll go up and see Sarah. I still need to get my stuff together." she stated.

"I'll help you get the corn in, Todd. You and Sarah can come to my house until the snakes leave if you want to." Matthew offered. He felt like a coward for not helping Todd kill the snakes but if the shoe fit, he guessed he'd just have to wear it.

Todd grinned at Matthew. "That's all right buddy, me'n Lum and Ned can handle the corn, no more than there is of it. Besides, you're on your honeymoon."

"That doesn't matter, if you need the help." Matthew assured him.

"I don't." Todd said firmly. "As for Sarah and the snakes, I just came up with a great idea."

"What's that?" Matthew asked.

"We never had time for much of a honeymoon ourselves. If she won't come out of the bedroom, it's my duty as a husband to see that she don't get lonesome up there." Todd replied, with a wicked grin.

"Now you're talking." Matthew said, giving Todd a brotherly slap on the back. "Well, if you won't let me help you with the corn, I guess I'll go help Wynn get her things together."

"Good idea. I'd like to visit longer but I guess I'd better go help Ned and Lum. I reckon the next thing I need to do is build another outhouse. I'm just proud of one thing." Todd said with a grin.

"What's that?" Matthew asked.

"That I wasn't in it when that tree fell." Todd replied as he left the porch.

Matthew ascended the stairs and heard Wynn and Sarah talking in the master bedroom. He tapped lightly on the door and Sarah called for him to come in. She sat in the middle of the bed, fully dressed. "What's this I hear about you being penned up by a bunch of snakes?" he asked his sister-in-law.

Sarah gave him a sheepish grin. "I know it's silly but I can't help it. I'm scared to death of snakes." she admitted.

"Me too." Matthew said.

"Oh come on. You're just saying that to make me feel better."

Sarah said skeptically.

Matthew shook his head. "I wish I was but it's the God's truth." he said sincerely. "Actually I'm only scared of two kinds." he continued, with a grin.

"What kind is that?" Sarah asked.

"Live ones and dead ones." Matthew replied.

"Oh you!" Sarah cried out, but laughed until her eyes were wet.

Wynn stood up when they had all stopped laughing. "I guess this ain't getting my things together. We'll come back in and see you before we go." she promised Sarah.

Once they were in Wynn's room, Matthew sat down on the bed to watch her pack. "I was going to put my clothes in crocus bags but since we brought the buggy, I'll put them in my trunk." she said.

Wynn opened the trunk that sat at the foot of her bed and began filling it with clothes from the wardrobe. Matthew had never thought of Wynn as being clothes conscious but her dresses must have numbered over two dozen and many of them were high quality. Once the dresses and petticoats were packed, she hardly had room for the drawer full of work britches and the things from the dresser. The trunk was large but he was still surprised that she managed to get everything in it and close the lid. She set half a dozen hat boxes on the bed and looked around the room. "Well I guess that's about it for now. I can get my musket and the deer skin when I come to get my horse." she said.

"What about your bed?" Matthew asked.

"I'll leave it here. It's not really big enough for the two of us." she replied.

"Wynn, my curiosity is killing me. What happened to that square of wallpaper over there?" Matthew asked.

"We couldn't get any kind of paper here during the war. I used that piece of wallpaper to write to Todd when our Daddy died." she explained. "Nearly every house around here has squares cut out of the wallpaper, it's the only kind we could find."

"I see." Matthew said. "now that you've got that trunk packed, how are we going to get it down the stairs?"

Wynn laughed. "It's not as heavy as it looks. I can carry half, if you take the other." she said confidently.

Matthew eyed her slight frame with a skeptical look. "This I've gotta see." he said.

"I really can." Wynn assured him. "Me and Todd used to carry it back and forth when we were at the academy."

To Matthew's surprise, she held up her end of the trunk quite well. When it was loaded into the buggy, they went back for the hat boxes. "Remind me not to make you too mad at me." Matthew teased.

Wynn turned to him with a raised eyebrow. "Why's that?" she asked innocently.

Matthew laughed. "Any woman who is as strong as you are might just beat the tar out of me."

Wynn giggled. "I've been mad enough at you to kill you a time or two already but I'd think twice before I started beating on you." she said seriously.

"You knocked the heck out of me one time, as I recall." Matthew said with a laugh.

"And you deserved it." Wynn replied.

Matthew turned serious. "You may not believe this, but I can't for the life of me, remember what it was I done."

Wynn tilted her chin up and assumed a haughty expression. "Why Suh, you merely endangered my honor." she said, with an exaggerated drawl.

"And you teased me unmercifully. I guess you knew I was too drunk to be any real danger to you." he said with a laugh.

"Why Suh, I've nevah behaved in any mannah less than a lady." she drawled.

"The heck you ain't. And if you ever get to be too much like one, I'll turn you over my knee." Matthew said with a laugh.

They stopped by the master bedroom to bid Sarah good-bye on the way out with the hat boxes. Her eyes were twinkling with suppressed laughter and they surmised correctly that she had heard their whole conversation.

On the way back, they stopped by to inspect the damage to Willy and Lissa's cabin. The one they had moved into was the best of the two cabins and it would be easier to fix the windows in it than repair the roof on the other one. Willy had apparently come to the same conclusion, for he was busily moving the panes of glass from the windows of the one to the other. "Lissa say she like dis house fine, it be alright wid you Missa Matthew.

"Suits me," Matthew agreed. "You can fix it up however you

217

want to."

"Yassuh." Willy agreed happily. "You cares if I tears down de ol house an' use de lumbah to make a poach? Lissa say she sho' do like to sit on de poach in de cool ob de day."

"Go ahead Willy, I've got two or three pounds of nails at the house. Come and get them and whatever tools you'll need." Matthew said.

"I sho' will. Thank you Missa Matthew." Willy said, tipping his hat respectfully.

Matthew and Wynn got back to the house with just enough daylight to spare to move both their possessions into the master bedroom. When it was arranged to suit Wynn, she stood back to admire it. "Now this room just suits me." she said with satisfaction.

"Me too, especially the bed." Matthew agreed with a wicked grin. The big four poster bed did indeed dominate the room. It was oversized and the feather mattress looked inviting.

"Why didn't you use this room to start with?" Wynn asked.

"It's a room for two people. I wouldn't have felt right in it alone." Matthew explained.

"I think," Wynn said wistfully, "that this room has never known anything but love. Mrs. Marlow was crazy about that husband of hers."

"It's too bad. I guess just about everyone lost someone in the war." Matthew replied quietly.

"It's true. Sarah lost an older brother. Did you know that?" Wynn asked.

"No, she has a younger brother still at home doesn't she?"

"Yeah, he's a nice boy, kind of quiet and shy but as good as they come." Wynn replied.

"Yes, I remember him. I met him and Sarah's parents at the wedding. Her parents are getting up in years aren't they. Or at least I thought they looked a little old to have a boy still in school." Matthew said.

"Yes they are. Sarah's younger brother was born when her mother was up in her forties. I guess it happens like that sometimes. Her father's at least fifteen years older than her mother." Wynn replied.

"My parents were both over forty when I was born." Matthew said. "People shouldn't have children at that age."

"I agree. Children should be born while the parents are still young and two or three is enough." Wynn said.

"But people don't have much say so about how many or when they come. " Matthew put in.

Wynn grinned. "They do if they're smart. I don't intend to wear myself out having children. Like Mrs. Marlow, would you have ever guessed she was only thirty? Seven children in seven years will make an old woman out of any woman. I'm not going to do that to myself." Wynn stated firmly.

"Well, that's all well and good but what's to stop it? Other than separate bedrooms maybe." Matthew replied.

Wynn smiled. "There's a way. Granny told me about it. Black women know a lot about such things."

"And it works?" Matthew asked.

"Sure it works. Granny only had two children and Todd's and my mother was only expecting once. It worked for them." Wynn said.

"You're not doing whatever it is now are you?" Matthew asked.

"No, and I won't. At least not until I give you at least one child. I know it will never make up for the son you lost but maybe it'll help." Wynn promised.

"I'd like that." Matthew said simply. He pulled Wynn into his arms and rested his cheek, on the top of her head. Her words had touched him to the depths of his being. He was only now beginning to comprehend the meaning of what love was all about. Until now, he had not realized how barren of it his life had always been. To his parents, he was nothing more than the long awaited heir to Silver Oaks. To Elizabeth, he was nothing more than the man she must marry in order fulfill her duties as a daughter of the South. Now that he thought about it, it was love that had brought him here to this time and this place and to this woman that he held in his arms. Love was a Confederate soldier that had carried him out of a Yankee prison, holding him with as much tender care as a woman would hold a child. Love was a black giant of a man, who had wept with him when all was lost and had stayed behind to guard his fortune when all others had gone. Love was a woman whose heart could ache for him when he was nothing more than a ragged stranger. It was a woman who could teach him how to laugh and play. Love was caring more for another human being than one did for oneself.

Wynn, perhaps sensing the depths of his emotions, hugged him almost fiercely before stepping back to look up into his eyes. For a moment, he lost himself, looking so deeply into the black depths of her eyes that the world around him seemed to disappear. He saw himself mirrored there in her eyes.

Wynn reached up to touch his cheek, breaking the spell. "What are you thinking Matthew?" she asked softly.

"Only that I love you." he replied.

Her soft laughter rang out in the stillness of the room. "You looked so serious for a moment. I was beginning to wonder." she teased.

"Love is a serious matter." he said solemnly. His face suddenly split into a wide grin. "And so is supper. Are you going to feed me woman?"

"I'll think about it." she replied playfully.

Chapter 41

Matthew and Wynn went to bed soon after supper and the evening chores were done. As soon as the candle was blown out and they were settled into bed, the hogs began raising a ruckus under the house. "What are they doing, having a shindig under there?" Wynn asked.

"Sounds like it." Matthew replied.

"Well, at least we don't have to worry about snakes under the house, as long as the hogs are under there." Wynn stated.

"What's that got to do with whether we have snakes or not?" Matthew asked.

"Hogs love nothing better than killing and eating snakes. Too bad Todd ain't got some on his place, they'd wipe out those snakes in no time." Wynn replied.

Matthew sat up in bed. "You're kidding! You don't mean to tell me hogs kill snakes."

"Sure they do. I bet you haven't seen one snake on this place since you moved in." Wynn assured him.

"Now that I think about it, I haven't. I saw one chicken snake a while back and I killed it to hang in a tree but it's the only one I've seen." Matthew replied thoughtfully.

"See what I mean." Wynn said.

"Yeah, but don't the hogs get snake bit?" he asked.

Wynn laughed. "Not very often but if they do the poison can't get through all that fat." she replied.

"Well I guess I learn something new every day." Matthew said in wonder.

"Didn't you have hogs on your plantation in Georgia?" Wynn asked. "Anyone that ever had much dealings with hogs would know they eat snakes."

"Sure, we had hogs but where we lived, snakes never were very much of a problem." Matthew argued.

"Maybe that's why." Wynn said, with a laugh.

"Maybe you're right." Matthew conceded seriously. He broke into a laugh. "Here it is our second night together and we're spending it having an in-depth discussion on the subject of hogs. Surely we can think of something better to do."

"Like what?" Wynn asked, in pretended innocence.

"Like this!" 'Matthew growled and proceeded to show her.

For the second morning in a row, they were awakened by a loud banging on the front door. Matthew crawled out of bed reluctantly and pulled on his pants. "If that's Willy again, I just might kill him." he stated crossly. Though Wynn had slept soundly all night long, he had slept poorly. The hogs had awakened him several times during the night and he was ready to butcher them all.

Wynn, on the other hand, seemed to bounce out of bed, bright eyed and full of energy. Matthew envied her ability to sleep so soundly. She pulled on her nightgown and wrapper and was ready to accompany him to the door.

To their surprise, it was Todd and Sarah who stood on the porch, rather than Willy. Todd's face bore the expression of a man who was at his wits end and Sarah stood behind him, with a satchel in her hand and looking mad enough to chew nails.

"What on earth?" Matthew asked.

"Sarah says she ain't going home until the snakes are gone. Y'all mind if she stays here?" Todd asked.

"Of course not. Y'all come in." Matthew replied.

Sarah, looking mad enough to kill, stomped into the house, pushing past Matthew and Wynn, who still stood in the doorway. Rather than get run over, they made room for her. "Damn snakes" she muttered, as she pushed past them. Matthew and Wynn exchanged a look. This couldn't be little Sarah, using a four letter word.

Todd motioned for Matthew to follow him out into the yard and Wynn followed Sarah into the house.

Once in the yard, Todd didn't stop until he and Matthew were both concealed from the house, behind the stable.

"What happened?" Matthew asked. "I thought you had the situation all worked out."

"I did." Todd replied. "Things were going real good. I finally got her to come down from the bedroom to cook supper. It was great. She fixed a special meal and used the best china and silver. We ate by candlelight and I thought I was in for a real special evening."

"Sounds good, so far." Matthew said.

"Yeah, well you know how Sarah is. No way will that woman go to bed with dirty dishes in the kitchen. If she hadn't insisted on doing the dishes before we went to bed, everything would've been fine." Todd replied.

"I don't see any problem with that." Matthew said.

"I didn't either. Actually the trouble started when she went to throw out the dish water." Todd suddenly doubled over in a fit of helpless laughter, clutching his sides in mirth.

"What's so funny?" Matthew asked, with a grin.

Todd gasped for breath and wiped his eyes. "Well, actually it ain't funny but in a way, it's the funniest damn thing I ever seen in my life. I shouldn't laugh. Sarah was scared to death. She almost stepped on a rattlesnake when she went out on the porch." Todd broke into another fit of helpless laughter.

Matthew looked at Todd as if he had taken leave of his senses. "Good God, what's funny about that?" he asked incredulously.

Todd gained control of his laughter, long enough to continue. "Well, she'd been holding her water all day 'cause she didn't want to leave the house and damned if she didn't wet all over herself. That made her mad and she threw the dishpan, water and all at the snake. Apparently the snake decided it was dryer in the yard and left. Hell, by the time I got there to see what the racket was all about, that sweet little wife of mine was cussing like a sailor! I didn't even know she knew such words. Well, anyway, I got tickled. She looked so funny, standing there in a puddle of pee and cussing to beat the band. That was a bad mistake on my part. The more I laughed, the madder she got. What it boils down to is, she ain't talking to me no more, except to tell me she's leaving and not coming back until the snakes are gone. She said she might not even come back then. She spent the night locked up in the bedroom, with the lamp burning and I had to sleep in the spare bedroom."

"Well Todd! How many snakes do you have over there?" Matthew asked, holding his sides and laughing.

"I don't know. Between me and Lum and Ned, we done killed four rattlers and three cottonmouths. I can tell there's still more under the house. I threw a rock under there and I could hear the rattles buzzing. Todd replied.

"Hell, I don't blame Sarah. I'd have moved out a long time ago." Matthew said.

"Well, I guess I don't blame her either. When you see her, don't you dare laugh. She'll know I told you and kill both of us." Todd said seriously.

Matthew grinned and shrugged. "I'll try." he promised. "But it won't be easy. What are you going to do now?"

"I've got two choices. I can wait till the snakes leave and risk Sarah divorcing me or I can get rid of those snakes in a hurry. The only thing I can think of is to borrow a few of your hogs. I never seen such a ruckus over a few little snakes in my life!" Todd said seriously.

Matthew gave Todd a black look. "After last night, I'd damn near give them to you. The bastards kept me awake all night. They've set up housekeeping under the bedroom floor again." he complained.

"Well, at least the snakes ain't particularly noisy." Todd replied. "I thought you had them all neatly penned up back up yonder behind the house."

"I did," Matthew replied, "but the pen is right under a big oak tree and I figured they'd be safer through the storm, if I let them out."

"You've got a point there. It sure would be easier to get them over to my place though, if they were still in the pen."

"Yeah, I guess it would. It took Lum and me a good hour and a half to get them penned up the first time." Matthew replied.

Todd grinned. "Them hogs'll trot right along behind you just like a dog, if you'll walk along real unconcerned and drop an ear of corn now and then. I smell ham cooking, I do believe that sister of mine's cooking breakfast. By the way, did the hogs keep her awake too?" Todd asked.

Matthew gave his brother-in-law another black look. "You've got to be kidding. That woman could sleep through a dynamite blast."

Todd raised an eyebrow. "Yeah, she always could. I used to be the same way before the war, now I wake up if a flea on one of the dogs in the yard so much as sneezes."

"I'm the same way. I can't say as I ever heard a flea sneeze before though." Matthew said, with a chuckle. "Come on in the house. Maybe Wynn's got Sarah calmed down by now and she should have breakfast about ready."

"I sure as heck hope so. Sarah's usually as good natured as they come, but lately she's been as cross as a wet setting hen." Todd said flatly.

Matthew shrugged sympathetically. "That's probably why." he said.

By now, they were on their way across the yard to the kitchen but Todd stopped Matthew with a tug on his arm. "What do you mean?" he asked.

Matthew turned to Todd, with a grin. "I mean, that when that sweet little old hen of yours gets through setting, she'll get over being so cross."

Todd looked and sounded like a man, who had just been punched in the stomach. He bent over slightly and clutched his middle, as the air rushed out between his closed lips and his eyes opened wide. He gaped at Matthew in open-mouthed surprise. "Good God! You don't reckon?" he exclaimed.

This was too much for Matthew and he threw back his head and roared with laughter. He nearly choked as Todd's hand clamped down over his open mouth. "Shh dammit, she'll hear you." Todd cautioned.

Matthew put his own hand over his mouth and turned nearly purple as he struggled for self-control. He lost the battle entirely and fairly whooped with laughter. "Wet setting hen!" he managed to gasp out at last.

Todd gave him a look of sudden comprehension and the two of them stood where they were and laughed until their sides ached and tears ran down their faces.

When they had at last found some measure of self-control, they became aware of the shrieks of feminine laughter coming from the vicinity of the kitchen. They exchanged a look and burst through the kitchen door in time to hear Sarah gasp out between giggles. "That

224

rattlesnake thought for sure that another hurricane had hit."

Matthew and Todd doubled over once more with laughter, clutching their aching ribs. Wynn and Sarah were both red eyed from laughing until they cried. Sarah, laughing hardest of all, kept egging it on. "I guess he figured the yard couldn't be any wetter than the porch." she gasped.

It was a good thing that Wynn already had breakfast on the table or it would have been burned. As it was, it was nearly cold by the time they could all stop laughing long enough to eat.

Getting the hogs the two miles between Matthew's place and Todd's took most of the remainder of the morning. The weather was exceptionally bright and clear after the storm and pleasantly cool. Wynn remained behind with Sarah and when the hogs were delivered safely, Matthew and Todd stood a safe distance away from the house in the now nearly dry yard, to see what would happen.

The hogs predictably, after nosing around a bit, headed straight under the house. In a moment, it began to sound like a small war as the hogs began to discover the snakes. A great deal of grunting and bumping could be heard and then a cottonmouth crawled rapidly across the yard. Matthew made short work of it with his pistol and good-naturedly passed it to Todd. "You get the next one." he said.

"It's a good thing you ain't as scared of snakes as you make out like you are." Todd replied. Another snake crawled out from under the house and Todd shot at it three times before hitting it. He handed the pistol back to Matthew.

"There's a lot of difference between facing a snake from ten feet away with a loaded gun and crawling around under the house with them." Matthew said. He shot at yet another snake and killed it cleanly. He handed the pistol back to Todd.

"Damn, I never seen anything like it. You're one hell of a shot with a pistol Matthew. How the hell do you expect me to do any good with only one cartridge left in this thing?" he asked.

"You're the artillery man, not me. I've got more bullets in my pocket. Just pretend the head of the next snake you see is the eye of a damn Yankee, it improves the aim considerably." Matthew replied, with a grin.

Todd laughed. "Give me a rifle or a ten-pounder and I'll show you a hit every time, but I never was too good with a pistol." As soon as another snake crawled out from under the house, fleeing from the hogs, Todd took careful aim and fired. The snake's head separated neatly from it's body. "Well I'll be damned, it works." Todd said, in surprise.

Matthew reloaded the pistol but no more snakes were seen.

Chapter 42

"By dark it ought to be safe for Sarah to come back home. I think I'll take a ride and see how much the water's gone down and check on the cattle. You could go with me on Wynn's horse and then ride him on home for her when we're done." Todd suggested

Matthew went with Todd to the stable to saddle the horses. "You know, if we bred this boy to our own gray mares, we'd get a couple of fine colts." he said.

"Just what I was thinking." Todd agreed. Wynn's gray stallion and our mares would probably produce some of the best horse flesh in Marion County."

"They're bound to." Matthew said. "I've got to make a living somehow and I figure I'll concentrate on raising stock. Cattle, hogs and horses mostly. I want to get another bull, a good one, maybe a Brahma. I hear they do well here and produce good calves when they're bred to these part long-horns they raise here."

"Sounds like a good plan to me." Todd said. "I reckon I'll stick to raising crops. I just naturally like to watch things grow and my land's more suited to it than yours."

"I know, I think I'll plant hay and corn for stock feeding and just enough other stuff to keep the pantry full. I hate to push a plow nearly as bad as I hate Yankees and snakes." Matthew said, with a grin.

"That's where you and I differ. I kind'a like to plow. It gives me time to think my own thoughts." Todd replied.

They spent the remainder of the day riding over the two farms. The springs were full almost to overflowing and the river was up. Enough of both their herds of cattle were seen to assure them that they had fared the storm all right.

By suppertime, they arrived back at Matthew's farm. Sarah was once more her usual cheerful self and the two women had apparently enjoyed their day.

Conversation around the supper table centered mostly on talk of the storm and plans for the two farms. Todd said that he and Sarah would probably take his corn to the new mill across the river to have it ground. "The way I've got it figured," he said, "there ain't enough of it to be worth hauling to Jacksonville. Matthew, what do you think about me trading you enough corn to feed your stock through the winter for that sow of yours with the litter of pigs?" he asked.

Matthew thought a minute. "That sounds fair enough to me. You've got yourself a trade." he agreed.

Soon after supper was over, Todd and Sarah went back home. Matthew and Wynn stood on their front porch watching them leave, cozily riding double on Todd's gray mare. "I thought Todd never would get her convinced that the snakes were gone." Wynn said, with a laugh.

"She may wish that she had the snakes back instead of the hogs, after they keep her awake all night." Matthew replied.

"Um well, they didn't bother me. By the way, did you know that four more ducks showed up while you were gone?" Wynn asked. As if on cue, the six ducks flew up onto the wash shelf at the end of the porch.

"Well how about that!" Matthew exclaimed. He was obviously pleased but Wynn grabbed a broom and began shooing the ducks off the porch.

"Get down from there!" she ordered, swinging the broom with enough force to knock the water bucket off of the shelf.

"Leave them alone, they're not hurting anything." Matthew said.

Wynn gave him a dirty look. "The heck they ain't. I've done had to scrub the duck sh... uh, mess off the porch three times today already." she complained.

"Surely six little old ducks can't sh... uh, mess that much." Matthew said with a grin.

Wynn put both hands on her hips and gave him a disgusted look. "Matthew the word is shit, mess is what it makes on the floor and wash shelf." Suddenly realizing what she had said, Wynn covered her mouth with one hand and began to giggle.

"You believe in calling a spade a shovel, don't you?" Matthew asked and laughed.

"I reckon." Wynn agreed. "I do wish the nasty things would stay off of the porch though."

Matthew shrugged. "Just keep them run off, they'll get the idea in no time." he assured her. "Have you got any hot water left? I need to shave, I got off this morning without getting around to it. On second thought, if you can stand these bristles for a while, I might grow back my beard."

"I'd like that but my face can't take anymore getting scratched up right now. Besides, as hot as it is, it'd itch you to death right now." Wynn said.

Matthew gave her a hug and planted a kiss on each of her reddened cheeks. "It would be a shame to scratch up that pretty face any more than it is. Your cheeks are still red from yesterday." he said sympathetically.

"I told Sarah, it was sunburn but she didn't believe me." Wynn said with a grin. "Did you notice Todd's growing a mustache?"

"Yeah." Matthew suddenly laughed. "You should have seen his face when I said something about Sarah was expecting."

"I guess he didn't know. I don't reckon Sarah did either until we got to talking about it and started figuring things up. We think it'll come about the end of March or early April." Wynn said.

"That'll be nice. I kind of like the idea of being an uncle." Matthew said happily.

Wynn went into the house and came back in a few minutes with a kettle full of hot water. Matthew had gone to the well and Wynn gave the ducks a disgusted look as they scattered off of the wash shelf at the sight of her. They flew off across the yard, quacking loudly and beating the air with their wings. "You'd better go!" she snapped.

Matthew came around the corner of the house, with a full bucket of water and just missed being run over by the flying ducks as he went by. He prudently said nothing and neither did Wynn.

"I'm going to heat some more water for my bath. Are you going to wash out here, or should I heat enough for both of us?" Wynn asked.

"I'll wash out here, you go ahead. After that, I think I'll walk over to Willy's. I need to tell him we're going to start fixing the roofs tomorrow. That's a bad leak we've got in the corner of the front room.'" Matthew told her.

"Take your time Matthew, I'll be a while." Wynn said, with a mysterious grin.

Matthew got back from Willy's just after dark. The only light in the entire house came from beneath the bedroom door. He entered the

228

dimly lit room to find Wynn seated at the dressing table, brushing out her hair.

The nightgown that she wore was pink and totally transparent. His heart leapt at the sight of her and he stood in the doorway drinking in her beauty with his eyes. She stood up and twirled around the room, making the thin fabric of the gown float around her and her smile was one of pure seduction. Matthew reached out and caught her as she danced by. "Do you like it?" she asked. "I intended to wear it the first night but we never got around to dressing for bed. Then I had to iron it after Sarah tied it in knots."

"I love it." Matthew stated. "You smell good too." he said, sniffing appreciatively.

"I'm not wearing perfume." she said.

"No, it doesn't smell like perfume, more like cinnamon and cloves." Matthew said thoughtfully. "What is it?"

"My soap, I guess. I always make a few bars just for me and I scent them with cinnamon and oil of cloves. There's crushed orange blossoms in it too. I made some for Sarah that smells like gardenias." Wynn explained.

"I thought she always wore perfume. It suits her. What would you put in a soap for me and Todd?" he asked.

Wynn snuggled close to him and thought for a minute. "For you, I'd use wintergreen and pine and maybe a touch of lemon. I think about the same for Todd, except I'd use bayberry instead of pine."

Matthew was quickly losing interest in the subject of soap making, as his hands roamed over her silk clad body. "That's interesting." he mumbled, in such a way as to leave her wondering if he meant her, or her method of soap making. In a little while he left no doubt in her mind as to which one he found the most interesting.

The following day, work on the farm returned to normal. Matthew, with Willy's help, repaired the damages from the storm and began piling up the fallen limbs for burning. Wynn kept busy all day in the house with Lissa and by the end of the day, she had come a long way towards getting things arranged the way she wanted them.

Late in the day, when supper was over, Matthew and Wynn sat on the front porch in the cool of the day. Since the hurricane, the biting insects were less plentiful and the air was crystal clear and sweet to breathe. A small puddle still remained in a low place near the stable and the six ducks fought among themselves for room to splash around in it. A pair of cardinals flew down from the top of the chinaberry tree to compete with the ducks for possession of the puddle. The bright red feathers of the males seemed all the more brilliant when seen next to the snowy white ducks. Matthew sat watching them with a bemused grin. He was drowsy and utterly content.

"Just look at those ducks." Wynn said. "You'd think they had never messed up a thing in their lives, the way they carry on so innocent like."

"Still wanting to roost on the wash shelf, are they?" Matthew asked sleepily. "You got a lot done today. Is Lissa working out to suit you?"

"Lissa's all right." Wynn replied. "We've been sorting through all that junk in the back bedroom. It's funny, the things that accumulate on a place over the years. I threw a lot of it away but some of it I hung on to."

"I never got around to digging through all that stuff. I'm surprised that you found anything in there that was worth keeping." Matthew said.

"Not much of it was. I gave a bunch of old clothes to Lissa, to make her and Willy a quilt. There was even a few things, they might be able to wear. I actually found one thing that was a real treasure. That old wooden crate in the corner was packed full of books. I haven't had anything new to read in years. Some of the stuff that I thought was beyond saving, Lissa wouldn't let me throw away. She's convinced that Willy can fix anything. Those two old porch rockers with the broken seats and a box of old hardware, she insisted I should keep." Wynn yawned and set aside the basket of mending she was working on.

"Well, if Willy can fix that stuff, we might as well give it to him. Most of that old hardware would need a blacksmith to fix it, I doubt if he can do much with it." Matthew said.

"What got me was that old piece of a shotgun, she insisted that Willy could fix." Wynn said, with a laugh.

Matthew's half closed eyes opened with interest. "What kind is it?" he asked.

Wynn shrugged. "I don't know. It ain't even got a stock and one of the hammers is broken off. The barrels are rusty too. As hard as guns are to come by these days, I wish Willy really could fix it."

230

"He might could at that, if it had a stock. I lent him my old musket when the wolves were plaguing us and he brought it back looking and working like a new gun."

"Well, this one's beyond fixing, even I can tell that. It's so rusty, it's froze up." Wynn got up from her chair. "Just a minute and I'll go get it and show you." she said. She returned a moment later and handed him what was left of the double-barrel. "See what I mean?" she asked.

Matthew turned it over and over in his hands and squinted to read the writing on the rusty chamber. "Humm, this gun isn't very old. It looks like they just put it aside when the stock got broken. It looks like somebody used it to drive stakes in the ground, to break both the stock and the hammer like that." he observed.

"What a waste." Wynn said.

"Just for the heck of it, I think I'll turn this over to Willy and see what he does with it." Matthew said, with a grin.

"Yeah, well, I guess it wouldn't hurt anything but there sure isn't much there to work with." Wynn said skeptically.

"That's a fact. I'll just throw it in with the other stuff in that box and see what he does with it. Maybe he can get some use out of all that junk. I need to go pay them their wages for the month and I'll take the box with me. I'll go while you take your bath, save the water for me. I won't be long." Matthew said.

He returned a half-hour later as Wynn was finishing her bath. They ended up making love, standing upright in the middle of the bedroom floor.

Later, as they lay together in the big four poster bed, Wynn asked sleepily, "What did Willy think of the box of junk?"

Matthew chuckled softly. "He was tickled pink. You know how blacks are. He had a fit over that old piece of a shotgun. He said he could fix it up as good as new. I don't how, but it'll be interesting to see what he does."

"Uh-Yeah, I guess so." Wynn replied. She snuggled closer to his side and fell asleep.

Matthew lay awake a few minutes longer, enjoying the feel of her in his arms. In a while, he too slept.

By noon the next day, Matthew was beginning to wish that he had never thought of giving the shotgun to Willy. It was all Willy could talk about. He speculated for hours on what kind of wood

231

would make the best stock and described in endless detail how he planned to fashion a new hammer.

Matthew finally sent Willy off to set fence posts on his own and he spent the afternoon picking up yet more limbs and tearing down what was left of the chicken pen. The gate of the hog pen was damaged in the storm and Matthew tried to repair it. He couldn't get it to hang straight and wished that he had left that chore for Willy.

Chapter 43

Matthew and Wynn had an early supper and went over to Todd's to retrieve their hogs and collect the corn they had taken in trade for the sow and pigs.

The hogs were nowhere in sight, when they arrived but trotted in from the woods as Todd celled them with a high pitched, "Pig, pig, pig, sueee!"

"Now wait a minute here." Todd said. "There's supposed to be six of these boogers, not counting the pigs ain't there?" he asked.

"Yeah," Matthew replied. "I don't see but five though. I wonder where the other one got off to. These hogs usually stick pretty close together. You don't reckon one of them got snake bit, do you?" he asked.

"Not likely." Todd said. "I see Ned and Lum coming in from the woods, they've been out cutting myrtle bushes to get rid of the fleas. Maybe they've seen the other hog, most likely it just wandered off."

As the two Negroes came nearer, it became apparent that they were in too much of a hurry to just be coming in from completing a task. Both men were walking briskly and carrying a bundle of myrtle branches over their shoulders.

"I wonder what their hurry is." Todd said. "I know we've got a problem with fleas but there ain't that big a rush to get the myrtle out. I don't know if we're jinxed or what. First it was the snakes under the house, then it was the hogs, now the place is infested with fleas. If it ain't one thing it's another." Todd lamented.

As the two Negroes came within calling distance, Todd yelled out, "Hey, y'all seen anything of a stray hog while you were out?"

Ned and Lum broke into a run, when they saw the two white men standing in the yard. "Yassuh!" Lum called out. "You an' Massa best

232

be comin', somethin' strange be goin' on heah." They trotted into the yard and dropped the bundles of myrtle branches onto the ground.

"Massa Todd, somethin' done be kilt one ob Missa Matthew's hawgs. It sho' don't look right. You bes' be seein' dis fo' yo' selves." Ned said, scratching his woolly head and looking upset and puzzled.

"What does it look like?" Matthew asked. Just then, Wynn and Sarah came out of the house to join the men. "Something killed one of my hogs." Matthew explained to the two women.

"Yo hawg done be all chewed up. Dey is bear tracks an' man tracks. It be de stranges' thing I evah see." Lum said.

"A bear!" Todd exclaimed. "I guess that explains it. Y'all sure it wasn't your tracks you seen, as well as the bear's?" he asked the two black men.

Ned and Lum looked insulted. "Cose not Missa Todd!" Lum said emphatically.

"Well, I guess we'd better go take a look." Matthew replied.

They all followed Lum and Ned to the edge of where the hammock met the woods and found the remains of the dead hog in a small clearing

What they saw was indeed strange. The hog was partially eaten by a bear, as the tracks confirmed. From the looks of the carcass, the hog had not been killed by the bear, but from having it's throat cut. Mingled with the tracks of the bear, were those of two men. "This is the damnedest thing I ever seen." Todd stated.

"Yeah, what do you make of it Todd?" Matthew asked.

Todd studied the tracks and the carcass at length. "Looks to me like, a couple of men killed this hog and then the bear smelled the blood and when he come to see what it was, the men ran off." he said.

"That's the way I see it." Matthew agreed. "As you said before, Todd, if it's not one thing, it's another. It looks like we've got some hog thieves on our hands and a bear with a newly developed taste for fresh pork."

"Kind of makes you wonder what's next, don't it? Lum, you reckon that bloodhound of yours can trail that bear?" Todd asked.

"I don' know Missa Todd. Dis dog done be trained to hunts de run away slaves, not hunts de game." Lum replied skeptically.

"Well, maybe he'll trail one or the other. Matthew, what do you say we go hunting first thing in the morning? It's too late to do much now but I reckon they ain't got too much of a head start." Todd suggested.

"My thoughts exactly, I'm not sure which one to hunt first, the bear or the men." Matthew said, with a grin.

"I'd like to catch up with all three. I reckon the bear was just doing what comes natural but I hate a thief worse than anything, next to Yankees and snakes, that is."

Wynn studied the sky overhead. "It don't look like there's any chance of rain tonight. The trail should be still fresh in the morning. I'll fix us some food to take with us, no telling how long this will take."

She looked at Sarah, who was looking a little green in the face, at the sight of the mutilated hog. "You all right Sarah?" she asked in concern.

Sarah squared her shoulders. "Yeah, the least little thing makes me queasy anymore. Y'all aren't going to go off bear hunting, and leave me here by myself, are you? Not with strange men around and all."

"You've got a point there Sarah." Todd said, hugging her close to his side. "Somebody'll have to stay with you."

Sarah looked at all of them and it was obvious that none of them wanted to stay behind. "I'm going too." she announced. "It ain't fair for y'all to have all the fun."

"Now wait a minute!" Todd exclaimed. "This ain't going to be no picnic, we're in for some pretty rough going and you ain't in no condition to be traipsing around all over the woods." he told Sarah firmly.

Sarah raised her chin and took on a stubborn look.

"I'm strong and healthy and this baby's a long way off yet. I reckon it won't hurt me." she argued.

Todd recognized the look and gave in. "Well, alright but I don't want to hear no unnecessary complaining and you'll have to keep quiet."

"Look, if Wynn can keep up with you men, so can I. I'm no sissy." Sarah said, with her chin still tilted at a stubborn angle.

"I said you could go. Now stop arguing woman." Todd snapped.

Sarah looked chastened but didn't change her mind.

Matthew, understanding Sarah's feelings perhaps a little better than Todd, sought to make things easier for her. "Sarah, you can use my brown mare, she rides like a rocking chair." he offered.

234

"Thank you Matthew." Sarah said sweetly. She gave Todd a sour expression and turned to Wynn. "You got some britches I can borrow?" she asked.

"Sure." Wynn replied. She grinned at Sarah with a conspiratorial grin. "You want homespun or denim?" she asked.

"It don't much matter." Sarah replied. "Matthew, if you're going to take your pistol, can I use your musket?" she asked.

"Sure Sarah," Matthew agreed. He turned away to hide the twinkle in his eyes. The idea of Sarah on a hunt was amusing. The way he had it figured, Todd would have to bring her home before half a day had gone by. He caught Todd's eye and winked.

Todd returned the wink but turned away quickly so that Sarah wouldn't catch him.

Matthew and Wynn by now were running late and it was after dark by the time they got the hogs home and the corn unloaded. In spite of the late hour, Willy was still working on something. He had a lantern lit and was busily running the shotgun barrels over the wheel of the grinder.

"What on earth are you doing?" .Matthew asked.

Willy stopped grinding long enough to answer. "I'se just gettin' de rust off dease heah barrels." he replied. "I'se gwine go home now. I don' wants to bothah you an' Miz Wynn." he said politely.

"That's all right Willy, go ahead. We'll be up for a while yet." Matthew said. He went on to explain about the dead hog and the hunt they were planning.

"You might want to go see if Granny and Pearl are alright, sometime during the day tomorrow. They might want to stay over at your place if we're not back by dark." Matthew suggested.

"I sho' will Missa Matthew." Willy agreed. "What else you be wantin' done?" he asked.

"Finish up that stretch of fence we've got started and anything else you see that needs done. If I'm gone overnight, I'll need you to feed the stock. Oh, by the way, be sure to give the ducks some corn." Matthew replied pleasantly.

"Yassuh." Willy agreed.

Preparations for the hunt took another two hours, so that it was quite late by the time they got to bed.

"How do you reckon Sarah will make out on the hunt?" Matthew asked.

"Don't sell her short Matthew. She may just surprise you." Wynn replied sleepily.

"Maybe." Matthew conceded but he had his doubts. Tired from the long day, he surprised himself by falling asleep without first making love to Wynn.

They awakened early enough the next morning to make up for lost time before going to Todd's. Sarah had promised to have breakfast ready for them when they arrived.

True to her word, Sarah had made pancakes and fried a platter of sausage. "I'm glad it's fall." she said. "We're getting low on sausage and the syrup's last year's boiling, it's getting kind of strong."

"Well, it won't be long." Todd said. "Maybe we'll get a frost in late October and then we can grind the cane. The sausage may be a problem though. Those wild pigs Wynn caught this summer may not be fat enough to butcher by then. The six of them that the panther didn't get won't be enough by the time we divide the meat up between all of us. It won't be enough to feed ten people through the winter."

When breakfast was over, they set out. They led Todd's pack of hunting dogs and Lum's bloodhound to the place where the carcass of the hog lay. The bear had made another meal of the hog during the night and Todd's pack of dogs went crazy over the scent. "That makes me feel like a fool." Todd said. "If I'd been thinking straight, I'd have remembered that bears always come back to something like this. I could've got him easy, just by setting by until he come back for another meal."

"Well, I reckon he couldn't have gone very far away. We might as well turn the dogs loose and see if we can run up on him." Matthew said.

All of the dogs started off together, barking frantically with the excitement of the fresh scent of the bear in their noses. They followed the dogs off into the woods at a slower pace but keeping close enough to see where they were going. No more than a quarter of a mile from the carcass of the dead hog, Lum's bloodhound split, off from the rest of the pack. "Now where's that dog going?" Todd asked Matthew.

"There's no telling." Matthew replied. When he reached the place where the bloodhound had left the pack he studied the ground thoroughly, riding off a few feet in the direction the dog had taken. "Well, how about that?" he said. "That bloodhound's found the trail of the two men and the rest of them are still following the bear."

236

"We can't all hunt both." Todd said.

"Yeah, there's too much of us in one bunch as it is. If it's all the same to you, we'll follow the bloodhound and Lum can go with us." Matthew suggested. To his way of thinking, it would be better if Todd and Sarah were to hunt the bear. He figured that the bear was probably closer to home and the hunt would be easier on Sarah.

Todd obviously was thinking along the same lines. "Sounds good to me. Y'all be careful." With a wave of his hand, Todd along with Sarah and Ned, rode off on the trail of the bear.

Chapter 44

The trail of the men was not as fresh as that of the bear and the bloodhound followed it at a slow trot. Matthew and Wynn, along with Lum followed at a leisurely pace. The two men had made very little effort, if any, to hide their tracks. They were taking a route through an immense stretch of forest and were keeping to the more open areas. It was easy going, both for the men and the three mounted riders that followed them.

The three of them were beginning to enjoy the hunt as much for the sake of the outing, as the challenge of finding the hog thieves. The day was hot but not too uncomfortably so and they were shaded most of the time by tall pine trees and an occasional oak or blackjack.

For the most part, the trail skirted the gall berry and palmetto thickets as it meandered along in the path of least resistance. It sought out the islands of scrub oak and a few high palm hammocks Deer and squirrel were plentiful and Matthew marked the place in his mind, as a good area for future hunting.

Along towards midday, they came upon the spot where the hog thieves had spent the night. A campfire was built under the spreading limbs of a huge old oak tree that must have been growing there for at least three-quarters of a century. The trunk of the tree was nearly five feet thick, straight through the middle.

"This looks like as good a place as any to stop for dinner." Matthew said. He dismounted and searched the area carefully for any tell-tale signs the men might have left, but found nothing other than where they had spent the night in a pile of oak leaves. "Where do you reckon they're headed?" he asked Wynn.

She stopped momentarily in her search through the knapsack full of food. "It looks to me like they're headed towards Ocala in a roundabout way. I somehow get the idea that they're on the run from more people than just us." she replied.

"I think so too, otherwise they would've taken the road." Matthew agreed. "There's been reports of things being stolen in this area as well as across the river. One of the men from Conner told Todd that somebody had pilfered meat from his smokehouse and that he'd heard of some things coming up missing around Sharpes Ferry."

"It sounds to me like they may be just hungry. I reckon a lot of folks are on hard times since the war." Wynn said and began gathering up wood for a fire.

"Let me and Lum do that." Matthew said. "It's true, there is a lot of people on hard times, but that's no excuse to steal. I doubt if anyone around here would let anyone go hungry. Most people are willing to share whatever they have, just for the asking. I think that whoever it is, is just too sorry to work." he concluded and began to gather firewood.

Lum, who had kept quiet up until then, added his opinion. "Massa, you done hit de nail on de head. What I be thinkin' is dis, dem tracks be kinda walked ovah at de heels, like dey be black men. I done be seen dem kind befoah. Dat kind is mean an' dey's lazy. Dat kind be nothin' but trouble."

"Yeah, we had a couple like that at Silver Oaks a few years back, didn't we. They gave my daddy so much trouble that he came the nearest to whipping a couple of them as I ever seen him come. Remember, that was the two that tried to run and was killed by the dogs the slave catchers used to trail them." Matthew said to Lum.

"Yassuh. I remembers them." Lum replied. "Dey be de ones what ol' Massa done bought at Suh-vanna. Dey be trouble from de staht. None ob de black folks what be boan on de place evah cause no trouble. Ol' Massa, he b'lieved in treatin' us like we be human bein's."

"He did at that, Lum." Matthew agreed.

Wynn soon had the fire started and proceeded to drop slices of smoked bacon into the pan. When they were fried to a crisp golden brown, she made up a batter and fried hushpuppies. The meal was simple but, they ate with good appetites.

"Funny, how good something like this tastes in the woods." Wynn observed. "I'd rather eat most anything out like this than cake or pudding at home. Even cold biscuits and corn bread tastes good out like this."

"I can't argue with that." Matthew said. "I've eaten some of the sorriest food I'd ever seen around a campfire and thought it was good. We used to eat a lot of strange food in the army and were always glad to get it. I remember one time when the regiment was camped at Chattanooga, a bunch of the boys in my company sat traps and caught a mess of raccoons and possums. They tasted so good, you'd have thought we were eating the finest steaks."

Wynn grinned at the thought and was reminded of a story of her own. "One time, when me and Todd was around fourteen, our daddy took us with him on a panther hunt. The cat was a big old Tom, with a couple of toes missing and it had been killing Daddy's cows. Our daddy suffered something awful from rheumatism and he figured he'd kill two birds with one stone. He needed some panther grease for his aching joints and he was sick and tired of that cat killing his cattle. Well, that cat run us a merry chase before the dogs finally treed it in the river swamp. By then we were out of the food we'd brought with us and we hadn't been lucky enough to run up on any game. Well, my daddy shot that panther and we skinned it out and cooked steaks out of it over the fire. We enjoyed every bite of it. The meat was a little sweet tasting and kind of stringy but we were just hungry enough not to care. My daddy got a whole bottle of grease out of that panther and used it's hide for a saddle blanket for years before it finally wore out." Wynn had finished packing up the frying pan and other supplies as she talked and when she was done, she turned in time to see Matthew give her a funny look.

"It's the God's truth." she assured him.

"I don't doubt that." Matthew replied. "It's just that the idea of eating panther meat sort of turns my stomach. But then, what can I say. I'm the man that once ate half raw rats and was glad to get them." The look on Matthew's face expressed better than words, how he felt about the whole thing.

Wynn wrinkled her nose in disgust at the thought of eating rats but tactfully said nothing. She glanced over at Lum and thought that his black face looked a little green tinged.

They continued to follow the trail until mid-afternoon and had just about decided to give up the search. The trail had doubled back on itself and was headed in the general direction of home. "Looks

239

like they're going right back where they came from." Matthew observed.

"Yeah, it does. Do you reckon they're going back to raid the farm again?" Wynn asked.

"I sure do. Look at that dog, the trail's definitely getting hotter." The bloodhound's pace had quickened and the tone of it's bark had changed. "In fact, I think we may be about to run right up on them." Matthew said tersely.

Lum sat up straighter on his mule and checked the caps on his sawed off shotgun. Matthew and Wynn were carrying loaded guns from the start but checked to make sure their ammunition was within easy reach.

In less than an hour, they crossed a natural clearing just in time to see the bloodhound break into a flat out run. The scent was now so strong that the dog didn't even need to put his nose to the ground.

The long legged dog quickly out-distanced them and for a while, they thought that they had lost both the dog and the trail. On the other side of the clearing, the underbrush grew thick, in a tangle of blackberry briers and dog fennels. It created an almost impenetrable barrier and they skirted the edge of the thicket and came out just above it and a little to the northeast. Not far away, they could hear the frantic baying of the bloodhound. From the sound of his bark, he was in hot pursuit of his quarry.

The three of them kicked their mounts into a trot and headed in as straight a course as was possible toward the sound of the dog. Before they had gone very far, the baying of the bloodhound had changed from the bell like tones of the chase, to the deep-throated bark that indicated that the quarry had treed.

They crossed yet another natural clearing and found the bloodhound running frantically around a quarter-acre size clump of palmettos.

"Dey be in dare all right." Lum said. He lifted the leather thong that held his shotgun around his neck, over his head and held it like a pistol in one hand.

"Wynn, you stay here and I'll go over that way." Matthew said and pointed to the right. "Lum, you go to the left and we'll see if we can talk them out of there."

Matthew and Lum dismounted, leaving the horse and mule with Wynn and proceeded on foot. In a short time, they had attained their positions and Matthew heard Lum calling off the bloodhound.

Matthew fired a shot from his pistol, over the palmetto thicket. "We've got you surrounded, if you want out of there alive, you'd better come out with your hands up!" he shouted.

The palmetto fronds in the middle of the thicket shook a little, as someone moved about but no one showed themselves.

Lum, on the other side of the thicket, held on tightly to the collar of the bloodhound, who was straining to get loose. "You skeestahs bes' get yo 'selves outta there. I'se gwine counts to ten, den I'se gwine turn dis heah dawg loose." he called out in warning. Lum began to count slowly from one to ten and by the time he reached nine, two black heads came cautiously up out of the palmettos.

The two black men were facing Lum when they stood up and they must have found the sight intimidating to say the least. Lum stood scowling at them from his impressive height of six foot six. His face looked like a cross between a bulldog and a thundercloud and he held the sawed-off shotgun pointed at them as one would point a pistol. Lum's contempt for a thief more than equaled Matthew's and for a moment he completely forgot that he was in the presence of a white lady. "You bastads get yo' black asses out heah 'fore I blows yo' nappy heads off!" he said.

The two men looked around them for a way out but were penned in by Matthew and his pistol on one side and Wynn with her musket on the other. They had no choice but to follow Lum's orders. With an eye out for snakes, they began making their way out of the thicket. "What you mean pointin' yo gun at us? We ain't done nothin'." the smaller of the two black men called out defiantly.

He was a big buck but the other one was even bigger. He stood nearly as tall as Lum but looked a lot less menacing.

"Sho' you ain't, 'cept try to steal a hawg." Lum answered.

"What you talkin 'bout? We ain't stole no hawg. You gots no right trackin' us down like we be runaways." the smaller man argued defiantly.

"Only reason you didn't be dat bear done scared you off. Jus' 'cause you free don't give you no right to be stealin' what ain't yo's." Lum replied.

The biggest of the two black men remained silent. He shuffled along with the other black man, with his head hung and looking as guilty as sin. The smallest still seemed bent on arguing. "You gots proof?" he asked Matthew as he walked up to stand by Lum.

"We can't prove anything." Matthew said. "But we know it was you. You'd better be getting out of this part of the country. If I see you two around here again there'll be hell to pay." Matthew's voice was as cold as ice.

The smaller black man eyed Matthew belligerently.

"We goes wheah we wants to. Ain't no white man gwine give us awduhs no mo'." he snapped out.

Lum's move was as fast as lightning. In a blur of motion, he had the smaller Negro by the shirt collar with one hand, holding him up until his feet no longer touched the ground. The other hand shoved the barrel of the sawed-off shotgun against the black throat so hard that the man's eyes were bugging out and his face was shining with sweat. "Now you listen heah! You talks to Massa Matthew dat way one mo' time I'se gwine blow yo' black head off yo' shouldahs. It'll be de las' words you evah speak 'cause I done be killed you." Lum snarled. The big buck turned gray in the face and Lum set him back on the ground.

"We jus' be hongry." he whined, when he could get his breath.

"You be hongry, you bes' be getting yo'self a job. You gwine get yo' black ass killed, you keep stealin' from de white folks." Lum warned.

Lum seemed to have the situation so well in hand that Matthew simply folded his arms across his chest and stood back to watch.

Now that the barrels of the shotgun no longer pressed against his neck, the smaller of the two black men grew defiant once more. "Who you think you is? You jus' a nigga like I is. What you mean tellin' me what I bes' be doin'." he asked insolently.

From the look on Lum's face, Matthew figured it was time to step in before his black friend committed murder. He leveled the pistol at both the men and there was cold steel in his voice as spoke. "Lum has every right. You're on his land. Now get yourselves out of here and don't come back. The next time, we won't stand around and talk about it. We'll just blow your thieving heads off and put you where you won't be causing us any more trouble."

Chapter 45

The smaller black man gave Matthew a defiant look but turned and walked away. The larger of the two men stood there shaking like a leaf in a high wind and when Matthew aimed his pistol at him, he sank to his knees. "Are you going to leave, or will Lum and I have to carry your dead body out of here on a rail?" Matthew asked.

For the first time, the big black man spoke. "I got no place to go, Missa. I not be de one what cut yo' hawg's throat, dat be dat no-good Ezra. I jus' be comin' 'long 'cause he say he gots food. I'se hongry, Missa." he said humbly.

"Yeah, but you went along with him when he decided that my hog would make y'all a good meal." Matthew snapped.

"Please Missa. I didn' know what I be getting' into. I didn' know Ezra gwine steal dat hawg till it done be too late. I don't wants to steal nothin', I'se jus' hongry. You not gwine kill po' ol' Jiggs is you?"

Matthew took pity on the wretched looking black man and lowered the pistol. "Like Lum said, you'd better go find yourself a job." he said.

Jiggs held out a black hand that shook in a gesture of pleading. "I'se done walked heah all de way from Jaw-ja huntin' work. White folks say dey gots enough hep an' don't need no 'notha black mouth to feed. I don' know nothin', Missa. I be fit fo' nothin' but a field hand. I gots me a strong back though. Least I has when I'se not stahvin'. Missa, I hates to beg but I'se not eat nothin' in a week and I'se not gots de strength to leab heah. I don't know what I'se gwine do." Jiggs pleaded pitifully.

Matthew looked the young black man over thoughtfully for a moment. "You want food and a place to stay bad enough to work for it?" he asked.

"Yassuh." Jiggs replied humbly.

"Wynn," Matthew called out. "Come bring this man those left over hushpuppies."

Obediently, she came and handed the cold, hard fried bread to Jiggs. He made short work of it and looked grateful enough to cry.

"This man tells me he's willing to work for room and board. What do you think, shall we give him a try?" Matthew asked.

"Whatever you say Matthew." Wynn replied.

Lum hung his shotgun back around his neck and reached to help

Jiggs up. "Dis-un may be all right Massa. He gibs you any trouble I'll run him off my own self." he said.

"That settles it then. Jiggs, you've got yourself a job. You work for me for room and board and if you do a good job and don't try to steal me blind, I just might pay you what I pay my other help." Matthew promised.

"I'se not scared of hard work Missa." Jiggs assured him. "You bes' be lookin' out for dat no-good Ezra. He be bad business, you ain't seen de last ob dat man yet." he warned.

"You let me worry about Ezra. I'll be keeping an eye out for him and one on you too. Just because I hired you doesn't mean that I trust you any farther than I can throw you." Matthew told the young black man.

Jiggs' black face was round and childishly innocent. He rolled his eyes at Matthew. "Missa, I'se gwine work hard. Jiggs ain't no thief. I 'preciates you givin' me a chance." he said sincerely.

"Well, we'll see." Matthew said. "My place is a couple of miles from here. You reckon you can walk that far?" he asked.

"Yassuh." Jiggs replied.

They were at the back of Lum's property where it joined Todd's and the distance was a little more than two miles. Jiggs tried hard to keep up but soon fell behind and was staggering with weakness. Lum helped him up on his mule and led it the rest of the way to Matthew's farm before going back to Todd's.

"Where are we going to put him?" Wynn asked.

"That other little shack down by Willy's. It's not very big but it'll be a roof over his head," Matthew replied. "I'll take him down and turn him over to Willy and Lissa for the time being."

Matthew suited action to words and soon returned.

"Did you get him settled in alright?" Wynn asked.

"Yeah, I just hope I've done the right thing. There's nothing much worse than a man that's sorry enough to steal." Matthew replied.

"I'm not too concerned." Wynn said. "I believe he was telling the truth."

"Well, time will tell I guess. That other buck is the one that worries me. Now that one's trouble if I ever saw it. Somebody will end up killing him before it's done with." Matthew said, with a frown.

"I wonder where Todd and Sarah got off to. I half-way thought they'd be back long before now." Wynn said.

"'I did too. I'd have thought they'd give up the chase by now but I guess there's no use to worry."

"I wouldn't if it wasn't for Sarah. I doubt if she's ever spent a night out in the open in her life." Wynn said.

"Todd can take care of her. If they're not back by this time tomorrow, then I'll start worrying." Matthew replied.

Several miles away, Todd and Sarah, along with Ned, still followed the pack of hunting dogs. Todd glanced over at Sarah, with a touch of admiration. They had followed hard on the heels of the dogs all day, through underbrush and thick trees. Not once during the entire day, had Sarah voiced any complaint. Looking at her now, Todd could see her unspoken weariness. Her face was flushed from the heat but a little white around her mouth. Her blond curls hung in damp ringlets and her shoulders were slumped.

The dogs had followed the trail of the bear to the edge of the river swamp, sniffed around a bit and followed the trail on in. Todd stopped at the edge of the swamp to wait for Sarah, who was lagging a little behind. "We might as well stop here and camp for the night. The bear's took to the swamp." he said.

Sarah breathed a sigh of relief but didn't complain. "Are we going after him in the morning?" she asked.

"Not unless you want to go in the swamp after him." Todd replied.

Sarah shrugged. "I'll let you know in the morning." She raised a leg a little stiffly to dismount but stood with her foot in one stirrup listening. "The dogs sound different, Todd." she said.

"They've got something at bay in there. I'll bet they've got that bear cornered. I reckon I'd better go see." Todd rode off into the swamp and didn't notice at first that Sarah had followed him. She was behind Ned and he was surprised when he looked back and saw her.

As they drew closer, the barking of the dogs began to change into yelps of pain. They were now riding through water that came half way up on the horse's legs and the going was made treacherous by the soft marshy ground and submerged cypress knees. "Sounds like that bear's giving the dogs a fit." Todd called back over his shoulder.

They rode out onto a patch of dry ground and found the dogs

battling, not the bear but a huge wild boar! One of the dogs lay dead and another bled from a cut that ran from it's breastbone to it's belly. Todd raised his musket and waited for a chance at a clear shot at the beast. The moment finally came and he sent a fifty caliber slug into the hog, just behind it's shoulder blade. The hog let out a high pitched squeal and thrashed around until it at last lay dead.

Todd dismounted to take a closer look at the wild hog. The boar was one of the biggest he had ever seen and had tusks that looked to be nearly four inches long.

Sarah ignored the hog and went to examine the dogs. "Todd, old Kate's pretty bad off." she said.

Todd came to take a closer look at the injured dog. "There ain't nothin' I can do but put her out of her misery." he said, with regret.

Sarah agreed sadly. "It's a shame but we can't let her suffer."

Todd reloaded his musket and in seconds the dog was at peace. Feeling a little sick, he turned his back on the dead dogs. Sarah was kneeling down beside the huge boar and she looked up at him with a tired smile. "That was some good shot. It looks like I won't have to worry about where next year's sausage will come from." she said.

Sarah's complement made Todd feel ten feet tall and he answered her smile with a grin of his own. "If it don't spoil before we can get it home." he replied.

Todd's horse would have nothing to do with having the huge boar on it's back. Ned's mule finally accepted it reluctantly and they began to make their way out of the swamp. Dusk was already setting in and it was hard to see in the deep shadows. As before, Sarah followed along behind the two men. The tired dogs were close on her heels, splashing and sometimes swimming as they followed.

Suddenly, off to their left, they heard a rattling of underbrush at the same time as the dogs went crazy in a frenzy of barking. A big black bear suddenly stepped out of the bushes a scant ten feet away from the startled Sarah. She let out a gasp but raised the musket to her shoulder and fired. The bear let out an enraged roar and ran off into the swamp and Sarah fell off the horse with a splash as she hit the murky water. The dogs took off after the bear and Todd leapt from his horse and came running to see about her. She gave him the surprise of his life as she sat up sputtering and wiping her wet hair out of her eyes. "Did I kill it?" she asked excitedly.

Todd knelt down and began feeling Sarah all over for broken

bones. "Good God woman! Are you alright?" he asked frantically.

Sarah slapped his hands away. "Sure I am. Did I get the bear?"

"You hit it." Todd said at last.

"But I didn't kill it. Oh damn!" Sarah said. She got up and began squeezing the water out of her clothes.

Todd, totally shaken, wiped his brow and took his musket with him to walk off in the direction the bear had taken when it disappeared. After only a few steps, he called out, "Sarah, you and Ned come here!"

The bear had run off no more than twenty yards before dropping dead. Sarah had somehow managed to shoot it right through the heart. "Looks like you got it after all, Honey. What I want to know is where you learned to shoot. I'd have figured you didn't know which end of a gun the bullet came out of." Todd said in amazement.

"I was raised with two brothers." she answered.

"You can tell Matthew his gun kicks like a mule."

Todd grinned. "You tell him. Heck, it ain't the gun's fault. You was just caught off balance."

"Yeah I was." Sarah said happily.

By the time they got the bear out of the swamp it was full dark. Todd cooked supper over the open campfire after ordering Sarah to rest. "You've done enough for one day." he said. As soon as the fire was going, Sarah went off into the bushes to get out of her wet clothes. She returned a couple of minutes later, wrapped in a blanket and walking slowly.

Sarah eased herself down on the ground, beside the camp fire and gave Todd a tired smile. "Can I complain now?" she asked sweetly.

Todd grinned at her and turned over the bacon he was frying in the skillet. "Go ahead." he invited.

"My shoulder hurts, my backside hurts, I got red bugs, I'm sunburned and I'm cold and I'm tired enough to die! Besides that I'm starving and I want a bath and..."

Todd stopped her with a wave of his hand. "That'll do for a start." he said, with a grin.

"But I'm not through!" Sarah insisted. "I'm wet, I'm mosquito bit, I just pulled a tick off my arm. My shoes are muddy and my hands are blistered and I've got saddle sores."

"You through?" Todd asked.

"Yeah, can I go again next time?" she asked.

Todd laughed until he cried and even Ned looked amused.

In spite of the long, hard day Sarah had spent, she ate a hearty supper and slept like a baby afterwards.

Todd woke her up early the next morning and watched silently as she eased herself up from her makeshift bed of blanket and pine needles. Holding her blanket around her with one hand, she bent with difficulty to retrieve her still wet and very muddy shoes and clothes. Without a word, she shuffled off into the bushes to dress.

Todd set the bacon to frying in the skillet and in a few minutes Sarah returned fully dressed. Her walk was as stiff as that of an old woman but still she voiced no complaint. He hardly recognized his usually impeccably groomed wife. Her mud streaked blond curls hung down in her face and her clothes were a sight to behold. The britches she had borrowed from Wynn were a couple of sizes too small and Todd thought, with a pleased grin, that britches on a woman weren't such a bad thing after all.

Still, without a word, Sarah left Todd to tend the breakfast and walking a little like Matthew's brown mare was still under her, went to admire the bear she had shot. The carcasses of the bear and hog were hanging in a tree and she walked all around them before returning to the campfire. "I had to make sure I didn't dream the whole thing." she said at last.

"I got a little trouble believing it too. You alright this morning?" he asked.

Sarah simply nodded, though it was obvious that not one muscle on her small body wasn't sore.

Todd gave her an admiring grin. "The heck you are. You're so sore you can't hardly walk." he said sympathetically.

"I've got places that hurt where I didn't even know I had places." she admitted. "I never had so much fun in my whole life though. No wonder you men like to hunt so much. I used to think Wynn was crazy for wanting to go along all the time, now I see why. Just looking at that bear makes me feel like I'm about ten feet tall."

"Well, you've got a right to feel that way." Todd agreed. "Just wait till you show Matthew and Wynn, they just won't believe it."

An hour later, just as the morning fog was beginning to burn off, Todd and Ned finally succeeded in loading the carcass of the hog onto the back of Ned's mule. It had stiffened. overnight and the only way they could load it was by spreading apart the rib cage and tying it astride the mule's back, with it's legs hanging down. The ugly head of the beast rested on the mule's broad hips facing backwards.

Getting the bear loaded was a different matter. Neither horse would have anything to do with it and Todd was quickly losing patience with the whole thing. After a considerable amount of cussing, he finally got the bear loaded on the back of Matthew's brown mare. He almost had it tied down when the mare took a fit of bucking and threw it right back off. "We'll just leave the damned thing!" Todd said in disgust.

Sarah set him straight in a hurry. "Oh no you don't! That's my bear and we're gonna get it home, if we have to drag it!" she insisted.

In the end, that's exactly what they did. The bear was drug home, trailing behind the brown mare on the end of a rope.

Chapter 46

Matthew walked out onto the front porch to shave, shirtless and still half asleep. Wynn had gotten up ahead of him and the tin wash basin was already filled with hot water. The whole shelf was wet, as well as the floor, from a recent scrubbing but Matthew thought little about it. He reached for the bar of homemade soap and began to lather his face. The six ducks lined themselves up as usual on the wash shelf and with much interested quacking, watched him shave.

To Matthew, the ducks were an endless source of amusement. By now, he was beginning to recognize them as individuals and had begun to call them by name. The big drake was Oscar and the five hens, he had named Flossie, Matilda, Sally and Sadie. The fifth was as yet still unnamed. He had just finished shaving and was feeding the ducks their usual morning handful of corn, when Wynn came out to tell him that breakfast was ready.

The moment she steeped out onto the porch, the six ducks flew off the wash shelf and waddled off across the yard, quacking in alarm.

"Dad gum it Matthew, I ought to kill you and them ducks! I spend half of every day running them off the porch and cleaning up after them and here you are, feeding them corn and encouraging them!" Wynn protested angrily. She stomped her foot for emphasis.

Matthew jumped guiltily and gave her a boyish grin. "Oscar and the girls like corn." he stated innocently.

"Oscar, huh! Well Mr. Kendall! You just better inform Oscar that if he don't stay off my porch and take his harem with him, he just might end up in a pot of duck soup." Wynn threatened. She turned on her heels and slammed back into the house.

No sooner had she left, than the six ducks flew back onto the wash shelf. Matthew grinned at Oscar, who was busily preening his feathers. "I reckon you heard that, Oscar. You'd better watch out, she may do it. You wouldn't look nearly so good in a pot of duck soup, now would you?" he asked.

Oscar cocked his head, as if trying to understand and Matthew made a half hearted attempt at shooing off the ducks. They obediently flew off the wash shelf, except for the one unnamed female, which stubbornly refused to move. "You're as stubborn as someone I know." Matthew said and threw her off the shelf. She landed in the yard, squawking indignantly and with a grin of pure mischief, Matthew promptly named her Wynn.

By the time breakfast was over, the subject of the ducks was forgotten. A days work was lost the day before, due to the impromptu manhunt and Matthew sought out Willy and the newly hired Jiggs to begin catching up on it. The plot of land that was set aside for the house garden was in need of plowing and this would be as good a day as any to get started on it. Jiggs, feeling much revived after a couple of meals and a night's sleep was set to work on it. Matthew and Willy spent the morning finishing up the last stretch of fence that surrounded the farm. The last of the barbed wire was strung just before noon and Matthew fastened it off with a look of satisfaction.

Feeling a little uneasy about Jiggs, Matthew returned to the house to check on him. Jiggs, with a plow hitched behind a mule, plodded along steadily and methodically. Most of the garden plot was now neatly laid out in rows and Matthew could find no fault with his work.

Over the noon meal, Wynn expressed her concern over Todd and Sarah. Matthew, feeling the same way, decided that they would go check on them.

Todd and Sarah were still gone when they arrived. Lum greeted them as they rode into the yard. "Dey mus' be on de way. De dawgs jus' come in and dey sho' looks like dey been into somethin'. Dey all cut up and plumb wo' out." he said.

Matthew examined the tired, muddy dogs and scratched his head in bewilderment. "What do you reckon they got into, that got them all cut up like that?" he asked.

"I don't know." Wynn replied. "Whatever it was, must have been big and mean. It looks like Kate and old Sam are missing. If Todd and Sarah don't show up soon, we'd better go hunt them. I sure hope Sarah's all right. I'd know if anything had happened to Todd." Wynn said worriedly.

She had just finished speaking when Lum pointed out across the clearing. "Heah dey come." he announced.

The small procession heading towards the house moved slowly. Ned was leading the mule, with the hog tied on it's back and Todd was leading Matthew's brown mare. Behind the brown mare, a blanket wrapped bundle bumped and bounced along the ground and Todd had to go back every so often and untangle it from various obstacles. Sarah was riding Todd's gray and as she came closer, it became evident that a dirtier, more bedraggled woman had never been seen. She was grinning from ear to ear and waved to them enthusiastically as she rode into the yard ahead of Todd and Ned.

"We were getting worried. What took y'all so long?" Matthew asked.

Sarah stayed on the gray mare and scratched at her rib cage. "Well, first Todd shot a wild hog and then I shot the bear and then we like to have never got them home. Matthew, your gun kicks like a mule and if that old mare of yours rides like a rocking chair, remind me to stay out of rocking chairs." she said with a grin.

"Now wait a minute! Did you say you shot the bear?" Matthew asked incredulously.

By now, Todd and Ned had reached the yard and Todd answered him. "She sure did! Got him with one shot too. You should have seen her!" he replied, with no attempt to even try to hide his pride.

"Well, how about that! Are you going to sit there all day, or are you going to get down and show us the bear?" Matthew teased his sister-in-law.

"Todd, come help me. I don't think I can move." Sarah said sheepishly.

Todd lifted her down from the saddle and had to hold onto her for a minute until she got her legs working well enough to stand on her own. "Now, let's show off your bear." he said with a grin.

The bear, not too badly damaged from being drug several miles in a blanket, was showed off and admired. Sarah accepted her praise gracefully and refused to let Todd's hog go unnoticed.

Wynn looked the huge boar over carefully and burst into a fit of giggles. "That mule looks like it's got two heads, one on each end." she explained.

"That's one of the biggest wild boars I ever seen." Matthew said, when they were through laughing. I'd sure hate to tangle with him without a gun."

"Yeah, me too." Todd agreed. "He killed one of my dogs and cut another one up so bad, I had to put it out of it's misery." He went on to tell the whole story of how the hog and the bear had met their fate. When he had finished, he asked, "Now, what about y'all. Did you run up on those two men?"

Matthew filled them in about the two Negroes and finished off by saying, "I'm probably a fool for taking that one on and I doubt if I've seen the last of the other one."

"You're probably right about that sorry Ezra. I've seen his kind before." Todd agreed.

Matthew and Wynn stayed to help process the meat. It was nearly dark by the time they had all of it ready to go into the smokehouse. The entire hog was ground into sausage and the meat from the bear was hung up to cure.

By suppertime, Granny had a pot roast from the bear cooked and ready to serve. The meat was as good as the finest beef and it had just enough of a wild taste to make it interesting.

Matthew and Wynn returned home later than their usual bedtime and found the front door of the house standing open. The interior of the house was a mess, as every one of the rooms had been gone through. After a thorough search, they found nothing missing except a few jars of canned goods from the pantry. An inspection of the smokehouse revealed that a ham and a slab of salt bacon were missing.

When the inspection was finished, Matthew said "It looks like Ezra's been up to his tricks again. What I don't understand is why he tore up everything in the house and didn't take any more than he did. He could have easily gotten away with one of the mules and our muskets. It just doesn't make sense."

"Maybe you'd better go check on Jiggs, Matthew." Wynn

suggested.

Matthew found Jiggs sound asleep at Willy's house and Willy was able to confirm that he was at home, the whole evening. More puzzled than ever, Matthew went back home to talk the matter over with Wynn. After much discussion and thought on the subject, they came to the same conclusion Their house was messed up as an expression of defiance and the thief had not been serious about stealing anything at all.

During the next week, life on the farm proceeded as usual. Jiggs was proving himself to be a willing worker and Matthew could still find no fault with him. Nothing else had gone missing and they were beginning to hope that the troublesome Ezra had left their part of the county. This hope was dispelled when Todd came to tell them that someone had tried to set fire to Lum's house the night before. The person was quickly driven off by Lum's bloodhound and the house had suffered little damage.

"This is getting plumb out of hand." Todd stated. "But we can't set up every night to guard our places."

"I agree." Matthew replied. "Something has to be done, but unless we catch that scoundrel red-handed, I don't know what it'll be."

"He's bound to slip up sometime. He's out for revenge since you and Lum got the best of him. I never believed in whipping blacks but I sure would like to take a few strips of hide off that one." Todd said grimly.

"I've got an idea." Matthew said thoughtfully. "Between you and me and the four hired hands, we could take turns standing guard at night."

"That might work. You reckon you can trust that new one you hired?" Todd asked.

"I think so, he's been working a lot harder than I've been asking him to and he seems mighty grateful for what little I've done for him. I found out a little more about him this week. He had his shirt off the other day and he's got scars on his back that looks like someone once whipped him to within an inch of his life. Well, I asked him about it and he told me that he got that whipping for preaching to the other slaves. It seems his former owner didn't hold with blacks having religion." Matthew replied.

"That's a hell of a note." Todd stated.

"Yeah, it is." Matthew said. "Back to what we were talking about, it'll be a lot of trouble to take turns staying up like that, but it'll be worth it if we can catch that son-of-a-bitch."

For the next two weeks, they took turns standing guard but nothing out of the ordinary took place. Still, they decided to continue to keep watch.

Willy came over one morning after standing guard all night, to show Matthew the shotgun he had finished working on. The shotgun looked like a new one and Matthew was amazed. Willy had fashioned a new stock out of wild cherry wood and had forged a new hammer. The barrels were free of rust and gleamed with a fresh coat of oil. "I can't believe this is the same gun, Willy. Have you shot it yet?" Matthew asked.

"Nawsuh." Willy replied. "I gots no powdah nor nothin'."

Matthew grinned. "I've got what you need Willy. Wynn found the shot for it in a tin can, and a sack of wadding. I'll loan you some powder and we'll see if this thing will shoot."

A few minutes later, the shotgun stood the test after being loaded and fired. The new hammer worked perfectly and Matthew gave Willy enough powder to go squirrel hunting. Willy returned a few hours later, triumphantly carrying a sack of squirrels. He offered them to Matthew, but Matthew refused to take them.

Chapter 47

After another week of having no trouble, they slackened their guard and after yet another week, dropped it entirely. Matthew and Todd, by mutual agreement had stayed near by, being careful not to leave Wynn and Sarah alone. Both of them had business to attend to in Ocala, but kept putting it off. By the end of September, they could delay no longer.

Together, they set out soon after breakfast. It was a good day for a ride and the two men were enjoying their outing. The matched pair of grays stepped along at a lively pace and their riders talked amiably as they rode along.

"How much do you reckon that roll of gator skins will bring?" Matthew asked.

"I'm not sure." Todd replied, "I hope that they'll bring enough to set aside for me a new rifle. I figure my share of what we make off the skins and whatever I get out of the cane might be enough, if I'm lucky and syrup sells high this year."

"Maybe that shipment of rifles finally came in at the hardware store. I'm kind of anxious to see what they've got." Matthew replied.

"Me too. Using this damn musket is driving me crazy." Todd said.

"Well, one thing about it. If you come up a little short, I can always let you have the difference." Matthew offered.

"That's a tempting offer Matthew but I don't believe in owing anybody, not even you. I appreciate the offer though." Todd replied.

Todd suddenly pulled sharply on the reins and stopped in the middle of the road. He sat there for a few seconds, looking thoughtful and rubbing his cheek.

Matthew stopped also and turned in the saddle to look back at him. "What's the matter Todd? Did something sting you?" he asked.

"It's Wynn, something's wrong at home!" Todd exclaimed.

Before Todd could think any farther, Matthew had turned his gray mare around in the road and was heading back the way they had come at a full gallop. In a matter of seconds, Todd followed close on his heels but was unable to catch up.

Cold fear wrapped itself around Matthew's heart as he raced along. Surely the dreams that he still had all too often should have been warning enough to keep him from leaving her alone. He kicked the well-trained gray savagely in her ribs and she obediently gave him all that she had.

Matthew could hear the hoof beats of Todd's horse a few feet behind him and without turning around called out. "Can you tell what the trouble is?" he yelled.

"No," Todd yelled back. "She's scared now but alright."

In spite of Todd's reassuring words, Matthew continued to ride towards home at breakneck speed.

Wynn and Sarah had stayed behind at Matthew's house. It was a good chance to spend the day together, sewing quilt scraps and catching up on their girl talk. The two women sat together on the front porch, contentedly sewing and comparing notes on each other's husband.

"Matthew couldn't care less about how the house is kept." Wynn said. "He actually encourages those ducks to get on the porch. I'm a

255

good mind to quit cleaning up after them and see what he does."

"That just might work." Sarah replied. "After he goes out to shave a few mornings and finds a mess in his wash pan, he might get the idea."

"I think I'll try it." said Wynn.

"Todd's as bad as Matthew. I guess you ought to know, since he's your brother. You should have seen him the other day, using one of my pots to melt down lead for musket balls. I had to throw the pot away when he got through with it." Sarah complained.

"Yeah," Wynn agreed. "Men are a mess all right. But I sure would hate to live without Matthew, now that I've got used to having him around. We get along real good, for the most part."

"So does Todd and me. Now that I'm expecting, he wants to treat me like I'm made of glass sometimes. I keep telling him I'm not going to break." Sarah said.

Wynn gave Sarah a puzzled look. "I haven't noticed him doing that. I noticed he didn't say a word, the other day when he saw you lugging in that bucket of water."

Sarah shrugged and looked a little embarrassed. "It ain't in the day time that he treats me like glass." she admitted.

"Oh, I see." Wynn said, in sudden understanding. "I suppose it's the nature of a man to be more gentle, when a woman's in a delicate condition."

"Maybe so. But I'll admit I miss the times when he was like something wild. He never lets himself get carried away anymore. You know what I mean, don't you?" Sarah asked.

"I think so." Wynn replied. "I never know what to expect with Matthew. Sometimes he's like a summer rain and then again, he's like a hurricane."

Sarah sat up straighter in her chair and leaned forward to look in the direction of the lane that led to the house. "Someone's coming Wynn. Who is that?" she asked.

Wynn leaned forward to look and after a moment, said with some alarm, "It's that sorry Ezra! He would show up with the men gone off to town. Willy and Jiggs are out in the shed working on a wagon wheel. I guess with them here, we'll be alright, though I hate to depend on black men to protect me when it comes to one of their own kind."

Ezra staggered into the yard as bold as brass. He was obviously drunk and in a belligerent mood. With an insolent look, he stepped up onto the porch.

"What do you want?" Wynn asked coldly.

"I wants me a job. You done give Jiggs work. I needs me a job too." Ezra said.

"We haven't got any work for the likes of you. You'd better be on your way before Matthew gets back." Wynn stated firmly.

"You gots food? You gwine gimme somethin' to eat?" he asked, in mock meekness.

"Not on your life. I don't share my food with people that would rather steal it." Wynn snapped.

"Den I guesses I'se jus' gwine have to hep myself." Ezra said insolently. With that, he walked boldly off the porch and headed straight for the kitchen. Wynn and Sarah, not knowing what else to do, followed close on his heels.

Lissa, who was cooking dinner let out a screech and ran out the back door as Ezra burst through the front. Without a word, the black man headed straight for the stove and began eating right out of the pots. Wynn grabbed a rolling pin off of the table and raised it high but just as she was going to bring it down on Ezra's head, he moved. The rolling pin struck his shoulder a glancing blow and he turned on Wynn in a fury of drunken rage.

"Ezra don't take no such treatment from de white folks no mo'." he shouted. "I'se gwine show you white bitches what de black man be good fo'!" In an instant, he had Wynn down on the floor and was tearing at her clothes with both hands.

Wynn struggled but found that she was no match for the big black man. She managed to scratch his face and received a resounding slap across the face. Meanwhile, Sarah had tried pulling him off and trying to beat him off with her fists. By now, Ezra was insanely obsessed with his purpose and paid no attention to the screams of the two women, nor their feeble attempts to stop him. In desperation, Sarah looked for the rolling pin but it had rolled underneath the hot stove. Her eyes fell on the butcher knife lying on the kitchen table and she picked it up. Holding it in both hands, Sarah raised the knife to stab Ezra right in the middle of his broad back.

Before she could bring it down, Jiggs burst through the open door running. The huge black man grabbed Ezra by the shirt collar and picking him up bodily, flung him across the room. Ezra hit the wall,

257

next to the door with a thud and for a moment simply stood there with a look of shocked surprise on his face. Then, he went limp but strangely enough, seemed to hang there slumped against the wall.

Wynn was the first to recover and stood up on shaking legs, pulling the tattered remnants of her dress together with one hand. Sarah dropped down weakly into one of the kitchen chairs and Jiggs stood in the middle of the floor with both fists clinched and looking mad enough to kill.

Still holding her dress together, Wynn slowly crossed the room to take a closer look at Ezra. Just as she reached him, Willy ran up to the open door, carrying his shotgun. Lissa came right behind him with her hand over her mouth and looking scared to death. "It's alright Willy. Jiggs got here in time." Wynn said.

Willy lowered the shotgun and handed it to Lissa to hold. Panting for breath from running after the shotgun, Willy stepped inside. "You alright Miz Wynn?" he asked.

"I'm alright Willy, but see what's the matter with him." she said, indicating Ezra.

Willy took one look at Ezra and looked back at Wynn. His eyes looked as big as saucers and his black face had gone a little gray. "Miz Wynn, dis man be done daid."

Wynn's knees buckled and she sank to the floor. "But he's standing up Willy." she said incredulously.

Willy reached out with both hands and pulled Ezra's body away from the wall. It crumpled face down on the floor, revealing the bloody hole in it's back. A long spike had at some time, been driven into the wall next to the door, put there for the purpose of hanging one's coat or hat. It was this that had killed Ezra.

Sarah gasped and made her way to the door to be sick. Wynn remained on the floor and Jiggs still stood where he was, looking dazed. Lissa covered her face with her apron and began to wail.

Wynn arose from the floor and went to put her arms around the violently shaking Sarah. Jiggs had turned almost white and started to run out the door but Willy stopped him. "You ain't gwine go no-wheah." he stated.

"Let me go Willy, I'se done kilt a man and de law gwine come hang po' ol' Jiggs. Don't mattah no how, I'se gwine go to hell. De Lawd, he say a man what kills anotha gwine burn. Oh Lawd!" Jiggs moaned.

"Not for defending a white woman." Wynn assured him. "Besides, what the law don't know won't hurt them."

"You not gwine turn Jiggs in?" he asked pitifully.

"Of course not. It was an accident Jiggs." Wynn told him.

"I'se gwine go to hell, Miz Wynn." Jiggs lamented.

"For goodness sake, Jiggs. People don't go to hell for killing someone like that." Wynn indicated Ezra's body with a wave of her hand. She reached for Matthew's work shirt that was hanging across the back of one of the kitchen chairs and put it on over her torn dress. "Let's get out of here. I need some air and we've got to think what to do about this."

Later, they had all gathered on the kitchen porch and were making a valiant effort to calm down. Willy was awkwardly soothing Lissa. Wynn and Sarah sat on the edge of the porch holding hands. Jiggs paced back and forth across the length of the porch, wringing his hands and alternately worrying about his lost soul and the law. He suddenly stopped pacing and pointed down the lane. "Oh Lawd!" he cried out. "Heah de law come now."

Sure enough, the sound of rapidly beating hooves could be heard coming up the lane. Wynn and Sarah stood up and in a matter of seconds, Matthew and Todd rode into the yard at a full gallop. Matthew was down off the gray before it even slowed down, and running across the yard towards Wynn. She met him half way and threw herself into his waiting arms. He held her tight and the beating of his heart was so hard that the vibrations of it shook both of them. Sarah had rushed into Todd's arms a moment later and it was a while before the two women could explain what had happened.

When the story was all told and Matthew and Todd had looked the dead body of Ezra over, Jiggs approached Matthew and fell down on his knees before him. "I'se sorry Missa Matthew. You wants to get de shuff, you goes ahead. Ol' Jiggs done kilt a man an' ol' Jiggs gwine go to hell. You wants to whip ol' Jiggs, ol Jiggs jus' get what he deserve." He remained on his knees, with his head hung and his hands clasped in his lap.

Matthew knelt down in front of the desolate black man. "You done a brave thing Jiggs. Nobody's going to get the sheriff and nobody's going to whip you. As for going to hell, God takes it into consideration when it's an accident like this. You've done no more wrong than Todd and me, when we killed people in the war. You can

259

rest assured that you've gained my gratitude for the rest of your natural life. You have a home and a job on this farm as long as you want it. You deserve a medal Jiggs, not a whipping." Matthew said sincerely.

Jiggs raised his bowed head to look Matthew in the eye. "I'se done what I gots to do. Dat Ezra done be hurtin' yo' woman. Nobody gwine be messin' wid yo' woman, I can hep' it. You done hep out ol' Jiggs when he be needin' it. I sho' didn't go to kill dat man though. I be mad 'nuff to kill him but I sho' didn't go to. De good Lawd gwine send me to hell. I'se sho' sorry Missa Matthew." Jiggs said sadly.

Matthew reached to put his hands on Jiggs' shoulders. "Sorry Jiggs? There's nothing to be sorry for. If Ezra had done what he intended to do to my wife, then there would be something to be sorry for. The Bible says an eye for an eye and a tooth for a tooth. Ezra just got what he deserved and it was God's doing, not yours." Matthew assured him.

This seemed to satisfy Jiggs and the big black man began to sob as the feeling of guilt was lifted from his shoulders. Matthew, already touched beyond measure at Jiggs' loyalty, pulled him close and hugged him like a brother.

Matthew stood up. "Now Jiggs, you and Willy get this thing out of my kitchen and take it to the sink hole and bury it with the rest of the rabid varmints. What happened here today is our business and nobody else's, understand." There was steel in Matthew's voice as he spoke.

Willy and Jiggs obeyed quietly and Lissa rushed to scrub the bloodstains off the wall with a mixture of lye.

"I'd have never thought Jiggs had it in him." Matthew said finally.

"Me either." Todd agreed. "I guess it just goes to show you, you can't judge a book by its cover."

Chapter 48

Soon after, Todd took Sarah home. "She's still pretty upset." he said. "I guess our business in town will just have to wait another day."

As soon as they had gone, Matthew took Wynn in his arms once more. "Are you sure you're alright Honey?" he asked worriedly. Wynn's cheek was still red and swollen where Ezra had slapped her and Matthew ran his fingers across it gently.

"I'm fine." she assured him.

"When I think what could have happened to you, it makes my blood run cold." Matthew replied.

Wynn hugged him close. "Well it didn't, thanks to Jiggs."

Matthew looked down at her with pain filled gray eyes. "I never should have left you alone." he said regretfully.

"Matthew, you had no way of knowing. Don't blame yourself. I wasn't alone, there was four other people here besides me." she reassured him.

"He pulled her close once more and rested his chin on the top of her head. "What you need is one of those little Derringers that you can keep on you all the time and maybe a small dagger that you can strap to your leg." he said.

Wynn gave a small laugh. "You worry too much Matthew. I'd feel like a fool going around all the time, armed to the hilt."

"Maybe so and maybe I do worry too much. I have nightmares about losing you." Matthew admitted.

"I could lose you too, Matthew. Life's a gamble but we can't go around worrying about it all the time. We'd go crazy." Wynn told him.

"You drive me crazy anyway woman." Matthew said fiercely. He pulled her closer still and kissed her with a passion that took her breath away. Her gasp of surprise was followed quickly by a tiny moan and she pulled away from him breaking the kiss. She looked around quickly to see if they were alone.

"Matthew Kendall, have you no shame? It's broad daylight." she teased.

"So it is. Let's see now, Lissa's in the kitchen, so that won't do. Willy and Jiggs are still gone. The stable loft just might do the trick if we don't make too much noise."

Like mischievous children they sneaked into the stable, hand in hand. The door squeaked on its hinges as Matthew closed it behind them and Wynn peeked through the cracks to see if anyone had heard.

The air in the loft was hot and sweet smelling from the hay. Wynn came into his arms with a passion that matched his own. "I need you woman!" Matthew growled. "God, how I need you." With impatient hands, she loosened the buckle on his belt, reaching greedily to hold the proof of his desire in her hands. The fire in their veins drove them on and they mated like wild things, quick and hard driven in the heat of the loft.

Five minutes after entering the stable, they slipped back into the yard, blinking in the bright sun and exchanging a secret smile. Wynn brushed hay from Matthew's sweaty back and he picked stray pieces of it from her hair.

"Remind me to drive you crazy more often Matthew." Wynn said, with a grin.

"I don't have to remind you. You come by it naturally." Matthew replied.

"How much longer do you think it'll take Willy and Jiggs?" Wynn asked.

"They should be back any time now. Why don't you go change your dress and I'll go rub down the gray. I left her in a lather, that mare about run her heart out." Matthew said.

That night, after supper was over, Matthew and Wynn sat on the front porch. "I think I'll go pay Willy and Jiggs their wages. It's a little early but after what Jiggs done today I want to give him a bonus as a reward." Matthew said.

"That a good idea Matthew and he deserves it, but can we afford it?" Wynn asked.

Matthew only nodded and went into the house to get their pay. Not even Wynn knew where he kept his money hidden. He left with it in his pocket and returned a short time later.

"What did Jiggs say when you gave him his reward?" Wynn asked.

"It was the dangdest thing I ever saw. That big black man that just this morning killed a man was so pleased that he broke down and cried like a baby. He said, he'd never had any money in his whole life and I guess what I gave him seemed like a fortune." Matthew replied.

"How much did you give him, Matthew?" Wynn asked.

"A twenty dollar gold piece." he answered.

"Whew, I guess that did seem like a fortune to an ex-slave." Wynn said. "Matthew I don't begrudge what you gave him one bit, so don't misunderstand me. What I can't understand is how you never seem to run out of money. We haven't brought in one crop or even sold a hog since we've been here."

"You let me worry about the finances, woman. We've got enough to hold us for a while. It may be a couple of years before this farm is self supporting." Matthew told her.

Wynn said nothing more but was unusually quiet the rest of the evening. Just before they went into the house to go to bed, a thunder storm came up. It lasted for only a few minutes but left behind it air that was noticeably cooler. Wynn shivered and snuggled closer to Matthew on the porch swing. "I think we may be in for our first cold snap." she said.

Matthew snuggled her even closer and nodded. "It's still too early for frost." he replied.

"Yeah, that'll come later in the month or maybe not even till November. It'll be a little chilly tonight and be as hot as ever tomorrow."

"Just right for snuggling up in a nice warm feather bed." Matthew said contentedly.

"Umm hmm." Wynn agreed.

When Matthew went out early the next morning to shave, there was a decided chill in the air. Wynn had filled the tin wash pan with hot water as usual but hadn't cleaned out the basin or scrubbed off the shelf. Matthew looked at the basin of fouled water in disgust and threw it out into the yard. The ducks came running as usual to line up on the wash shelf. Matthew cleaned out the basin and proceeded to shave in what felt like ice water. He fed the ducks their usual handful of corn and went inside for breakfast.

Wynn kept watching him but he said nothing about the mess on the porch.

For three days running, the situation went from bad to worse. Matthew decided that he'd either have to give up shaving or pen up the ducks. In the end, he did both. On the same day that he started to grow back his beard, he and Willy built a duck pen, where the chicken pen had once stood. He penned up Oscar and his harem and the remaining rooster and two hens as well.

There was no doubt in his mind what Wynn was up to. She'd hated the ducks and their mess from the start. Now that he had begun to realize what she was up against and he couldn't say that he blamed her. He had learned long ago that in any conflict there were but two choices. A man had either to fight or surrender and it was a wise man

263

that could tell which was the most prudent action.

Matthew stood back to watch the ducks explore their new domain. Being penned up didn't seem to bother them in the least.

Wynn came across the yard and stood beside him, looking at the ducks. Matthew half way expected her to begin gloating over her victory but to his surprise she only said, "They need something to swim in. There's a big old wash tub in the shed that we ain't using. It just might do the trick."

"It might at that. Are you sure you don't need it for anything else?" Matthew asked.

"I'm sure. By the way, in all the excitement the other day, I forgot to tell you. Sarah said there's a man at Starke's Ferry that's got a litter of puppies to give away." she replied.

Matthew rubbed thoughtfully at the stubble on his chin. "Well, I wouldn't mind having a couple of puppies to train. Did she say what kind they are?"

"A mix, I think she said they're a cross between blue tick and some big yellow dog that took up on the place a while back. If you want pure breeds those puppies probably aren't what you're looking for." Wynn replied.

"Well, I guess it wouldn't hurt to go look at them. I may ride over there tomorrow if I have time."

"I wish you would. I hear they've got some young guava trees started. Maybe you could talk them out of a seedling for us to plant up by the well. Guava trees need a lot of water to start out."

"I never ate a guava but I guess if you like them, a tree would be nice. I've been thinking, I may just take a couple of those puppies no matter what they look like. Even the most worthless mutt will bark when a stranger comes around. That trouble we had with Ezra sure made me wish that we had something on the place to at least bark when someone or something was prowling around at night."

"I know what you mean." Wynn agreed. "By the way, did Todd find him a rifle when y'all went to Ocala the other day. I was so busy when you got back, I forgot to ask. you."

"No, the shipment still hasn't come in. By the way, remind me to give you your share or the gator money. I keep forgetting to give it to you."

"We're both getting awful forgetful, I guess we just got too much on our minds. Did you get that letter off to the lawyer in Georgia?"

264

she asked.

"Yeah, I'm kind of anxious to hear from him. I need to know about the taxes on the Silver Oaks land and I asked him to tell me if Elizabeth's folks had come back to that part of the country. I'm not sure where I stand legally as her heir." Matthew replied.

"I never thought about that. Was any of the property out there in her name?" Wynn asked.

"No, not actually. She stood to inherit her folk's plantation when they passed on. It was burnt to the ground, just like Silver Oaks, so she wouldn't have ended up with much anyway. I believe her folks hold some property in New Orleans. That's where they went when the war ended up on their doorsteps." Matthew explained.

"I see." Wynn replied. "I don't understand much about such matters." she admitted.

"In this case, I don't either. As her widower, I hold certain rights but in the end, the final decision will be up to her folks." he said.

Chapter 49

The next afternoon, Matthew set out to drive the buggy to Starkes Ferry. The entire day was overcast and dreary, with intermittently falling rain and gray skies. As a result, the deeply rutted sand road was muddy and resembled a washboard. The wheels of the buggy bumped along, causing the conveyance to rattle and shake enough to set Matthew's teeth on edge. Rain, or no rain, he was beginning to wish that he had rode the gray, rather than hitching her to the buggy. But then, he reasoned, if he were to bring home a couple of puppies, it would be impossible on horseback. This ride over to Starkes Ferry was something that he could have put off until another day and he wished now, wholeheartedly, that he had.

The day had gotten off on the wrong foot from the start, with the soot in the cook stove chimney catching fire and filling the kitchen with smoke and ashes. The resulting mess and inconvenience had set Wynn off into a foul mood, so that she was snappish and irritable.

To make matters worse, the ducks had escaped from their pen during the night and wreaked their usual havoc on Wynn's clean porch. Matthew had finally soothed her ruffled feathers by having Jiggs catch them all up again and clip their wings, so that they could no longer fly. The chore of scrubbing the porch had fallen to him, since Lissa was busy helping Wynn clean the kitchen. Willy had fallen heir to cleaning the stovepipe and had reported that it would do for a while but would have to be replaced.

Matthew had figured that, for one morning, he had seen enough aggravation but as fate would have it, there was still more to come. In the midst of all the scrubbing that the house had suddenly required, the rope on the well pulley had broken, sending the bucket to the bottom of the well and Wynn into yet another fit of temper.

Getting the bucket out of the well and rigging up the pulley with new rope took most of the rest of the morning. By the time he had gotten it accomplished, Matthew was wet and miserable.

Dinner was delayed when Lissa had scalded her hand and in the ensuing excitement, the biscuits were burned. By the time dinner was over, Lissa had gone home to nurse her burned hand and Wynn had broken a bowl of bean soup all over the floor. When the dishes had finally been washed and yet another mess cleaned up, Wynn had taken to her bed pleading a headache.

So it was, that Matthew had decided that rain or no rain, it was a good time to be elsewhere. A sudden gust of wind blew rain into his face and he pulled the brim of the black felt hat he was wearing down lower over his eyes. In spite of the rain, the day was still hot and the dampness along with the heat, set his face to itching beneath his fledgling beard. Irritably, he scratched his chin and eyed the long puddle that stretched before him in the road. Such puddles, or mud holes to be more exact, seldom posed any problem if one was not driving a loaded wagon.

The gray took the mud hole in stride, although at one point the wheels of the buggy were more than half submerged. As soon as the mud hole was left behind, the right front wheel of the buggy set up an annoying squeaking. The sound was aggravating to Matthew's already raw nerves but he thought little of it. Most likely it was caused by a little sand getting into the hub.

A quarter of a mile later, Matthew found out that not stopping to investigate the squeak was a bad mistake. In the middle of yet another mud hole, the offending wheel came off. The buggy tilted sharply to the right, sending Matthew off the seat and depositing him into the mud hole with a splash The well trained gray came instantly to a halt and looked back over her shoulder at the crazily tilted buggy and the man that was trying to extract himself from the puddle.

A sharp pain in the middle of Matthew's back sat him back down in the muddy water. He let out a groan of half pain and half disgust. At this point, his usually even temper deserted him. In a loud lengthy speech, he informed the startled gray of a few pertinent facts she had heretofore been ignorant of. According to him, the mud hole's mother was a she dog and was surely damned to hell for it. The buggy was possessed of various perverted sexual habits, along with having a dog for a mother and it too was doomed to hell. Matthew at last spent the worst of his wrath in his tirade of verbal abuse against the uncaring buggy.

He jammed his soaked hat back on his head and attempted once more to rise, this time with more success. The pain in his back wouldn't allow him to straighten up but by bending awkwardly at the waist, he was able to walk. Still mumbling obscenities, he looked the situation over and decided that it was hopeless. With much pain and difficulty, he unhitched the gray. Fortunately, he was closer to home than to Starkes Ferry. His intention was to ride the gray home bare backed and send Willy and Jiggs back for the buggy. After several unsuccessful attempts to mount the gray, he found that this too would be impossible. Any attempt to climb onto the gray's back was followed by a stabbing pain in his own. The only course left for him was to walk back home and lead the mare.

By the time he had covered the first half-mile, walking had become pure torment and he was beginning to wonder if he had injured himself worse than he had thought. Gritting his teeth against the pain and muscle spasms in his back, he continued on. He had no choice but to keep moving.

By moving at a snail's pace and stopping often to rest, Matthew at last made it home. Seeing no sign of life when he at last reached the house, he hitched the gray to the porch rail and made his way painfully into the house. As he entered the door, a muscle spasm seized him and he leaned against the door frame, calling out loudly for Wynn.

She answered him from the vicinity of the master bedroom. "Just a minute Matthew." she called back.

He stood there scowling, resting his weight against the door frame and watching the puddles of rainwater that dripped from his clothes grow at his feet. "Fine!" he muttered. "Now she'll be mad about the tracked up floor."

Wynn came into the front room, dressed in gown and wrapper and rubbing sleep from her eyes. Her face was a little puffy and her eyes were red. "Now what the heck ails you?" Matthew snapped.

Wynn lifted her head in surprise, not yet having looked at him. "I'm fine Matthew, but what on earth happened to you?" she asked, in alarm.

Matthew managed a wry grin. "Oh nothing much. A wheel came off the wagon and dumped me in a mud hole. I fell wrong and managed to throw my back out. I just walked five miles in the rain because I couldn't get this dilapidated body of mine up on the horse. Other than that, everything's just fine." he replied sarcastically.

"And I thought I was having a bad day." Wynn said. "Does it hurt much?" she asked.

Matthew made an effort to straighten up but only succeeded in setting off another muscle spasm. "Only if I move or breathe, or something." he replied, with a touch of irony.

"You are hurt Matthew. Come get out of those wet clothes before you catch your death of cold." Wynn said sympathetically. Her face reflected her growing concern.

"I'm alright Honey." Matthew tried to reassure her. "I just need some dry clothes and a little rest and I'll be as good as new." Another muscle spasm hit him and spoiled the effect of his words.

Wynn was immediately at his side. "Sure you are. Here let me help you." she said. She suited action to words and helped him to the master bedroom. With quick efficiency, she stripped the wet, muddy clothes from his body and bathed him with tepid water from the pitcher on the washstand.

In spite of the pain in his back, Matthew was beginning to enjoy the whole thing. No one had fussed this much over him since he was a child. Almost before he knew it, he was stretched out on the feather bed and Wynn was tucking pillows behind his back to make him more comfortable. "That's better." he said "You need to find Willy and Jiggs and send them after the buggy."

Wynn gave the pillows one last pat and straightened the sheet that covered him. "Let me change clothes first. I think Willy and Jiggs are at the quarters. There ain't much they can do around here on a day like this." she said. "I'll go see if I can find them."

She stripped off her dressing gown and draped it carelessly over

268

the back of the vanity chair. In one quick movement, she pulled her nightgown over her head and stood naked except for her ruffled drawers. In spite of his pain, Matthew eyed her appreciatively. Wynn ignored him and proceeded to dress herself. In a matter of minutes, she was fully clothed and had left the room.

Matthew settled himself more comfortably against the pillows and began to doze. As long as he kept perfectly still, the pain was almost nonexistent.

In what seemed like no time, Wynn returned. The soft click of the bedroom door closing behind her awakened Matthew and without thinking, he made an effort to sit up. The resulting muscle spasm had him back against the pillows in an instant.

Wynn gave him a worried look and set down the tray she was carrying. "They're on their way." she said. "Willy asked me if the wheel was broken or just came off. I told him I didn't know and he said not to worry, he'd get it fixed."

"I don't doubt it. What that man can't fix isn't worth fixing to start with." Matthew replied.

"That's the truth. Do you reckon you could roll over so I can get to your back?" she asked. "Lissa sent some kind of liniment that she makes up for Willy. She swears it'll fix you right up."

With considerable effort, Matthew managed to turn over onto his stomach and Wynn began to massage the strong smelling liquid into his back. The liniment was apparently as strong as it smelled, for very quickly his whole back began to burn. The heat of it was soothing however, and he let her continue without complaint. As she rubbed, the tied up muscles began to relax by degrees. He closed his eyes and sighed with pleasure.

"Is that helping any?" Wynn asked.

"Umm, yeah, that feels good. Your day hasn't been much better than mine, has it." he murmured.

Wynn's hands on his back slowed and became almost still. "Some days, everything just seems to go wrong. I sort of figured it was just me. I get like this sometimes." She breathed a long sigh and continued to rub his back.

"Why do I get the feeling that there's more bothering you than just an unusually aggravating day?" Matthew asked quietly.

Wynn's hands stopped entirely and she sat down beside him on the bed. "It's nothing Matthew. I'm just being silly I guess. You know how women are." Her words were spoken lightly but the tenseness in her body told a different story.

Matthew turned on his side, already much relieved of his pain and wrapped an arm around her waist. "That time of month?" he asked.

Her breath came out in a shuddering sigh. "Yeah." she answered.

"Are you hurting?" he asked.

"No more than usual. It's just...well, oh Matthew, I'm just so damn disappointed." She began to cry softly and reached to wipe her eyes.

Matthew caught her wrist. "Don't do that. You'll get liniment in your eyes. Now what's disappointed you enough to be worth, crying about?" he asked.

Wynn wiped her eyes on the sleeve of her dress instead.

"Don't you see Matthew? I'm not expecting." she replied.

"Well, no." Matthew said, slightly puzzled. "But it's not worth crying about, is it?"

Wynn turned to him with tears streaming down her face. "It is worth crying about Matthew. I want so much to give you another son."

Matthew pulled her down to him until her head rested beside his on the pillow. "And you will." he reassured her. "We have years to start a family in. Right now, I'm enjoying having you to myself."

"I don't know why, Matthew. I can't even stand myself lately." Wynn said sadly.

"Be careful how you talk about my wife." he said gently.

"It's true." she insisted.

"How do you figure that?" he asked.

"I guess I'm just not much of a wife." she replied.

Matthew took in a slow breath, to help him hang onto his patience. "I've found no fault with you." he said.

"But I hate it Matthew! I hate cooking and cleaning and staying in the house all the time. I feel like I'm in a cage." she wailed.

Matthew gave a small laugh. "I wondered how long it would last. I knew you hated those things long before I even met you. Why do you think I keep paying Lissa?"

Wynn raised up to look at him in surprise. "Then why did you let me knock myself out, trying to be a housewife?" she asked incredulously.

"I left it up to you. If I'd wanted a cook and a housekeeper I didn't have to marry you to get one. I have Lissa to do that kind of thing." Matthew explained.

Wynn's smile was like sunshine coming out after a rain. "You didn't get much of a lady when you married me, did you?" she asked.

"What I got was a perfect combination." Matthew said seriously. "I got a partner and best friend who also happens to be a part time lady and full time seductress."

Wynn sniffed and another tear rolled down her cheek.

"Now what's wrong?" he asked.

"I got liniment in my eye." she explained.

Matthew chuckled sympathetically. "And your head hurts and your tummy hurts and you feel like hell. Go wash your hands and let's take a nap." he ordered.

"But what about supper? Lissa's going to be out of commission with her hand for a while." Wynn objected.

"We'll eat canned goods later. Now hush and come to bed." Mathew ordered.

Wynn washed her hands and joined him in the bed. Soon, they were both fast asleep.

Chapter 50

Their nap turned into a night's sleep and as a result, they awakened early the next morning. Matthew's back was stiff and sore but much improved. Wynn had awakened in good spirits and in spite of her tirade about cooking and house work, prepared a better than average breakfast.

The rain that had fallen all the day before and most of the night had stopped. The air after the rain was crystal clear and a little chilly, below a brilliant blue bowl of a sky.

Willy and Jiggs arrived at their usual time, as well as Lissa, who swore her hand was much improved. When they arrived, Matthew was sitting on the front porch steps, cleaning his pistol. "Did you boys have any trouble getting the buggy home?" he asked.

"Nawsuh." Willy replied. "Dat nut done be come off an' we done had us a time huntin' it."

"Was it hard to fix?" Matthew asked.

271

"Nawsuh, Jiggs jus' lif's it up an' I put de wheel on an' tightened de nut." Willy replied.

Matthew gave them both a wide grin. "You boys done a good job." he said sincerely.

"Thank ya, Missa Matthew. You jus' lets us know what it is you needs done. Me'n Jiggs'll take care ob it. You needs to res' yo back." Willy offered.

"I'll do that." Matthew replied.

After the rain, the fields were just right for plowing and Matthew set Jiggs to work on it. Jiggs seemed to genuinely enjoy the field work best of all. Single handedly, he had already cultivated nearly twelve acres to be sown in hay next spring. Willy, on the other hand, proved more useful at other things. Not only was he a capable blacksmith, he was exceptionally talented at building or repairing almost anything. Willy was by nature, almost fanatical about everything being in good working order.

Quite often, he saw the need of things being done, that had never crossed Matthew's mind. This morning, Willy had arrived with a new idea and full of enthusiasm.

"You knows dat cane grinda' you got in de shed? I gots me an idea how I could be turnin' it into a mo-chine dat hep de women folks wash de clothes." Willy said, his black eyes dancing with enthusiasm.

Matthew raised a skeptical eyebrow, but was curious about what Willy intended to do. "How would it work, Willy?" he asked.

With much walking about and motioning with his hands, Willy described it. "De mule, he walks round and turns de geahs and de geahs turns dis paddle in de wash pot. Dat stirs de clothes 'round. I gets dat all worked out, I'se gwine see can I make de thang what wring de watah out ob de clothes."

Matthew still didn't understand how it would work. However, he could anticipate no future need for the cane grinder, so he decided to let Willy try it. If the contraption actually did work, Wynn would probably enjoy it. "Well, while you're at it, make sure you move it up close to the well, then they won't have to haul water so far." he suggested.

"Dat be a good idea, Missa Matthew. You cares if I gets stahted on dat dis mawnin?" Willy asked eagerly.

"Go ahead Willy." Matthew said with a grin.

Willy went off to the shed, whistling happily as he went.

272

Wynn came to join him on the front porch, looking as pretty and fresh as the rain washed morning. Matthew greeted her with a smile as she came to sit beside him on the steps. She reached out to give the half inch long whiskers of his new beard an affectionate tug. "Did that dip in the mud hole hurt your pistol?" she asked.

"Nothing a good cleaning and oiling won't cure. I'm just about finished." he replied. He gave it a final once over with the oily rag, reloaded it and replaced it in it's holster.

"Don't you ever get tired of wearing that thing?" Wynn asked.

"I wore one for most of the four years I was in the army. I got so used to it, I'd feel naked without it." Matthew replied.

"I guess you would." Wynn agreed. "Is your back still feeling better?"

"Yeah. It's sore as all get out but I think it'll be all right." he replied.

"That's good." Wynn cocked her head in a listening attitude and said, "I thought I just heard a horse whinny, down at the road. I wonder who could be coming this way, this early in the morning."

"There's no telling. Maybe it's someone from across the river getting an early start to Ocala." Matthew said with a shrug. He began to gather up his gun cleaning equipment but stopped to listen. "It sounds like whoever it is just turned down our road. I wonder who it is."

Wynn shook her head. "It couldn't be Todd, he always cuts across the field." she replied.

Matthew stiffened perceptibly, as a rider rounded the bend in the lane. The blue of a Yankee uniform was unmistakable, even at that distance. Behind the mounted rider, a man dressed like a common farmer stumbled along at the end of a rope. As the pair drew nearer, Matthew could see that the man on foot, obviously a prisoner of the Yankee, was shackled at both wrists and ankles with heavy chains.

Wynn turned her eyes from the pair on the road to look at Matthew. The soft gray of his eyes had darkened to the color of tempered steel and the line of his jaw had squared beneath it's covering of whiskers. "Is that a Yankee, Matthew? What do you suppose that man done, that he's in chains?" she asked.

Matthew continued to sit where he was. His body appeared relaxed to a casual observer but the look in his eyes was chilling to behold. Wynn's questions went unanswered. "Let me handle this." he said, in a voice that indicated he would accept no argument.

The blue clad soldier rode into the yard and stopped. The unfortunate prisoner, who stumbled along behind him, fell to his knees as soon as he stopped. Without so much as offering a greeting to Matthew, the soldier turned in the saddle to snarl back at his captive. "On your feet you Rebel bastard!" he snapped. The man in chains slowly struggled to his feet and stood wavering with exhaustion.

"I'll thank you to watch your language in front of my wife." Matthew said coldly.

The Yankee turned insolent eyes on Wynn and looked her over from head to toe. "Beg your pardon lady." he said with a leer. "You crackers got any water? Me and my horse are thirsty."

Matthew continued to sit where he was, a little slouched and with his hands resting loosely on his knees. "The bucket's over there." he said, indicating the wash shelf. "Help yourself."

The Union soldier dismounted, looking annoyed that he wasn't being waited on. As his feet hit the ground, his exhausted prisoner's knees buckled once more. With an ugly scowl, the blue clad soldier walked heavily back to where his prisoner knelt on the ground. He drew a long saber from its scabbard and used it to prick the prisoner between the shoulder blades. "On your feet scum!" he growled.

Matthew was on his feet in a move that was as quick as lightning. For a moment his gray eyes blazed with such hate that the soldier stepped back a full pace before sheathing the saber. The ragged prisoner struggled once more to his feet and gave Matthew a look of warning.

Matthew drew in a slow breath, feeling like an actor in a scene that had yet to play itself out. "Get your water Yankee and get off my property. You abuse that man one more time within my sight and there's going to be hell to pay." he said coldly.

"Obstructing an officer of the U.S. government is against the law. This man is guilty of treason and I'll treat him as I see fit." the soldier replied.

Matthew leaned against one of the posts that supported the porch roof and said nothing.

Looking superior, the soldier walked heavily across the yard and up the porch steps, as if he owned the place. The scabbard that held his saber clanked loudly as it hit against each step in turn. The silence was so great that each step taken by the soldier's booted feet across the porch sounded as loud as thunder.

From where Matthew stood, he could see not only the Yankee soldier but Willy standing near the shed and Lissa, peeking out from behind the kitchen door. The prisoner was hungrily eyeing the water bucket with hopeless eyes.

The Union soldier took two swallows from the dipper and spat the rest out. He turned his back on the wash shelf and clumped noisily back across the porch.

"Don't you crackers know to keep fresh water in your bucket?" he asked rudely. He descended the steps, purposely crowding Wynn where she sat.

Wynn gave him an annoyed look and spoke for the first time since the pair had arrived. "What about him? Aren't you going to give him any water?" she asked.

"Mind your own business girlie. Rebel bastards that commit treason don't need no water." he replied.

Wynn's black eyes flashed with sudden temper and she came instantly to her feet.

When Matthew moved, it came as a surprise to even Wynn. One second, he was slouched against the post and the next there was a sickening crack as his fist slammed against the jaw of the startled Yankee. The Union soldier landed five feet away, on his back in the yard, shaking his head and spitting out broken teeth.

"I told you to watch your language around my wife." Matthew snapped.

The soldier came instantly to his feet and came at Matthew with a roar of pure rage. With a move as lithe as that of a cat, Matthew dodged the Yankee's first wild swing and countered it with a fist into the man's unsuspecting belly. The Yankee promptly bent double and Matthew set him straight again with another blow to his jaw. Matthew stood back, rubbing his bleeding knuckles, as the Yankee caught his breath. In a sudden move, Matthew's enraged opponent caught him in a flying tackle, sending them both to the ground. Matthew, pinned beneath the slightly larger man, was temporarily at a disadvantage.

The Yankee got in a couple of telling blows, before Matthew managed to throw him off. He rolled out from under the Yankee, slightly dazed but recovered in time to continue the scuffle.

Matthew had two advantages over the bigger man. He had not yet lost his temper and he was quicker, both with his fists and on his feet. Still, at one point, the Yankee managed to land a blow to Matthew's chin that rattled his teeth and left him momentarily stunned. He found himself sprawled on the ground and shook his head to clear it. Just as Matthew's vision cleared, the Yankee drew his saber. Wynn came seemingly out of nowhere and clung to the Yankee's arm for dear life. The soldier shook her off as if she were no more than an annoying insect. In an instant, the tip of the saber was pressed against her chest. "Stay out of my way you Rebel bitch!" he growled.

At this point, Matthew saw red. A cry escaped from his throat that was a cross between a Rebel yell and the scream of an enraged panther. So quickly did he move, that the Yankee never knew what hit him. The saber flew off harmlessly across the yard and Matthew's fists slammed into him again and again. Totally beyond reasonable thought Matthew continued to pummel the Yankee, long after the fight had gone out of him.

Gradually, he became aware of Wynn trying to pull him off of the now helpless Yankee. For a moment, he continued to sit astride his beaten foe, panting for breath and wiping blood and sweat from his eyes. Finally, he got to his feet and stood looking down at the soldier with utter contempt. "This man needs some water, Wynn. Go get him some." he commanded.

On shaking legs, Wynn rushed to obey. When she came back with the bucket, Matthew took it from her and dumped it's entire contents into the Yankee's battered face. Matthew handed the bucket back to her calmly and waited for the Yankee to finish waking up.

The soldier regained consciousness quickly and managed to sit up. "You awake now, Blue Belly?" Matthew asked.

The Yankee only looked at him and dug around in his mouth in search of a broken tooth. In a move that was both sudden and unexpected, the soldier reached for and drew the revolver on his hip. Matthew, moving even faster, kicked it out of his hand.

"Good." Matthew said quietly. "I think that when a man dies, he ought to know who it was that killed him and why." He drew his pistol unhurriedly from it's holster and pointed it at the Yankee with deadly intent.

"You wouldn't shoot a representative of the U.S. government, would you?" the soldier asked, in a show of false confidence.

"You're right, maybe I wouldn't. Lord knows the U.S. government's been good to me." Matthew replied. With calm deliberation, he pulled back the hammer on the .44.

The Yankee's pretense of calm left him and he cowered back away from the pistol. "Please don't." he begged.

"Yeah, you're right, maybe I should reconsider. Shooting's too good for the likes of you. But then I'm a kind man. Wasn't it your Mr. Lincoln that said 'With malice towards none and with charity towards all?' Right pretty words, even if they were penned by a Yankee hand. Just to show you that I'm still a loyal American citizen, I'm going to honor those words and not give you what you deserve." Matthew replied, almost sweetly.

The Yankee's eyes showed his relief at Matthew's words but filled once more with dread as he continued.

"What you deserve is being marched fifteen miles in the condition you're in now, with no food and no water. You deserve to be stabbed in the back with a bayonet until you damn near bleed to death. Then when you get so weak that you fall down, you need to find out what it feels like to lose your life, when your only crime is not being able to walk any farther. You deserve to have your eyes gouged out and your ears cut off, just for kicks. That, my fine representative of the U.S. government is what you deserve. But, as I said, I'm a kind man and I hold no malice. For you, I'll make it quick and easy. No hours of torture for you, as you deserve, just a simple bullet through that ugly head of yours. There comes a time, Sergeant Saber, when hell must be paid."

The light of recognition that showed in the soldier's eyes was gratifying and Matthew pulled his swollen lips into a grin. "You remember, do you?" he asked. The Yankee nodded slowly. "I'll never forget you, or your kindness." Matthew continued, almost sweetly. "I'm giving you the honor of at least knowing why you died and who killed you."

The silence was broken by the sound of the .44 pistol, shattering the stillness of the morning. The hole that appeared suddenly between the Yankee's eyes looked almost innocent in comparison to the mass of brains and gore that spilled out of the bigger hole in the back of his head. For a matter of seconds, the body jerked and writhed before it was still.

Chapter 51

Matthew slowly became aware once more of his surroundings. Everything seemed to be moving in slow motion, as if he were in a dream. The sound of Wynn's startled scream reached his consciousness. Willy, running across the yard, seemed to be moving at no more than a snail's pace. Lissa's screech from the vicinity of the kitchen door sounded as if it were miles away. Only the prisoner, still tethered at the end of the rope behind the Yankee's horse, seemed unperturbed. He looked at Matthew with an expression that was a curious combination of gratitude and respect.

Matthew lowered the pistol and blew the smoke from the end of the barrel as calmly as if he had only shot a mad dog or a snake. He holstered the pistol and turned first to Willy. "Go get Jiggs and get that piece of garbage out of my yard." he commanded coolly. "On second thought, that piece of trash can wait. Get the chains off that man and hurry up about it."

Willy, looking awe-struck, obeyed without question.

Matthew's eyes next fell on Lissa. "Go get Jiggs" he ordered the cowering black girl. She too rushed to obey. Blood and sweat trickled once more into his eyes and he wiped it away before turning at last to Wynn. She stood white faced, with her hand over her mouth, staring in horror at the body of the dead Yankee. "Matthew you killed him." she said in disbelief.

Matthew had no more than opened his mouth to answer her, when he was interrupted by the clatter of hoof beats coming into the yard. In a heartbeat, Todd was down from his horse and looking the situation over. "Well, I'll be damned." he said. "I never figured, when you said you'd get that bastard that you'd ever get the chance. And I thought our days of killing Yankees was over. Just goes to show you what I know. What are you going to do with that bastard now?" Todd asked.

"Put him somewhere that the sun don't shine." Matthew replied.

The full impact of the situation was beginning to hit Todd and he gave Matthew a worried look. "You just might end up in the county jail, if this gets out buddy." he said.

"I don't anticipate that it will." Matthew replied, without concern.

"Well, you done the world a favor when you got rid of that one." Todd said. He turned to Wynn. "What are you looking so green around the gills for? You've seen dead people before." he scolded.

"Not killed in cold blood, I haven't." she replied sickly. "He had him beat, Todd and just gunned him down like he was a dog."

Todd raised an eyebrow at his sister and putting his arm around her, marched her into the house. "Little sister, it's about time you put yourself in his shoes. You've seen the scars from that bastard's bayonet yourself, but what you didn't see was how much pleasure that rotten son-of-a-bitch got out of murdering the ones of us that couldn't walk. Those poor wretches never had a chance. But let me tell you something, that ain't all. What if you came home and found all that you owned was totally destroyed and your husband and mother brutally killed by men just like that one? What if it had been you in that Yankee prison, guarded by men just like that one out there. What if it were you that nearly starved at their hands. A place like that can do strange things to a man. What I want to know, before you start condemning your husband, is just how much would it take to make you do what he just done?"

Wynn reached for her brother and hid her face against his shoulder. "I understand now, Todd. If the Yankees had done that to me, I'd go on a killing spree that would never end." she replied honestly.

"I only lost the use of two fingers and the right to own slaves. That man out there lost it all. I'm not the one that needs your understanding, Wynn." Todd told her gently.

Wynn drew in a deep breath, stood back and squared her shoulders. "He has it. Thank you Todd." she said. Together they walked out to join Matthew in the yard.

He was kneeling down, talking quietly to the man who was the Yankee's prisoner. Wynn came to stand behind him and rested her hand on his shoulder. He glanced up at her and a look of mutual understanding passed between them. "Wynn, I want you to take this man in the house as soon as Willy gets these chains off and see that he has what he needs. Todd and I have to get rid of that piece of filth over there. If anyone comes around, you make sure that this man is well hidden." Matthew ordered.

"I'll take care of him. You and Todd will be careful won't you?" she asked worriedly.

"Don't worry, no one knows they even came this way. This is..., well you don't need to know his name, only that he's connected with

Jeff Davis." Matthew turned to the man. "Sir, my wife, Wynn."

The blond haired stranger nodded cordially. "My pleasure Ma'am." he said.

Willy came out of the shed and tipped his hat respectfully to the stranger. "Missa, it gwine take a hammah an' chisel to get dem chains loose. You gwine has to go to de shed." he said.

"Whatever it takes fellow, these things have about rubbed the hide off of my ankles." The blond haired man stood up with Matthew's help and allowed Willy to help him to the shed. As he passed by the body of the dead Yankee, he paused and deliberately spat upon the corpse.

Matthew turned to Todd. "You ready to help me haul off this trash?" he asked.

Todd nodded. "Yeah, but I sure as hell hate to get my hands dirty fooling with that scum. I think I hear Lum coming. He was behind me on that old mule of his, when we heard the shot and I took off and left him."

As Lum rode into the yard he looked at the body of the dead Yankee and got down unhurriedly from the mule. "Lawsy Massa, I be knowin' you be shootin' at dat Yankee an' not no snake, I done been heah in mo' ob a hurry." he said.

"That's what it was Lum, just a snake." Matthew said. "Me and Todd are going to haul it off."

Lum looked at Matthew's pale battered face and bleeding knuckles. "Massa, I knows jus' what to do wid dat snake. I gets Jiggs to hep me an' we go an' feed dat skeestah to dat ol' bull gatah, down yondah in de swamp."

Matthew managed a grin that set his busted lips to bleeding. "You do that Lum, and make sure you do it good. That snake doesn't need to be seen lying around in these parts."

"Yassuh, we knows jus' de place." Lum replied.

In no time at all, the two huge black men had loaded the body of the Yankee on Lum's mule and were on their way through the woods in the direction of the swamp. Wynn led the Yankee's horse into the stable and shut the door, while Todd covered the bloodstains in the yard with a shovel and tamped down the wet sand, until no sign of what had occurred remained. The sound of Willy's hammer rang in the stillness as he pounded at the shackles on the fugitive's wrists.

"Well, that's over." Wynn said.

280

Matthew turned his back on both of them and walked slowly toward the house. As he stepped up onto the porch, he was suddenly seized with such violent trembling and weakness, that he had to cling to the post for support. Wynn reached him as he slowly slid down the length of it and dropped his head down onto his knees.

A tangled web of emotions swept through Matthew all at once and a familiar darkness began to descend. He'd known the darkness before. In the Federal prison and in the field hospital in Virginia, it was a welcome thing. A way to shut out the world. As he felt it closing in, a part of him reached for and welcomed it, while yet another part struggled to push it away. Strength came to him now, as it hadn't in the past. Todd's strong hand on his shoulder held him fast, while Wynn's arms surrounded and sheltered him. Gradually, awareness returned and he became conscious of Wynn's soft weeping. He slowly raised his head and met Todd's concerned gaze. "You alright buddy?" Todd asked.

"Yeah." Matthew managed to reply.

"Here, let's go inside and let Wynn take care of those cuts." Todd said and reached down to help Matthew up. Once on his feet, Matthew wavered slightly As it had once before in the past, Todd's strong arm came around him, lending him support. Wynn on the other side, added her support to that of her brother's.

A few minutes later, Matthew had once more regained control of his turbulent emotions. He sat at the kitchen table while Wynn bathed his cuts. Todd sat across the kitchen table from him and listened quietly as Matthew explained in detail, what had occurred.

"I thought there was something familiar about that fellow." Todd said, after Matthew had finished. "From what I hear, every member of Jeff Davis' cabinet was charged with treason. The face is familiar but I can't put a name to it."

"I can, but I won't." Matthew replied. "The fewer people that know who he is, the better. He said he got caught down south a ways. He was trying to get to the coast to catch a ship to Cuba. We'll hide him out here for a couple of days, until he's ready to travel."

"He's an important man then, is he? Did he actually do anything wrong?" Wynn asked.

"Nothing more than me or Todd. His only crime was holding a higher than usual position in the government of the Confederacy." Matthew explained.

The kitchen door opened after a brief knock and Willy escorted the raggedly dressed, blond haired man into the room.

"Thank you Willy." Matthew said. "I want you to guard that stable if anyone comes around. No one is to see that horse under any circumstances."

"Yas Suh." Willy replied. He left the room with a respectful tipping of the wide brimmed palmetto hat that covered his head.

Lissa, still looking wide eyed from the events of the morning, spooned food onto a plate and placed it on the table before their unexpected guest.

He sat down wearily and although he must have been ravishingly hungry, he took the time to say to Lissa, "Thank you girl." He turned to Wynn. "And you Ma'am."

"You're welcome." Wynn replied.

The stranger turned then to Matthew. "I don't believe I caught your name, sir. Since I owe you my life I'd be pleased to know just who it is that I owe it to." he said.

Matthew reached out his hand to shake that of his guest. "Captain Matthew Kendall of the Seventh Georgia." he replied. "I don't see that you owe me anything. What happened out there was a personal matter. However if it bought your freedom, as well as settling a score for me, then perhaps it was worth it."

"Kendall?" he said thoughtfully. "Yes, I've heard of you by that name too. It was me who signed the citation recommending you for a decoration for bravery after the first battle at Manassas, or what the Yankees called the Battle of Bull Run."

"That's the first I've heard of it." Matthew said.

"Unfortunately a lot of correspondence got lost during the war. I'm sorry you never received it. You deserved it and a whole lot more."

"What did you do Matthew?" Wynn asked. "And what did you mean Mr... Sir, when you said you knew of him by his name too?"

Matthew replied first. "Nothing much, the best I can remember." he said, looking uncomfortable.

"Your husband is too modest, my dear." the stranger replied to Wynn. "I was referring to your husband's nickname. Many people knew him better as The Cat."

Todd, who was sitting next to Wynn at the table, looked at Matthew in open-mouthed surprise. "My God! You? Surely not!" he exclaimed.

"Matthew, you never told me you had a nickname." Wynn accused. "How did you get it?"

Matthew only shook his head. "I only heard it once or twice myself. I have no idea where it came from."

"That's easy to answer, Captain Kendall. It refers to your habit of always landing on your feet, no matter what, kind of scrape you got into. I must say, the name struck fear into many a Yankee's heart, at least those that didn't heed your warnings."

Matthew gave his guest a blank look and he continued. "They learned very quickly, that when The Cat said there would be hell to pay, they'd better listen. Your campaign against the Yankee partisan rangers was well known at the Capitol. It impressed Jeff Davis that you were such a gentleman about it. First you warned them and if they didn't cease whatever skullduggery they were up to, they got scratched by The Cat. As the story goes, the scream of the Rebel Cat was one of the last things they ever heard."

"You can't believe everything you hear." Matthew said.

"Well, story or not, let me answer your wife's first question about the citation. I read the report signed by General Bartow's second in command. Bartow's dying words were for the regiment to hold up the colors at all costs. Well, according to the report, your husband not only held up the colors, Mrs. Kendall, he defended them with nothing more than an empty gun."

Wynn looked at Matthew as if she had never seen him before. "You did that Matthew?" she asked incredulously.

"I seem to remember that I ended up carrying the colors at least once that day. Mostly I remember the heat. It was the hottest day I ever seen. I lost as many men out of my company to heat stroke as I did to battle. It's a wonder we won that one at all." Matthew said depreciatingly. "They should rename it the battle of Break and Run. Both sides certainly done their share of it that day."

Chapter 52

Matthew's guest patted his now full stomach in satisfaction and laughed heartily at Matthew's unintentional joke. "Mrs. Kendall, that was the best meal I've had in weeks. Thank you very much." he said to Wynn.

"You're more than welcome Mr. umm-, it's awkward not knowing what to call you." she replied.

After a moment's thought, his face lit up with a glow of satisfied amusement. "I arrived here in chains, dying for a drink of water. I suppose that with a little imagination, you could get Linc Waters out of that."

"Well, Linc Waters it is then." Matthew said with a grin.

Wynn rose gracefully from her chair, very much the lady in the presence of what was turning out to be an honored guest. "Lissa, would you get the back bedroom ready and prepare a bath for Mr. Waters. I'm sure he could use some rest."

Lissa, a little surprised at the behavior of both her employer and his wife, answered respectfully, "Yassum, Miz Wynn." and hurried to obey.

"I think I hear Lum and Jiggs coming back." Matthew said, and went to the door to take a look.

Lum greeted him with a satisfied smirk. "Dat ol' gatah say he likes de dinnah you done sent."

"Well, I hope it doesn't make him sick. What's that you've got there?" he asked.

Lum handed the rolled up bundle of clothing to Matthew. "It be a shame to waste deez clothes. I gots it in my head dat man in dare might jus' find dis stuff useful."

"Now there's an idea, Lum. A Yankee uniform might just be the ticket out of here." Matthew said. "Here Wynn, see about getting this stuff clean." he said, as he handed the bundle to her.

"Lum, go find Willy and tell him to come here, would you." Matthew said.

Lum, noticing the difference in Matthew's manner, said nothing but sought out Willy as Matthew had said. Lum couldn't decide if it was an order or a request.

In a matter of minutes, Lum, Willy, Lissa and Jiggs were assembled together in the kitchen. Wynn sat at the table with the newly christened Mr. Waters and Todd, wondering what would come next.

Matthew stood up at the head of the table. "What happened here today is no light matter. I've broken the law, but I want you all to know that my conscience is clear." Matthew's eyes swept over the

284

small assembly, catching and holding each of their gazes in turn. "Todd, I'm going to ask you not to tell Sarah about this. Knowing it will do her no good and the fewer people who know about it, the better. Wynn, I think you already know how important it is, that this not get around." He paused. "Now, for the rest of you," Matthew continued, meaning the Negroes, "each of you has shown me your loyalty in one way or another. I have no doubts about Lum, or the rest of you, for that matter. What happened today is to go no farther than this room and I believe that will be the case. But, if it does and word leaks out," he paused for emphasis, "there's going to be hell to pay. That's all I have to say."

Matthew's small speech was followed by total silence in the room. Wynn made a minute study of the boards on the top of the kitchen table. Todd's gaze was locked unmoving on the window across the room. Mr. Waters appeared to be almost dozing and the Negroes all stood with their arms hanging loosely at their sides and their eyes downcast.

Lissa was the first to move or make a sound. Her black hand, still bandaged from yesterday's burn, flew up to cover her mouth and a small sob broke from her throat.

Matthew's eyes, still uncharacteristically hard, turned on her sharply. "Have you got a problem with that Lissa?" he asked, almost sharply.

Lissa jumped when he spoke and her eyes flew up for a second to look at him, before once more seeking the floor. "Can I be sayin' somethin', Missa Matthew?" she asked meekly.

Matthew continued to stare at her sternly, but nodded.

Lissa reached for Willy's hand to draw courage from him, before she spoke. "Missa Matthew, dey's not be one soul in dis room, what wouldn't hab kilt dat Yankee dey selves, you say you wants it done, 'ceptin' maybe Missa Watahs. What I means is dis, Missa Matthew; you don't gotta be tellin' us what we's already knows." Lissa wiped a tear off her black cheek and fell silent.

"You can add Mr. Waters to that list girl." Mr. Waters replied. "Had I the chance, I'd have drawn great pleasure from doing the job myself."

It was Matthew's turn to drop his gaze. "Lissa's right. I owe you all an apology." he said.

The sun seemed to come out in the room as six pairs of eyes

brightened simultaneously. Todd stood up. "Well, I don't know about the rest of you but I've got work to do. Me and Lum just came by to borrow your can of axle grease, we're all out." he said.

"Help yourself, Todd. Willy'll get it for you." Matthew said.

"Yas suh, Missa Todd. I gets it. I'se got work I gots to do too." Willy replied.

After everyone had gone except for Wynn, Matthew and Mr. Waters, Lissa announced that his room was ready, as well as his bath. When he too had gone, Wynn dismissed Lissa. "Go home and take care of your hand." she told the black girl gently. "I'll take care of dinner. You can come back in time to help with supper if you feel like it."

Now that they were alone, Wynn reached for Matthew's hand. "There's blood on your shirt Matthew, come let me get you another one."

Matthew went with her into the master bedroom and removed the soiled shirt, while Wynn went to get another one from the wardrobe. He handed her the dirty one, in exchange for the clean one. "Thank you." he said, almost formally.

Wynn gave him a worried look. "Matthew, you're not yourself yet." she said gently.

"Oh, then who am I?" he asked as he put on the clean shirt and began buttoning it.

Wynn stared up at him worriedly. "Matthew, I don't know. That's what scares me. I thought I knew the man I married, but I'm finding out that I don't know you at all."

"Why, because I executed that scum?" he asked.

Taking a deep breath to calm herself, Wynn answered him. "No Matthew, I understand that. It's everything else. You've never told me much about the war and I can understand that too. I know that it was hell for you, but I never thought much about the part you played in it. I suppose I thought that you were just an ordinary soldier, like Todd." she explained.

Matthew's eyes were almost cold as he stared down at his wife. "I was." he answered.

Wynn's gaze met his unwaveringly. "I'm beginning to think, Matthew, that there is nothing ordinary about you and never has been." she said.

"What makes you think that?" he asked.

286

Wynn reached for a button on his shirt and began to fiddle with it. She stared at the button, instead of his face. "When I met you, you were wearing the uniform of a private, wasn't it?" she asked.

"It wasn't mine. Just something they gave me in the field hospital to cover my bones." he replied.

Wynn glanced up at him, but went back to her study of the shirt button. "I see that now. I suppose it just comes as a surprise to me that instead of marrying an ordinary soldier, I find out I've married a legend. I knew you to be a gentleman, even when you were dressed in rags. That scared me bad enough, just worrying about whether or not I was good enough for a man of your station. Now, there's this."

Matthew breathed a long sigh and took her hand, stopping her fiddling with his shirt button. He said nothing, until she looked up at him. "Legends have a way of growing out of almost nothing in war time. You said a moment ago that you didn't know me. Well, maybe you don't. Maybe I'm a little bit of it all, the plantation heir, the company commander, the ex-Confederate soldier. Shake it all up and what do you get?" he asked.

Wynn drew in another deep breath and changed the subject. "What did you feel, when you killed that man?" she asked. instead of answering him.

"What did I feel?" Matthew repeated the question. "Four or five things." he said with a shrug.

"Were any of them good?" Wynn asked.

Matthew raised an eyebrow and gave her a satisfied grin. "Hell yes, it felt good!"

Wynn's lips tilted up in a small smile. "I understand that, I think. Like shooting a dog that killed someone's child?"

Matthew nodded. "Yeah, exactly." he replied.

"You're beginning to sound more like the Matthew I know." Wynn said.

Matthew gave her an affectionate hug. "You're right Honey, I'm not myself. I don't know why this thing has me so shook up. I knew the moment I saw that man again, that I had to kill him. Still, I wasn't sure I would go through with it, until he went a step too far."

"When was that?" Wynn asked.

"Do you remember the other day, just before we went into the stable? Remember that I told you I had nightmares where I saw you dead?" he asked.

287

"Yes, I remember you saying that." Wynn replied.

"In my nightmares, it's always been a Yankee soldier with a sword or saber. I'd see Elizabeth, the way she died. Then it would be you I'd see there on the ground. Can you imagine what seeing that Yankee aiming his saber at your breast did to me?" Matthew asked.

"Oh Matthew! It made you crazy for a while, didn't it?" Wynn asked.

"No. The crazy part was over when I got through whipping him. I was perfectly rational, when I blew his brains out. Does that shock you?"

"No, not now." Wynn replied.

"But it did, didn't it?" Matthew asked quietly.

Wynn reached to brush back the lock of hair that had fallen onto his forehead. "You're a kind man, Matthew, a gentle man."

"Am I?" he asked. "I think not, Wynn. I've got a river of hate inside of me that's as deep and twisted as the Ocklawaha. Hate is an ugly thing. A man can bury it in a hidden corner of himself and pretend that is isn't there, but it never goes away. You look at me with those Indian black eyes of yours and tell me I'm a kind and gentle man. But what do you know of me?" Matthew asked. His gray eyes were bleak, with a hard and haunted sadness.

Wynn reached for his hand and pressed his skinned and swollen knuckles against her lips. "Only what I've seen, Matthew." she said gently.

Matthew said nothing, he only pulled her close once again.

She pulled away to look up at him again. "When I was a little girl, I once heard my mother say that my father was a strongly gentle man. She had the Cherokee way of turning phrases like that and I was too young to fully understand what she meant until years later. You're like him, Matthew, in a lot of ways. I've seen you come from being a man beaten down to the very ground by life, into one who can stand tall." she said sincerely.

Matthew's gray eyes darkened as he looked into the softness of Wynn's. "They left me nothing but my pride and then set out to destroy even that. How much pride can a man have when the only brains and guts that he has are the ones that are stuck to his boots? You told me once that it only took backbone to begin building a new life. Another time, you said that all any of us could do was to go on living until we died. What choice is there but to do the best we can?"

288

he said quietly.

Wynn's face lit up with a small victorious smile. "There you have it, Matthew. A weaker man would have been destroyed, but you survived. They never destroyed your pride or broke your spirit." she said sincerely.

"My dear wife." Matthew said in a voice that hardly sounded like his own. "I hope to God that someday I'll actually become the man you see when you look at me." He turned slowly and left the room.

Chapter 53

Wynn busied herself throughout the rest of the day attending to various household tasks. Several times as she went about her work, she glanced out the front room window. Matthew had sat on the front porch, hardly moving, throughout most of the afternoon. Her smooth brow creased with worry each time she looked at him. Not since he had first arrived had she seen him staring off into nothing as he did now.

Wynn was looking out the window yet again, when a small sound behind her caused her to turn. The man who stood there scarcely resembled the stranger who had arrived that morning in ragged clothes and shackled with chains. He was clean and freshly shaven and the trim Union uniform fit him as if it was made for him.

"Mr. Waters, I hardly knew you in that uniform." she said.

"I appreciate you cleaning and pressing it for me. Do you suppose you could call me Linc? I might as well get used to the name, I'll probably be using it for a long time." He walked past her to look out the window. "Has anyone been around?" he asked.

"No, not a soul. If there was, they wouldn't have gotten past Matthew." she assured him.

"That, my dear, I can well believe. It would be a foolish man indeed, that would even try. Captain Kendall is a man I'd hate to know I'd ever tried to cross." Linc said seriously.

"Mr. Waters... Linc. I'd offer you some coffee but it's still as scarce as hen's teeth here. I do have some tea, if you'd care for some." Wynn peeked out the window once more and again, a small frown crossed her brow.

"That would be nice, Mrs. Kendall." Linc replied.

"I'm not used to being called Mrs. Kendall yet. We've only been married a few weeks. If I'm to call you Linc, then you might as well call me Wynn." she said.

"I'd be honored Ma'am." he replied.

Wynn led the way to the kitchen and put a kettle of water on the stove to heat.

"Pardon me for saying so; but I could hardly help but notice that something is troubling you. If it's my presence here, I will try to make my stay as short as possible." Linc said politely.

Wynn sat down at the table in a chair directly opposite from him. "That you're here doesn't bother me in the least. To be perfectly honest, what's bothering me is Matthew. I think what happened has upset him." Wynn confided.

Linc nodded. "And understandably so, my dear." he replied.

Something in Linc Water's manner and expression seemed to inspire confidence and Wynn confided in him further. "I guess so. But I don't think he's upset about killing that man, it's more than that. Killing that Yankee only set off something deeper." she said worriedly.

Linc Waters gave her an understanding smile. "The war left scars on us all. Wounds heal my dear, but now and again something will come along that opens them all up again. At such times, a man must bleed and from what I've seen, from such bleeding there comes healing." He reached across the table to pat her hand in a gesture of reassurance.

"I understand that. It's just that the man you seem to know and the one I seem to know are not the same." Wynn said with concern.

"Ah, I see, you're having trouble comprehending that other life, that other side of the coin. We're all a combination of many selves, my dear. We are for the most part molded and shaped by where we are and what's happening in our lives at any given time. The self we show the world is the one that circumstances makes of us. We become whoever we must be, to do whatever must be done. Yet, all in all, each aspect of a person makes up the sum total of the whole." Linc explained.

"You're a wise man, Linc Waters, or whoever you are." Wynn said with a smile.

"Sometimes, I wonder about that. I never thought I'd see the day I'd be hunted down for treason in a country that I hold more dear than my own life. Don't worry about Captain Kendall my dear, he's the stuff this country is made of. Allow him his grief for what is past and what might have been. He's earned the right." Linc's pale blue eyes reflected some of the same pain she had seen earlier in Matthew's.

Wynn nodded and stood up to prepare the tea. Matthew entered the kitchen just as she was pouring it into cups.

Matthew met his guest's eyes with a look of amusement. "I never figured I'd see the day when the likes of you would be dressed in Union blue." he said.

"Nor did I." Linc replied. "At least not again. I once wore it with pride, when we were at war with Mexico."

"So you gave up soldiering for politics." Matthew said. He sat down opposite Linc, in the chair Wynn had just vacated.

"I'm still trying to decide which was the most hazardous." Linc said. "A soldier usually knows who his enemies are. A politician has to be wary of most men and quite often, most women."

"I suppose it has its drawbacks." Matthew agreed.

"That it does." Linc replied.

"Have you given any thought as to how you're going to get to the coast?" Matthew asked.

"I think so. What I intend to do is ride out of here in this Yankee uniform on that Yankee horse, with a pocketful of Yankee credentials. If I don't run into some southern boy that don't like the color of my clothes, I just might make it." Linc said, with a touch of irony.

"It's a good plan, it just might work at that." Matthew agreed. "You never did say how it was that you came to be captured."

Linc shrugged his shoulders. "Some people will do anything for a price. In my case, it was a woman."

"A woman betrayed you?" Wynn asked.

"Not any woman, my dear. The lovely lady was my wife. It seems that when I ceased to be an influential man, my use to her ended. When I found myself without honor and without funds, she sold me to the highest bidder." Linc's voice was calm but his eyes revealed his anger and pain.

"I'm sorry." Wynn stated simply.

"Her time will come." Linc replied. "Enough about that. Sit down my dear and have your tea." he invited. "Aren't you going to have some, Captain?"

"I never learned to like the stuff." Matthew replied.

"I suppose one could say it's an acquired taste. I believe you said you were with the Seventh Georgia. How did you come to end up here?" Linc asked.

Matthew explained the events that had led to his arrival in Florida.

"I'd like to see this spring you were talking about. Do you suppose it would be possible?" Linc asked, when Matthew was through speaking.

"I don't see why not. The only place between here and there belongs to Wynn's brother. It should be safe enough." Matthew replied.

Right after supper that evening, Todd came back to return Matthew's can of axle grease. Matthew walked with him to the shed, to put it away.

"All right, spit it out Todd." Matthew said. "You know I have two cans of this stuff, so there was no need to make a special trip to bring it back. I sort of thought you'd be here sooner. Your curiosity must be killing you."

Todd placed the can of axle grease on the shelf and turned to his brother-in-law. "Dammit Matthew, what the hell is this?" he asked. "How do you think it makes me feel to find out after knowing you all this time, that my best friend is The Cat. Hell, you're even married to my sister and it was plain that she didn't know anything about it either. I'd have never figured I'd see the day when you hid something like that from the people who care the most about you. For two cents, I'd punch hell out of you, but then maybe I'd better be careful. I'd sure as hell hate to get scratched by The Cat!" Todd concluded bitterly.

"Tell me one thing Todd. What good would it have done you to have known?" Matthew asked.

"Well hell, none I guess. But what's that got to do with you holding out on me?" Todd asked in return.

Matthew shrugged his shoulders. "Todd, what difference does it make?"

For a split second, the hurt behind Todd's anger showed in his eyes. "I thought you trusted me." he replied.

"Twice with my life. Trust has nothing to do with it. I just didn't see any point in it, that's all." Matthew said.

"No point!" Todd snapped. "No point, hell! How do you think I feel, finding out second hand that my brother-in-law is a hero?" he asked.

Matthew's gray eyes, one half closed from his fight with the Yankee, captured and held Todd's before he spoke. "Hero, Todd? Was it a hero that was so done in by a little bump on the head that he damn near got himself killed at Chickamauga? Did that rack of bones you carried out of that Yankee prison look like a hero. That sure as hell wasn't a case of The Cat landing on his feet. Let me tell you something else. I sure as hell didn't look like a hero when the Yankees took Lookout Mountain. I high-tailed it out of there just like everybody else. Hell Todd, I don't even know how all that bullshit about The Cat got started. I overheard my men call me that a time or two, behind my back. I wasn't even sure they were talking about me." Matthew explained.

Todd just shook his head and gave Matthew a wry grin. "Damned if you don't beat all I've ever seen. One of the men that served under you got transferred to my Artillery Division. You was all he could talk about. Hell, Matthew. I know what you done by heart, I heard it enough times. The only reason I didn't know it was you was because he never referred to you as anything but The Cat." Todd said.

"Todd, I followed orders like everybody else. We were sent to do a job and we done it the best we could. Success in a mission like that is ninety percent luck and ten percent leadership. On second thought, luck has nothing to do with it at all. It's being blessed with having some of the best soldiers in the Confederate army to serve with you. I was glad that we were successful but I honestly never thought much about it." Matthew said seriously.

Todd shook his head and grinned. "Like your friend Mr. Waters said, you're too modest. And you accused me once of understating a situation."

"You did." Matthew replied. "And I found out one thing, you do have some damn big mosquitoes here in Florida."

Todd laughed and changed the subject. "You reckon you'll have any trouble from what happened today?" he asked.

"No. Like I said, no one even knows they came this way. That Yankee wasn't connected with the government. He wasn't even still in the army. He was nothing more than a common bounty hunter looking for a reward. I doubt seriously if he'll ever be missed."

Matthew replied.

"I hope you're right." Todd said. "It does worry me some though."

The two men talked for a few minutes longer and Todd made his departure.

Chapter 54

Linc remained with Matthew and Wynn another day before making his departure under the cover of darkness the following night. He mounted the Yankee's brown horse, wincing with displeasure as he tried to settle himself more comfortably on the McClellan saddle. He tipped his hat to Wynn and reached to shake Matthew's hand. "I hope you folks know that you have my eternal gratitude for what you've done. Someday when things die down a bit you'll be hearing from me." he promised. He saluted Matthew smartly and rode away.

They stood watching until he was out of sight and Wynn reached for Matthew's hand. "Who was he?" she asked.

Matthew squeezed her hand. "Just another Confederate, who gave it all for something that can never be." he replied.

Wynn shivered and drew closer to him for warmth. "Do you think he'll be back this way?" she asked.

"Maybe. It's cold tonight, I think we'll have frost by morning." Matthew replied

"I hope so. Todd's cane ought to be all right. It's the only crop I've ever seen that kept on growing after being flattened like it was." Wynn said.

Matthew pulled her close and planted a kiss on her forehead. "It's Rebel cane darlin'. I guess it's like the rest of us. It has no choice but to keep growing."

Wynn gave Matthew a hug to signify her agreement. "Matthew, I've been meaning to ask you something for the last couple of days now." she said.

"What's that?" Matthew prompted.

Wynn laughed. "How's your back?" she asked.

Matthew chuckled softly. "My back is fine, but my chin is sore as hell." he replied.

"Which brings to mind another question." Wynn said.

Matthew took her hand and they began walking back towards the house. "What question is that?" he asked.

"Only this, what are you going to do if someone comes around asking questions?" Wynn asked worriedly.

They entered the house and Matthew didn't answer immediately. He knelt before the front room fireplace set a match to the fat lightered splinters he had placed there earlier. The wood caught immediately, dispelling the darkness with flickering light. The dancing glow of the flames sent shadows across the room and lit up his face as he stood up and brushed his hands on his pant legs. "Chances are they won't." he replied, at last.

Wynn shivered and moved the settee closer to the fireplace. She sat down and began to unlace her shoes. "But if they do?" she prompted. She pulled off one shoe and began unlacing the other one.

Matthew rested an arm on the mantle and stared down thoughtfully into the flames. "Let them ask their questions, I suppose and behave like nothing did happen." he replied.

Wynn said nothing more and removed the other shoe. She curled up with her feet under her skirt and patted the place next to her on the settee.

Matthew sat down beside her and rested the ankle of one foot on the other knee. "I wish you wouldn't let all this worry you," he said, after a time.

"I can't help it Matthew. If they found out what you did, you could go to jail, even hang." Wynn shivered at the thought.

Matthew reached for her hand and began caressing her fingers with his thumb. "If," and he emphasized the word if, "they did, I probably would, but they won't."

"Now how can you be so sure?" Wynn fretted.

"I suppose I can't. But let me assure you of one thing. Never again will any man or group of men, put me behind prison walls." The steel in his voice made Wynn shiver yet again.

"The subject's closed. We won't discuss it again." Matthew stated firmly.

Wynn said nothing and leaned to rest her head on his broad shoulder. "The fire feels good." she said, in an effort to change the subject.

"If there's frost tonight, I suppose we should go help Todd get the cane in." Matthew said.

"He'll need all the help he can get. He's going to grind it at home this year. We used to take our cane to the big cane mill across the river, before the Yankees burned it. It was quite a shindig. Everyone from miles around would gather over there and it would take two or three days to get all the cane ground and the syrup made." There was a wistful note in Wynn's voice as she spoke.

"This place seems so untouched by the war, at least compared to some." Matthew commented.

"I suppose it does, if you weren't here to see it like it was." Wynn replied.

Matthew leaned forward and stared into the flames in the fireplace. "Was it worth the price Wynn? This country that our ancestors fought so hard for, they'd turn over in their graves, if they could see it divided like it is now. This war may be officially over but it's still going on. I doubt that there will ever be a true understanding between the North and the South. How many years will it take Wynn, to put us all back together? Before God, it's going to take more than just living under one flag to unite us all again." he said sadly.

Matthew stood up and once more rested his arm on the mantle. The flickering flames lit his face and reflected in his serious gray eyes, that now burned with emotion. "I long for it, Wynn. For the day when the states of the Confederacy are no longer bastard sons, but honored heirs to a nation united in the eyes of God and the world." he said, with feeling.

Wynn arose from the settee and came to stand looking up at him. The tears on her cheeks took him by surprise. "What's this?" he asked. With a callused fingertip, he caught one of the crystal drops and pressed it to his lips. Wynn breathed in a quivering sigh and smiled through her tears.

"You don't know how glad your words make me feel." she said softly.

Matthew looked blankly into her eyes, wondering what he had said that had moved her to tears. "I don't understand." he said at last.

Wynn rested the palms of her hands on his shirt front and continued to look into his eyes. "The other day Matthew, the way you talked to that man before you killed him. You said things that sounded like you hated the United States and all that it stood for."

Matthew gave her a small smile. "No Wynn, not the United States. Only a piece of rot who claimed to represent it. Not all of them are bad. Some of the men I fought against were honorable, principled men who fought for a cause they believed in." he said softly.

Wynn cupped his face with both hands, looking into his eyes intently. "If men like you can heal from their wounds, then so can our country. I've seen the healing that's come about in you and our nation will heal too." she said earnestly.

Matthew drew her into his arms. "It'll be a long time before we're well again, this country and me. The bitterness is like poison and this nation is full of it, just as I am." he said bleakly.

"Matthew, we've got to put it all behind us. Hate never solved anything." Wynn replied softly.

"I know that." Matthew said. "It's something all of us have to learn. We fought in the end, with nothing more than our own stubborn blindness to keep us going, that and our Southern pride."

Wynn gave him a hard hug. "Matthew, I think I like this new you I'm seeing." she said.

His hands began pulling the pins from her hair, but his mind was elsewhere. "Hell Wynn, what you're seeing isn't the new me, it's the old one. It's funny how just a little nudge can do that. I've been running around giving my help orders like they were still slaves, instead of hired help. A part of me that got lost has come back and I'm not sure I even want it. I was an arrogant man, Wynn and I don't want to be that way again. The Yankee prison destroyed my self-respect, not the war. The war taught me things about myself that I sometimes lose sight of. Sometimes, I'm not even sure who I am."

Wynn leaned back to look up at him. "I don't understand." she said.

Matthew shook his head. "I'm not sure I do either." he said vaguely.

Wynn pressed her body close to him. "It'll all work out Matthew. You'll see."

His fingers tangled into the long silky strands of her hair. "It will, won't it." It was neither a question nor a statement.

True to their predictions, the next morning presented them with a world that was white with frost. Matthew arose before Wynn to light a fire in the kitchen stove, before going to the porch, to wash his face.

Above the frost coated ground rose a sky that was deep blue and cloudless. The cold air was so still that not even the moss that hung from the trees moved.

The water in the bucket on the wash shelf was filmed over with a coating of ice that shattered when he dipped into it with the dipper. He took a long drink of the icy water before filling the tin pan and splashing his face with it.

Matthew lingered on the front porch, coatless in the frosty air. He shivered slightly, yet felt invigorated. A feeling of peace and contentment filled him as he heard the sound of metal on metal coming from the vicinity of the kitchen. The smell of frying bacon blended with the smell of wood smoke in the crystal clear air. He drew in a deep breath of it and leaned against the post by the steps. His gaze took in the hammock on the other side of his own cleared fields. Off in the distance, he heard the bellowing of one of his steers and closer by, the grunting of the hogs in the pen.

The front door opened behind him and Wynn crossed the porch to stand at his side. She pulled her shawl closer around her shoulders and reached to put an arm around his waist. Matthew drew her closer to his side and glanced down at her with a smile of utter contentment on his face. She returned the smile and rested her head against his shoulder.

"It's going to be a nice day." she said at last.

Matthew's gray eyes lit with a smile, even before it reached his lips. "It's a good day for a new beginning." he replied quietly.

Wynn's eyes asked the question that her lips never spoke.

"It's all behind me, Wynn. All the hate, all the bitterness. Lum and Jiggs hauled it away." he said.

"Is the war finally over for you Matthew?" Wynn asked.

Matthew nodded. "It was over when I put an end to that Yankee scum. It's taken me a couple of days to figure that out. There were two kinds of men in the war, Wynn. There were men like myself and Todd, who fought for what we believed in. We fought against others on the other side that felt the same way. Each side felt like they were right. Then there was the other kind of man, Wynn. Men like the one I shot. We had them on both sides. There are some things that a man does in a war, that is nothing more than what he has to do, yet there's honor in what he does. There's no honor in men like the one I killed. It was his kind that I campaigned so hard against. It was men like that, who killed innocent women and children and murdered helpless men. They made the prisons on both sides nothing more than hell

298

holes. I have no hate for the men on the other side, who only fought for what they thought was right."

Matthew was silent for a moment, then continued. "I've been trying ever since it happened, to figure out why I collapsed when it was all over. Heaven knows, that wasn't the first man I ever killed, though I hope it will be the last. I finally figured it out, Wynn. It was the hate going out of me. It was a cleansing that gave me back my self-respect and left me free and whole again. Yes Wynn, the war is finally over." Matthew concluded.

"The South still has a long row to hoe." Wynn said.

Matthew spoke softly. "I don't know what the future will bring us, but together we can face anything. With you at my side, I know that I can. It's been a long road for me, my love. I've come all the way from hell to Marion County and here I'll stay."

Thank you for buying this book. To order additional copies, fill out or duplicate this page and send it with the appropriate payment amount in the form a U. S. Postal money order for orders of any quantity. Florida residents please include 7% sales tax.

Quantity	Price each
1	$14.95
2-5	$13.95
6+	$12.95

Bulk buyers and booksellers should call for discount rates.

Name: _____

Address: _____

_____

City: _____

State: _____   Zip: _____

Number of books ordered: _____

Shipping and handling ($1.90 per book) _____

Sales tax 7% (Florida residents only) _____

Total order _____

Send form and payment to:
BenAura Publishing
P.O. Box 606
Anthony, FL 32617

This is book one of a trilogy. Book two should be available in the spring of 2004 and book 3 about 4-6 months after that.

Please feel free to contact us at (352) 402-0926 or by mail at the address above or email us at benaura@earthlink.net.